LEGENDS OF THE MIDDLE AGES

This edition published 2025
by Living Book Press
Copyright © Living Book Press, 2025

ISBN: 978-1-76153-407-2 (hardcover)
         978-1-76153-408-9 (softcover)

First published in 1896.

This edition is based on the 1924 printing by American Book Company.

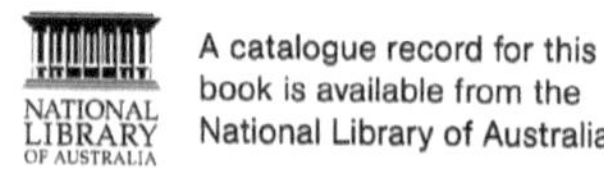
A catalogue record for this book is available from the National Library of Australia

LEGENDS OF THE MIDDLE AGES

by

HELENE A. GUERBER

DEDICATED
TO MY SISTER,
ADELE E. GUERBER

Contents

1.	BEOWULF.	6
2.	GUDRUN.	19
3.	REYNARD THE FOX.	32
4.	THE NIBELUNGENLIED.	50
5.	LANGOBARDIAN CYCLE OF MYTHS.	81
6.	THE AMBLINGS.	95
7.	DIETRICH VON BERN.	103
8.	CHARLEMAGNE AND HIS PALADINS.	123
9.	THE SONS OF AYMON.	145
10.	HUON OF BORDEAUX.	154
11.	TITUREL AND THE HOLY GRAIL.	173
12.	MERLIN.	195
13.	THE ROUND TABLE.	205
14.	TRISTAN AND ISEULT.	225
15.	THE STORY OF FRITHIOF.	237
16.	RAGNAR LODBROK.	260
17.	THE CID.	272
18.	GENERAL SURVEY OF ROMANCE LITERATURE.	290

CORONATION OF CHARLEMAGNE.—Levy.

"Saddle the Hippogriffs, ye Muses nine,
And straight we'll ride to the land of old Romance"

WIELAND

"Men lykyn jestis for to here,
And romans rede in diuers manere

"Of Brute that baron bold of hond,
The first conqueroure of Englond;
Of kyng Artour that was so riche,
Was non in his tyme him liche.

"How kyng Charlis and Rowlond fawght
With sarzyns nold they be cawght;
Of Tristrem and of Ysoude the swete,
How they with love first gan mete;

"Stories of diuerce thynggis,
Of pryncis, prelatis, and of kynggis;
Many songgis of diuers ryme,
As english, frensh, and latyne."
Curser Mundi.

PREFACE.

The object of this work is to familiarize young students with the legends which form the staple of mediaeval literature.

While they may owe more than is apparent at first sight to the classical writings of the palmy days of Greece and Rome, these legends are very characteristic of the people who told them, and they are the best exponents of the customs, manners, and beliefs of the time to which they belong. They have been repeated in poetry and prose with endless variations, and some of our greatest modern writers have deemed them worthy of a new dress, as is seen in Tennyson's "Idyls of the King," Goethe's "Reineke Fuchs," Tegnér's "Frithiof Saga," Wieland's "Oberon," Morris's "Story of Sigurd," and many shorter works by these and less noted writers.

These mediaeval legends form a sort of literary quarry, from which, consciously or unconsciously, each writer takes some stones wherewith to build his own edifice. Many allusions in the literature of our own day lose much of their force simply because these legends are not available to the general reader.

It is the aim of this volume to bring them within reach of all, and to condense them so that they may readily be understood. Of course in so limited a space only an outline of each legend can be given, with a few short quotations from ancient and modern writings to illustrate the style of the poem in which they are embodied, or to lend additional force to some point in the story.

This book is, therefore, not a manual of mediaeval literature, or a series of critical essays, but rather a synopsis of some of the epics and romances which formed the main part of the culture of those days. Very little prominence has been given to the obscure early versions, all disquisitions have been carefully avoided, and explanations have been given only where they seemed essential.

The wealth and variety of imagination displayed in these legends will, I hope, prove that the epoch to which they belong has been greatly maligned by the term "dark ages," often applied to it. Such was the favor which the legendary style of composition enjoyed with our ancestors that several of the poems analyzed in this volume were among the first books printed for general circulation in Europe.

Previous to the invention of printing, however, they were familiar to rich and poor, thanks to the scalds, bards, trouvères, troubadours, minstrels, and minnesingers, who, like the rhapsodists of Greece, spent their lives in wandering from place to place, relating or reciting these tales to all they met in castle, cottage, and inn.

A chapter on the Romance literature of the period in the different countries of Europe, and a complete index, will, it is hoped, fit this volume for handy reference in schools and libraries, where the author trusts it may soon find its own place and win a warm welcome.

CHAPTER I

BEOWULF.

"List! we have learnt a tale of other years,
Of kings and warrior Danes, a wondrous tale,
How aethelings bore them in the brunt of war."
Beowulf (Conybeare's tr.).

The most ancient relic of literature of the spoken languages of modern Europe is undoubtedly the epic poem "Beowulf," which is supposed to have been composed by the Anglo-Saxons previous to their invasion of England. Although the poem probably belongs to the fifth century, the only existing manuscript is said to date from the ninth or tenth century.

This curious work, in rude alliterative verse (for rhyme was introduced in England only after the Norman Conquest), is the most valuable old English manuscript in the British Museum. Although much damaged by fire, it has been carefully studied by learned men. They have patiently restored the poem, the story of which is as follows:

Hrothgar (the modern Roger), King of Denmark, was a descendant of Odin, being the third monarch of the celebrated dynasty of the Skioldungs. They proudly traced their ancestry to Skeaf, or Skiold, Odin's son, who mysteriously drifted to their shores. He was then but an infant, and lay in the middle of a boat, on a sheaf of ripe wheat, surrounded by priceless weapons and jewels. As the people were seeking for a ruler, they immediately recognized the hand of Odin in this mysterious advent, proclaimed the child king, and obeyed him loyally as long as he lived. When he felt death draw near, Skeaf, or Skiold, ordered a vessel to be prepared, lay down in the midst on a sheaf of grain or on a funeral pyre, and drifted out into the wide ocean, disappearing as mysteriously as he had come.

Such being his lineage, it is no wonder that Hrothgar became a mighty chief; and as he had amassed much wealth in the course of a long life of warfare, he resolved to devote part of it to the construction of a magnificent hall, called Heorot, where he might feast his retainers and listen to the heroic lays of the scalds during the long winter evenings.

> "A hall of mead, such as for space and state
> The elder time ne'er boasted; there with free
> And princely hand he might dispense to all
> (Save the rude crowd and men of evil minds)
> The good he held from Heaven. That gallant work,
> Full well I wot, through many a land was known
> Of festal halls the brightest and the best."
> *Beowulf (Conybeare's tr.).*

The inauguration of this hall was celebrated by a sumptuous entertainment; and when all the guests had retired, the king's body-guard, composed of thirty-two dauntless warriors, lay down in the hall to rest. When morning dawned, and the servants appeared to remove the couches, they beheld with horror the floor and walls all stained with blood, the only trace of the knights who had gone to rest there in full armor.

Gigantic, blood-stained footsteps, leading directly from the festive hall to the sluggish waters of a deep mountain lake, or fiord, furnished the only clew to their disappearance. Hrothgar, the king, beholding these, declared that they had been made by Grendel, a descendant of the giants, whom a magician had driven out of the country, but who had evidently returned to renew his former depredations.

> "A haunter of marshes, a holder of moors.
> .   .   .   .   .   Secret
> The land he inhabits; dark, wolf-haunted ways
> Of the windy hillside, by the treacherous tarn;
> Or where, covered up in its mist, the hill stream
> Downward flows."
> *Beowulf (Keary's tr.).*

As Hrothgar was now too old to wield a sword with his former skill, his first impulse was, of course, to offer a princely reward to any man brave enough to free the country of this terrible scourge. As soon as this was known ten of his doughtiest knights volunteered to camp in the hall on the following night, and attack the monster Grendel should he venture to reappear.

But in spite of the valor of these experienced warriors, and of the efficacy of their oft-tried weapons, they too succumbed. A minstrel, hiding in a dark corner of the hall, was the only one who escaped Grendel's fury, and after shudderingly describing the massacre he had witnessed, he fled in terror to the kingdom of the Geates (Jutes or Goths). There he sang his lays in the presence of Hygelac, the king, and of his nephew Beowulf (the Bee Hunter), and roused their deepest interest by describing the visit of Grendel and the vain but heroic defense of the brave knights. Beowulf, having listened intently, eagerly questioned the scald, and, learning from him that the monster still haunted those regions, impetuously declared his intention to visit Hrothgar's kingdom, and show his valor by fighting and, if possible, slaying Grendel.

> "He was of mankind
> In might the strongest,
> At that day
> Of this life,
> Noble and stalwart.
> He bade him a sea ship,
> A goodly one, prepare.
> Quoth he, the war king,
> Over the swan's road,
> Seek he would
> The mighty monarch,
> Since he wanted men."
>
> *Beowulf* (Longfellow's tr.).

Although very young, Beowulf was quite distinguished, and had already won great honors in a battle against the Swedes. He had also proved his endurance by entering into a swimming match with Breka, one of the lords at his uncle's court. The two champions had started

out, sword in hand and fully armed, and, after swimming in concert
for five whole days, they were parted by a great tempest.

> "Then were we twain there on the sea
> Space of five nights, till the floods severed us,
> The welling waves. Coldest of weathers,
> Shadowy night, and the north wind
> Battelous shocked on us; wild were the waters,
> And were the mere-fishes stirred up in mind."
> *Beowulf.*

Breka was driven ashore, but the current bore Beowulf toward
some jagged cliffs, where he desperately clung, trying to resist the fury
of the waves, and using his sword to ward off the attacks of hostile
mermaids, nicors (nixies), and other sea monsters. The gashed bodies of these slain foes soon drifted ashore, to Hygelac's amazement;
but when Beowulf suddenly reappeared and explained that they had
fallen by his hand, his joy knew no bounds. As Breka had returned
first, he received the prize for swimming; but the king gave Beowulf
his treasured sword, Nägeling, and praised him publicly for his valor.

Beowulf had successfully encountered these monsters of the deep
in the roaring tide, so he now expressed a hope that he might prevail
against Grendel also; and embarking with fourteen chosen men, he
sailed to Denmark, where he was challenged by the coast guard and
warmly welcomed as soon as he had made his purpose known.

> "'What men are ye,
> War gear wearing,
> Host in harness,
> Who thus the brown keel
> Over the water street
> Leading, come
> Hither over the sea?'"
> *Beowulf* (Longfellow's tr.).

Hrothgar received Beowulf most hospitably, but vainly tried
to dissuade him from his perilous undertaking. Then, after a
sumptuous banquet, where the mead flowed with true northern
lavishness, Hrothgar and his suite sadly left the hall Heorot in

charge of the brave band of strangers, whom they never expected to see again.

As soon as the king had departed, Beowulf bade his companions lie down and sleep in peace, promising to watch over them, yet laying aside both armor and sword; for he knew that weapons were of no avail against the monster, whom he intended to grapple with hand to hand should it really appear.

> "'I have heard
> That that foul miscreant's dark and stubborn flesh
> Recks not the force of arms:—such I forswear,
> Nor sword nor burnish'd shield of ample round
> Ask for the war; all weaponless, hand to hand
> (So may great Higelac's smile repay my toil)
> Beowulf will grapple with the mighty foe.'"
>   *Beowulf* (Conybeare's tr.).

The warriors had no sooner stretched themselves out upon the benches in the hall than, overcome by the oppressive air as well as by mead, they sank into a profound sleep. Beowulf alone remained awake, watching for Grendel's coming. In the early morning, when all was very still, the giant appeared, tore asunder the iron bolts and bars which secured the door, and striding into the hall, enveloped in a long, damp mantle of clammy mist, he pounced upon one of the sleepers. He tore him limb from limb, greedily drank his blood, and devoured his flesh, leaving naught but the head, hands, and feet of his unhappy victim. This ghastly repast only whetted the fiend's ravenous appetite, however, so he eagerly stretched out his hands in the darkness to seize and devour another warrior. Imagine his surprise and dismay when he suddenly found his hand caught in so powerful a grasp that all his efforts could not wrench it free!

Grendel and Beowulf struggled in the darkness, overturning tables and couches, shaking the great hall to its very foundations, and causing the walls to creak and groan under the violence of their furious blows. But in spite of Grendel's gigantic stature, Beowulf clung so fast to the hand and arm he had grasped that Grendel, making a desperate effort to free himself by a jerk, tore the whole limb out of its socket! Bleeding and mortally wounded, he then beat a hasty retreat to his marshy den, leaving a long, bloody trail behind him.

> "Soon the dark wanderer's ample shoulder bore
> A gaping wound, each starting sinew crack'd,
> And from its socket loosed the strong-knit joint.—
> The victory was with Beowulf, and the foe,
> Howling and sick at heart, fled as he might,
> To seek beneath the mountain shroud of mist
> His joyless home; for well he knew the day
> Of death was on him, and his doom was seal'd."
> *Beowulf* (Conybeare's tr.).

As for Beowulf, exhausted but triumphant, he stood in the middle of the hall, where his companions crowded around him, gazing in speechless awe at the mighty hand and limb, and the clawlike fingers, far harder than steel, which no power had hitherto been able to resist.

At dawn Hrothgar and his subjects also appeared. They heard with wonder a graphic account of the night's adventures, and gazed their fill upon the monster's limb, which hung like a trophy from the ceiling of Heorot. After the king had warmly congratulated Beowulf, and bestowed upon him many rich gifts, he gave orders to cleanse the hall, to hang it with tapestry, and to prepare a banquet in honor of the conquering hero.

While the men were feasting, listening to the lays of the scalds, and carrying the usual toasts, Wealtheow, Hrothgar's beautiful wife, the Queen of Denmark, appeared. She pledged Beowulf in a cup of wine, which he gallantly drained after she had touched it to her lips. Then she bestowed upon him a costly necklace (the famous Brisinga-men, according to some authorities)[1] and a ring of the finest gold.

> "'Wear these,' she cried, 'since thou hast in the fight
> So borne thyself, that wide as ocean rolls
> Round our wind-beaten cliffs his brimming waves,
> All gallant souls shall speak thy eulogy.'"
> *Beowulf* (Conybeare's tr.).

---

[1] See Guerber's Myths of Northern Lands, p. 127.

When the banquet was ended, Hrothgar escorted his guests to more pleasant sleeping apartments than they had occupied the night before, leaving his own men to guard the hall, where Grendel would never again appear. The warriors, fearing no danger, slept in peace; but in the dead of night the mother of the giant, as grewsome and uncanny a monster as he, glided into the hall, secured the bloody trophy still hanging from the ceiling, and carried it away, together with Aeschere (Askher), the king's bosom friend.

When Hrothgar learned this new loss at early dawn he was overcome with grief; and when Beowulf, attracted by the sound of weeping, appeared at his side, he mournfully told him of his irretrievable loss.

> " 'Ask not after happiness;
> Sorrow is renewed
> To the Danes' people.
> Aeschere is dead,
> Yrmenlaf's
> Elder brother,
> The partaker of my secrets
> And my counselor,
> Who stood at my elbow
> When we in battle
> Our mail hoods defended,
> When troops rushed together
> And boar crests crashed.'"
>
> *Beowulf* (Metcalfe's tr.).

The young hero immediately volunteered to finish his work and avenge Aeschere by seeking and attacking Grendel's mother in her own retreat; but as he knew the perils of this expedition, Beowulf first gave explicit directions for the disposal of his personal property in case he never returned. Then, escorted by the Danes and Geates, he followed the bloody track until he came to a cliff overhanging the waters of the mountain pool. There the bloody traces ceased, but Aeschere's gory head was placed aloft as a trophy.

> "Now paused they sudden where the pine grove clad
> The hoar rock's brow, a dark and joyless shade.

> Troublous and blood-stain'd roll'd the stream below.
> Sorrow and dread were on the Scylding's host,
> In each man's breast deep working; for they saw
> On that rude cliff young Aeschere's mangled head."
> *Beowulf* (Conybeare's tr.).

Beowulf gazed down into the deep waters, saw that they also were darkly dyed with the monster's blood, and, after taking leave of Hrothgar, bade his men await his return for two whole days and nights ere they definitely gave him up for lost. He then plunged bravely into the bloody waters, swam about seeking for the monster's retreat, and dived deep. At last, descrying a phosphorescent gleam in the depths, he quickly made his way thither, shrewdly conjecturing that it must be Grendel's hiding place. But on his way thither he was repeatedly obliged to have recourse to his sword to defend himself against the clutches of countless hideous sea monsters which came rushing toward him on all sides.

> "While thro' crystal gulfs were gleaming
> Ocean depths, with wonders teeming;
> Shapes of terror, huge, unsightly,
> Loom'd thro' vaulted roof translucent."
> J.C. JONES, *Valhalla*.

A strong current seized Beowulf, and swept him irresistibly along into the slimy retreat of Grendel's mother. She clutched him fast, wrestled with him, deprived him of his sword, flung him down, and finally tried to pierce his armor with her trenchant knife. Fortunately, however, the hero's armor was weapon-proof, and his muscles were so strong that before she could do him any harm he had freed himself from her grasp. Seizing a large sword hanging upon a projection of rock near by, he dealt her a mighty blow, severing her head from the trunk at a single stroke. The blood pouring out of the cave mingled with the waters without, and turned them to such a lurid hue that Hrothgar and his men sorrowfully departed, leaving the Geates alone to watch for the return of the hero, whom they feared they would never see again.

Beowulf, in the mean while, had rushed to the rear of the cave, where, finding Grendel in the last throes, he cut off his head also.

He seized this ghastly trophy and rapidly made his way up through the tainted waters, which the fiery blood of the two monsters had so overheated that his sword melted in its scabbard and naught but the hilt remained.

> "That stout sword of proof,
> Its warrior task fulfill'd, dropp'd to the ground
> (So work'd the venom of the felon's blood)
> A molten mass."
> *Beowulf* (Conybeare's tr.).

The Geates were about to depart in sorrow, notwithstanding the orders they had received, when they suddenly beheld their beloved chief safe and sound, and bearing the evidences of his success. Then their cries of joy echoed and reechoed from the neighboring hills, and Beowulf was escorted back to Heorot, where he was almost overwhelmed with gifts by the grateful Danes. A few days later Beowulf and his companions returned home, where the story of their adventures, and an exhibition of all the treasures they had won, formed the principal topics of conversation.

Several years of comparative peace ensued, ere the land was invaded by the Friesians, who raided the coast, burning and plundering all in their way, and retreated into their ships before Hygelac or Beowulf could overtake and punish them. The immediate result of this invasion was a counter-movement on Hygelac's part. But although he successfully harried Friesland, he fell into an ambush just as he was about to leave the country, and was cruelly slain, his nephew Beowulf barely escaping a similar untoward fate.

When the little army of the Geates reached home once more, they either buried or consumed Hygelac's remains, with his weapons and battle steed, as was customary in the North. This ceremony ended, Queen Hygd, overwhelmed with grief, and fearing the almost inevitable dissensions arising during the long minority of an infant king, convened the popular assembly known as the Thing, and bade the people set her own child's claims aside in favor of Beowulf. This proposal was hailed with enthusiasm; but Beowulf refused to usurp his kinsman's throne, and raising Hardred, Hygelac's infant son, upon his shield, he declared

FUNERAL OF A NORTHERN CHIEF.—Cormon.

that he would protect and uphold him as long as he lived. The people, following his example, swore fealty to the new king, and faithfully kept this oath until he died.

Hardred, having attained his majority, ruled wisely and well; but his career was cut short by the sons of Othere, the discoverer of the North Cape. These youths had rebelled against their father's authority and taken refuge at Hardred's court; but when the latter advised a reconciliation, the eldest youth angrily drew his sword and slew him.

This crime was avenged, with true northern promptitude, by Wiglaf, one of the king's followers; and while the second youth effected an escape, Beowulf was summoned by the Thing to accept the now vacant throne. As there were none to dispute his claims, the hero no longer refused to rule, and he bravely defended his kingdom against Eadgils, Othere's second son. Eadgils was now king of Sweden, and came with an armed host to avenge his brother's death; but he only succeeded in losing his own life.

A reign of forty years of comparative peace brought Beowulf to extreme old age. He had naturally lost much of his former vigor, and was therefore somewhat dismayed when a terrible, fire-breathing dragon took up its abode in the mountains near by, where it gloated over a hoard of glittering gold.

> "The ranger of the darksome night,
> The Firedrake, came."
> *Beowulf* (Conybeare's tr.)

A fugitive slave, having made his way unseen into the monster's den during one of its temporary absences, bore away a small portion of this gold. On its return the Firedrake discovered the theft, and became so furious that its howling and writhing shook the mountain like an earthquake. When night came on its rage was still unappeased, and it flew all over the land, vomiting venom and flames, setting houses and crops afire, and causing so much damage that the people were almost beside themselves with terror. Seeing that all their attempts to appease the dragon were utterly fruitless, and being afraid to attack it in its lair, they finally implored Beowulf to deliver them as he had delivered the Danes, and to slay this oppressor, which was even worse than the terrible Grendel.

Such an appeal could not be disregarded, and in spite of his advanced years Beowulf donned his armor once more. Accompanied by Wiglaf and eleven of his bravest men, he then went out to seek the monster in its lair. At the entrance of the mountain gorge Beowulf bade his followers pause, and advancing alone to the monster's den, he boldly challenged it to come forth and begin the fray. A moment later the mountain shook as the monster rushed out breathing fire and flame, and Beowulf felt the first gust of its hot breath, even through his massive shield.

> "First from his lair
> Shaking firm earth, and vomiting as he strode
> A foul and fiery blast, the monster came."
> *Beowulf* (Conybeare's tr.).

A desperate struggle followed, in the course of which Beowulf's sword and strength both failed him. The Firedrake coiled its long, scaly folds about the aged hero, and was about to crush him to death when the faithful Wiglaf, perceiving his master's imminent danger, sprang forward and attacked the monster so fiercely as to cause a diversion and make it drop Beowulf to concentrate its attention upon him.

Beowulf, recovering, then drew his dagger and soon put an end to the dragon's life; but even as it breathed its last the hero sank fainting to the ground. Feeling that his end was near, he warmly thanked Wiglaf for his timely aid, rejoiced in the death of the monster, and bade his faithful follower bring out the concealed treasure and lay it at his feet, that he might feast his eyes upon the glittering gold he had won for his people's use.

> "Saw then the bold thane
> Treasure jewels many,
> Glittering gold
> Heavy on the ground,
> Wonders in the mound
> And the worm's den,
> The old twilight flier's,
> Bowls standing;
> Vessels of men of yore,
> With the mountings fall'n off.

> There was many a helm
> Old and rusty,
> Armlets many
> Cunningly fastened.
> He also saw hang heavily
> An ensign all golden
> High o'er the hoard,
> Of hand wonders greatest,
> Wrought by spells of song,
> From which shot a light
> So that he the ground surface
> Might perceive,
> The wonders overscan."
>
> *Beowulf* (Metcalfe's tr.).

The mighty treasure was all brought forth to the light of day, and the followers, seeing that all danger was over, crowded round their dying chief. He addressed them affectionately, and, after recapitulating the main events his career, expressed a desire to be buried in a mighty mound on a projecting headland, which could be seen far out at sea, and would be called by his name.

> "'And now,
> Short while I tarry here—when I am gone,
> Bid them upon yon headland's summit rear
> A lofty mound, by Rona's seagirt cliff;
> So shall my people hold to after times
> Their chieftain's memory, and the mariners
> That drive afar to sea, oft as they pass,
> Shall point to Beowulf's tomb.'"
>
> *Beowulf* (Conybeare's tr.).

These directions were all piously carried out by a mourning people, who decked his mound with the gold he had won, and erected above it a Bauta, or memorial stone, to show how dearly they had loved their brave king Beowulf, who had died to save them from the fury of the dragon.

CHAPTER II

GUDRUN.

Maximilian I., Emperor of Germany, rendered a great service to posterity by ordering that copies of many of the ancient national manuscripts should be made. These copies were placed in the imperial library at Vienna, where, after several centuries of almost complete neglect, they were discovered by lovers of early literature, in a very satisfactory state of preservation. These manuscripts then excited the interest of learned men, who not only found therein a record of the past, but gems of literature which are only now beginning to receive the appreciation they deserve.

Among these manuscripts is the poem "Gudrun," belonging to the twelfth or thirteenth century. It is evidently compiled from two or more much older lays which are now lost, which are alluded to in the Nibelungenlied. The original poem was probably Norse, and not German like the only existing manuscript, for there is an undoubted parallel to the story of the kidnaping of Hilde in the Edda. In the Edda, Hilde, the daughter of Högni, escapes from home with her lover Hedin, and is pursued by her irate father. He overtakes the fugitives on an island, where a bloody conflict takes place, in which many of the bravest warriors die. Every night, however, a sorceress recalls the dead to life to renew the strife, and to exterminate one another afresh.

The poem "Gudrun," which is probably as old as the Nibelungenlied, and almost rivals it in interest, is one of the most valuable remains of ancient German literature. It consists of thirty-two songs, in which are related the adventures of three generations of the heroic family of the Hegelings. Hence it is often termed the "Hegeling Legend."

The poem opens by telling us that Hagen was the son of Sigeband, King of Ireland, which was evidently a place in Holland, and not the well-known Emerald Isle. During a great feast, when countless guests were assembled around his father's hospitable board, this prince, who was then but seven years of age, was seized by a griffin and rapidly borne away.

> "Young Hagen, loudly crying, was filled with dire dismay;
> The bird with mighty pinions soared high with him away."
>
> *Gudrun* (Dippold's tr.).

The cries of the child, and the arrows of Sigeband's men at arms, were equally ineffectual in checking the griffin, which flew over land and sea, and finally deposited its prey in its nest on the top of a great cliff on a desert island. One of the little griffins, wishing to reserve this delicate morsel for its own delectation, caught the boy up in its talons and flew away to a neighboring tree. The branch upon which it perched was too weak to support a double load, however, and as it broke the frightened griffin dropped Hagen into a thicket. Undismayed by the sharp thorns, Hagen quickly crept out of the griffin's reach and took refuge in a cave, where he found three little girls who had escaped from the griffins in the same way.

One of these children was Hilde, an Indian princess; the second, Hildburg, daughter of the King of Portugal; and the third belonged to the royal family of Isenland. Hagen immediately became the protector of these little maidens, spending several years in the cave with them. He ventured out only when the griffins were away, to seek berries or shoot small game with a bow which he had made in imitation of those he had seen in his father's hall.

Years passed by before Hagen found the corpse of an armed warrior, which had been washed ashore during a storm. To appropriate the armor and weapons for which he had so long and vainly sighed was the youth's first impulse; his second was to go forth and slay the griffins which had terrorized him and his little companions for so many years. The griffins being disposed of, the young people roamed about the island at will, keeping a sharp lookout for any passing vessel which might convey them home. At last a sail came in sight! Hagen, the first to see it, climbed up on a rock and shouted with all his young strength to attract the crew's attention.

> "With might young Hagen shouted, and did not cease to shout,
> Howe'er the roaring tempest the wild waves tossed about."
>
> *Gudrun* (Dippold's tr.).

The sailors reluctantly drew near, gazing fearfully upon the three maidens, who, clad in furs and moss, resembled mermaids or wood nymphs. But when they heard their story they gladly took them on board. It was only when the island was out of sight, and when they were in mid-ocean, that Hagen discovered that he had fallen into the hands of Count Garadie, his father's inveterate enemy, who now proposed to use his power to treat the young prince as a slave. But Hagen's rude fare, and the constant exposure of the past few years, had so developed his strength and courage that he now flew into a Berserker rage,[2] flung thirty men one after another into the sea, and so terrified his would-be master that he promised to bear him and the three maidens in safety to his father's court.

As Sigeband had died without leaving any other heir, Hagen was warmly welcomed home, and ascending the vacant throne, he took to wife Hilde, the fair maiden with whom he had shared his game and berries for so many years. The royal couple were very happy, and Hagen ruled so wisely that he became a terror to his enemies and a blessing to his own subjects. Even when engaged in warfare he proved himself an upright and generous man, never attacking the poor and weak.

> "On warlike enterprises into his enemies' land
> He spared the poor from ravage of fire with powerful hand;
> Whenever he encountered a warrior overbearing,
> He broke his burgs and slew him with dire revenge unsparing."
>
> *Gudrun* (Dippold's tr.).

Hagen and Hilde eventually became the parents of an only daughter, who was called by her mother's name, and grew up so beautiful that many suitors soon came to Ireland to ask for her hand. Hagen, who loved his daughter dearly and was in no haste to part from her, first replied that she was far too young to think of marriage; but when

2   See Guerber's Myths of Northern Lands, p. 29.

this plea was disputed he declared that Hilde should only marry a man who would defeat her father in single fight.

As Hagen was unusually tall and strong, as well as uncommonly brave, he was considered well-nigh invincible. The suitors, dismayed at this declaration, reluctantly withdrew, even though they were all valiant men. In those days Hettel (who corresponds to Hedin in the Edda story) was king of northern Germany and of the Hegelings. He too heard marvelous accounts of Hilde's beauty, and, as he was still unmarried, longed to secure her as wife. But knowing that Hagen, in his anger, was likely to slay any ambassador who came to his court with a proposal of marriage, Hettel vowed that he would rather forego the alliance than run the risk of losing any of his tried friends and faithful servants.

> "Then said the royal Hetel: 'The people all relate
> That whosoe'er will woo her incurs her father's hate,
> And for the maid has perished full many a noble knight;
> My friends shall never suffer for me such woeful plight.'"
> Gudrun (Dippold's tr.).

His faithful followers, Wat, Horant, and Frute, perceiving that his heart was set upon the maiden, finally volunteered to go and get her, saying that they could easily bear her away by stratagem, although they did not dare to ask for her openly. So they loaded their vessel with merchandise, hid their weapons, so that they should be taken for the traders they professed to be, and sailed boldly into Hagen's port, where, spreading out their wares, they invited all the people to buy.

Attracted by the extraordinary bargains they offered, the people came in crowds, and soon all the inhabitants of Balian were busy talking about the strange peddlers and praising their wares. These stories soon came to the ears of both queen and princess, who, summoning the merchants into their presence, asked who they were and whence they came.

All three replied that they were warriors, and that, being banished from Hettel's court, they had been forced to take up their present occupation to make a living. To prove the truth of their assertions,

Wat exhibited his skill in athletic sports, while Horant delighted all the ladies by his proficiency in the art of minstrelsy.

> "When now the night was ended and there drew near the dawn,
> Horant began his singing, so that in grove and lawn
> The birds became all silent, because he sang so sweetly;
> The people who were sleeping sprang from their couches fleetly.
>
> "The cattle in the forests forsook their pasture ground;
> The creeping creatures playing among the grass around,
> The fishes in the water,—all in their sports were ceasing.
> The minstrel might most truly rejoice in art so pleasing.
>
> "Whate'er he might be singing, to no one seemed it long;
> Forgotten in the minster were priest and choral song,
> Church bells no longer sounded so sweetly as before,
> And every one who heard him longed for the minstrel sore."
> *Gudrun* (Dippold's tr.).

These soft strains so pleased the younger Hilde that she soon sent for the minstrel again, and Horant, finding her alone, made use of this opportunity to tell her of Hettel's love and longing. She was so touched by this declaration of love that he easily won from her a promise to flee with him and his companions as soon as a suitable opportunity occurred.

The pretended merchants, having now achieved the real object of their journey, disposed of their remaining wares. They then invited the king and his family to visit their ship, and cleverly managing to separate the willing princess from her parents and train, they sailed rapidly away, leaving the angry father to hurl equally ineffectual spears, curses, and threats after them.

The Hegelings sailed with their prize direct to Waleis, in Holland (near the river Waal), where the impatient Hettel came to meet them, and tenderly embraced his beautiful young bride. There their hasty nuptials were celebrated; but, as they were about to sail away on the morrow, Hettel became aware of the rapid approach of a large fleet. Of course the foremost vessel was commanded by Hagen, who had immediately started out in pursuit of his kidnaped daughter. Landing, with all his forces, he challenged his new-made son-in-law to fight.

"King Hagen, full of anger, leaped forward in the sea.
Unto the shore he waded; no braver knight than he!
Full many pointed arrows against him were seen flying,
Like flakes of snow, from warriors of Hetel's host defying."
Gudrun (Dippold's tr.).

The result of this battle was that Hettel was wounded by Hagen, who, in his turn, was injured by Wat, and that the distracted Hilde suddenly flung herself between the contending parties, and by her tears and prayers soon brought about a reconciliation. Hagen, who had tested the courage of his new son-in-law and had not found it wanting, now permitted his daughter to accompany her husband home to Matelan, where she became the mother of a son, Ortwine, and of a daughter, Gudrun, who was even fairer than herself.

Ortwine was fostered by Wat, the dauntless hero, who taught him to fight with consummate skill; while Hilde herself presided over the education of Gudrun, and made her so charming that many suitors soon came, hoping to find favor in her eyes. These were Siegfried, King of Moorland, a pagan of dark complexion; Hartmut, son of Ludwig, King of Normandy; and, lastly, Herwig of Zealand. Although the latter fancied that he had won some favor in the fair Gudrun's sight, Hettel dismissed him as well as the others, with the answer that his daughter was yet too young to leave the parental roof.

Herwig, who was not ready to give the maiden up, then remembered that Hettel had won his own bride only after he had measured his strength with her father's; so he collected an army, invaded Matelan, and proved his courage by encountering Hettel himself in the fray. Gudrun, who stood watching the battle from the palace window, seeing them face to face, loudly implored them to spare each other, an entreaty to which they both lent a willing ear.

"Fair Gudrun saw the combat, and heard the martial sound.
Like to a ball is fortune, and ever turns around.

"Then from the castle chamber the royal maid cried out:
'King Hetel, noble father, the blood flows all about
Athwart the mighty hauberks. With gore from warlike labor
The walls are sprinkled. Herwig is a most dreadful neighbor.'"
Gudrun (Dippold's tr.).

Herwig had in this encounter proved himself no despicable foe; so Hettel, preferring to have him as a friend, no longer opposed his betrothal, but even promised that the wedding festivities should be celebrated within a year. Herwig tarried in Matelan with his betrothed until he heard that Siegfried, King of Moorland, jealous of his successful wooing of Gudrun, had invaded his kingdom and was raiding his unprotected lands.

These tidings caused the brave young warrior to bid Gudrun a hasty farewell and sail home as quickly as possible, Hettel promising to follow him soon and help him repel the invaders, who were far superior in number to his small but oft-tried host. While Herwig and Hettel were thus occupied in warring against one of the disappointed suitors, Hartmut, the other, hearing that they were both away, invaded Matelan and carried off Gudrun and all her attendants to Normandy. He paused only once on his way thither to rest for a short time on an island called Wülpensand, at the mouth of the Scheldt.

The bereaved Hilde, who had seen her beloved daughter thus carried away, promptly sent messengers to warn Hettel and Herwig of Gudrun's capture. These tidings put an immediate stop to their warfare with Siegfried, who, joining forces with them, sailed in pursuit of the Normans in the vessels of a party of pilgrims, for they had none of their own ready for instant departure.

Hettel, Herwig, and Siegfried reached Wülpensand before the Normans had left it, and there took place a frightful conflict, in the course of which King Ludwig slew the aged Hettel. The conflict raged until nightfall, and although there were now but few Hegelings left, they were all ready to renew the struggle on the morrow. What was not their chagrin, therefore, on discovering that the Normans had sailed away with their captives during the night, and were already out of sight!

It was useless to pursue them with so small an army; so the Hegelings sorrowfully returned home, bearing Hettel's lifeless body back to the disconsolate Hilde. Then they took counsel, and discovered that so many able fighting men had perished during the last war that they would be obliged to wait until the rising generation was able to bear arms before they could invade Normandy with any hope of success.

"Then spoke old Wat, the hero: 'It never can befall
Before this country's children have grown to manhood all.'"
Gudrun (Dippold's tr.).

Gudrun, in the mean while, had arrived in Normandy, where she persisted in refusing to marry Hartmut. On her way thither the haughty princess had even ventured to remind King Ludwig that he had once been her father's vassal, and so roused his anger that he threw her overboard. But Hartmut immediately plunged into the water after her, rescued her from drowning, and when he had again seen her safe in the boat, angrily reproved his father for his hasty conduct.

"He said: 'Why would you drown her who is to be my wife,
The fair and charming Gudrun? I love her as my life.
Another than my father, if he had shown such daring,
Would lose his life and honor from wrath of mine unsparing.'"
Gudrun (Dippold's tr.).

After this declaration on the part of the young heir, none dared at first treat Gudrun with any disrespect; and Gerlinda and Ortrun, the mother and sister of Hartmut, welcomed her as she landed on their shores. Gerlinda's friendliness was a mere pretense, however, for she hated the proud maiden who scorned her son's proffered love. She therefore soon persuaded her son to give the gentle captive entirely into her charge, saying that she would make her consent to become his bride. Hartmut, who was about to depart for the war, and who little suspected his mother's cruel intentions, bade her do as she pleased; and he was no sooner out of sight than poor Gudrun was degraded to the rank of a servant, and treated with much harshness and often with actual violence.

During three whole years Gudrun endured this cruelty in silence; but when Hartmut returned she was restored to her former state, although she still persisted in refusing his passionate suit. Discouraged by her obstinacy, the young man weakly consented to abandon her again to Gerlinda's tender mercies. The princess was now made to labor harder than ever, and she and Hildburg, her favorite

GUDRUN AND THE SWAN.—Kepler.

companion and fellow captive, were daily sent down to the shore to wash the royal linen.

It was winter, the snow lay thick on the ground, and Gudrun and her companion, barefooted and miserably clad, suffered untold agonies from the cold. Besides, they were nearly exhausted, and the hope of rescue, which had sustained them during the past twelve years, had almost forsaken them. Their deliverance was near, however, and while Gudrun was washing on the shore, a mermaid, in the guise of a swan, came gently near her and bade her be of good cheer, for her sufferings would soon be at an end.

> "'Rejoice in hope,' then answered the messenger divine;
> 'Thou poor and homeless maiden, great joy shall yet be thine.
> If thou wilt ask for tidings from thy dear native land,
> To comfort thee, great Heaven has sent me to this strand.'"
> *Gudrun* (Dippold's tr.).

The swan maiden then informed her that her brother Ortwine had grown up, and that he would soon come with brave old Wat and the longing Herwig to deliver her.

The next day, in spite of the increased cold, Gerlinda again roughly bade the maidens go down to the shore and wash, refusing to allow them any covering except one rough linen garment.

> "They then took up the garments and went upon their way.
> 'May God let me,' said Gudrun, 'remind you of this day.'
> With naked feet they waded there through the ice and snow:
> The noble maids, all homeless, were filled with pain and woe."
> *Gudrun* (Dippold's tr.).

Gudrun and Hildburg had barely begun their usual task, however, ere a small boat drew near, in which they recognized Herwig and Ortwine. All unconscious of their identity at first, the young men inquired about Gudrun. She herself, to test their affection, replied that the princess was dead, and did not allow them to catch a glimpse of her face until she beheld Herwig's emotion at these tidings, and heard him protest that he would be faithful to her unto death.

> "There spoke the royal Herwig: 'As long as lasts my life,
> I'll mourn for her; the maiden was to become my wife.'"
> *Gudrun* (Dippold's tr.).

The lovers, who had been equally true, now fell into each other's arms. Ortwine was overjoyed at finding his sister and her companion, having long secretly loved the latter, so he poured out an avowal of his passion, and won from Hildburg a promise to be his wife. The first moments of joyful reunion over, Herwig would fain have carried Gudrun and Hildburg back to camp with him; but Ortwine proudly declared that he had come to claim them openly, and would bear them away from Normandy honorably, in the guise of princesses, rather than by stealth.

Promising to rescue them on the morrow, the young men took leave of the maidens. Hildburg conscientiously finished her task, but Gudrun proudly flung the linen into the sea and returned to the palace empty-handed, saying that it did not become her to do any more menial labor, since she had been kissed by two kings. Gerlinda, hearing her confess that she had flung the linen into the sea, ordered her to be scourged; but when Gudrun turned upon her and proudly announced that she would take her revenge on the morrow, when she would preside over the banquet hall as queen, Gerlinda concluded that she had decided to accept Hartmut.

The mother, therefore, flew to him to impart the joyful tidings. In his delight he would fain have embraced Gudrun, who, however, haughtily bade him refrain from saluting a mere washerwoman. Becoming aware only then of her sorry plight, the prince withdrew, sternly ordering that her maidens should again be restored to her, that her every command should be fulfilled as if she were already queen, and that all should treat her with the utmost respect. These orders were executed without delay, and while Hartmut was preparing for his wedding on the morrow, Gudrun, again clad in royal attire, with her maidens around her, whispered the tidings of their coming deliverance. Morning had barely dawned when Hildburg, gazing out of the window, saw the castle entirely surrounded by the Hegelings' forces; and at cockcrow old Wat's horn pealed forth a loud defiance, rousing the Normans from pleasant dreams, and calling them to battle instead of to the anticipated wedding.

"The morning star had risen upon the heavens high,
When to the castle window a beauteous maid drew nigh,
In order to espy there and watch the break of day,
Whereby from royal Gudrun she would obtain rich pay.

"There looked the noble maiden and saw the morning glow.
Reflected in the water, as it might well be so,
Were seen the shining helmets and many bucklers beaming.
The castle was surrounded; with arms the fields were gleaming."
Gudrun (Dippold's tr.).

The battle was very fierce, and the poem enumerates many of the cuts and thrusts given and received. Clashing swords and streams of gore now monopolize the reader's attention. In the fray Herwig slew King Ludwig. Gudrun was rescued by Hartmut from the hands of Gerlinda, who had just bidden her servants put her to death, so that her friends should not take her alive. Next the Norman prince met his rival and fought bravely. He was about to succumb, however, when his sister Ortrun, who throughout had been gentle and loving to Gudrun, implored her to save her brother's life. Gudrun, touched by this request, called out of the casement to Herwig, who, at a word from her, sheathed his sword, and contented himself with taking Hartmut prisoner.

The castle was duly plundered, the whole town sacked, and Wat, bursting into the palace, began to slay all he met. The women, in terror, then crowded around Gudrun, imploring her protection. Among these were Ortrun and Gerlinda; but while Gudrun would have protected the former at the cost of her life, she allowed Wat to kill the latter, who had deserved such a death in punishment for all her cruelty.

When the massacre was over, the victors celebrated their triumph by a grand banquet, at which Gudrun, fulfilling her boast, actually presided as queen.

"Now from the bitter contest the warriors rested all.
There came the royal Herwig into King Ludwig's hall,
Together with his champions, their gear with blood yet streaming.
Dame Gudrun well received him; her heart with love was teeming."
Gudrun (Dippold's tr.).

When the banquet was over, the Hegelings set sail, taking with them the recovered maidens, all the spoil they had won, and their captives, Hartmut and Ortrun; and on reaching Matelan they were warmly welcomed by Hilde, who was especially rejoiced to see her daughter once more.

> "The queen drew near to Gudrun. Could any one outweigh
> The joy they felt together, with any wealth or treasure?
> When they had kissed each other their grief was changed to pleasure."
> *Gudrun* (Dippold's tr.).

Shortly after their return home a fourfold wedding took place. Gudrun married her faithful Herwig, Ortwine espoused Hildburg, Siegfried consoled himself for Gudrun's loss by taking the fair Ortrun to wife, and Hartmut received with the hand of Hergart, Herwig's sister, the restitution not only of his freedom but also of his kingdom.

At the wedding banquet Horant, who, in spite of his advanced years, had lost none of his musical skill, played the wedding march with such success that the queens simultaneously flung their crowns at his feet,—an offering which he smilingly refused, telling them that crowns were perishable, but that the poet's song was immortal.

> "The aged minstrel drew his harp still closer to his breast,
> Gazed at the jeweled coronets as this thought he expressed:
> 'Fair queens, I bid you wear them until your locks turn gray;
> Those crowns, alas! are fleeting, but song will live alway.'"
> NIENDORF (H.A.G.'s tr.).

CHAPTER III.

REYNARD THE FOX.

Among primitive races, as with children, animal stories are much enjoyed, and form one of the first stages in literature. The oldest of these tales current in the middle ages is the epic of Reineke Fuchs, or Reynard the Fox. This poem was carried by the ancient Franks across the Rhine, became fully acclimated in France, and then returned to Germany by way of Flanders, where it was localized.

After circulating from mouth to mouth almost all over Europe, during many centuries, it was first committed to writing in the Netherlands, where the earliest manuscript, dating from the eleventh or twelfth century, gives a Latin version of the tale.

"The root of this saga lies in the harmless natural simplicity of a primeval people. We see described the delight which the rude child of nature takes in all animals,—in their slim forms, their gleaming eyes, their fierceness, their nimbleness and cunning. Such sagas would naturally have their origin in an age when the ideas of shepherd and hunter occupied a great portion of the intellectual horizon of the people; when the herdman saw in the ravenous bear one who was his equal, and more than his equal, in force and adroitness, the champion of the woods and wilds; when the hunter, in his lonely ramble through the depths of the forest, beheld in the hoary wolf and red fox, as they stole along,—hunters like himself,—mates, so to say, and companions, and whom he therefore addressed as such.... So that originally this kind of poetry was the exponent of a peculiar sort of feeling prevailing among the people, and had nothing whatever to do with the didactic or satiric, although at a later period satiric allusions began to be interwoven with it."

The story has been rewritten by many poets and prose writers. It has been translated into almost every European language, and was remodeled from one of the old mediaeval poems by Goethe, who has given it the form in which it will doubtless henceforth be known. His poem "Reineke Fuchs" has been commented upon by Carlyle and translated by Rogers, from whose version all the following quotations have been extracted.

As was the custom among the Franks under their old Merovingian rulers, the animals all assembled at Whitsuntide around their king, Nobel the lion, who ruled over all the forest. This assembly, like the Champ de Mars, its prototype, was convened not only for the purpose of deciding upon the undertakings for the following year, but also as a special tribunal, where all accusations were made, all complaints heard, and justice meted out to all. The animals were all present, all except Reynard the fox, who, it soon became apparent, was accused of many a dark deed. Every beast present testified to some crime committed by him, and all accused him loudly except his nephew, Grimbart the badger.

> "And yet there was one who was absent,
> Reineke Fox, the rascal! who, deeply given to mischief,
> Held aloof from half the Court. As shuns a bad conscience
> Light and day, so the fox fought shy of the nobles assembled.
> One and all had complaints to make, he had all of them injured;
> Grimbart the badger, his brother's son, alone was excepted."

The complaint was voiced by Isegrim the wolf, who told with much feeling how cruelly Reynard had blinded three of his beloved children, and how shamefully he had insulted his wife, the fair lady Gieremund. This accusation had no sooner been formulated than Wackerlos the dog came forward, and, speaking French, pathetically described the finding of a little sausage in a thicket, and its purloining by Reynard, who seemed to have no regard whatever for his famished condition.

The tomcat Hintze, who at the mere mention of a sausage had listened more attentively, now angrily cried out that the sausage which Wackerlos had lost belonged by right to him, as he had concealed it in the thicket after stealing it from the miller's wife. He added that he too had had much to suffer from Reynard, and was supported by the panther, who described how he had once found the miscreant cruelly beating poor Lampe the hare.

"Lampe he held by the collar,
Yes, and had certainly taken his life, if I by good fortune
Had not happened to pass by the road. There standing you see him.
Look and see the wounds of the gentle creature, whom no one
Ever would think of ill treating."

The king, Nobel, was beginning to look very stern as one after another rose to accuse the absent Reynard, when Grimbart the badger courageously began to defend him, and artfully turned the tables upon the accusers. Taking up their complaints one by one, he described how Reynard, his uncle, once entered into partnership with Isegrim. To obtain some fish which a carter was conveying to market, the fox had lain as if dead in the middle of the road. He had been picked up by the man for the sake of his fur, and tossed up on top of the load of fish. But no sooner had the carter's back been turned than the fox sprang up, threw all the fish down into the road to the expectant wolf, and only sprang down himself when the cart was empty. The wolf, ravenous as ever, devoured the fish as fast as they were thrown down, and when the fox claimed his share of the booty he had secured, Isegrim gave him only the bones.[3]

Not content with cheating his ally once, the wolf had induced the fox to steal a suckling pig from the larder of a sleeping peasant. With much exertion the cunning Reynard had thrown the prize out of the window to the waiting wolf; but when he asked for a portion of the meat as reward, he was dismissed with nothing but the piece of wood upon which it had been hung.

The badger further proceeded to relate that Reynard had wooed Gieremund seven years before, when she was still unmated, and that if Isegrim chose to consider that an insult, it was only on a par with the rest of his accusations, for the king could readily see that Reynard was sorely injured instead of being guilty.

Then, encouraged by the favorable impression he had produced, Grimbart airily disposed of the cases of Wackerlos and Hintze by proving that they had both stolen the disputed sausage, after which he went on to say that Reynard had undertaken to instruct Lampe the hare in psalmody, and that the ill treatment which the panther had described was only a little wholesome castigation inflicted by the teacher upon a lazy and refractory pupil.

3   For Russian version see Guerber's Contes et Légendes, vol. i., p. 93.

> "Should not the master his pupil
> Sometimes chastise when he will not observe, and is stubborn in evil?
> If boys were never punished, were thoughtlessness always passed over,
> Were bad behavior allowed, how would our juveniles grow up?"

These plausible explanations were not without their effect, and when Grimbart went on to declare that, ever since Nobel proclaimed a general truce and amnesty among all the animals of the forest, Reynard had turned hermit and spent all his time in fasting, almsgiving, and prayer, the complaint was about to be dismissed.

Suddenly, however, Henning the cock appeared, followed by his two sons, Kryant and Kantart, bearing the mangled remains of a hen upon a bier. In broken accents the bereaved father related how happily he had dwelt in a convent henyard, with the ten sons and fourteen daughters which his excellent consort had hatched and brought up in a single summer. His only anxiety had been caused by the constant prowling of Reynard, who, however, had been successfully at a distance by the watchdogs. But when the general truce had been proclaimed, the dogs were dismissed. Reynard, in the garb of a monk, had made his way into the henyard to show Henning the royal proclamation with the attached seal, and to assure him of his altered mode of living.

Thus reassured, Henning had led his family out into the forest, where, alas! Reynard was lurking, and where he killed all but five of Henning's promising brood. They had not only been killed, but devoured, with the exception of Scratch-foot, whose mangled remains were laid at the monarch's feet in proof of the crime, as was customary in the mediaeval courts of justice.

The king, angry that his truce should thus have been broken, and sorry for the evident grief of the father, ordered a sumptuous funeral for the deceased, and commanded that a stone should be placed upon her grave, bearing the epitaph:

> "'Scratch-foot, daughter of Henning, the cock, the best of the hen tribe.
> Many an egg did she lay in her nest, and was skillful in scratching.
> Here she lies, lost, alas! to her friends, by Reineke murdered.
> All the world should know of his false and cruel behavior,
> As for the dead they lament.' Thus ran the words that were written."

Then the king, having taken advice with his council, solemnly bade Brown the bear proceed immediately to Malepartus, Reynard's home, and summon him to appear at Reynard and court forthwith, to answer the grave charges which had been made against him. But he warned his messenger to behave circumspectly and to beware of the wiles of the crafty fox. The bear rather resented these well-meant recommendations, and, confidently asserting his ability to take care of himself, set out for Reynard's abode.

On his way to the mountains he was obliged to pass through an arid, sandy waste, and reached Malepartus weary and overheated. Standing before the fortress, which rejoiced in many labyrinthine passages, he loudly made known his errand; and when Reynard, peeping cautiously out, had ascertained that Brown was alone, he hastened out to welcome him.

With great volubility the fox commiserated his long journey, and excused the delay in admitting him under plea of an indisposition caused by eating too much honey, a diet which he abhorred.

At the mere mention of honey the bear forgot all his fatigue, and when his host lamented the fact that he had nothing else to offer him, he joyfully declared no food could suit him better, and that he could never get enough of it.

> "'If that is so,' continued the Red one, 'I really can serve you,
> For the peasant Rüsteviel lives at the foot of the mountain.
> Honey he has, indeed, such that you and all of your kindred
> Never so much together have seen.'"

Oblivious of everything else at the thought of such a treat, Brown the bear immediately set out in Reynard's company, and they soon came to the peasant's yard, where a half-split tree trunk lay in full view. Reynard then bade his companion thrust his nose well down into the hollow and eat his fill of honey. As soon as he saw that the bear had thrust not only his nose, but both fore paws, into the crack, Reynard cleverly removed the wedges, the tree clapped together, and he left the bear a prisoner and howling with pain.

These sounds soon attracted the peasant's attention, and he and his companions all fell upon the captive bear with every imaginable weapon, and proceeded to give him a sound beating. Frantic with pain and terror, the unfortunate bear finally succeeded in wrenching himself free, at the cost of the skin on his nose and fore paws, and,

BROWN THE BEAR CAUGHT IN THE LOG.—Wagner.

after tumbling the fat cook into the water, swam down the stream and landed in a thicket to bewail his misfortunes. Here he was found by the fox, who added insult to injury by making fun of him, and reproved him for his gluttony, until the bear again plunged into the stream and swam away.

Then, painfully making his way back to Nobel, Brown presented himself at court all bleeding and travel-stained, and poured forth a doleful account of his mission.

The king, after consulting with his principal courtiers, declared it the right of any man to be thrice summoned, and, conceding that the bear's manners were not of a conciliatory nature, selected Hintze the cat to bear his message to Malepartus. The cat, disheartened by unfavorable omens, was nevertheless compelled to go on this unwelcome journey.

Reynard welcomed him cordially, promised to accompany him to court on the morrow, and then asked what kind of refreshment he could offer. When Hintze had confessed his preference for mice, the fox replied that it was very fortunate, as there were plenty of them in the parson's barn. Hintze immediately asked to be led thither, that he might eat his fill.

> "'Pray do me the kindness
> Hence to lead and show me the mice, for far above wild game
> Give me a mouse for delicate flavor.'"

Reynard then conducted Hintze to the parson's barn, and pointed out a little opening through which he had passed to steal chickens, and where he knew that Martin, the parson's son, had laid a trap to catch any intruder. Hintze at first demurred, but, urged by Reynard, crept in and found himself caught in a noose. Reynard, pretending to take the cat's moans for cries of joy, banteringly inquired whether that was the way they sang at court, as the caterwauling grew louder.

These sounds finally reached the ears of little Martin, who, accompanied by his father, came into the barn to catch the intruder. Poor Hintze, frightened at the sight of the bludgeon the parson carried, flew at his legs, scratching and biting him, until the saintly man fainted. Then, taking advantage of the confusion, Hintze managed to slip out of the noose and effect his escape. He returned to court minus one eye, and there poured out the story of his wrongs.

The wrath of the king was now terrible to behold, and assembling his council, he bade them decide how he should punish the wretch who had twice ill treated his messengers. Grimbart the badger, seeing that public opinion was decidedly against his relative, now begged that a third summons should be sent, and offered to carry the message himself. He furthermore declared that, even according to their own showing, the cat and bear had come to grief through their greediness; and then he promptly departed.

Grimbart found Reynard in the bosom of his family, delivered his message, and frankly advised the fox to obey the king's summons and appear at court, where, perchance, he might yet manage to save himself; while if he remained at home the king would besiege his fortress and slay him and all his family. Reynard listened favorably to this advice, and, after bidding his wife a tender farewell, and committing his beloved children to her care, he set out with Grimbart to go to court.

On the way the recollection of his many transgressions began to lie very heavily upon his heart. The fear of death quickened his conscience, and, longing to make his peace with Heaven, he expressed a great wish to confess his sins and receive absolution. As no priest was near at hand, he begged Grimbart the badger to listen to him, and penitently confessed all the misdeeds we have already recounted. He also added that he once bound Isegrim to the rope of the convent bell at Elkinar, where his frantic tugging rang the bell, until the monks, crowding around him, cudgeled him severely. Reynard related, too, how he once induced Isegrim to enter the priests' house through a window and crawl along some beams in search of ham and bacon. As the wolf was carefully feeling his way, however, the mischievous fox pushed him and made him fall on the sleeping people below, who, awakening with a start, fell upon him and beat him. These and sundry other sins having duly been confessed, the badger bade the fox chastise himself with a switch plucked from the hedge, lay it down in the road, jump over it thrice, and then meekly kiss that rod in token of obedience. Then he pronounced Reynard absolved from his former sins, and admonished him to lead an altered life in future.

"'My uncle, take care that your future amendment
In good works be visible. Psalms you should read, and should visit
Churches with diligence; fast at the seasons duly appointed;
Him who asks you point out the way to; give to the needy
Willingly; swear to forsake all evil habits of living,
All kinds of theft and robbing, deceit and evil behavior.
Thus can you make quite sure that you will attain unto mercy!'"

The fox solemnly promised amendment, and with sanctimonious mien continued his journey. But as he and the badger passed a convent, and some plump hens crossed their path, Reynard forgot all his promises and began to chase the chickens. Sharply recalled to a sense of duty by Grimbart, Reynard reluctantly gave up the chase, and the two proceeded without further drawback to the court, where Reynard's arrival created a great sensation.

"When at the Court it was known that Reineke really was coming,
Ev'ry one thronged out of doors to see him, the great and the little.
Few with friendly intent; for almost all were complaining.
This, however, in Reineke's mind was of little importance;
Thus he pretended, at least, as he with Grimbart the badger,
Boldly enough and with elegant mien now walked up the high street.
Jauntily swung he along at his ease, as if he were truly
Son of the king, and free and quit of ev'ry transgression.
Thus he came before Nobel the king, and stood in the palace
In the midst of the lords; he knew how to pose as unruffled."

With consummate skill and unparalleled eloquence and impudence, Reynard addressed the king, lauding himself as a faithful servant, and commiserating the fact that so many envious and backbiting people were ready to accuse him. Nobel the king, in whose mind the recollection of the treatment inflicted upon Brown the bear and Hintze the cat was still very vivid, answered him sternly, and told him that it would be difficult for him to acquit himself of those two charges, to say nothing of the many others brought against him. Reynard, still undismayed, demanded with well-feigned indignation whether he was to be held responsible for the sins of those messengers whose misfortunes were attributable to their gluttonous and thievish propensities only.

But in spite of this specious pleading, all the other animals came crowding around with so many grievous charges that matters began to look very dark indeed for the fox. In spite of all Reynard's eloquence, and of the fluent excuses ever on his tongue, the council pronounced him guilty, and condemned him to die an ignominious death. Reynard's enemies rejoiced at this sentence, and dragged him off with cheerful alacrity to the gallows, where all the animals assembled to witness his execution.

On the way to the place of punishment Reynard tried to think of some plan by means of which he could save himself even at the eleventh hour; and knowing that some scheme would occur to him if he could only gain a little time, he humbly implored permission to make a public confession of his manifold sins ere he paid the penalty of his crimes. Anxious to hear all he might have to say, the king granted him permission to speak; and the fox began to relate at length the story of his early and innocent childhood, his meeting and alliance with Isegrim the wolf, and his gradual induction by him into crooked paths and evil ways. He told, too, how the cruel wolf, presuming on his strength, had ever made use of it to deprive him, the fox, of his rightful share of plunder; and concluded by saying that he would often have suffered from hunger had it not been for the possession of a great treasure of gold, which had sufficed for all his wants.

> "Thanks be to God, however, I never suffered from hunger;
> Secretly have I fed well by means of that excellent treasure,
> All of silver and gold in a secret place that securely
> Hidden I keep; with this I've enough. And, I say it in earnest,
> Not a wagon could carry it off, though sevenfold loaded."

At the word "treasure" Nobel pricked up his ears and bade Reynard relate how this hoard was obtained and where it was concealed. The artful fox, seeing the king's evident interest, rapidly prepared more lies, and, speaking to the king and queen, declared that ere he died it would be better for him to reveal the carefully guarded secret of a conspiracy which would have resulted in the king's death had it not been for his devotion.

The queen, shuddering at the mere thought of the danger her royal consort had run, now begged that Reynard might step down from the scaffold and speak privately to her and to Nobel. In this interview Reynard, still pretending to prepare for immediate death, told how he discovered a conspiracy formed by his father, Isegrim the wolf, Brown the bear, and many others, to slay the king and seize the scepter. He described the various secret conferences, the measures taken, and his father's promise to defray all the expenses of the enterprise and to subsidize mercenary troops by means of the hoard of King Ermenrich, which he had discovered and concealed for his own use.

Reynard then continued to describe his loyal fears for his beloved sovereign, his resolve to outwit the conspirators, and his efforts to deprive them of the sinews of war by discovering and abstracting the treasure. Thanks to his ceaseless vigilance, he saw his father steal forth one night, uncover his hoard, gloat over the gold, and then efface the traces of his search with the utmost skill.

> "'Nor could one,
> Not having seen, have possibly known. And ere he went onwards
> Well he understood at the place where his feet had been planted,
> Cleverly backwards and forwards to draw his tail, and to smooth it,
> And to efface the trace with the aid of his mouth.'"

Reynard then told the king how diligently he and his wife, Ermelyn, labored to remove the gold and conceal it elsewhere, and how the conspiracy came to naught when no gold was found to pay the troops. He mournfully added that his loyalty further deprived him of a loving father, for the latter had hung himself in despair when he found his treasure gone and all his plans frustrated. With hypocritical tears he then bewailed his own fate, saying that, although ready to risk all for another, there was no one near him to speak a good word for him in his time of bitterest need.

The queen's soft heart was so touched by this display of feeling that she soon pleaded for and obtained Reynard's pardon from Nobel, who freely granted it when the fox promised to give him his treasure. Most accurately now he described its place of concealment, but said that he could not remain at court, as his presence there was an insult to royalty, seeing that he was under the Pope's ban and must make a pilgrimage ere it could be removed.

The king, after imprisoning Isegrim, Brown, and Hintze (the chief conspirators according to Reynard's tale), and ascertaining that the place the fox so accurately described really existed, bade Reynard depart, and at his request procured for him a fragment of Brown's hide to make a wallet, and a pair of socks from Isegrim and his wife, who were very loath to part with their foot covering. The king, queen, and court then accompanied Reynard a short way on the first stage of his journey, and turned back, leaving Bellyn the ram and Lampe the hare to escort him a little farther. These innocent companions accompanied Reynard to Malepartus, and while Bellyn waited patiently without, Lampe entered the house with Reynard. Lady Ermelyn and her two young sons greeted Reynard with joy, listened breathlessly to the account of his adventures, and then helped him to slay and eat Lampe, who, he declared, had brought all these evils upon him.

Reynard and his family feasted upon the body of poor Lampe the hare, whose head was then securely fastened in the wallet made of Brown's skin. This the fox carefully carried out and placed upon Bellyn's back, assuring him volubly the while that it contained important dispatches, and that in order to insure him a suitable reward for his good offices he had told Nobel the king that the ram had given him valuable assistance in preparing the contents of the wallet.

> "'Yet, as soon as you see the king, and to still better favor
> Wish to attain with him, 'twere well to bring to his notice
> That you have sagely given advice in composing the letters,
> Yea, and the writer have help'd.'"

Thus instructed, and reassured concerning the absence of Lampe, whom Reynard described as enjoying a chat with Ermelyn, Bellyn bounded off to court, where he did not fail to vaunt that he had helped Reynard prepare the contents of the wallet. Nobel publicly opened it, and when he drew out Lampe's bleeding head his anger knew no bounds. Following the advice of his courtiers, Bellyn, in spite of all his protestations, was given in atonement to the bear and the wolf, who the king now feared had been unjustly treated. They were then released from imprisonment and reinstated to royal favor, and twelve days of festivity ensued.

In the midst of the dance and revelry a bloody rabbit appeared to accuse Reynard of tearing off one of his ears, while the garrulous crow, Merkinau, related how the same unscrupulous wretch had pretended death merely to befool Sharfenebbe, his wife, and induce her to come near enough for him to bite off her head. Nobel the king, upon hearing these complaints, immediately swore that within six days he would besiege Reynard in his castle, would take him prisoner, and would make him suffer the penalty of his crimes.

Isegrim the wolf and Brown the bear rejoiced at these tidings, while Grimbart the badger, seeing the peril his uncle had incurred, hastened off secretly to Malepartus to warn him of his danger and support him by his advice. He found Reynard sitting complacently in front of his house, contemplating two young doves which he had just secured as they were making their first attempt to fly. Grimbart breathlessly related the arrival of Bellyn, the royal indignation at the sight of Lampe's head, and the plan for surrounding and capturing Reynard in his safe retreat.

In spite of this disquieting news Reynard's composure did not desert him; but after vowing that he could easily acquit himself of these crimes if he could only win the king's ear for a moment, he invited his kinsman to share his meal and taste the delicate morsels he had secured. Grimbart the badger, seeing that the fox was not inclined to flee, now advised him not to await the king's coming and expose his wife and children to the horrors of a siege, but boldly to return to court.

> "'Go with assurance before the lords, and put the best face on
> Your affairs. They will give you a hearing. Lupardus was also
> Willing you should not be punish'd before you had fully
> Made your defense, and the queen herself was not otherwise minded.
> Mark this fact, and try to make use of it.'"

Once more Reynard bade a tender farewell to his wife and sons, resisting all the former's entreaties to seek safety in flight, and, relying upon his cunning, set out with Grimbart to visit the court. On his way he again pretended repentance for his former sins, and resuming his confession at the point where he had broken off, he told how maliciously he had secured a piece of the bear's hide for a wallet, and socks from Isegrim and his wife. He then went on to relate just how he had murdered Lampe, charged the innocent Bellyn with the ambiguous message which had cost him his life, torn off one of the rabbit's ears, and eaten the crow's wife. Lastly, he confessed how he had gone out in company with the wolf, who, being hungry and seeing a mare with a little foal, had bidden Reynard inquire at what price she would sell it. The mare retorted that the price was written on her hoof. The sly fox, understanding her meaning, yet longing to get his companion into trouble, pretended not to know how to read, and sent the wolf to ascertain the price. The result was, of course, disastrous, for the mare kicked so hard that the wolf lay almost dead for several hours after.

> "So he went and asked the lady, 'What price is the filly?
> Make it cheap.' Whereupon she replied, 'You've only to read it;
> There you will find the sum inscribed on one of my hind feet.'
> 'Let me look,' continued the wolf; and she answered, 'With pleasure.'
> "Then she lifted upwards her foot from the grass; it was studded
> With six nails. She struck straight out, and not by a hair's breadth
> Missed she her mark. She struck on his head, and straightway he fell down,
> Lying as dumb as the dead."

Waxing more and more eloquent as they drew nearer court and his fears increased, Reynard began to moralize. He excused himself for Lampe's murder on the plea of the latter's aggravating behavior, said that the king himself was nothing but a robber living by rapine, and proceeded to show how even the priests were guilty of manifold sins, which he enumerated with much gusto.

They had scarcely finished this edifying conversation when they came across Martin the ape, on his way to Rome; and Reynard hastened to implore him to secure his release from the Pope's ban, through the intercession of the ape's uncle, the cardinal, whose interest it was to serve him. Martin the ape not only promised his good offices at the papal court, but bade Reynard not hesitate to consult his wife should he find himself in any predicament at court.

Thus supported, Reynard again made his appearance at court, to the utter amazement and surprise of all; and although, he was well aware that his situation was more dangerous than ever, his assurance did not seem at all impaired. Kneeling with pretended humility before the king, he artfully began his address by lamenting the fact that there were so many unscrupulous people ever ready to accuse the innocent; and when the king angrily interrupted him to accuse him of maiming the rabbit and devouring the crow, he began his defense.

First Reynard explained that since Martin the ape had undertaken to free him from his ban, his journey to Rome was of course unnecessary. Then he related how the rabbit, dining at his house, had insulted and quarreled with his children, from whose clutches he had had much trouble to save him. The crow's death was caused by a fish bone she had swallowed. Bellyn, the traitor, had slain Lampe himself, and evidently put his head in the wallet instead of some treasures which Reynard had intrusted to their care for the king and queen.

The king, who had listened impatiently to all this discourse, angrily retired, refusing to believe a word, while Reynard sought the ape's wife, Frau Rückenau, and bade her intercede for him. She entered the royal tent, reminded the king of her former services, and seeing his mood somewhat softened, ventured to mention how cleverly Reynard once helped him to judge between the rival claims of a shepherd and a serpent. The latter, caught in a noose and about to die, had implored a passing shepherd to set it free. The peasant had done so after exacting a solemn oath from the serpent to do him no harm. But the serpent, once released, and suffering from the pangs of hunger, threatened to devour the peasant. The latter called the raven, wolf, and bear, whom he met by the way, to his aid; but as they all hoped to get a share of him, they all decided in favor of the serpent's claim to eat him.

The case by this time had become so intricate that it was laid before the king, who, unable to judge wisely, called Reynard to his aid. The fox declared that he could only settle so difficult a matter when plaintiff and defendant had assumed the relative positions which they occupied at the time of dispute. Then when the snake was safely in the noose once more, Reynard decided that, knowing the serpent's treachery, the peasant might again set him loose, but need not do so unless he chose.

REYNARD PREPARING FOR BATTLE.—Kaulbach.

"'Here now is each of the parties
Once again in his former state, nor has either the contest
Won or lost. The right, I think, of itself is apparent.
For if it pleases the man, he again can deliver the serpent
Out of the noose; if not, he may let her remain and be hang'd there.
Free he may go on his way with honor and see to his business,
Since she has proved herself false, when she had accepted his kindness;
Fairly the man has the choice. This seems to me to be justice,
         True to the spirit. Let him who understands better declare it.'"

The king, remembering this celebrated judgment, and skillfully reminded by Frau Rückenau of the bear's and the wolf's rapacity, consented at last to give Reynard a second hearing. The fox now minutely described the treasures he sent to court,—a magic ring for the king, and a comb and mirror for the queen. Not only was the fable of the judgment of Paris engraved on the latter, but also that of the jealous donkey, who, imitating his master's lapdog, and trying to climb into his lap, received nothing but blows. There was also the story of the cat and the fox, of the wolf and the crane, and, lastly, the account of the miraculous way in which his father, a noted leech, had saved Nobel's sire by making him eat the flesh of a wolf just seven years old.

The pleader then reminded the king of a noted hunting party, where Isegrim, having secured a boar, gave the king one quarter, the queen another, reserved a half for himself, and gave the fox nothing but the head. This division was of course very disloyal, and the fox showed that he thought so by dividing a calf more equitably; i.e., giving the queen one half, the king the other, the heart and liver to the princes, the head to the wolf, and reserving only the feet for himself.

Reynard prided himself upon these tokens of loyalty, and then, seeing that he had made a favorable impression, he volunteered, in spite of his small size, to meet the wolf in battle and leave the vindication of his claims to the judgment of God. This magnanimous behavior filled the king with admiration, and the trial was appointed for the following day, the intervening hours being granted to both combatants for preparation. Reynard, still advised by Frau Rückenau, was shaved smooth, rubbed with butter until he was as slippery as could be, and instructed to feign fear and run fleetly in front of the wolf, kicking up as much sand as possible, and using his brush to dash it into his opponent's eyes and thus blind him.

The combat took place. The wolf, blinded by the sand in his eyes, was so infuriated that he finally pounced upon the fox, who, however, managed yet to get the upper hand and come off victor, generously granting life to his foe, whom he had nearly torn and scratched to pieces. Reynard, having thus won the victory, enjoyed the plaudits of the crowd, while the wolf, being vanquished, was publicly derided, and borne off by his few remaining friends to be nursed back to health, if possible.

> "Such is ever the way of the world. They say to the lucky,
> 'Long may you live in good health,' and friends he finds in abundance.
> When, however, ill fortune befalls him, alone he must bear it.
> Even so was it here; each one of them wish'd to the victor
> Nearest to be, to show himself off."

The king pronounced Reynard guiltless of all charges, and made him one of his privy councilors. But the fox, after thanking the king for his favors, humbly besought permission to return home, where his wife was awaiting him, and departed, escorted by a deputation of his friends.

According to some versions of the tale, Reynard contented himself with blinding the wolf and maiming him for life; according to others, he bided his time, and when the king was ill, told him that nothing could save him short of the heart of a wolf just seven years old. Of course no wolf of the exact age could be found but Isegrim, so he was sacrificed to save the king, who recovered. As for Reynard, he enjoyed great honor as long as he lived, and his adventures have long been the delight of the people, whom his tricks never failed to amuse.

> "Highly honor'd is Reineke now! To wisdom let all men
> Quickly apply them, and flee what is evil, and reverence virtue!
> This is the end and aim of the song, and in it the poet
> Fable and truth hath mixed, whereby the good from the evil
> Ye may discern, and wisdom esteem; and thereby the buyers
> Of this book in the ways of the world may be daily instructed.
> For it was so created of old, and will ever remain so.
> Thus is our poem of Reineke's deeds and character ended.
> May God bring us all to eternal happiness. Amen!"

CHAPTER IV.

THE NIBELUNGENLIED.

Germany's greatest epic is, without doubt, the ancient poem entitled "Nibelungenlied," or the "Lay," "Fall," or "Calamity of the Nibelungs." Although nothing certain is known concerning the real authorship of this beautiful work, it is supposed to have been put into its present form either by the Austrian minstrel von Kürenberg or by the German poet von Ofterdingen, some time previous to the year 1210, the date inscribed on the oldest manuscript of that poem now extant.

According to the best authorities on ancient German literature, the "Nibelungenlied" is compiled from preëxisting songs and rhapsodies, forming five distinct cycles of myths, but all referring in some way to the great treasure of the Nibelungs. One of these cycles is the northern Volsunga Saga,[4] where Sigurd, Gudrun, Gunnar, Högni, and Atli, the principal characters, correspond to Siegfried, Kriemhild, Gunther, Hagen, and Etzel of the "Nibelungenlied." The story of the German poem, which can be given only in outline, is as follows:

Dankrat and Ute, King and Queen of Burgundy, were the fortunate parents of four children: three sons, Gunther, Gernot, and Giselher; and one beautiful daughter, Kriemhild. When the king died, his eldest son, Gunther, succeeded him, and reigned wisely and well, residing at Worms on the Rhine, his capital and favorite city.

As was customary in those days, Kriemhild lived a peaceful and secluded life, rarely leaving her mother's palace and protection. But one night her slumbers, which were usually very peaceful, were disturbed by a tormenting dream, which, upon awaking, she hastened to confide to her mother, thinking that, as Ute was skilled in magic and dreams, she might give a favorable interpretation and thus rid her of her haunting fears.

4   See Guerber's Myths of Northern Lands, p. 225.

> "A dream was dreamt by Kriemhild, the virtuous and the gay,
> How a wild young falcon she train'd for many a day,
> Till two fierce eagles tore it."
>> *Nibelungenlied* (Lettsom's tr.).

Ute declared that the falcon her daughter had seen in her dream must be some noble prince, whom she would love and marry; while the two eagles were base murderers, who would eventually slay her beloved. Instead of reassuring Kriemhild, this interpretation only saddened her the more, and made her loudly protest that she would rather forego all the joys of married estate than have to mourn for a beloved husband.

In those days there flourished farther down the Rhine the kingdom of the Netherlands, governed by Siegmund and Siegelind. They were very proud of their only son and heir, young Siegfried, who had already reached man's estate. To celebrate his knighthood a great tournament was held at Xanten on the Rhine, and in the jousting the young prince won all the laurels, although great and tried warriors matched their skill against his in the lists.

The festivities continued for seven whole days, and when the guests departed they were all heavily laden with the costly gifts which the king and queen had lavished upon them.

> "The gorgeous feast it lasted till the seventh day was o'er.
> Siegelind, the wealthy, did as they did of yore;
> She won for valiant Siegfried the hearts of young and old,
> When for his sake among them she shower'd the ruddy gold.
> "You scarce could find one needy in all the minstrel band;
> Horses and robes were scatter'd with ever-open hand.
> They gave as though they had not another day to live;
> None were to take so ready as they inclin'd to give."
>> *Nibelungenlied* (Lettsom's tr.).

After the departure of all these guests, young Siegfried sought his parents' presence, told them that he had heard rumors of the beauty and attractions of Kriemhild of Burgundy, and declared his wish to journey thither to secure her as his wife.

In vain the fond parents tried to prevail upon him to remain quietly at home; the young hero insisted so strongly that he finally won their consent to his immediate departure. With eleven companions, all decked out in the richest garments that the queen's chests could furnish, the young prince rode down the Rhine, and reached Worms on the seventh day.

The arrival of the gallant little troop was soon noted by Gunther's subjects, who hastened out to meet the strangers and help them dismount. Siegfried immediately requested to be brought into the presence of their king, who, in the mean while, had inquired of his uncle, Hagen, the names and standing of the newcomers. Glancing down from the great hall window, Hagen said that the leader must be Siegfried, the knight who had slain the owners of the Nibelungen hoard and appropriated it for his own use, as well as the magic cloud-cloak, or Tarnkappe, which rendered its wearer invisible to mortal eyes.[5] He added that this same Siegfried was ruler of the Nibelungen land, and the slayer of a terrible dragon, whose blood had made him invulnerable, and he concluded by advising Gunther to receive him most courteously.

> "Yet more I know of Siegfried, that well your ear may hold:
> A poison-spitting dragon he slew with courage bold,
> And in the blood then bath'd him; thus turn'd to horn his skin,
> And now no weapons harm him, as often proved has been.
> "Receive then this young hero with all becoming state;
> 'Twere ill advis'd to merit so fierce a champion's hate.
> So lovely is his presence, at once all hearts are won,
> And then his strength and courage such wondrous deeds have done."
> *Nibelungenlied (Lettsom'str.).*

In obedience to this advice, Gunther went to meet Siegfried and politely inquired the cause of his visit. Imagine his dismay, therefore, when Siegfried replied that he had come to test the Burgundian's vaunted strength, and to propose a single combat, in which the victor might claim the lands and allegiance of the vanquished. Gunther recoiled from such a proposal, and as none of his warriors seemed inclined to accept the challenge, he and his brother hastened to disarm Siegfried's haughty mood by their proffers of unbounded hospitality.

---

5   For various legends of this cycle see Guerber's Legends of the Rhine, article Xanten.

Siegfried sojourned for nearly a year at Gunther's court, displaying his skill in all martial exercises; and although he never caught a glimpse of the fair maiden Kriemhild, she often admired his strength and manly beauty from behind the palace lattice.

One day the games were interrupted by the arrival of a herald announcing that Ludeger, King of the Saxons, and Ludegast, King of Denmark, were about to invade Burgundy. These tidings filled Gunther's heart with terror, for the enemy were very numerous and their valor was beyond all question. But when Hagen hinted that perhaps Siegfried would lend them a helping hand, the King of Burgundy seized the suggestion with joy.

As soon as Siegfried was made aware of the threatened invasion he declared that if Gunther would only give him one thousand brave men he would repel the foe. This offer was too good to refuse; so Gunther hastily assembled a chosen corps, in which were his brothers Gernot and Giselher, Hagen and his brother Dankwart, Ortwine, Sindolt, and Volker,—all men of remarkable valor.

> "'Sir king,' said noble Siegfried, 'here sit at home and play,
> While I and your vassals are fighting far away;
> Here frolic with the ladies and many a merry mate,
> And trust to me for guarding your honor and estate.'"
> *Nibelungenlied* (Lettsom's tr.).

This little force, only one thousand strong, then marched bravely out of Worms, passed through Hesse, and entered Saxony, where it encountered the enemy numbering no less than twenty thousand valiant fighting men. The battle was immediately begun; and while all fought bravely, none did such wonders as Siegfried, who made both kings prisoners, routed their host, and returned triumphant to Worms, with much spoil and many captives.

A messenger had preceded him thither to announce the success of the expedition, and he was secretly summoned and questioned by Kriemhild, who, in her joy at hearing that Siegfried was unharmed and victorious, gave the messenger a large reward.

"Then spake she midst her blushes, 'Well hast thou earn'd thy meed,
Well hast thou told thy story, so take thee costliest weed,
And straight I'll bid be brought thee ten marks of ruddy gold.'
No wonder, to rich ladies glad news are gladly told."
Nibelungenlied (Lettsom's tr.).

Kriemhild then hastened to her window, from whence she witnessed her hero's triumphant entrance, and heard the people's acclamations of joy. The wounded were cared for, the captive kings hospitably entertained and duly released, and great festivities were held to celebrate the glorious victory. Among other entertainments the knights tilted in the tournaments, and, by Gernot's advice, Ute, Kriemhild, and all the court ladies were invited to view the prowess of the men at arms. It was thus that Siegfried first beheld Kriemhild, and as soon as he saw her he gladly acknowledged that she was fairer than he could ever have supposed.

"As the moon arising outglitters every star
That through the clouds so purely glimmers from afar,
E'en so love-breathing Kriemhild dimm'd every beauty nigh.
Well might at such a vision many a bold heart beat high."
Nibelungenlied {Lettsom's tr.}.

Siegfried's happiness was complete, however, when he was appointed the escort of this peerless maiden; and on the way to and from the tournament and mass he made good use of his opportunity to whisper pretty speeches to Kriemhild, who timidly expressed her gratitude for the service he had rendered her brother, and begged that he would continue to befriend him. These words made Siegfried blush with pride, and then and there he registered a solemn vow to fulfill her request.

"'Ever,' said he, 'your brethren I'll serve as best I may,
Nor once, while I have being, will head on pillow lay
Till I have done to please them whate'er they bid me do;
And this, my Lady Kriemhild, is all for love of you.'"
Nibelungenlied (Lettsom's tr.).

The festivities being ended, Gunther bestowed many gifts on the departing guests; but when Siegfried would also have departed he entreated him to remain at Worms. This the young hero was not at all loath to do, as he had fallen deeply in love with the fair Kriemhild, whom he was now privileged to see every day.

The excitement consequent on the festivities had not entirely subsided in Worms when King Gunther declared his desire to win for his wife Brunhild, a princess of Issland, who had vowed to marry none but the man who could surpass her in casting a spear, in throwing a stone, and in jumping.

> "Then spake the lord of Rhineland: 'Straight will I hence to sea,
> And seek the fiery Brunhild, howe'er it go with me.
> For love of the stern maiden I'll frankly risk my life;
> Ready am I to lose it, if I win her not to wife.'"
> *Nibelungenlied* (Lettsom's tr.).

In vain Siegfried, who knew all about Brunhild, tried to dissuade him; Gunther insisted upon departing, but proposed to Siegfried to accompany him, promising him as reward for his assistance Kriemhild's hand as soon as the princess of Issland was won. Such an offer was not to be refused, and Siegfried immediately accepted it, advising Gunther to take only Hagen and Dankwart as his attendants.

After seeking the aid of Kriemhild for a supply of rich clothing suitable for a prince going a-wooing, Gunther and the three knights embarked on a small vessel, whose sails soon filled, and which rapidly bore them flown the Rhine and over the sea to Issland. When within sight of its shores, Siegfried bade his companions all carefully agree in representing him to the strangers as Gunther's vassal only. Their arrival was seen by some inquisitive damsels peering out of the windows of the castle, and reported to Brunhild, who immediately and joyfully concluded that Siegfried had come to seek her hand in marriage. But when she heard that he held another man's stirrup to enable him to mount, she angrily frowned, wondering why he came as a menial instead of as a king. When the strangers entered her hall she would have greeted

Siegfried first had he not modestly drawn aside, declaring that the honor was due to his master, Gunther, King of Burgundy, who had come to Issland to woo her.

Brunhild then haughtily bade her warriors make all the necessary preparations for the coming contest; and Gunther, Hagen, and Dankwart apprehensively watched the movements of four warriors staggering beneath the weight of Brunhild's ponderous shield. Then they saw three others equally overpowered by her spear; and twelve sturdy servants could scarcely roll the stone she was wont to cast.

Hagen and Dankwart, fearing for their master,—who was doomed to die in case of failure,—began to mutter that some treachery was afoot, and openly regretted that they had consented to lay aside their weapons upon entering the castle. These remarks, overheard by Brunhild, called forth her scorn, and she contemptuously bade her servants bring the strangers' arms, since they were afraid.

> "Well heard the noble maiden the warrior's words the while,
> And looking o'er her shoulder, said with a scornful smile,
> 'As he thinks himself so mighty, I'll not deny a guest;
> Take they their arms and armor, and do as seems them best.
> "'Be they naked and defenseless, or sheath'd in armor sheen,
> To me it nothing matters,' said the haughty queen.
> 'Fear'd yet I never mortal, and, spite of yon stern brow
> And all the strength of Gunther, I fear as little now.'"
> *Nibelungenlied* (Lettsom's tr.).

While these preliminaries were being settled, Siegfried had gone down to the ship riding at anchor, and all unseen had donned his magic cloud-cloak and returned to the scene of the coming contest, where he now bade Gunther rely upon his aid.

> "'I am Siegfried, thy trusty friend and true;
> Be not in fear a moment for all the queen can do.'
> "Said he, 'Off with the buckler, and give it me to bear;
> Now what I shall advise thee, mark with thy closest care.
> Be it thine to make the gestures, and mine the work to do.'"
> *Nibelungenlied* (Lettsom's tr.).

GUNTHER WINNING HIS BRIDE.—Keller

In obedience to these directions, Gunther merely made the motions, depending upon the invisible Siegfried to parry and make all the attacks. Brunhild first poised and flung her spear with such force that both heroes staggered and almost fell; but before she could cry out victory, Siegfried had caught the spear, turned it butt end foremost, and flung it back with such violence that the princess fell and was obliged to acknowledge herself outdone.

Nothing daunted, however, by this first defeat, she caught up the massive stone, flung it far from her, and leaping after it, alighted beside it. But even while she was inwardly congratulating herself, and confidently cherishing the belief that the stranger could not surpass her, Siegfried caught up the stone, flung it farther still, and grasping Gunther by his broad girdle, bounded through the air with him and landed far beyond it. Brunhild was outdone in all three feats, and, according to her own promise, belonged to the victor, Gunther, to whom she now bade her people show all due respect and homage.

> "Then all aloud fair Brunhild bespake her courtier band,
> Seeing in the ring at distance unharm'd her wooer stand:
> 'Hither, my men and kinsmen, low to my better bow.
> I am no more your mistress; you're Gunther's liegemen now.'"
> *Nibelungenlied* (Lettsom's tr.).

The warriors all hastened to do her bidding, and escorted their new lord to the castle, whither, under pretext of fitly celebrating her marriage, Brunhild summoned all her retainers from far and near. This rally roused the secret terror of Gunther, Hagen, and Dankwart, for they suspected some act of treachery on the part of the dark-browed queen. These fears were also, in a measure, shared by Siegfried; so he stole away, promising to return before long with a force sufficient to overawe Brunhild and quell all attempt at foul play.

Siegfried, having hastily embarked upon the little vessel, swiftly sailed away to the Nibelungen land, where he arrived in an incredibly short space of time, presented himself at the gates of his castle, and forced an entrance by conquering the giant porter, and Alberich, the dwarf guardian of his treasure. Then making himself known to his followers, the Nibelungs, he chose one thousand of them to accompany him back to Issland to support the Burgundian king.

The arrival of this unexpected force greatly surprised Brunhild. She questioned Gunther, and upon receiving the careless reply that they were only a few of his followers, who had come to make merry at his wedding, she gave up all hope of resistance. When the usual festivities had taken place, and the wonted largesses had been distributed, Gunther bade his bride prepare to follow him back to the Rhine with her personal female attendants, who numbered no less than one hundred and sixty-eight.

Brunhild regretfully left her own country, escorted by the thousand Nibelung warriors; and when they had journeyed nine days, Gunther bade Siegfried spur ahead and announce his safe return to his family and subjects. Offended by the tone of command Gunther had assumed, Siegfried at first proudly refused to obey; but when the king begged it as a favor, and mentioned Kriemhild's name, he immediately relented and set out.

> "Said he, 'Nay, gentle Siegfried, do but this journey take,
> Not for my sake only, but for my sister's sake;
> You'll oblige fair Kriemhild in this as well as me.'
> When so implored was Siegfried, ready at once was he.
> "'Whate'er you will, command me; let naught be left unsaid;
> I will gladly do it for the lovely maid.
> How can I refuse her who my heart has won?
> For her, whate'er your pleasure, tell it, and it is done.'"
> *Nibelunglied* (Lettsom's tr.).

Kriemhild received this messenger most graciously, and gave immediate orders for a magnificent reception of the new queen, going down to the river to meet and greet her in the most cordial and affectionate manner.

A tournament and banquet ensued; but as they were about to sit down to the latter, the impatient Siegfried ventured to remind Gunther of his promise, and claim the hand of Kriemhild. In spite of a low-spoken remonstrance on Brunhild's part, who said that he would surely never consent to give his only sister in marriage to a menial, Gunther sent for Kriemhild, who blushingly expressed her readiness to marry Siegfried if her brother wished. The marriage was immediately celebrated, and the two bridal couples sat side by side.

But while Kriemhild's fair face was radiant with joy, Brunhild's dark brows were drawn close together in an unmistakable and ominous frown.

The banquet over, the newly married couples retired; but when Gunther, for the first time alone with his wife, would fain have embraced her, she seized him, and, in spite of his vigorous resistance, bound him fast with her long girdle, suspended him from a nail in the corner of her apartment, and, notwithstanding his piteous entreaties, let him remain there all night long, releasing him only a few moments before the attendants entered the nuptial chamber in the morning. Of course all seemed greatly surprised to see Gunther's lowering countenance, which contrasted oddly with Siegfried's radiant mien; for the latter had won a loving wife, and, to show his appreciation of her, had given her as wedding gift the great Nibelungen hoard.

In the course of the day Gunther managed to draw Siegfried aside, and secretly confided to him the shameful treatment he had received at his wife's hands. When Siegfried heard this he offered to don his cloud-cloak once more, enter the royal chamber unperceived, and force Brunhild to recognize her husband as her master, and never again make use of her strength against him.

In pursuance of this promise Siegfried suddenly left Kriemhild's side at nightfall, stole unseen into the queen's room, and when she and Gunther had closed the door, he blew out the lights and wrestled with Brunhild until she begged for mercy, promising never to bind him again; for as Siegfried had remained invisible throughout the struggle, she thought it was Gunther who had conquered her.

> "Said she, 'Right noble ruler, vouchsafe my life to spare;
> Whatever I've offended, my duty shall repair.
> I'll meet thy noble passion; my love with thine shall vie.
> That thou canst tame a woman, none better knows than I.'"
> *Nibelungenlied* (Lettsom's tr.).

Still unperceived, Siegfried now took her girdle and ring, and stole out of the apartment, leaving Gunther alone with his wife; but, true to her promise, Brunhild ever after treated her husband with due respect, and having once for all been conquered, she entirely lost the fabulous strength which had been her proudest boast, and was no more powerful than any other member of her sex.

After fourteen days of rejoicing, Siegfried and Kriemhild (the latter escorted by her faithful steward Eckewart) journeyed off to Xanten on the Rhine, where Siegmund and Siegelind received them joyfully, and even abdicated in their favor.

Ten years passed away very rapidly indeed. Siegfried became the father of a son, whom he named Gunther, in honor of his brother-in-law, who had called his heir Siegfried; and when Siegelind had seen her little grandson she departed from this world. Siegfried, with Kriemhild, his father, and his son, then went to the Nibelungen land, where they tarried two years.

In the mean while Brunhild, still imagining that Siegfried was only her husband's vassal, secretly wondered why he never came to court to do homage for his lands, and finally suggested to Gunther that it would be well to invite his sister and her husband to visit them at Worms. Gunther seized this suggestion gladly, and immediately sent one of his followers, Gary, to deliver the invitation, which Siegfried accepted for himself and his wife, and also for Siegmund, his father.

As they were bidden for midsummer, and as the journey was very long, Kriemhild speedily began her preparations; and when she left home she cheerfully intrusted her little son to the care of the stalwart Nibelung knights, little suspecting that she would never see him again.

On Kriemhild's arrival at Worms, Brunhild greeted her with as much pomp and ceremony as had been used for her own reception; but in spite of the amity which seemed to exist between the two queens, Brunhild was secretly angry at what she deemed Kriemhild's unwarrantable arrogance.

One day, when the two queens were sitting together, Brunhild, weary of hearing Kriemhild's constant praise of her husband, who she declared was without a peer in the world, cuttingly remarked that since he was Gunther's vassal he must necessarily be his inferior. This remark called forth a retort from Kriemhild, and a dispute was soon raging, in the course of which Kriemhild vowed that she would publicly assert her rank by taking the precedence of Brunhild in entering the church. The queens parted in hot anger, but both immediately proceeded to attire themselves with the utmost magnificence, and, escorted by all their maids, met at the church door. Brunhild there bade Kriemhild stand aside and make way for her superior; but this order so angered the Nibelungen queen that the dispute was resumed in public with increased vehemence and bitterness.

In her indignation Kriemhild finally insulted Brunhild grossly by declaring that she was not a faithful wife; and in proof of her assertion she produced the ring and girdle which Siegfried had won in his memorable encounter with her, and which he had imprudently given to his wife, to whom he had also confided the secret of Brunhild's wooing.

Brunhild indignantly summoned Gunther to defend her, and he, in anger, sent for Siegfried, who publicly swore that his wife had not told the truth, and that Gunther's queen had in no way forfeited her good name. Further to propitiate his host, Siegfried declared the quarrel to be disgraceful, and promised to teach his wife better manners for the future, advising Gunther to do the same with his consort.

> "'Women must be instructed,' said Siegfried the good knight,
> 'To leave off idle talking and rule their tongues aright.
> Keep thy fair wife in order. I'll do by mine the same.
> Such overweening folly puts me indeed to shame.'"
> *Nibelungenlied* (Lettsom's tr.).

To carry out this good resolution he led Kriemhild home, where, sooth to say, he beat her black and blue,—an heroic measure which Gunther did not dare to imitate.

Brunhild, smarting from the public insult received, continued to weep aloud and complain, until Hagen, inquiring the cause of her extravagant grief, and receiving a highly colored version of the affair, declared that he would see that she was duly avenged.

> "He ask'd her what had happen'd—wherefore he saw her weep;
> She told him all the story; he vow'd to her full deep
> That reap should Kriemhild's husband as he had dar'd to sow,
> Or that himself thereafter content should never know."
> *Nibelungenlied* (Lettsom's tr.).

To keep this promise, Hagen next tried to stir up the anger of Gunther,
Gernot, and Ortwine, and to prevail upon them to murder Siegfried; but
Giselher reproved him for these base designs,
and openly took Siegfried's part, declaring:
"'Sure 'tis but a trifle to stir an angry wife.'"
Nibelungenlied (Lettsom's tr.).

But although he succeeded in quelling the attempt for the time
being, he was no match for the artful Hagen, who continually reminded
Gunther of the insult his wife had received, setting it in the worst
possible light, and finally so worked upon the king's feelings that he
consented to a treacherous assault.

Under pretext that his former enemy, Ludeger, was about to attack
him again, Gunther asked Siegfried's assistance, and began to prepare
as if for war. When Kriemhild heard that her beloved husband was
about to rush into danger she was greatly troubled. Hagen artfully
pretended to share her alarm, and so won her confidence that she
revealed to him that Siegfried was invulnerable except in one spot,
between his shoulders, where a lime leaf had rested and the dragon's
blood had not touched him.

"'So now I'll tell the secret, dear friend, alone to thee
(For thou, I doubt not, cousin, wilt keep thy faith with me),
Where sword may pierce my darling, and death sit on the thrust.
See, in thy truth and honor how full, how firm, my trust!
"'As from the dragon's death-wounds gush'd out the crimson gore,
With the smoking torrent the warrior wash'd him o'er,
A leaf then 'twixt his shoulders fell from the linden bough.
There only steel can harm him; for that I tremble now.'"
Nibelungenlied (Lettsom's tr.).

Pretending a sympathy he was far from feeling, and disguising his
unholy joy, Hagen bade Kriemhild sew a tiny cross on Siegfried's doublet
over the vulnerable spot, that he might the better protect him in case of
danger, and, after receiving her profuse thanks, returned to report the
success of his ruse to the king. When Siegfried joined them on the morrow, wearing the fatal marked doublet, he was surprised to hear that the
rebellion had been quelled without a blow; and when invited to join in a
hunt in the Odenwald instead of the fray, he gladly signified his consent.

After bidding farewell to Kriemhild, whose heart was sorely oppressed by dark forebodings, he joined the hunting party. He scoured the forest, slew several boars, caught a bear alive, and playfully let him loose in camp to furnish sport for the guests while the noonday meal was being prepared. Then he gaily sat down, clamoring for a drink. His exertions had made him very thirsty indeed, and he was sorely disappointed when told that, owing to a mistake, the wine had been carried to another part of the forest. But when Hagen pointed out a fresh spring at a short distance, all his wonted good humor returned, and he merrily proposed a race thither, offering to run in full armor, while the others might lay aside their cumbersome weapons. This challenge was accepted by Hagen and Gunther. Although heavily handicapped, Siegfried reached the spring first; but, wishing to show courtesy to his host, he bade him drink while he disarmed. When Gunther's thirst was quenched, Siegfried took his turn, and while he bent over the water Hagen treacherously removed all his weapons except his shield, and gliding behind him, drove his spear through his body in the exact spot where Kriemhild had embroidered the fatal mark.

Mortally wounded, Siegfried made a desperate effort to avenge himself; but finding nothing but his shield within reach, he flung it with such force at his murderer that it knocked him down. This last effort exhausted the remainder of his strength, and the hero fell back upon the grass, cursing the treachery of those whom he had trusted as friends.

> "Thus spake the deadly wounded: 'Ay, cowards false as hell!
> To you I still was faithful; I serv'd you long and well;—
> But what boots all?—for guerdon treason and death I've won.
> By your friends, vile traitors! foully have you done.
> "Whoever shall hereafter from your loins be born,
> Shall take from such vile fathers a heritage of scorn.
> On me you have wreak'd malice where gratitude was due;
> With shame shall you be banish'd by all good knights and true.'"
> *Nibelungenlied* (Lettsom'str.).

But even in death Siegfried could not forget his beloved wife; and laying aside all his anger, he pathetically recommended her to Gunther's care, bidding him guard her well. Siegfried expired as soon as these words were uttered; and the hunters silently gathered around his corpse, regretfully contemplating the fallen hero, while they took counsel together how they might keep the secret of Hagen's treachery. They finally agreed to carry the body back to Worms and to say that they had found Siegfried dead in the forest, where he had presumably been slain by highwaymen.

> "Then many said, repenting, 'This deed will prove our bale;
> Still let us shroud the secret, and all keep in one tale,—
> That the good lord of Kriemhild to hunt alone preferr'd,
> And so was slain by robbers as through the wood he spurr'd.'"
> *Nibelungenlied* (Lettsom's tr.).

But although his companions were anxious to shield him, Hagen gloried in his dastardly deed, and secretly bade the bearers deposit Siegfried's corpse at Kriemhild's door after nightfall, so that she should be the first to see it there when on her way to early mass. As he fully expected, Kriemhild immediately recognized her husband, and fell senseless upon him; but when she had recovered consciousness she declared, while loudly bewailing her loss, that Siegfried was the victim of an assassination.

> "'Woe's me, woe's me forever! sure no fair foeman's sword
> Shiver'd thy failing buckler; 'twas murder stopp'd thy breath.
> Oh that I knew who did it! death I'd requite with death!'"
> *Nibelungenlied* (Lettsom's tr.).

By her orders a messenger was sent to break the mournful tidings to the still sleeping Siegmund and the Nibelungs. They hastily armed and rallied about her, and would have fallen upon the Burgundians, to avenge their master's death, had she not restrained them, bidding them await a suitable occasion, and promising them her support when the right time came.

The preparations for a sumptuous funeral were immediately begun, and all lent a willing hand, for Siegfried was greatly beloved at Worms. His body was therefore laid in state in the cathedral, where all came to view it and condole with Kriemhild; but when Gunther drew near to express his sorrow, she refused to listen to him until he promised that all those present at the hunt should touch the body, which at the murderer's contact would bleed afresh. All stood the test and were honorably acquitted save Hagen, at whose touch Siegfried's blood began to flow.

> "It is a mighty marvel, which oft e'en now we spy,
> That when the blood-stain'd murderer comes to the murder'd nigh,
> The wounds break out a-bleeding; then too the same befell,
> And thus could each beholder the guilt of Hagen tell."
> *Nibelungenlied* (Lettsom's tr.).

Once more Kriemhild restrained the angry Nibelung warriors from taking immediate revenge, and, upheld by Gernot and Giselher, who really sympathized with her grief, she went through the remainder of the funeral ceremonies and saw her hero duly laid at rest.

Kriemhild's mourning had only begun. All her days and nights were now spent in bitter weeping. This sorrow was fully shared by Siegmund, who, however, finally roused himself and proposed a return home. Kriemhild was about to accompany him, when her relatives persuaded her to remain in Burgundy. Then the little band which had come in festal array rode silently away in mourning robes, the grim Nibelung knights muttering dark threats against those who had dealt so basely with their beloved master.

> "'Into this same country we well may come again
> To seek and find the traitor who laid our master low.
> Among the kin of Siegfried they have many a mortal foe.'"
> *Nibelungenlied* (Lettsom's tr.).

Eckewart the steward alone remained with Kriemhild, with a faithfulness which has become proverbial in the German language, and prepared for his mistress a dwelling close by the cathedral, so that she might constantly visit her husband's tomb. Here Kriemhild spent three years in complete seclusion, refusing to see Gunther, or the detested Hagen; but they, remembering that the immense Nibelungen hoard was hers by right, continually wondered how she could be induced to send for it. Owing to Hagen's advice, Gunther, helped by his brothers, finally obtained an interview with, and was reconciled to, his mourning sister, and shortly after persuaded her to send twelve men to claim from Alberich, the dwarf, the fabulous wealth her husband had bestowed upon her as a wedding gift.

> "It was made up of nothing but precious stones and gold;
> Were all the world bought from it, and down the value told,
> Not a mark the less thereafter were left than erst was scor'd.
> Good reason sure had Hagen to covet such a hoard.
>
> "And thereamong was lying the wishing rod of gold,
> Which whoso could discover, might in subjection hold
> All this wide world as master, with all that dwelt therein.
> There came to Worms with Gernot full many of Albric's kin."
> *Nibelungenlied* (Lettsom's tr.).

But although this wealth is said to have filled nearly one hundred and fifty wagons, Kriemhild would gladly have given it all away could she but have seen her husband by her side once more. Not knowing what else to do with it, she gave away her gold right and left, bidding all the recipients of her bounty pray for Siegfried's soul. Her largesses were so extensive that Hagen, who alone did not profit by her generosity, and who feared the treasure might be exhausted before he could obtain a share, sought out Gunther and told him that Kriemhild was secretly winning to her side many adherents, whom she would some day urge to avenge her husband's murder by slaying her kindred.

While Gunther was trying to devise some plan to obtain possession of the hoard, Hagen boldly seized the keys of the tower where it was kept, secretly removed all the gold, and, to prevent its falling into any hands but his own, sank it in the Rhine near Lochheim.

> "Ere back the king came thither, impatient of delay,
> Hagen seized the treasure, and bore it thence away.
> Into the Rhine at Lochheim the whole at once threw he!
> Henceforth he thought t'enjoy it, but that was ne'er to be.
>
> "He nevermore could get it for all his vain desire;
> So fortune oft the traitor cheats of his treason's hire.
> Alone he hop'd to use it as long as he should live,
> But neither himself could profit, nor to another give."
> *Nibelungenlied* (Lettsom's tr.).

SIEGFRIED'S BODY BORNE HOME BY THE HUNTSMEN.—Pixis.

When Gunther, Gernot, and Giselher heard what Hagen had done, they were so angry that he deemed it advisable to withdraw from court for a while. Kriemhild would fain have left Burgundy forever at this fresh wrong, but with much difficulty was prevailed upon to remain and take up her abode at Lorch, whither Siegfried's remains were removed by her order.

Thirteen years had passed by since Siegfried's death in the Odenwald when Etzel, King of Hungary, who had lost his beautiful and beloved wife, Helche, bade one of his knights, Rüdiger of Bechlaren, ride to Worms and sue for the hand of Kriemhild in his master's name.

Rüdiger immediately gathered together a suitable train and departed, stopping on the way to visit his wife and daughter at Bechlaren. Passing all through Bavaria, he arrived at last at Worms, where he was warmly welcomed, by Hagen especially, who had formerly known him well.

In reply to Gunther's courteous inquiry concerning the welfare of the King and Queen of the Huns, Rüdiger announced the death of the latter, and declared that he had come to sue for Kriemhild's hand.

"Thereon the highborn envoy his message freely told:
'King, since you have permitted, I'll to your ears unfold
Wherefore my royal master me to your court has sent,
Plung'd as he is in sorrow and doleful dreariment.

"'It has been told my master, Sir Siegfried now is dead,
And Kriemhild left a widow. If thus they both have sped,
Would you but permit her, she the crown shall wear
Before the knights of Etzel; this bids me my good lord declare.'"
Nibelungenlied (Lettsom's tr.).

Gunther gladly received this message, promised to do all in his power to win Kriemhild's consent, and said that he would give the envoy a definite answer in three days' time. He then consulted his brothers and nobles as to the advisability of the proposed alliance, and found that all were greatly in favor of it save Hagen, who warned them that if Kriemhild were ever Queen of the Huns she would use her power to avenge her wrongs.

This warning was, however, not heeded by the royal brothers, who, seeking Kriemhild's presence, vainly tried to make her accept the Hun's proposal. All she would grant was an audience to Rüdiger, who laid before her his master's proposal, described the power of the Huns, and swore to obey her in all things would she but consent to become his queen.

> "In vain they her entreated, in vain to her they pray'd,
> Till to the queen the margrave this secret promise made,—
> He'd 'full amends procure her for past or future ill.'
> Those words her storm-tost bosom had power in part to still."
> *Nibelungenlied* (Lettsom's tr.).

After receiving this promise, Kriemhild signified her consent, and immediately prepared to accompany Rüdiger to King Etzel's court. Eckewart and all her maidens accompanied her, with five hundred men as a bodyguard; and Gernot and Giselher, with many Burgundian nobles, escorted her to Vergen on the Danube, where they took an affectionate leave of her, and went back to their home in Burgundy.

From Vergen, Kriemhild and her escort journeyed on to Passau, where they were warmly welcomed and hospitably entertained by good Bishop Pilgrim, brother of Queen Ute. He would gladly have detained them, had not Rüdiger declared that his master impatiently awaited the coming of his bride, which had duly been announced to him.

A second pause was made at Bechlaren, Rüdiger's castle, where Kriemhild was entertained by his wife and daughter, Gotelinde and Dietelinde, and where the usual lavish distribution of gifts took place. Then the procession swept on again across the country and down the Danube, until they met King Etzel, whom Kriemhild graciously kissed, and who obtained a similar favor for his brother and a few of his principal nobles.

After witnessing some tilting and other martial games, the king and queen proceeded to Vienna, where a triumphal reception awaited them, and where their marriage was celebrated with all becoming solemnity and great pomp. The wedding festivities lasted seventeen days; but although all vied in their attempts to please Kriemhild, she remained sad and pensive, for she could not forget her beloved Siegfried and the happy years she had spent with him.

The royal couple next journeyed on to Gran, Etzel's capital, where Kriemhild found innumerable handmaidens ready to do her will, and where Etzel was very happy with his new consort. His joy was complete, however, only when she bore him a son, who was baptized in the Christian faith, and called Ortlieb.

Although thirteen years had now elapsed since Kriemhild had left her native land, the recollection of her wrongs was as vivid as ever, her melancholy just as profound, and her thoughts were ever busy planning how best to lure Hagen into her kingdom so as to work her revenge.

> "One long and dreary yearning she foster'd hour by hour;
> She thought, 'I am so wealthy and hold such boundless power,
> That I with ease a mischief can bring on all my foes,
> But most on him of Trony, the deadliest far of those.
>
> "'Full oft for its beloved my heart is mourning still;
> Them could I but meet with, who wrought me so much ill,
> Revenge should strike at murder, and life atone for life;
> Wait can I no longer.' So murmur'd Etzel's wife."
> *Nibelungenlied* (Lettsom's tr.).

Kriemhild finally decided to persuade Etzel to invite all her kinsmen for a midsummer visit, which the king, not dreaming of her evil purpose, immediately hastened to do. Two minstrels, Werbel and Swemmel, were sent with the most cordial invitation. Before they departed Kriemhild instructed them to be sure and tell all her kinsmen that she was blithe and happy, and not melancholy as of yore, and to use every effort to bring not only the kings, but also Hagen, who, having been at Etzel's court as hostage in his youth, could best act as their guide.

The minstrels were warmly received at Worms, where their invitation created great excitement. All were in favor of accepting it except Hagen, who objected that Kriemhild had cause for anger and would surely seek revenge when they were entirely in her power.

> "'Trust not, Sir King,' said Hagen, 'how smooth soe'er they be,
> These messengers from Hungary; if Kriemhild you will see,
> You put upon the venture your honor and your life.
> A nurse of ling'ring vengeance is Etzel's moody wife.'"
> *Nibelungenlied* (Lettsom's tr.).

But all his objections were set aside with the remark that he alone had a guilty conscience; and the kings bade the minstrels return to announce their coming, although Ute also tried to keep them at home. Hagen, who was no coward, seeing them determined to go, grimly prepared to accompany them, and prevailed upon them to don their strongest armor for the journey.

Gunther was accompanied by both his brothers, by Hagen, Dankwart, Volker (his minstrel), Gary, and Ortwine, and by one thousand picked men as escort. Before leaving he intrusted his wife, Brunhild, and his son to the care of Rumolt, his squire, and bidding farewell to his people, set out for Hungary, whence he was never to return.

In the mean while the Hungarian minstrels had hastened back to Gran to announce the guests' coming, and, upon being closely questioned by Kriemhild, described Hagen's grim behavior, and repeated his half-muttered prophecy: "This jaunt's a jaunt to death."

The Burgundians, who in this part of the poem are frequently called Nibelungs (because they now held the great hoard), reached the Danube on the twelfth day. As they found neither ford nor ferry, Hagen, after again prophesying all manner of evil, volunteered to go in search of a boat or raft to cross the rapid stream.

He had not gone very far before he heard the sound of voices, and, peeping through the bushes, saw some swan maidens, or "wise women," bathing in a neighboring fountain. Stealing up unperceived, he secured their plumage, which he consented to restore only after they had predicted the result of his journey. To obtain her garments, one of the women, Hadburg, prophesied great good fortune; but when the pilfered robes were restored, another, called Siegelind, foretold much woe.

> "'I will warn thee, Hagen, thou son of Aldrian;
> My aunt has lied unto thee her raiment back to get;
> If once thou com'st to Hungary, thou'rt taken in the net.
>
> "'Turn while there's time for safety, turn, warriors most and least;
> For this, and for this only, you're bidden to the feast,
> That you perforce may perish in Etzel's bloody land.
> Whoever rideth thither, Death has he close at hand.'"
> *Nibelungenlied* (Lettsom's tr.).

After adding that the chaplain alone would return alive to Worms, she told Hagen that he would find a ferryman on the opposite side of the river, farther down, but that he would not obey his call unless he declared his name to be Amelrich.

Hagen, after leaving the wise women, soon saw the ferryman's boat anchored to the opposite shore, and failing to make him come over for a promised reward, he cried out that his name was Amelrich. The ferryman immediately crossed, but when Hagen sprang into his boat he detected the fraud and began to fight. Although gigantic in size, this ferryman was no match for Hagen, who, after slaying him, took possession of the boat and skillfully ferried his masters and companions across the river.

In hope of giving the lie to the swan maidens, Hagen paused once in the middle of the stream to fling the chaplain overboard, thinking he would surely drown; but to his surprise and dismay the man struggled back to the shore, where he stood alone and unharmed, and whence he slowly wended his way back to Burgundy. Hagen now knew that the swan maidens' prophecy was destined to be fulfilled. Nevertheless he landed on the opposite shore, where he bade the main part of the troop ride on ahead, leaving him and Dankwart to bring up the rear, for he fully expected that Gelfrat, master of the murdered ferryman, would pursue them to avenge the latter's death. These previsions were soon verified, and in the bloody encounter which ensued, Hagen came off victor, with the loss of but four men, while the enemy left more than one hundred dead upon the field.

Hagen joined the main body of the army once more, passed on with it to Passau, where Bishop Pilgrim was as glad to see his nephews as he had been to welcome his niece, and from thence went on to the frontiers of Bechlaren. There they found Eckewart, who had been sent by Rüdiger to warn them not to advance any farther, as he suspected that some treachery was afoot.

> "Sir Eckewart replied:
> 'Yet much, I own, it grieves me that to the Huns you ride.
> You took the life of Siegfried; all hate you deadly here;
> As your true friend I warn you; watch well, and wisely fear.'"
> *Nibelungenlied* (Lettsom's tr.).

As the Burgundians would have deemed themselves forever disgraced were they to withdraw from their purpose, they refused to listen to this warning, and, entering Rüdiger's castle, were warmly received by him and his family. Giselher, seeing the beauty of the maiden Dietelinde, fell deeply in love with her, and prevailed upon the margrave to consent to their immediate marriage, promising, however, to claim and bear away his bride only upon his homeward journey. Once more gifts were lavished with mediaeval profusion, Gunther receiving a coat of mail, Gernot a sword, Hagen a shield, and the minstrel Volker many rings of red gold.

Rüdiger then escorted the Burgundians until they met the brave Dietrich von Bern (Verona), who also warned them that their visit was fraught with danger, for Kriemhild had by no means forgotten the murder of the husband of her youth.

His evil prognostications were also of no avail, and he sadly accompanied them until they met Kriemhild, who embraced Giselher only. Then, turning suddenly upon Hagen, she inquired aloud, in the presence of all the people, whether he had brought her back her own, the Nibelung hoard. Nothing daunted by this sudden query, Hagen haughtily answered that the treasure still lay deep in the Rhine, where he fancied it would rest until the judgment day.

> "'I' faith, my Lady Kriemhild, 'tis now full many a day
> Since in my power the treasure of the Nibelungers lay.
> In the Rhine my lords bade sink it; I did their bidding fain,
> And in the Rhine, I warrant, till doomsday 'twill remain.'"
> *Nibelungenlied* (Lettsom's tr.).

The queen turned her back contemptuously upon him, and invited her other guests to lay aside their weapons, for none might enter the great hall armed. This Hagen refused to allow them to do, saying that he feared treachery; and the queen, pretending great grief, inquired who could have filled her kinsmen's hearts with such unjust suspicions. Sir Dietrich then boldly stepped forward, defied Kriemhild, and declared that it was he who had bidden the Burgundians be thus on their guard.

> ""Twas I that the warning to the noble princes gave,
> And to their liegeman Hagen, to whom such hate thou bear'st.
> Now up, she-fiend! be doing, and harm me if thou dar'st!'"
> *Nibelungenlied* (Lettsom's tr.).

Although the thirst for revenge now made her a "she-fiend," as he termed her, Kriemhild did not dare openly to attack Dietrich, whom all men justly feared; and she quickly concealed her anger, while Etzel advanced in his turn to welcome his guests; and especially singled out Hagen, his friend's son. While many of the Burgundians accompanied the king into the hall, Hagen drew Volker aside, and, sitting down on a stone seat near Kriemhild's door, entered into a life-and-death alliance with him. Kriemhild, looking out of her window, saw him there and bade her followers go out and slay him; but although they numbered four hundred, they hung back, until the queen, thinking that they doubted her assertions, volunteered to descend alone and wring from Hagen a confession of his crimes, while they lingered within earshot inside the building. Volker, seeing the queen approach, proposed to Hagen to rise and show her the customary respect; but the latter, declaring that she would ascribe this token of decorum to fear alone, grimly bade him remain seated, and, when she addressed him, boldly acknowledged that he alone had slain Siegfried.

> "Said he, 'Why question further? that were a waste of breath.
> In a word, I am e'en Hagen, who Siegfried did to death.
>
> *   *   *   *   *
>
> "'What I have done, proud princess, I never will deny.
> The cause of all the mischief, the wrong, the loss, am I.
> So now, or man or woman, revenge it whoso will;
> I scorn to speak a falsehood,—I've done you grievous ill.'"
> *Nibelungenlied* (Lettsom's tr.).

But although the warriors had heard every word he said, and the queen again urged them on to attack her foe, they one and all withdrew after meeting one of Hagen's threatening glances. This episode, however, was enough to show the Burgundians very plainly what they could expect, and Hagen and Volker soon joined their companions, keeping ever side by side, according to their agreement.

> "Howe'er the rest were coupled, as mov'd to court the train,
> Folker and Hagen parted ne'er again,
> Save in one mortal struggle, e'en to their dying hour."
> *Nibelungenlied* (Lettsom's tr.).

After banqueting with Etzel the guests were led to their appointed quarters, far remote from those of their squires; and when the Huns began to crowd them, Hagen again frightened them off with one of his black looks. When the hall where they were to sleep was finally reached, the knights all lay down to rest except Hagen and Volker, who mounted guard, the latter beguiling the hours by playing on his fiddle.

Once, in the middle of the night, these self-appointed sentinels saw an armed troop draw near; but when they loudly challenged the foremost men, they beat a hasty retreat. At dawn of day the knights arose to go to mass, wearing their arms by Hagen's advice, keeping well together, and presenting such a threatening aspect that Kriemhild's men dared not attack them.

In spite of all these signs, Etzel remained entirely ignorant of his wife's evil designs, and continued to treat the Burgundians like friends and kinsmen.

> "How deep soe'er and deadly the hate she bore her kin,
> Still, had the truth by any disclos'd to Etzel been,
> He had at once prevented what afterwards befell.
> Through proud contemptuous courage they scorn'd their wrongs to tell."
> *Nibelungenlied* (Lettsom's tr.).

After mass a tournament was held, Dietrich and Rüdiger virtuously abstaining from taking part in it, lest some mishap should occur through their bravery, and fan into flames the smoldering fire of discord. In spite of all these precautions, however, the threatened disruption nearly occurred when Volker accidentally slew a Hun; and it was avoided only by King Etzel's prompt interference.

Kriemhild, hearing of this accident, vainly tried to use it as an excuse to bribe Dietrich, or his man Hildebrand, to slay her foe. She finally won over Blödelin, the king's brother, by promising him a fair bride. To earn this reward the prince went with an armed host to the hall where all the Burgundian squires were feasting under Dankwart's care, and there treacherously slew them all, Dankwart alone escaping to the king's hall to join his brother Hagen.

In the mean while Etzel was entertaining his mailed guests, and had sent for his little son, whom he placed in Gunther's lap, telling him that he would soon send the boy to Burgundy to be educated among his mother's kin.

All admired the graceful child except Hagen, who gruffly remarked that the child appeared more likely to die early than to live to grow up. He had just finished this rude speech, which filled Etzel's heart with dismay, when Dankwart burst into the room, exclaiming that all his companions had been slain, and calling to Hagen for aid.

> "'Be stirring, brother Hagen; you're sitting all too long.
> To you and God in heaven our deadly strait I plain:
> Yeomen and knights together lie in their quarters slain.'"
> *Nibelungenlied* (Lettsom's tr.).

The moment Hagen heard these tidings he sprang to his feet, drew his sword, and bade Dankwart guard the door and prevent the ingress or egress of a single Hungarian. Then he struck off the head of the child Ortlieb, which bounded into Kriemhild's lap, cut off the minstrel Werbel's hand, and began hewing right and left among the Hungarians, aided by all his companions, who manfully followed his example.

Dismayed at this sudden turn of affairs, the aged King Etzel "sat in mortal anguish," helplessly watching the massacre, while Kriemhild shrieked aloud to Dietrich to protect her from her foes. Moved to pity by her evident terror, Dietrich blew a resounding blast on his horn, and Gunther paused in his work of destruction to inquire how he might serve the man who had ever shown himself a friend. Dietrich answered by asking for a safe-conduct out of the hall for himself and his followers, which was immediately granted.

> "'Let me with your safe-conduct this hall of Etzel's leave,
> And quit this bloody banquet with those who follow me;
> And for this grace forever I'll at your service be.'"
> *Nibelungenlied* (Lettsom's tr.).

Dietrich von Bern then passed out of the hall unmolested, leading the king by one hand and the queen by the other, and closely followed by all his retainers. This same privilege was granted to Rüdiger and his five hundred men; but when these had all passed out, the Burgundians renewed the bloody fight, nor paused until all the Huns in the hall were slain, and everything was reeking with blood.

Then the Burgundians gathered up the corpses, which they flung down the staircase, at the foot of which Etzel stood, helplessly wringing his hands, and vainly trying to discover some means of stopping the fight.

Kriemhild, in the mean while, was actively employed in gathering men, promising large rewards to any one who would attack and slay Hagen. Urged on by her, Iring attempted to force an entrance, but was soon driven back; and when he would have made a second assault, Hagen ruthlessly slew him.

Irnfried the Thuringian, and Hawart the Dane, seeing him fall, rushed impetuously upon the Burgundians to avenge him; but both fell under Hagen's and Volker's mighty blows, while their numerous followers were all slain by the other Burgundians.

> "A thousand and four together had come into the hall;
> You might see the broadswords flashing rise and fall;
> Soon the bold intruders all dead together lay;
> Of those renown'd Burgundians strange marvels one might say."
> *Nibelungenlied* (Lettsom's tr.).

Etzel and the Huns were mourning over their dead; so the weary Burgundians removed their helmets and rested, while Kriemhild continued to muster new troops to attack her kinsmen, who were still strongly intrenched in the great hall.

> "'Twas e'en on a midsummer befell that murderous fight,
> When on her nearest kinsmen and many a noble knight
> Dame Kriemhild wreak'd the anguish that long in heart she bore,
> Whence inly griev'd King Etzel, nor joy knew evermore.
>
> "Yet on such sweeping slaughter at first she had not thought;
> She only had for vengeance on one transgressor sought.

She wish'd that but on Hagen the stroke of death might fall;
'Twas the foul fiend's contriving that they should perish all."
Nibelungenlied (Lettsom's tr.).

An attempt was now made by the Burgundians to treat with Etzel for a safe-conduct. Obdurate at first, he would have yielded had not Kriemhild advised him to pursue the feud to the bitter end, unless her brothers consented to surrender Hagen to her tender mercies. This, of course, Gunther absolutely refused to do; so Kriemhild gave secret orders that the hall in which the Burgundians were intrenched should be set on fire. Surrounded by bitter foes, blinded by smoke, and overcome by the heat, the Burgundians still held their own, slaking their burning thirst by drinking the blood of the slain, and taking refuge from the flames under the stone arches which supported the ceiling of the hall.

Thus they managed to survive that terrible night; but when morning dawned and the queen heard that they were still alive, she bade Rüdiger go forth and fight them. He refused until she reminded him or the solemn oath he had sworn to her in Worms before she would consent to accompany him to Hungary.

"'Now think upon the homage that once to me you swore,
When to the Rhine, good warrior, King Etzel's suit you bore,
That you would serve me ever to either's dying day.
Ne'er can I need so deeply that you that vow should pay.'"
Nibelungenlied (Lettsom's tr.).

Torn by conflicting feelings and urged by opposite oaths,—for he had also sworn to befriend the Burgundians,—Rüdiger now vainly tried to purchase his release by the sacrifice of all his possessions. At last, goaded to madness, he yielded to the king's and queen's entreaties, armed his warriors, and drew near the hall where his former guests were intrenched. At first they could not believe that Rüdiger had any hostile intentions; but when he pathetically informed them that he must fight, and recommended his wife and daughter to their care in case he fell, they silently allowed him and his followers to enter the hall, and grimly renewed the bloody conflict.

Rüdiger, after slaying many foes, encountered Gernot wielding the sword he had given him; and these two doughty champions finally slew each other. All the followers of Rüdiger also fell; and when Kriemhild, who was anxiously awaiting the result of this new attack in the court below, saw his corpse among the slain, she began to weep and bemoan her loss. The mournful tidings of Rüdiger's death soon spread all over the town, and came finally to the ears of Dietrich von Bern, who bade his man Hildebrand go and claim the corpse from his Burgundian friends.

Hildebrand went thither with an armed force, but some of his men unfortunately began to bandy words with the Burgundians, and this soon brought about an impetuous fight. In the ensuing battle all the Burgundians fell except Gunther and Hagen, while Hildebrand escaped sore wounded to his master, Dietrich von Bern. When this hero heard that his nephew and vassals were all slain, he quickly armed himself, and, after vainly imploring Gunther and Hagen to surrender, fell upon them with an armed force. The two sole remaining Burgundians were now so exhausted that Dietrich soon managed to take them captive. He led them bound to Kriemhild, and implored her to have pity upon them and spare their lives.

> "'Fair and noble Kriemhild,' thus Sir Dietrich spake,
> Spare this captive warrior, who full amends will make
> For all his past transgressions; him here in bonds you see;
> Revenge not on the fetter'd th' offenses of the free.'"
> *Nibelungenlied* (Lettsom's tr.).

By the queen's orders, Gunther and Hagen were confined in separate cells. There she soon sought the latter, promising him his liberty if he would but reveal the place where her treasure was concealed. But Hagen, mistrusting her, declared that he had solemnly sworn never to reveal the secret as long as one of his masters breathed. Kriemhild, whose cruelty had long passed all bounds, left him only to have her brother Gunther beheaded, and soon returned carrying his head, which she showed to Hagen, commanding him to speak. But he still refused to gratify her, and replied that since he was now the sole depositary of the secret, it would perish with him.

> "'So now, where lies the treasure none knows save God and me,
> And told it shall be never, be sure, she-fiend, to thee!'"
> *Nibelungenlied* (Lettsom's tr.).

This defiant answer so exasperated Kriemhild that she seized the sword hanging by his side,—which she recognized as Siegfried's favorite weapon,—and with her own hands cut off his head before Etzel or any of his courtiers could interfere. Hildebrand, seeing this act of treachery, sprang impetuously forward, and, drawing his sword, slew her who had brought untold misery into the land of the Huns.

> "The mighty and the noble there lay together dead;
> For this had all the people dole and drearihead.
> The feast of royal Etzel was thus shut up in woe,
> Pain in the steps of Pleasure treads ever here below.

> "'Tis more than I can tell you what afterwards befell,
> Save that there was weeping for friends belov'd so well;
> Knights and squires, dames and damsels, were seen lamenting all.
> So end I here my story. This is the Nibelungers' Fall."
> *Nibelungenlied* (Lettsom's tr.).

Although the "Nibelungenlied" proper ends here, an appendix, probably by another hand, called the "Lament," continues the story, and relates how Etzel, Dietrich, and Hildebrand, in turn, extolled the high deeds and bewailed the untimely end of each hero. Then this poem, which is as mournful as monotonous throughout, describes the departure of the messengers sent to bear the evil tidings and the weapons of the slain to Worms, and their arrival at Passau, where more tears were shed and where Bishop Pilgrim celebrated a solemn mass for the rest of the heroes' souls.

From thence the funeral procession slowly traveled on to Worms, where the sad news was imparted to the remaining Burgundians, who named the son of Gunther and Brunhild as their king, and who never forgot the fatal ride to Hungary.

CHAPTER V

LANGOBARDIAN CYCLE OF MYTHS.

Although the following tales of mythical heroes have some slight historical basis, they have been so adorned by the fancy of mediaeval bards, and so frequently remodeled with utter disregard of all chronological sequence, that the kernel of truth is very hard to find, and the stories must rather be considered as depicting customs and times than as describing actual events. They are recorded in the "Heldenbuch," or "Book of Heroes," edited in the fifteenth century by Kaspar von der Rhön from materials which had been touched up by Wolfram von Eschenbach and Heinrich von Ofterdingen in the twelfth century. The poem of "Ortnit," for instance, is known to have existed as early as the ninth century.

According to the poets of the middle ages, the Gepidae and the Langobards settled in Pannonia (Hungary and the neighboring provinces), where they were respectively governed by Thurisind and Audoin. The sons of these two kings, having quarreled for a trifle, met in duel soon after, and the Langobardian prince, having slain his companion, took possession of his arms, with which he proudly returned home.

But when, flushed with victory, he would fain have taken his seat at his father's board with the men at arms, Audoin gravely informed him that it was not customary for a youth to claim a place beside tried warriors until some foreign king had distinguished him by the present of a complete suit of armor. Angry at being thus publicly repulsed, Alboin, the prince, strode out of his father's hall, resolved to march into Thurisind's palace and demand of him the required weapons.

When the King of the Gepidae saw his son's murderer boldly enter his palace, his first impulse was to put him to death; but, respecting the rights of hospitality, he forbore to take immediate vengeance, and even bestowed upon him the customary gift of arms as he departed on the morrow, but warned him never to return, lest he should lose his life at the warriors' hands. On leaving the palace, however, Alboin bore away the image of little Rosamund, Thurisind's fair granddaughter, whom he solemnly swore he would claim as wife as soon as she was of marriageable age.

Alboin having thus received his arms from a stranger, the Langobards no longer refused to recognize him as a full-fledged warrior, and gladly hailed him as king when his father died.

Shortly after Alboin's accession to the throne, a quarrel arose between the Gepidae and the Langobards, or Lombards, as they were eventually called; and war having been declared, a decisive battle was fought, in which Thurisind and his son perished, and all their lands fell into the conqueror's hands. With true heathen cruelty, the Lombard king had the skulls of the Gepidae mounted as drinking vessels, which he delighted in using on all state and festive occasions. Then, pushing onwards, Alboin took forcible possession of his new realm and of the tearful young Rosamund, whom he forced to become his wife, although she shrank in horror from the murderer of all her kin and the oppressor of her people.

She followed him home, concealing her fears, and although she never seemed blithe and happy, she obeyed her husband so implicitly that he fancied her a devoted wife. He was so accustomed to Rosamund's ready compliance with his every wish that one day, after winning a great victory over the Ostrogoths, and conquering a province in northern Italy (where he took up his abode, and which bears the name of his race), he bade her fill her father's skull with wine and pledge him by drinking first out of this repulsive cup.

The queen hesitated, but, impelled by Alboin's threatening glances and his mailed hand raised to strike her, she tremblingly filled the cup and raised it to her lips. But then, instead of humbly presenting it to her lord, she haughtily dashed it at his feet, and left the hall, saying that though she had obeyed him, she would never again live with him as his wife,—a declaration which the warriors present secretly applauded, for they all thought that their king had been wantonly cruel toward his beautiful wife.

While Alboin was pondering how he might conciliate her without owning himself in the wrong, Rosamund summoned Helmigis, the king's shield-bearer, and finding that he would not execute her orders and murder his master in his sleep, she secured the services of the giant Perideus. Before the murder of the king became generally known, Rosamund and her adherents—for she had many—secured and concealed the treasures of the Crown; and when the nobles bade her marry a man to succeed their king, who had left no heirs, she declared that she preferred Helmigis.

The Langobardian nobles indignantly refused to recognize an armor-bearer as their king, and Rosamund, fearing their resentment, fled by night with her treasures, and took refuge with Longinus, viceroy of the Eastern emperor, who was intrenched in Ravenna. Captivated by the fugitive queen's exquisite beauty, no less than by her numerous treasures, Longinus proposed that she should poison Helmigis, and marry him. Rosamund obediently handed the deadly cup to her faithful adorer; but he drank only half its contents, and then, perceiving that he was poisoned, forced her, at the point of his sword, to drink the remainder, thus making sure that she would not long survive him.

Longinus, thus deprived of a beautiful bride, managed to console himself for her loss by appropriating her treasures, while the Langobardian scepter, after having been wielded by different kings, fell at last into the hands of Rother, the last influential monarch of a kingdom which Charlemagne conquered in 774.

Rother established his capital at Bari, a great seaport in Apulia; but although his wealth was unbounded and his kingdom extensive, he was far from happy, for he had neither wife nor child to share his home. Seeing his loneliness, one of his courtiers, Duke Berchther (Berchtung) of Meran, the father of twelve stalwart sons, advised him to seek a wife; and when Rother declared that he knew of no princess pretty enough to please his fastidious taste, the courtier produced the portrait of Oda, daughter of Constantine, Emperor of the East. Rother fell desperately in love with this princess at first sight. In vain Berchther warned him that the emperor had the unpleasant habit of beheading all his daughter's would-be suitors; Rother declared that he must make an attempt to secure this peerless bride, and was only with great difficulty persuaded to resign the idea of wooing in person.

When Berchther had prevailed upon him to send an imposing embassy of twelve noblemen, richly appareled, and attended by a

ASPRIAN SLAYING THE LION.—Keller.

large suite, Rother asked who would undertake the mission. All the warriors maintained a neutral silence, until seven of Berchther's sons volunteered their services, and then five other noblemen signified their readiness to accompany them.

To speed them on their way, Rother escorted them to the port, and, standing on the pier, composed and sang a marvelous song. He bade them remember the tune, and promised them that whenever they heard it they might be sure their king was very near.

Arrived at Constantinople, the ambassadors made known their errand, but were immediately cast into prison, in spite of the empress's intercession in their behalf. Here the noblemen languished month after month, in a foul dungeon, while Rother impatiently watched for their return. When a whole year had elapsed without his having heard any tidings, he finally resolved to go in disguise to Constantinople, to ascertain the fate of his men and win the lovely princess Oda for his bride.

Berchther, hearing this decision, vowed that he would accompany him; but although all the noblemen were anxious to escort their beloved king, he took only a few of them with him, among whom was Asprian (Osborn), king of the northern giants, with eleven of his tallest men.

Rother embarked with this little train, and sailed for Constantinople over the summer seas; and as he sat on deck, playing on his harp, the mermaids rose from the deep to sport around his ship. According to a prearranged plan, Rother presented himself before Constantine as a fugitive and outlaw, complaining bitterly of the King of the Lombards, who, he declared, had banished him and his companions. Pleased with the appearance of the strangers, Constantine gladly accepted their proffered services, and invited them to a banquet, in the course of which he facetiously described how he had received Rother's ambassadors, who were still languishing in his dampest dungeons. This boastful talk gradually roused the anger of the giant Asprian, who was but little accustomed to hide his feelings; and when the emperor's pet lioness came into the hall and playfully snatched a choice morsel out of his hand, he impetuously sprang to his feet, caught her in his powerful grasp, and hurled her against the wall, thus slaying her with a single blow.

Constantine was somewhat dismayed when he saw the strength, and especially the violence, of the new servants he had secured; but he wisely took no notice of the affair, and, when the banquet was ended, dismissed Rother and his followers to the apartments assigned them. The Lombard king now freely distributed the immense treasures he had brought with him, and thus secured many adherents at court. They sang his praises so loudly that at last the princess Oda became very anxious to see this noted outlaw.

Bribing Herlind, one of her handmaidens, to serve her secretly, Oda sent her to Rother to invite him to visit her. The maiden acquitted herself adroitly of this commission; but the Langobardian monarch, pretending exaggerated respect, declared that he would never dare present himself before her beautiful mistress, to whom, however, he sent many rich gifts, among which were a gold and a silver shoe. Herlind returned to her mistress with the gifts; but when Oda would fain have put on the shoes, she discovered that they were both for the same foot. She then feigned a resentment she was far from feeling, and bade the handmaiden order her father's new servant to appear before her without delay, bringing a shoe for her other foot, unless he wished to incur her lasting displeasure. Overjoyed at this result of his ruse, which he had foreseen, Rother entered the princess's apartments unnoticed, proffered his most humble apologies, fitted a pair of golden shoes on her tiny feet, and, taking advantage of his position as he bent on one knee before her, declared his love and rank, and won from Oda a solemn promise that she would be his wife.

The lovers spent some very happy hours together in intimate conversation, and ere Rother left the apartment he prevailed upon the princess to use her influence in behalf of his imprisoned subjects. She therefore told her father that her peaceful rest had been disturbed by dreams, in which heavenly voices announced that she should suffer all manner of evil unless Rother's ambassadors were taken from prison and hospitably entertained. Oda then wrung from Constantine a promise that the men should be temporarily released, and feasted at his own board that selfsame evening. This promise was duly redeemed, and the twelve ambassadors, freed from their chains, and refreshed by warm baths and clean garments, were sumptuously entertained at the emperor's table. While they sat there feasting, Rother entered the hall, and, hiding behind the tapestry hangings near the door, played the tune they had heard on the day of their departure. The hearts of the captives bounded for joy when they heard these strains, for they knew that their king was near and would soon effect their release.

A few days later, when the young ambassadors had fully recovered their health and strength, Constantine was dismayed to learn that Imelot, King of Desert Babylonia, was about to make war against him, and wondered how he could successfully encounter such a universally dreaded opponent. Rother, seeing his perplexity, immediately volunteered his services, adding that if Constantine liberated the ambassadors, who were mighty men of valor, and allowed them to fight, there would be no doubt of his coming off conqueror in the war. The Eastern emperor gladly followed this advice, and soon set out with Rother and all his companions. The two armies met one evening and encamped opposite each other, intending to begin the fight at sunrise on the morrow. During the night, however, Rother and his companions stole into the enemy's camp, slew Imelot's guards, and having bound and gagged him, Asprian carried him bodily out of his tent and camp, while his companions routed all the mighty Babylonian host.

A few hours later they returned to the camp of Constantine, where they lay down to rest. The emperor, entering their tent on the morrow to chide them for their laziness, saw the captive Imelot, and heard the story of the night's work. He was so delighted with the prowess of his allies that he gladly consented to their return to Constantinople to announce the victory, while he and his army remained to take possession of Desert Babylonia and of all of Imelot's vast treasures.

Rother and his companions returned in haste to Constantinople and rushed into the palace; but instead of announcing a victory they told the empress and Oda that Constantine had been defeated, that Imelot was on the way to seize the city, and that the emperor had sent them on ahead to convey his wife and daughter to a place of safety, with their most valuable treasures.

The empress and Oda, crediting every word of this tale, made immediate preparations for departure, and soon joined Rother on the pier, where his fast sailing vessel was ready to start. All the Langobardians had already embarked, and Rother escorted the princess on board, bidding the empress wait on the quay until he returned for her. But as soon as he and his fair charge set foot upon deck, the vessel was pushed off, and Rother called out to the distressed empress that he had deceived her in order to carry away her daughter, who was now to become the Langobardian queen.

Constantine, on his return, was of course very angry at having been so cleverly duped, and vainly tried to devise some plan for recovering the daughter whom he loved so well. When a magician came, therefore, and promised to execute his wishes, he gladly provided him with vessel and crew to sail to Bari. The magician, disguised as a peaceful merchant, spread out his wares as soon as he was anchored in port, and by a series of artful questions soon ascertained that Rother was absent, and that Oda was at home, carefully guarded by the principal nobles of the realm. When he also learned that one of these noblemen had a crippled child, the magician informed the people who visited his vessel to inspect his wares, that the most precious treasure in his possession was a magic stone, which, in a queen's hands, had the power of restoring cripples.

The rumor of this miraculous stone reached the court, and the nobleman persuaded the kind-hearted queen to go down to the vessel to try the efficacy of the stone. As soon as Oda was on board, the vessel set sail, bearing her away from her husband and back to her father's home, where she was welcomed with great demonstrations of joy.

Rother, coming back from the war shortly after her disappearance, immediately prepared a vessel to go in pursuit of her, selecting his giants and bravest noblemen to accompany him. Once more they landed at a short distance from Constantinople, and Rother bade his men hide in a thicket, while he went into the city, disguised as a pilgrim, and carrying under his robe a hunting horn, which he promised to sound should he at any time find himself in danger.

He no sooner entered the city than he noticed with surprise that all the inhabitants seemed greatly depressed. He questioned them concerning their evident sadness, and learned that Imelot, having effected his escape from captivity, had invaded the kingdom, and vowed that he would not retreat unless Oda married his ugly and hunchbacked son that very day.

These tidings made Rother press on to the palace, where, thanks to his disguise, he effected an easy entrance. Slipping unnoticed to his wife's side, he dropped into the cup beside her a ring upon which his name was engraved. Quick as a flash Oda recognized and tried to hide it; but her hunchbacked suitor, sitting beside her, also caught sight of it. He pointed out the intruder, cried that he was Rother in disguise, and bade his guards seize him and hang him. Rother, seeing that he was discovered, boldly stepped forward, declared that he had come to claim his wife, and challenged the cowardly hunchback, who, however, merely repeated his orders, and accompanied his guards to a grove outside the city to see his captive executed. Just as they were about to fasten the fatal noose around his neck, Rother blew a resounding blast upon his horn, in answer to which call his followers sprang out of their ambush, slew guards, Imelot, and hunchback, routed the imperial forces, recovered possession of Oda, and sailed home in triumph to Lombardy. Here Oda bore her husband a lovely little daughter called Helche (Herka), who eventually married Etzel (Attila), King of the Huns.

*　*　*　*　*

Another renowned Lombardian king is Ortnit (Otnit), whose realm included not only all Italy, from the Alps to the sea, but also the island of Sicily. He had won this province by his fabulous strength, which, we are told, was equivalent to that of twelve vigorous men.

In spite of all outward prosperity, Ortnit was lonely and unhappy. One day, while he was strolling along the seashore at sunset, he saw a misty castle rise slowly out of the waves. On its topmost tower he beheld a fair maiden, with whom he fell deeply in love at first sight. As he was gazing spellbound at the lady's beauty, castle and maiden suddenly vanished; and when Ortnit asked his uncle, Ylyas (Elias), Prince of the Reussen, what this fantastic vision might mean, he learned that the castle was the exact reproduction of the stronghold of Muntabure, and the maiden a phantom of Princess Sidrat, daughter of the ruler of Syria, which the Fata Morgana, or Morgana the fay, had permitted him to behold.

> "As the weary traveler sees,
>   In desert or prairie vast,
> Blue lakes, overhung with trees,
>   That a pleasant shadow cast;
>
> "Fair towns with turrets high,
>   And shining roofs of gold,
> That vanish as he draws nigh,
>   Like mists together rolled."
> LONGFELLOW, *Fata Morgana.*

Of course Ortnit vowed that he would go and ask the maiden's hand in marriage; and although his uncle warned him that Machorell, the girl's father, beheaded all his daughter's suitors, to use their heads as decorations for his fortifications, the young king persisted in this resolve.

Forced to go by sea in order to reach Syria, Ortnit had to delay his departure until suitable preparations had been made. During that time his mother vainly tried to dissuade him from the undertaking. Finally, seeing that nothing could deter him from going in search of the lovely maiden he had seen, she slipped a ring on his hand, and bade him ride out of town in a certain direction, and dismount under a lime tree, where he would see something marvelous.

> "'If thou wilt seek the adventure, don thy armor strong;
> Far to the left thou ride the towering rocks along.
> But bide thee, champion, and await, where grows a linden tree;
> There, flowing from the rock, a well thine eyes will see.
>
> "'Far around the meadow spread the branches green;
> Five hundred armed knights may stand beneath the shade, I ween.
> Below the linden tree await, and thou wilt meet full soon
> The marvelous adventure; there must the deed be done.'"
> *Heldenbuch* (Weber's tr.).

Ortnit obeyed these instructions, dismounted in a spot which seemed strangely familiar, and, gazing inquisitively around him, became aware of the presence of a lovely sleeping infant. But when he attempted to take it in his arms he found himself sprawling on the ground, knocked over by a single blow from the child's tiny fist. Furious at his overthrow, Ortnit began wrestling with his small assailant; but in spite of his vaunted strength he succeeded in pinioning him only after a long struggle.

Unable to free himself from Ortnit's powerful grasp, the child now confessed that he was Alberich, king of the dwarfs, and promised Ortnit a marvelous suit of armor and the sword Rosen—which had been tempered in dragons' blood, and was therefore considered invulnerable—if he would only let him go.

> "'Save me, noble Otnit, for thy chivalry!
> A hauberk will I give thee, strong, and of wondrous might;
> Better armor never bore champion in the fight.
>
> "'Not eighty thousand marks would buy the hauberk bright.
> A sword of mound I'll give thee, Otnit, thou royal knight;
> Through armor, both of gold and steel, cuts the weapon keen;
> The helmet could its edge withstand ne'er in this world was seen.'"
> *Heldenbuch* (Weber's tr.).

The king consented, but the moment he set the dwarf free he felt him snatch the ring his mother had given him off his hand, and saw him mysteriously and suddenly disappear, his voice sounding tauntingly now on one side, now on the other. Some parley ensued before the dwarf would restore the ring, which was no sooner replaced on the hero's hand than he once more found himself able to see his antagonist.

Alberich now gravely informed Ortnit that in spite of his infantile stature he was very old indeed, having lived more than five hundred years. He then went on to tell him that the king, whom Ortnit had until then considered his father, had no claim to the title of parent, for he had secretly divorced his wife, and given her in marriage to Alberich. Thus the dwarf was Ortnit's true father, and declared himself ready now to acknowledge their relationship and to protect his son.

After giving Ortnit the promised armor and sword, and directing him to turn the magic ring if ever he needed a father's aid, Alberich vanished. Ortnit, returning to town, informed his mother that he had seen his father; and as soon as the weather permitted he set sail for Suders (Tyre). Ortnit entered the harbor as a merchant, and exhibited his wares to the curious people, while Alberich, at his request, bore a challenge to Machorell, threatening to take Tyre and the castle of Muntabure unless he were willing to accept Ortnit as son-in-law.

The dwarf acquitted himself nobly of his task, and when Machorell scornfully dismissed him, he hastened back to Tyre, bidding Ortnit lose no time in surprising and taking possession of the city. This advice was so well carried out that Ortnit soon found himself master of the city, and marching on to Muntabure, he laid siege to the castle, restoring all his men as soon as they were wounded by a mere touch of his magic ring. Alberich, whom none but he could see, was allowed to lead the van and bear the banner, which seemed to flutter aloft in a fantastic way. The dwarf took advantage of this invisibility to scale the walls of the fortress unseen, and hurled down the ponderous machines used to throw stones, arrows, boiling pitch, and oil. Thus he greatly helped Ortnit, who, in the mean while, was performing unheard-of deeds of valor, which excited the admiration of Princess Sidrat, watching him from her tower.

Alberich next glided to this maiden's side, and bade her hasten to the postern gate early on the morrow, if she would see the king. As Ortnit had been told that he would find her there, he went thither in the early dawn, and pleaded his cause so eloquently that Sidrat eloped with him to Lombardy. There she became his beloved queen, was baptized in the Christian faith, and received the name of Liebgart, by which she was ever afterward known.

The happiness of Ortnit and Liebgart was very great, but the young queen did not feel that it was quite complete until a giant and his wife came from her father's court bringing conciliatory messages, and a promise that Machorell would visit his daughter in the early spring. They also brought countless valuable presents, among which were two huge eggs, which the giants said were priceless, as from them could be hatched magic toads with lodestones in their foreheads. Of course Liebgart's curiosity was greatly excited by this gift, and learning that the giant couple would see to the hatching of the eggs and the bringing up of the toads if a suitable place were only provided for them, she sent them into a mountain gorge near

Trient, where the climate was hot and damp enough for the proper hatching of the toads.

Time passed by, and the giantess Ruotze hatched dragons or lind-worms from the huge eggs. These animals grew with alarming rapidity, and soon the governor of the province sent word to the king that he could no longer provide food enough for the monsters, which had become the terror of the whole countryside. They finally proved too much even for the giants, who were obliged to flee. When Ortnit learned that ordinary weapons had no effect upon these dragons, he donned his magic armor and seized his sword Rosen. He then bade Liebgart a tender farewell, telling her that if he did not return she must marry none but the man who wore his ring, and sallied forth to deliver his people from the ravenous monsters whom he had thoughtlessly allowed to be bred in their midst.

Ortnit soon dispatched the giant and giantess, who would fain have hindered his entrance into the fatal gorge. Then he encountered the dwarf Alberich, and was warned that he would fall victim to the pestilent dragons, which had bred a number of young ones, destined, in time, to infest all Europe.

In spite of these warnings, Ortnit declared that he must do his best for the sake of his people; and having given the magic ring back to Alberich, he continued on his way. All day long he vainly sought the monsters in the trackless forest, until, sinking down exhausted at the foot of a tree, he soon fell asleep.

This slumber was so profound that it was like a lethargy, and the wild barking of his dog failed to waken him so that he could prepare for the stealthy approach of the great dragon. The monster caught the sleeping knight in his powerful claws, and dashed him against the rocks until every bone in his body was broken into bits, although the magic armor remained quite whole.

Then the dragon conveyed the corpse to his den, where the little dragons vainly tried to get at the knight to eat his flesh, being daunted by the impenetrable armor, which would not give way.

In the mean while Liebgart was anxiously awaiting the return of her beloved husband; but when she saw his dog steal into the palace in evident grief, she knew that Ortnit was dead, and mourned for him with many a tear. As he had left no heir to succeed him, the nobles soon crowded around Liebgart, imploring her to marry one of them and make him king of Lombardy; but she constantly refused to listen to their wooing.

Angry at her resistance, the noblemen then took possession of treasure, palace, and kingdom, and left poor Liebgart so utterly destitute that she was forced to support herself by spinning and weaving. She carried on these occupations for a long time, while patiently waiting for the coming of a knight who would avenge Ortnit's death, wear his ring, claim her hand in marriage, and restore her to her former exalted position as queen of Lombardy.

CHAPTER VI

THE AMBLINGS.

While Ortnit's ancestors were ruling over Lombardy, Anzius was Emperor of Constantinople. When about to die, this monarch confided his infant son, Hugdietrich, to the care of Berchther of Meran, the same who had accompanied Rother on his journey to Constantinople.

When Hugdietrich attained marriageable age, his tutor felt it incumbent upon him to select a suitable wife for him. One princess only, Hildburg, daughter of Walgund of Thessalonica, seemed to unite all the required advantages of birth, beauty, and wealth; but unfortunately this princess's father was averse to her marrying, and, to prevent her from having any lovers, had locked her up in an isolated tower, where none but women were ever admitted.

Berchther having informed his ward of his plan, and of the difficulties concerning its fulfillment, Hugdietrich immediately made up his mind to bring it about, even if he had to resort to stratagem in order to win his bride. After much cogitation he let his hair grow, learned all about woman's work and ways, donned female garments, and journeyed off to Thessalonica, where he presented himself before the king as a princess in distress, and claimed his chivalrous protection. Walgund welcomed the pretended princess warmly, and accepted her gifts of gold and embroidery. As soon as he had shown the latter to his wife and daughter, they expressed a lively desire to see the stranger and have her teach them to embroider also.

Hugdietrich, having thus effected an entrance into the princess's tower as embroidery teacher, soon managed to quiet Hildburg's alarm when she discovered that the pretended princess was a suitor in disguise, and wooed her so successfully that she not only allowed him to take up his abode in the tower, but also consented to a secret union. All went on very well for some time, but finally Hugdietrich felt it his duty to return to his kingdom; and parting from his young wife, he solemnly promised to return ere long to claim her openly.

On reaching home, however, he found himself unexpectedly detained by a war which had just broken out; and while he was fighting, Hildburg anxiously watched for his return. Month after month passed by without any news of him, till Hildburg, in her lonely tower, gave birth to a little son, whose advent was kept secret by the ingenuity and devotion of the princess's nurse.

When the queen presented herself at the door unexpectedly one day, this servant hastily carried the child out of the building, and set him down on the grass in the moat, intending to come and get him in a few moments. She could not do so, however, as the queen kept her constantly beside her, and prolonged her visit to the next day.

> "In the moat the new-born babe meanwhile in silence lay,
> Sleeping on the verdant grass, gently, all the day.
> From the swathing and the bath the child had stinted weeping;
> No one saw, or heard its voice, in the meadow sleeping."
> *Heldenbuch* (Weber's tr.).

When the faithful nurse, released at last, rushed out to find her charge, who could creep about, she could discover no trace of him; and not daring to confide the truth to Hildburg, she informed her that she had sent the child out to nurse.

A few days later, Berchther of Meran arrived at Thessalonica, saying that Hugdietrich had fallen in love with Hildburg on hearing a description of her charms from the exiled princess, his sister, and openly suing in his name for her hand. Instead of giving an immediate answer to this proposal, Walgund invited the ambassador to hunt with him in a neighboring forest on the morrow.

Accidentally separated from their respective suites, Walgund and Berchther came to a thicket near the princess's tower, and peering through the underbrush to discover the meaning of some strange sounds, they saw a beautiful little boy sitting on the grass, playfully handling some young wolf cubs, whose struggles he seemed not to mind in the least. While the two men were gazing spellbound at this strange sight, they saw the mother wolf draw near, ready to spring upon the innocent child and tear him limb from limb. As Berchther skillfully flung his spear past the child and slew the wolf, Walgund sprang forward and caught the babe in his arms, exclaiming that if he were only sure his grandchildren would be as handsome and fearless as this little boy, he would soon consent to his daughter's marriage.

As the child was so small that it still required a woman's tender care, Walgund next proposed to carry it to the tower, where his daughter and her attendants could watch over it until it was claimed; and as Berchther indorsed this proposal, it was immediately carried out. Hildburg received the charge with joy, revealed by her emotion that the child was her very own, and told her father all about her secret marriage with Hugdietrich, whom Walgund now graciously accepted as son-in-law.

In memory of this adventure the baby rescued from the beast of prey was called Wolfdietrich, and he and his mother, accompanied by a nobleman named Sabene, were escorted in state to Constantinople, where Hugdietrich welcomed them with joy. Here they dwelt in peace for several years, at the end of which, a war having again broken out, Hugdietrich departed, confiding his wife and son to the care of Sabene, who now cast aside all his pretended virtue. After insulting the queen most grossly, he began to spread lying reports about the birth of the young heir, until the people, doubting whether he might not be considered a mere foundling, showed some unwillingness to recognize him as their future prince.

Hugdietrich, returning home and hearing these remarks, also began to cherish some suspicions, and, instead of keeping Wolfdietrich at court, sent him to Meran, where Berchther brought him up with his twelve stalwart sons, every one of whom the young prince outshone in beauty, courage, and skill in all manly exercises.

In the mean while Hildburg had borne two other sons, Bogen and Waxmuth, to Hugdietrich; but seeing that Sabene was still trying to poison people's minds against the absent Wolfdietrich, and deprive him of his rights, she finally sought her husband, revealed the baseness of Sabene's conduct, and had him exiled. Hugdietrich's life was unfortunately cut short a few months after this, and when he felt that he was about to die, he disposed of all his property, leaving the sovereignty of Constantinople to Wolfdietrich, and making his younger sons kings of lands which he had conquered in the south.

As soon as he had breathed his last, however, the nobles of the land, who had all been won over by Sabene's artful insinuations, declared that they would never recognize Wolfdietrich as their ruler, but would recall Sabene watch over the two younger kings, and exercise the royal power in their name. These measures having been carried out, Sabene avenged himself by banishing Hildburg, who, turned out of the imperial palace at night, was forced to make her way alone and on foot to Meran, where her son Wolfdietrich received her gladly and promised to protect her with his strong right arm.

At the head of a small troop composed of Berchther and his sons, Wolfdietrich marched to Constantinople to oust Sabene; but, in spite of all his valor, he soon found himself defeated, and forced to retreat to the castle of Lilienporte. Here he intrenched himself, rejoicing at the sight of the strong battlements, and especially at the provisions stored within its inclosure, which would suffice for all the wants of the garrison for more than seven years.

In vain Sabene besieged this castle; in vain he constructed huge engines of war; the fortress held out month after month. At the end of the third year, Wolfdietrich, seeing that their provisions would not hold out forever, resolved to make his escape alone, and go in search of allies to save his trusty friends. He soon obtained the consent of Berchther and of his mother for the execution of this scheme.

While a skirmish was going on one day, Wolfdietrich escaped through the postern gate, and, riding into the forest, rapidly disappeared in the direction of Lombardy, where he intended to ask the aid of Ortnit. Riding through the deserts of Roumelia, where his guardian had bidden him beware of the enchantments of the witch Rauch-Else, he shared his last piece of bread with his faithful steed, and, faint with hunger and almost perishing with thirst, plodded painfully on.

Finally horse and rider could go no farther, and as the latter lay in a half swoon upon the barren soil, he was suddenly roused by the appearance of a hideous, bearlike female, who gruffly inquired how he dared venture upon her territory. The unhappy Wolfdietrich recognized Rauch-Else by the description his guardian, Berchther, had given of her, and would have fled, had strength remained him to do so; but, fainting with hunger, he could only implore her to give him something to eat.

At this appeal Rauch-Else immediately produced a peculiar-looking root, of which he had no sooner tasted than he felt as strong and rested as ever before. By the witch's advice he gave the remainder of the root to his horse, upon whom it produced the same magic effect; but when he would fain have expressed his gratitude and ridden away, Rauch-Else told him that he belonged to her by decree of fate, and asked him to marry her.

Not daring to refuse this proposal, which, however, was very distasteful indeed, Wolfdietrich reluctantly assented, expressing a wish that she were not quite so repulsive. No sooner were the words fairly out of his mouth than he saw her suddenly transformed into a beautiful woman, and heard her declare that his "yes" had released her from an evil spell, and allowed her to resume her wonted form and name, which was Sigeminne, Queen of Old Troy.

Slowly proceeding to the seashore, the young couple embarked in a waiting galley and sailed directly to Sigeminne's kingdom, where they lived happily together, Wolfdietrich having entirely forgotten his mother, tutor, and companions, who were vainly awaiting his return with an army to deliver them.

> "By the hand she led Wolfdietrich unto the forest's end;
> To the sea she guided him; a ship lay on the strand.
> To a spacious realm she brought him, hight the land of Troy."
> *Heldenbuch* (Weber's tr.).

Wolfdietrich's happiness, however, was not to endure long; for while he was pursuing a stag which his wife bade him secure for her, a magician named Drusian suddenly presented himself before Sigeminne and spirited her away.

Wolfdietrich, finding his wife gone, resolved to go in search of her, and not to rest until he had found her. Then, knowing that nothing but cunning could prevail against the magician's art, he donned a magic silken vest which his wife had woven for him, which could not be penetrated by weapon or dragon, and covering it with a pilgrim's garb, he traveled on until he came within sight of the castle of Drusian.

Worn out by his long journey, he sat down for a moment to rest ere he began the ascent of the steep mountain upon which the castle stood; and having fallen asleep, he was roughly awakened by a giant, who bore him off prisoner to the fortress, where he saw Sigeminne.

> "He led the weary pilgrim into the castle hall,
> Where brightly burned the fire, and many a taper tall.
> On a seat he sat him down, and made him right good cheer.
> His eyes around the hall cast the hero without fear."
> *Heldenbuch* (Weber's tr.).

Wolfdietrich concealed his face in the depths of his cowl, and remained quietly seated by the fire until evening came. Then the giant turned to the mourning queen, declaring that he had been patient long enough, and that she must now consent to marry him and forget her husband. Hardly had these words been spoken when Wolfdietrich, the pretended pilgrim, fell upon him, and refused to let him go until he had accepted his challenge for a fair fight and had produced suitable arms. The young hero selected an iron armor, in preference to the gold and silver mail offered him, and boldly attacked the giant, who finally succumbed beneath his mighty blows. Sigeminne, thus restored to her husband's arms, then returned with him to Old Troy, where they ruled happily together until she died of a mortal illness.

When she breathed her last, Wolfdietrich, delivered from the spell she had cast upon him by making him partake of the magic root, suddenly remembered his mother, Berchther, and his faithful companions, and, filled with compunction, hastened off to help them. On his way he passed through many lands, and finally came to a fortified town, whose walls were adorned with human heads set up on spikes. He asked a passer-by what this singular decoration might mean, and learned that the city belonged to a heathen king, Belligan, who made it a practice to slay every Christian who entered his precincts.

Wolfdietrich immediately resolved to rid the earth of this monster, and riding boldly into the city, he cried that he was ready to meet the king in his favorite game of dagger throwing. This challenge was promptly accepted, the preparations all made, and although the heathen king was protected by his daughter's magic spells, he could not withstand the Christian knight, who pierced him through and through, and left him dead.

> "Speedily Wolfdietrich the third knife heaved on high.
> Trembling stood Sir Belligan, for he felt his death was nigh.
> The pagan's heart asunder with cunning skill he cleft;
> Down upon the grass he fell, of life bereft."
> *Heldenbuch* (Weber's tr.).

But as Wolfdietrich attempted to leave the castle, waves suddenly surrounded him on all sides, threatening to drown him, until, suspecting that this phenomenon was produced by the princess's magic arts, he seized her and held her head under water until she died. Then the waves immediately subsided and permitted him to escape unharmed.

Wolfdietrich next came to some mountains, where he encountered a giantess, who told him the story of Ortnit's death, and so roused his compassion for the unfortunate Liebgart that he vowed to slay the dragon and avenge all her wrongs. To enable him to reach his destination sooner the giantess bore him and his horse over the mountains, fifty miles in one day, and set him down near Garden (Guarda), where he saw Liebgart and her sole remaining attendant sadly walking up and down.

Struck by Liebgart's resemblance to the dead Sigeminne, Wolfdietrich stood quietly in the shade long enough to overhear her sigh and say that she wished the brave Wolfdietrich would come along that way and avenge her husband's death.

In answer to these words the hero presented himself impetuously before her, swore he would do all in his power to fulfill her wishes, and having received from her fair hand a ring, which she declared would bring the wearer good luck, he hastened off to the mountain gorge to encounter the dragons. On the way thither, Wolfdietrich met Alberich, who cautioned him not to yield to the desire for slumber if he would overcome the foe; so pressing on in spite of almost overpowering lassitude, he met the dragon.

Notwithstanding all his efforts Wolfdietrich soon found himself carried off to the monster's cave, where he was flung down to serve as pasture for the young lind-worms. They would surely have devoured him had he not been protected by Sigeminne's magic shirt, which they could not pierce.

Looking about him for some weapon to defend himself with, Wolfdietrich suddenly saw Ortnit's ring and his sword Rosen, which he seized, and wielded the latter to such good purpose that he soon slew all the dragons. He then cut out their tongues, which he packed in a bag the dwarfs brought him, and triumphantly rode off to find Liebgart and tell her of his success. But, as he lost his way in the forest, it was several days before he reached the town where she dwelt, and as he rode through the gates he was indignant to hear that Liebgart was about to marry a knight by the name of Gerhart, who had slain the dragon, brought home its head, and claimed the fulfillment of an old promise she had made to marry her husband's avenger. Wolfdietrich spurred onward, entered the castle, denounced the impostor Gerhart, and proved the truth of his assertions by producing the dragons' tongues. Then, turning to the queen, Wolfdietrich stretched out his hand to her, humbly asking whether she would marry him. At that moment Liebgart saw Ortnit's ring glittering on his finger, and, remembering her husband's last words, immediately signified her consent.

The happy couple spent a whole year together in restoring order, peace, and prosperity to the Lombards, before Wolfdietrich left his wife to go and succor the companions whom he had neglected so long. Landing with his army near Constantinople, Wolfdietrich, disguised as a peasant, made his way into the city, and learned that Berchther and his sons had been put in prison. There the former had died, but the latter were still languishing in captivity. Wolfdietrich bribed the jailer to bear them a cheering message and strengthening food, and led his army against Sabene, whom he utterly routed.

After recovering possession of Constantinople, granting full forgiveness to his erring brothers, executing Sabene, and liberating his companions, to whom he intrusted the sovereignty of the empire, Wolfdietrich returned to Lombardy, and from thence proceeded with Liebgart to Romaburg (Rome), where he was duly crowned emperor.

To reward Herbrand, Berchther's eldest son, for his faithfulness, Wolfdietrich gave him the city of Garden and all its territories, a realm which subsequently was inherited by his son Hildebrand, a hero whom we shall have further occasion to describe.

Hache, another of Berchther's sons, received as his share all the Rhine land, which he left to his son, the trusty Eckhardt (Eckewart) who ever and anon appears in northern literature to win mortals back to virtue and point out the road to honor. Wolfdietrich and Liebgart were the happy parents of a son called Hugdietrich, like his grandfather; and this king's second son, Dietmar, was the father of the famous Dietrich von Bern, the hero of the next chapter of this volume.

CHAPTER VII.

DIETRICH VON BERN.

DIETRICH VON BERN, whose name is spelled in eighty-five different ways in the various ballads and chronicles written about him, has been identified with the historical Theodoric of Verona, whose "name was chosen by the poets of the early middle ages as the string upon which the pearls of their fantastic imagination were to be strung."

This hero is one of the principal characters in the ancient German "Book of Heroes," and his adventures, which are recorded in many ancient manuscripts, and more especially in the Wilkina saga, are about as follows:

Dietmar, the second son of Hugdietrich, or of Samson according to other authorities, became the independent ruler of Bern (Verona), and refused to recognize his elder brother, Ermenrich, Emperor of the West, as his liege lord. The young prince had married Odilia, the heiress of the conquered Duke of Verona, who bore him a son called Dietrich. Gentle and generous when all went according to his wishes, this child was uncontrollable when his anger was roused, and his breath then came from his lips in a fiery torrent, scorching his opponent, and consuming all inflammable articles.

When Dietrich was but five years of age his training was intrusted to Hildebrand, son of Herbrand, one of the Volsung race; and so well did the tutor acquit himself of this task that he soon made his pupil as accomplished a warrior as himself. Their tastes were, moreover, so similar that they soon became inseparable friends, and their attachment has become as proverbial among northern nations as that of David and Jonathan, Damon and Pythias, or Orestes and Pylades.

Hearing that a giant, Grim, and a giantess, Hilde, were committing great depredations in a remote part of his father's territories, and that no one had been able to rout or slay them, young Dietrich set out with Master Hildebrand to attack them. They had not ridden long in the forest before they became aware of the presence of a tiny dwarf, Alberich (Alferich, Alpris, or Elbegast), and pouncing upon him, they held him fast, vowing that he should recover his liberty only upon condition of pointing out the giants' lurking place.

The dwarf not only promised the desired information, but gave Dietrich the magic sword Nagelring, which alone could pierce the giants' skin. Then he led both heroes to the cave, where Grim and Hilde were gloating over a magic helmet they had made and called Hildegrim. Peering through a fissure of the rock, Hildebrand was the first to gaze upon them, and in his eagerness to get at them he braced his shoulder against the huge mass of stone, forced it apart, and thus made a passage for himself and for his impetuous young pupil.

As Nagelring, the magic sword, had been stolen from him, Grim attacked Dietrich with a blazing brand snatched from the fire, while Hildebrand and Hilde wrestled together. The encounter was short and fierce between the young hero and his gigantic opponent, who soon succumbed beneath Nagelring's sharp blows. Then Dietrich, turning, came just in time to save his master from Hilde's treacherous blade. But, although one stroke of Nagelring cut her in two, the heroes were dismayed to see the severed parts of her body knit together in a trice, and permit Hilde, whole once more, to renew the attack.

To prevent a repetition of this magical performance, Dietrich, after again cutting her in two, placed his sword between the severed parts, and, knowing that steel annuls magic, left it there until all power to unite was gone and Hilde was really dead. The two heroes then returned home in triumph with Nagelring and Hildegrim, the two famous trophies, which Dietrich took as his share of the spoil, leaving to Hildebrand an immense treasure of gold which made him the richest man of his day. This wealth enabled Hildebrand to marry the noble Ute (Uote or Uta), who helped him to bring up Dietrich's young brother, then but a babe.

Although the young prince of Bern imagined that he had exterminated all the giants in his land, he was soon undeceived; for Sigenot, Grim's brother, coming down from the Alps to visit him, and finding him slain, vowed to avenge his death. The brave young prince, hearing that Sigenot was terrorizing all the neighborhood, immediately set out

FALKE KILLS THE GIANT.—Keller.

to attack him, followed at a distance by Hildebrand and the latter's nephew, Wolfhart, who was always ready to undertake any journey, provided there was some prospect of a fight at the end.

Dietrich soon came to a forest, where, feeling hungry, he slew an elk and proceeded to roast some of its flesh upon a spit. While he was thus engaged he heard shrill cries, and looking up, he saw a giant holding a dwarf and about to devour him. Ever ready to succor the feeble and oppressed, Dietrich caught up his sword and attacked the giant, who made a brave but fruitless defense. The dwarf, seeing his tormentor dead, then advised Dietrich to fly in haste, lest Sigenot, the most terrible of all the mountain giants, should come to avenge his companion's murder. But, instead of following this advice, Dietrich persuaded the dwarf to show him the way to the giant's retreat.

Following his tiny guide, Dietrich climbed up the snow-clad mountains, where, in the midst of the icebergs, the ice queen, Virginal, suddenly appeared to him, advising him to retreat, as his venture was perilous in the extreme. Equally undeterred by this second warning, Dietrich pressed on; but when he came at last to the giant's abode he was so exhausted by the ascent that, in spite of all his courage, he was defeated, put in chains, and dragged into the giant's den.

Hildebrand, in the mean while, following his pupil, awaited his return at the foot of the mountains for eight days, and then, seeing that he did not appear, he strode up the mountain side. The giant encountered him, stunned him with a great blow, and dragged him into the den, where, thinking him senseless, he leisurely began to select chains with which to bind him fast. Hildebrand, however, sprang noiselessly to his feet, seized a weapon lying near, and stealing behind a pillar, which served him as a shield, he attacked Sigenot, and stretched him lifeless at his feet.

A moment later he heard Dietrich calling him from the depths of the cave. To spring forward and free his pupil from his chains was the work of a moment, and then, following the dwarf, who openly rejoiced at the death of his foe, the two heroes visited the underground kingdom. There they were hospitably entertained, their wounds were healed, and the king of the dwarfs gave them the finest weapons that they had ever seen.

While hunting in the Tyrolean mountains shortly after this encounter, Dietrich confided to Hildebrand that he had fallen in love with the ice fairy, Virginal, and longed to see her again. This confidence was suddenly interrupted by the appearance of a dwarf, who presented himself as Bibung, the unconquerable protector of Queen Virginal, but who in the same breath confessed that she had fallen into the hands of the magician Ortgis. The latter kept her imprisoned in one of her own castles, and at every new moon he forced her to surrender one of the snow maidens, her lovely attendants, whom he intended, to devour as soon as they were properly fattened.

Dietrich's eyes flashed with anger when he heard of his lady-love's distress, and bidding the dwarf show him the way, he forthwith set out to rescue her. They had not gone very far before they beheld the ice queen's palace glittering far above their heads; and as they eagerly climbed upward to reach it, they heard cries of terror, and saw a beautiful girl rush down the pathway, closely pursued by the magician and his mounted train.

Dietrich allowed the maiden to pass him, and then stepped boldly into the middle of the path, where he and Hildebrand soon succeeded in slaying the magician and all his men. Jambas, the son of Ortgis, alone effected his escape; but Dietrich and his master closely pursued him, took forcible possession of his castle, set the captive snow maidens free, and fearlessly slew all the monsters which Jambas conjured up to destroy them. Then, resuming their interrupted journey, Dietrich and Hildebrand soon came face to face with the self-styled unconquerable guardian of the ice queen. He had been hiding during the fray, and now implored them to hasten forward, as his mistress was besieged by Jambas. The magician's son was anxious to secure Virginal and all her maidens, but his principal aim was to appropriate the great carbuncle shining in the queen's crown, as it gave the possessor full power over the elements, the mountains, and all who ventured within reach of them.

Thus urged to greater speed, the heroes toiled upward faster and faster, and soon came near the glittering castle of Jeraspunt, and the besiegers. The latter were on the point of overpowering the garrison and gaining possession of the queen. When Dietrich saw her on the battlement, wringing her hands in despair, he rushed impetuously forward, crying that he had come to save her. He struck right and left, and did such good execution with his sword that the mountains shook, the icebergs cracked, and great avalanches, rolling down into the abysses, carried with them the bodies of the slain which he hurled down from the drawbridge.

In a very short time the enemy was completely routed, and Dietrich was joyfully welcomed by Virginal, who, touched by his devotion, consented to forsake her glittering castle, relinquish her sway over the mountains, and to follow him down into the green valley. Their wedding was celebrated in Jeraspunt, which was all hung in bridal white; and the ice queen and her maidens wore misty veils and crowns of glittering diamonds, which sparkled and flashed and lit up the whole scene with fairylike splendor. Some versions of the story tell, however, that the queen soon grew homesick down in the green valley, and, deserting her hero husband, returned to her palace on the mountain top, where she still rules supreme.

Dietrich's numerous adventures soon became the theme of the wandering bards and minstrels, and thus the rumor of his courage came to the ears of Heime, the son of the northern stud keeper Studas. After distinguishing himself at home by slaying a dragon, this youth obtained from his father the steed Rispa and the sword Blutgang, with which he set out to test Dietrich's courage, vowing that he would serve him forever if conquered by him.

> "King Tidrick sits intill Bern;
> He rooses [boasts] him of his might;
> Sae mony has he in battle cow'd,
> Baith kemp [rough] and doughty knight."
> *The Ettin Langshanks* (Jamieson's tr.).

Heime soon reached Bern, boldly challenged Dietrich, and when defeated entered his service, after procuring for his master's exclusive use the matchless steed Falke, which could carry even such a gigantic man as Dietrich without showing any signs of fatigue, and which served him faithfully for many a year.

The rumor of Dietrich's courage also came to Heligoland, where Wieland (Wayland, or Völund), the smith, dwelt with his son Wittich (Witig). The latter, determined to cross swords with the hero of Bern, persuaded his father to give him the celebrated sword Mimung, by the help of which he hoped to overcome every foe. Wieland also fashioned a complete suit of armor for his son, gave him much good advice, and parted from him, bidding him to prove himself worthy of his ancestors, and to call upon his grandmother, the mermaid Wachilde, if he were ever in great distress.

Thus instructed Wittich departed, and on the way to Bern fell in with Hildebrand, Heime, and Hornbogi, another of Dietrich's noted warriors. They concealed their names, encouraged the stranger to talk, and soon learned where he was going and on what errand. Master Hildebrand, hearing of the magic sword, and anxious to preserve his pupil from its blows, allowed Wittich to fight single-handed against twelve robbers in a mountain pass. As the youth disposed of them all without receiving a scratch, Hildebrand substituted his own sword blade for that which Wittich bore, one night while the latter was peacefully sleeping at an inn. This exchange remained unnoticed until Wittich arrived in Bern. There, while fighting with Dietrich, the blade suddenly snapped in two.

Loudly reproaching his father, Wieland, for having provided him with such an unreliable weapon, Wittich was about to announce himself conquered, when Hildebrand, realizing that he had not acted honorably, gave him back his own blade. Dietrich, to his surprise and dismay, found himself conquered in this second encounter, and was forced to acknowledge that he owed his life only to Wittich's magnanimity. But the northern hero soon confessed in his turn that had it not been for his magic sword he would have been obliged to yield to Dietrich, and voluntarily offered his services to him, thus becoming one of his train.

> "Sae gladly rode they back to Bern;
> But Tidrick maist was glad;
> And Vidrich o' his menyie a'
> The foremost place aye had."
>
> *The Ettin Langskanks* (Jamieson's tr.).

Dietrich's next adventure, which is recorded in the "Eckenlied," was with the giant Ecke, who held Bolfriana, the widowed Lady of Drachenfels, and her nine daughters, in his power. The hero of Bern encountered the giant by night, and, in spite of his aversion to fighting at such a time, was compelled to defend himself against the giant's blows. He was about to succumb when his steed Falke, scenting his danger, broke loose from the tree to which it had been tied, and stamped Ecke to death.

Dietrich now rode on to Drachenfels, where he encountered Fasolt, Ecke's brother, and, after defeating him also, and delivering the captive ladies, went back to Bern, where Fasolt joined his chosen warriors. Dietrich, moreover, delivered the knight Sintram from the jaws of a dragon, and made him one of his followers. Then, having appropriated Ecke's sword, the great Eckesax, Dietrich was about to give Nagelring to Heime; but hearing that the latter had stood idly by while Wittich fought single-handed against twelve robbers, he banished him from his presence, bidding him never return until he had atoned for his dishonorable conduct by some generous deed.

Heime, incensed at this dismissal, sulkily withdrew to the Falster wood on the banks of the Wisara (Weser), where he became chief of a body of brigands, ruthlessly spoiled travelers, and daily increased the hoard he was piling up in one of his strongholds.

But, although Dietrich thus lost one of his bravest warriors, his band was soon reënforced by Hildebrand's brother Ilsan, who, although a monk, was totally unfitted for a religious life, and greatly preferred fighting to praying. There also came to Bern Wildeber (Wild Boar), a man noted for his great strength. He owed this strength to a golden bracelet given him by a mermaid in order to recover her swan plumage, which he had secured.

As Dietrich was once on his way to Romaburg (Rome), whither his uncle Ermenrich had invited him, he accepted the proffered service and escort of Dietlieb the Dane. This warrior, seeing that the emperor had forgotten to provide for the entertainment of Dietrich's suite, pledged not only his own steed and weapons, but also his master's and Hildebrand's, leading a jolly life upon the proceeds.

When the time of departure came, and Dietrich called for his steed, Dietlieb was forced to confess what he had done. The story came to Ermenrich's ears, and he felt called upon to pay the required sum to release his guest's weapons and steeds, but contemptuously inquired whether Dietlieb were good at anything besides eating and drinking, wherein he evidently excelled. Enraged by this taunt, Dietlieb challenged Ermenrich's champion warrior, Walther von Wasgenstein (Vosges), and

THE VICTORIOUS HUNS.—Checa.

beat him at spear and stone throwing. He next performed feats hitherto unheard of, and won such applause that Ermenrich not only paid all his debts, but also gave him a large sum of money, which this promising young spendthrift immediately expended in feasting all the men at arms.

Dietlieb's jests and jollity so amused Isung, the imperial minstrel, that he left court to follow him to the land of the Huns, where the fickle youth next offered his services to Etzel (Attila). The King of the Huns, afraid to keep such a mercurial person near him, gave him the province of Steiermark (Styria), bidding him work off all surplus energy by defending it against the numerous enemies always trying to enter his realm.

Some time after this, Dietlieb returned to his old master in sorrow, for his only sister, Kunhild (Similde, or Similt), had been carried away by Laurin (Alberich), king of the dwarfs, and was now detained prisoner in the Tyrolean mountains, not far from the vaunted Rose Garden. This place was surrounded by a silken thread, and guarded most jealously by Laurin himself, who exacted the left foot and right hand of any knight venturing to enter his garden or break off a single flower from its stem.

As soon as Dietrich heard this, he promised to set out and rescue the fair Kunhild. He was accompanied by Dietlieb, Hildebrand, Wittich, and Wolfhart; and as they came to the Rose Garden, all the heroes except Dietrich and Hildebrand began to trample the dainty blossoms, and tried to break the silken cord.

> "Wittich, the mighty champion, trod the roses to the ground,
> Broke down the gates, and ravaged the garden far renowned;
> Gone was the portals' splendor, by the heroes bold destroyed;
> The fragrance of the flowers was past, and all the garden's pride."
> *Heldenbuch* (Weber's tr.).

While they were thus employed, the dwarf Laurin donned his glittering girdle of power, which gave him the strength of twelve men, brandished a sword which had been tempered in dragons' blood and could therefore cut through iron and stone, and put on his ring of victory and the magic cap of darkness, Tarnkappe (Helkappe).

Dietrich, carefully instructed by Hildebrand, struck off this cap, and appropriated it, as well as the girdles of strength and the ring of victory. He was so angry against Laurin for resisting him that the dwarf king soon fled to Dietlieb for protection, promising to restore Kunhild, unless she preferred to remain with him as his wife.

This amicable agreement having been made, Laurin led the knights down into his subterranean palace, which was illuminated by carbuncles, diamonds, and other precious stones. Here Kunhild and her attendant maidens, attired with the utmost magnificence, welcomed them hospitably and presided at the banquet.

> "Similt into the palace came, with her little maidens all;
> Garments they wore which glittered brightly in the hall,
> Of fur and costly ciclatoun, and brooches of the gold;
> No richer guise in royal courts might mortal man behold."
> *Heldentuch* (Weber's tr.).

The wines, however, were drugged, so the brave knights soon sank into a stupor; and Laurin, taking a base advantage of their helplessness, deprived them of their weapons, bound them fast, and had them conveyed into a large prison. Dietlieb was placed in a chamber apart, where, as soon as he recovered his senses, Laurin told him that he and his companions were doomed to die on the morrow.

At midnight Dietrich awoke. Feeling himself bound, his wrath burned hot within him, and his breath grew so fiery that it consumed the ropes with which he was pinioned. He then released his captive companions, and, while they were bewailing their lack of weapons, Kunhild stealthily opened the door. Noiselessly she conducted them into the great hall, bade them resume possession of their arms, and gave each a golden ring, of dwarf manufacture, to enable them to see their tiny foes, who were else invisible to all of mortal birth.

Joined by Dietlieb, who had also been liberated by Kunhild, the knights now roused Laurin and his host of giants and dwarfs, and, after an encounter such as mediaeval poets love to describe at great length, routed them completely. Laurin was made prisoner and carried in chains to Bern, where Kunhild, now full of compassion for him, prevailed upon Dietrich to set him free, provided he would forswear all his malicious propensities and spend the remainder of his life in doing good.

When this promise had been given, Laurin was set free; and after marrying Kunhild, he went to live with her in the beautiful Rose Garden and the underground palace, which peasants and simple-hearted Alpine hunters have often seen, but which the worldly wise and skeptical have always sought in vain.

The mere fact of his having come off victor in one Rose Garden affair made Dietrich hail with joy the tidings brought by a wandering minstrel, that at Worms, on the Rhine, Kriemhild (Grimhild, Gutrun, etc.), the Burgundian princess, had a similar garden. This was guarded by twelve brave knights, ever ready to try their skill against an equal number of warriors, the prize of the victor being a rose garland and kisses from the owner of this charming retreat.

Eager to accept this challenge, Dietrich selected Hildebrand, Wittich, Wolfhart, and five other brave men; but as he could think of no others worthy to share in the adventure, Hildebrand suggested that Rüdiger of Bechlaren, Dietlieb of Steiermark, and his own brother, the monk Ilsan, would be only too glad to help them. This little band soon rode into Worms, where Dietrich and his men covered themselves with glory by defeating all Kriemhild's champions, and winning the rose garlands as well as the kisses.

The knights, if we are to believe the ancient poem, appreciated the latter reward highly, with the exception of the rude monk Ilsan, who, we are told, scrubbed the princess's delicate cheek with his rough beard until the blood flowed.

> "And when Chrimhild, the queen, gave him kisses fifty-two,
> With his rough and grisly beard full sore he made her rue,
> That from her lovely cheek 'gan flow the rosy blood:
> The queen was full of sorrow, but the monk it thought him good."
> *Heldenbuch* (Weber's tr.).

Then Ilsan carried his garlands back to the monastery, where he jammed them down upon the monks' bald pates, laughing aloud when he saw them wince as the sharp thorns pierced them.

On his way home Dietrich visited Etzel, King of the Huns, and further increased his train by accepting the services of Amalung, Hornbogi's son, and of Herbrand the wide-traveled. On his arrival at

Bern, he found that his father, Dietmar, was dead, and thus Dietrich became King of the Amaling land (Italy).

Shortly after his accession to the throne, he went to help Etzel, who was warring against Osantrix, King of the Wilkina land (Norway and Sweden). With none but his own followers, Dietrich invaded the Wilkina land, and throughout that glorious campaign old Hildebrand rode ever ahead, bearing aloft his master's standard, and dealing many memorable blows.

In one encounter, Wittich was thrown from his horse and stunned. Heime, who had joined the army, seeing him apparently lifeless, snatched the sword Mimung out of his nerveless grasp and bore it triumphantly away. Wittich, however, was not dead, but was soon after made prisoner by Hertnit, Earl of Greece, Osantrix's brother, who carried him back to the capital, where he put him in prison.

When the campaign against the Wilkina men was ended, Dietrich and his army returned to Bern, leaving Wildeber in Hungary to ascertain whether Wittich were really dead, or whether he still required his companions' aid.

Wishing to penetrate unrecognized into the enemy's camp, Wildeber slew and flayed a bear, donned its skin over his armor, and, imitating the uncouth antics of the animal he personated, bade the minstrel Isung lead him thus disguised to Hertnit's court.

This plan was carried out, and the minstrel and dancing bear were hailed with joy. But Isung was greatly dismayed when Hertnit insisted upon baiting his hunting hounds against the bear; who, however, strangled them all, one after another, without seeming to feel their sharp teeth. Hertnit was furious at the loss of all his pack, and sprang down into the pit with drawn sword; but all his blows glanced aside on the armor concealed beneath the rough pelt. Suddenly the pretended bear stood up, caught the weapon which the king had dropped, and struck off his head. Then, joining Isung, he rushed through the palace and delivered the captive Wittich; whereupon, seizing swords and steeds on their way, they all three rode out of the city before they could be stopped.

When they arrived in Bern they were warmly welcomed by Dietrich, who forced Heime to give the stolen Mimung back to its rightful owner. The brave warriors were not long allowed to remain inactive, however, for they were soon asked to help Ermenrich against his revolted vassal, Rimstein. They besieged the recalcitrant knight in his stronghold of Gerimsburg, which was given to Walther von Wasgenstein, while Wittich was rewarded for his services by the hand of Bolfriana, the Lady of Drachenfels, and thus became the vassal of Ermenrich.

The estates of Ermenrich were so extensive and so difficult to govern that he was very glad indeed to secure as prime minister a capable nobleman by the name of Sibich. Unfortunately, this Sibich had a remarkably beautiful wife, whom the emperor once insulted during her husband's absence. As soon as Sibich returned from his journey his wife told him all that had occurred, and the emperor's conduct so enraged the minister that he vowed that he would take a terrible revenge.

The better to accomplish his purpose, Sibich concealed his resentment, and so artfully poisoned Ermenrich's mind that the latter ordered his eldest son to be slain. To get rid of the second prince, Sibich induced him to enter a leaky vessel, which sank as soon as he was out at sea. Then, when the prime minister saw the third son, Randwer, paying innocent attentions to his fair young stepmother, Swanhild, daughter of Siegfried and Kriemhild, he so maliciously distorted the affair that Ermenrich ordered this son to be hung, and his young wife to be trampled to death under the hoofs of wild horses.

Sibich, the traitor, having thus deprived the emperor of wife and children, next resolved to rob him of all his kin, so that he might eventually murder him and take undisputed possession of the empire. With this purpose in view, he forged letters which incited the emperor to war against his nephews, the Harlungs. These two young men, who were orphans, dwelt at Breisach, under the guardianship of their tutor, the faithful Eckhardt. They were both cruelly slain, and the disconsolate tutor fled to the court of Dietrich, little thinking that Ermenrich would soon turn upon this his last male relative, also.

Dietrich, forsaken by Virginal, and anxious to marry again, had, in the mean while, sent his nephew Herbart to Arthur's court in the Bertanga land (Britain), to sue for the hand of Hilde, his fair young daughter. But Arthur, averse to sending his child so far away, would not at first permit the young ambassador to catch a glimpse of her face, and sent her to church guarded by ten warriors, ten monks, and ten duennas.

In spite of all these safeguards, Herbart succeeded in seeing the princess, and after ascertaining that she was very beautiful, he secured a private interview, and told her of his master's wish to call her wife. Hilde, wishing to know what kind of a man her suitor was, begged Herbart to draw his portrait; but finding him unprepossessing, she encouraged Herbart to declare his own love, and soon eloped with him.

Dietrich had no time to mourn for the loss of this expected bride, however, for the imperial army suddenly marched into the Amaling land, and invested the cities of Garden, Milan, Raben (Ravenna), and Mantua. Of course these successes were owing to treachery, and not to valor, and Dietrich, to obtain the release of Hildebrand and a few other faithful followers, who had fallen into the enemy's hands, was forced to surrender Bern and go off into exile.

As he had thus sacrificed his kingdom to obtain their freedom, it is no wonder that these men proudly accompanied him into banishment. They went to Susat, where they were warmly welcomed by Etzel and Helche (Herka), his wife, who promised to care for Diether, Dietrich's brother, and have him brought up with her own sons.

There were in those days many foreigners at Etzel's court, for he had secured as hostages Hagen of Tronje, from the Burgundians; the Princess Hildegunde, from the Franks; and Walther von Wasgenstein from the Duke of Aquitaine.

During the twenty years which Dietrich now spent in the land of the Huns fighting for Etzel, peace was concluded with Burgundy and Hagen was allowed to return home. Walther of Aquitaine (or von Wasgenstein), whose adventures are related in a Latin poem of the eighth or ninth century, had fallen in love with Hildegunde. Seeing that Etzel, in spite of his promises to set them both free, had no real intention of doing so, he and his ladylove cleverly effected their escape, and fled to the Wasgenstein (Vosges), where they paused in a cave to recruit their exhausted strength. Gunther, King of Burgundy, and Hagen of Tronje, his ally, hearing that Walther and Hildegunde were in the neighborhood, and desirous of obtaining the large sum of gold which they had carried away from Etzel's court, set out to attack them, with a force of twelve picked men. But Hildegunde was watching while Walther slept, and, seeing them draw near, warned her lover. He, inspired by her presence, slew all except Gunther and Hagen, who beat a hasty retreat.

They did not return to Worms, however, but lay in ambush beside the road, and when Walther and Hildegunde passed by they attacked the former with great fury. In spite of the odds against him, the poem relates that Walther triumphantly defeated them both, putting out one of Hagen's eyes and cutting off one of Gunther's hands and one of his feet.

The conflict ended, Hildegunde bound up the wounds of all three of the combatants, who then sat down to share a meal together, indulged in much jocularity about their wounds, and, parting amicably, sought their respective homes. Walther and Hildegunde were next joyously welcomed by their relatives, duly married, and reigned together over Aquitaine for many a long year.

In the mean while Dietrich had been engaged in warring against Waldemar, King of Reussen (Russia and Poland), in behalf of Etzel, who, however, forsook him in a cowardly way, and left him in a besieged fortress, in the midst of the enemy's land, with only a handful of men. In spite of all his courage, Dietrich would have been forced to surrender had not Rüdiger of Bechlaren come to his rescue. By their combined efforts, Waldemar was slain, and his son was brought captive to Susat.

Dietrich and his noble prisoner were both seriously wounded; but while Queen Helche herself tenderly cared for the young prince of Reussen, who was her kinsman, Dietrich lay neglected and alone in a remote part of the palace. The young prince was no sooner cured, however, than he took advantage of Etzel's absence to escape, although Helche implored him not to do so, and assured him that she would have to pay for his absence with her life.

In her distress Helche now thought of Dietrich, who, weak and wounded, rose from his couch, pursued the fugitive, overtook and slew him, and brought his head back to her. The Queen of the Huns never forgot that she owed her life to Dietrich, and ever after showed herself his faithful friend.

Twenty years had passed since Dietrich left his native land ere he asked to return. Helche promised him the aid of her sons, Erp and Ortwine, whom she armed herself, and furnished one thousand men.

THE TOMB OF THEODORIC.

Etzel, seeing this, also offered his aid, and Dietrich marched back to the Amaling land with all his companions, and with an army commanded by the two Hun princes and Rüdiger's only son, Nudung.

The van of the army took Garden and Padauwe (Padua), and with Dietrich at its head made a triumphant entrance into Bern. But, hearing that Ermenrich was coming against him, Dietrich now went to meet him, and fought a terrible battle near Raben in 493. The hero of Bern distinguished himself, as usual, in this fray, until, hearing that Nudung, the two Hun princes, and his young brother, Diether, had all been slain, he became almost insane with grief.

In his fury he wildly pursued Wittich, his former servant and Diether's murderer, and would have slain him had the latter not saved himself by plunging into the sea. Here his ancestress, the swan maiden Wachilde, took charge of him, and conveyed him to a place of safety. Then, although victorious, Dietrich discovered that he had no longer enough men left to maintain himself in his reconquered kingdom, and mournfully returned to Susat with the bodies of the slain.

It was during his second sojourn at the court of the Huns that Dietrich married Herrat (Herand), Princess of Transylvania, a relative of Helche. The latter died soon after their union. Three years later Etzel married Kriemhild, Siegfried's widow; and now occurred the fall of the brave Nibelung knights, recorded in the "Nibelungenlied." Dietrich, as we have seen, took an active part in the closing act of this tragedy, and joined in the final lament over the bodies of the slain.

Ten years after the terrible battle of Raben, Dietrich again resolved to make an attempt to recover his kingdom, and set out with only a very few followers. As Ermenrich had succumbed, either under the swords of Swanhild's brothers, as already related, or by the poison secretly administered by the traitor Sibich, the crown was now offered to Dietrich, who was glad to accept it.

All the lost cities were gradually recovered, and Hildebrand, coming to Garden, encountered his son Hadubrand (Alebrand), who, having grown up during his absence, did not recognize him, and challenged him to fight. Mighty blows were exchanged between father and son, each of whom, in the pauses of the combat, anxiously besought the other to reveal his name. It was only when their strength was exhausted that Hadubrand revealed who he was, and father and son, dropping their bloody swords, embraced with tears.

> "So spake Hadubrand,
> Son of Hildebrand:
> 'Said unto me
> Some of our people,
> Shrewd and old,
> Gone hence already,
> That Hildebrand was my father called,—
> I am called Hadubrand.
> Erewhile he eastward went,
> Escaping from Odoaker,
> Thither with Theodoric
> And his many men of battle,
> Here he left in the land,
> Lorn and lonely,
> Bride in bower,
> Bairn ungrown,
> Having no heritage.'"
>
> *Song of Hildebrand* (Bayard Taylor's tr.).

Hildebrand then rejoined his wife, Ute, and Dietrich, having slain the traitor Sibich, who had made an attempt to usurp the throne, marched on to Romaburg (Rome), where he was crowned Emperor of the West, under the name of Theodoric. Some time after his accession, Dietrich lost his good wife Herrat, whom, according to some accounts, he mourned as long as he lived. According to others he married again, taking as wife Liebgart, widow of Ortnit.

Etzel, according to this version, having been lured by Aldrian, Hagen's son, into the cave where the Nibelungen hoard was kept, was locked up there, and died of hunger while contemplating the gold he coveted. His estates then became the property of Dietrich, who thus became undisputed ruler of nearly all the southern part of Europe.

In his old age Dietrich, weary of life and imbittered by its many trials, ceased to take pleasure in anything except the chase. One day, while he was bathing in a limpid stream, his servant came to tell him that there was a fine stag in sight. Dietrich immediately called for his horse, and as it was not instantly forthcoming, he sprang upon a coal-black steed standing near, and was borne rapidly away.

The servant rode after as fast as possible, but could never overtake Dietrich, who, the peasants aver, was spirited away, and now leads the Wild Hunt upon the same sable steed, which he is doomed to ride until the judgment day.

In spite of this fabulous account, however, the tomb of Theodoric is still to be seen near Verona, but history demonstrates the impossibility of the story of Dietrich von Bern, by proving that Theodoric was not born until after the death of Attila, the unmistakeable original of the Etzel in the "Heldenbuch."

CHAPTER VIII.

CHARLEMAGNE AND HIS PALADINS.

One of the favorite heroes of early mediaeval literature is Charlemagne, whose name is connected with countless romantic legends of more or less antique origin. The son of Pepin and Bertha the "large footed," this monarch took up his abode near the Rhine to repress the invasions of the northern barbarians, awe them into submission, and gradually induce them to accept the teachings of the missionaries he sent to convert them.

As Charlemagne destroyed the Irminsul, razed heathen temples and groves, abolished the Odinic and Druidic forms of worship, conquered the Lombards at the request of the Pope, and defeated the Saracens in Spain, he naturally became the champion of Christianity in the chronicles of his day. All the heroic actions of his predecessors (such as Charles Martel) were soon attributed to him, and when these legends were turned into popular epics, in the tenth and eleventh centuries, he became the principal hero of France. The great deeds of his paladins, Roland, Oliver, Ogier the Dane, Renaud de Montauban, and others, also became the favorite theme of the poets, and were soon translated into every European tongue.

The Latin chronicle, falsely attributed to Bishop Turpin, Charlemagne's prime minister, but dating from 1095, is one of the oldest versions of Charlemagne's fabulous adventures now extant. It contains the mythical account of the battle of Roncesvalles (Vale of Thorns), told with infinite repetition and detail so as to give it an appearance of reality.

Einhard, the son-in-law and historian of Charlemagne, records a partial defeat in the Pyrenees in 777-778, and adds that Hroudlandus was slain. From this bald statement arose the mediaeval "Chanson de Roland," which was still sung at the battle of Hastings. The probable author of the French metrical version is Turoldus; but the poem, numbering originally four thousand lines, has gradually been lengthened, until now it includes more than forty thousand. There are early French, Latin, German, Italian, English, and Icelandic versions of the adventures of Roland, which in the fourteenth and fifteenth centuries were turned into prose, and formed the basis of the "Romans de Chevalerie," which were popular for so many years. Numerous variations can, of course, be noted in these tales, which have been worked over again by the Italian poets Ariosto and Boiardo, and even treated by Buchanan in our day.

It would be impossible to give in this work a complete synopsis of all the *chansons de gestes* referring to Charlemagne and his paladins, so we will content ourselves with giving an abstract of the most noted ones and telling the legends which are found in them, which have gradually been woven around those famous names and connected with certain localities.

We are told that Charlemagne, having built a beautiful new palace for his use, overlooking the Rhine, was roused from his sleep during the first night he spent there by the touch of an angelic hand, and, to his utter surprise, thrice heard the heavenly messenger bid him go forth and steal. Not daring to disobey, Charlemagne stole unnoticed out of the palace, saddled his steed, and, armed cap-a-pie, started out to fulfill the angelic command.

He had not gone far when he met an unknown knight, evidently bound on the same errand. To challenge, lay his lance in rest, charge, and unhorse his opponent, was an easy matter for Charlemagne. When he learned that he had disarmed Elbegast (Alberich), the notorious highwayman, he promised to let him go free if he would only help him steal something that night.

Guided by Elbegast, Charlemagne, still incognito, went to the castle of one of his ministers, and, thanks to Elbegast's cunning, penetrated unseen into his bedroom. There, crouching in the dark, Charlemagne overheard him confide to his wife a plot to murder the emperor on the morrow. Patiently biding his time until they were sound asleep, Charlemagne picked up a worthless trifle, and noiselessly made his way out, returning home unseen. On the morrow, profiting by the knowledge thus obtained, he cleverly outwitted the conspirators, whom he restored to favor only after they had solemnly sworn future loyalty. As for Elbegast, he so admired the only man who had ever succeeded in conquering him that he renounced his dishonest profession to enter the emperor's service.

In gratitude for the heavenly vision vouchsafed him, the emperor named his new palace Ingelheim (Home of the Angel), a name which the place has borne ever since. This thieving episode is often alluded to in the later romances of chivalry, where knights, called upon to justify their unlawful appropriation of another's goods, disrespectfully remind the emperor that he too once went about as a thief.

When Charlemagne's third wife died, he married a beautiful Eastern princess by the name of Frastrada, who, aided by a magic ring, soon won his most devoted affection. The new queen, however, did not long enjoy her power, for a dangerous illness overtook her. When at the point of death, fearful lest her ring should be worn by another while she was buried and forgotten, Frastrada slipped the magic circlet into her mouth just before she breathed her last.

Solemn preparations were made to bury her in the cathedral of Mayence (where a stone bearing her name could still be seen a few years ago), but the emperor refused to part with the beloved body. Neglectful of all matters of state, he remained in the mortuary chamber day after day. His trusty adviser, Turpin, suspecting the presence of some mysterious talisman, slipped into the room while the emperor, exhausted with fasting and weeping, was wrapped in sleep. After carefully searching for the magic jewel, Turpin discovered it, at last, in the dead queen's mouth.

> "He searches with care, though with tremulous haste,
> For the spell that bewitches the king;
> And under her tongue, for security placed,
> Its margin with mystical characters traced,
> At length he discovers a ring."
> SOUTHEY, *King Charlemain.*

To secure this ring and slip it on his finger was but the affair of a moment; but just as Turpin was about to leave the room the emperor awoke. With a shuddering glance at the dead queen, Charlemagne flung himself passionately upon the neck of his prime minister, declaring that he would never be quite inconsolable as long as he was near.

Taking advantage of the power thus secured by the possession of the magic ring, Turpin led Charlemagne away, forced him to eat and drink, and after the funeral induced him to resume the reins of the government. But he soon wearied of his master's constant protestations of undying affection, and ardently longed to get rid of the ring, which, however, he dared neither to hide nor to give away, for fear it should fall into unscrupulous hands.

Although advanced in years, Turpin was now forced to accompany Charlemagne everywhere, even on his hunting expeditions, and to share his tent. One moonlight night the unhappy minister stole noiselessly out of the imperial tent, and wandered alone in the woods, cogitating how to dispose of the unlucky ring. As he walked thus he came to a glade in the forest, and saw a deep pool, on whose mirrorlike surface the moonbeams softly played. Suddenly the thought struck him that the waters would soon close over and conceal the magic ring forever in their depths; and, drawing it from his finger, he threw it into the pond. Turpin then retraced his steps, and soon fell asleep. On the morrow he was delighted to perceive that the spell was broken, and that Charlemagne had returned to the old undemonstrative friendship which had bound them for many a year.

> "Overjoy'd, the good prelate remember'd the spell,
> And far in the lake flung the ring;
> The waters closed round it; and, wondrous to tell,
> Released from the cursed enchantment of hell,
> His reason return'd to the king."
> SOUTHEY, *King Charlemain.*

Charlemagne, however, seemed unusually restless, and soon went out to hunt. In the course of the day, having lost sight of his suite in the pursuit of game, he came to the little glade, where, dismounting, he threw himself on the grass beside the pool, declaring that he would fain linger there forever. The spot was so charming that he even gave orders, ere he left it that night, that a palace should be erected there for his use; and this building was the nucleus of his favorite capital, Aix-la-Chapelle (Aachen).

"But he built him a palace there close by the bay,
And there did he love to remain;
And the traveler who will, may behold at this day
A monument still in the ruins at Aix
Of the spell that possess'd Charlemain."
SOUTHEY, *King Charlemain.*

According to tradition, Charlemagne had a sister by the name of Bertha, who, against his will, married the brave young knight Milon. Rejected by the emperor, and therefore scorned by all, the young couple lived in obscurity and poverty. They were very happy, however, for they loved each other dearly, and rejoiced in the beauty of their infant son Roland, who even in babyhood showed signs of uncommon courage and vigor.

One version of the story relates, however, that Milon perished in a flood, and that Bertha was almost dying of hunger while her brother, a short distance away, was entertaining all his courtiers at his board. Little Roland, touched by his mother's condition, walked fearlessly into the banquet hall, boldly advanced to the table, and carried away a dishful of meat. As the emperor seemed amused at the little lad's fearlessness, the servants did not dare to interfere, and Roland bore off the dish in triumph.

A few minutes later he reentered the hall, and with equal coolness laid hands upon the emperor's cup, full of rich wine. Challenged by Charlemagne, the child then boldly declared that he wanted the meat and wine for his mother, a lady of high degree. In answer to the emperor's bantering questions, he declared that he was his mother's cupbearer, her page, and her gallant knight, which answers so amused Charlemagne that he sent for her. He then remorsefully recognized her, treated her with kindness as long as she lived, and took her son into his own service.

Another legend relates that Charlemagne, hearing that the robber knight of the Ardennes had a priceless jewel set in his shield, called all his bravest noblemen together, and bade them sally forth separately, with only a page as escort, in quest of the knight. Once found, they were to challenge him in true knightly fashion, and at the point of the lance win the jewel he wore. A day was appointed when, successful or not, the courtiers were to return, and, beginning with the lowest in rank, were to give a truthful account of their adventures while on the quest.

All the knights departed and scoured the forest of the Ardennes, each hoping to meet the robber knight and win the jewel. Among them was Milon, accompanied by his son Roland, a lad of fifteen, whom he had taken as page and armor-bearer. Milon had spent many days in vain search for the knight, when, exhausted by his long ride, he dismounted, removed his heavy armor, and lay down under a tree to sleep, bidding Roland keep close watch during his slumbers.

Roland watched faithfully for a while; then, fired by a desire to distinguish himself, he donned his father's armor, sprang on his steed, and rode into the forest in search of adventures. He had not gone very far when he saw a gigantic horseman coming to meet him, and, by the dazzling glitter of a large stone set in his shield, he recognized in him the invincible knight of the Ardennes. Afraid of nothing, however, the lad laid his lance in rest when challenged to fight, and charged so bravely that he unhorsed the knight. A fearful battle on foot ensued, where many gallant blows were given and received; yet the victory finally remained with Roland. He slew his adversary, and wrenching the jewel from his shield, hid it in his breast. Then, riding rapidly back to his sleeping father, Roland laid aside the armor, and removed all traces of a bloody encounter. When Milon awoke he resumed the quest, and soon came upon the body of the dead knight. When he saw that another had won the jewel, he was disappointed indeed, and sadly rode back to court, to be present on the appointed day.

Charlemagne, seated on his throne, bade the knights appear before him, and relate their adventures. One after another strode up the hall, followed by an armor-bearer holding his shield, and all told of finding the knight slain and the jewel gone, and produced head, hands, feet, or some part of his armor, in token of the truth of their story. Last of all came Milon, with lowering brows, although Roland walked close behind him, proudly holding his shield, in the center of which the jewel shone radiant. Milon related his search, and reported that he too had found the giant knight slain and the jewel gone. A shout of incredulity made him turn his head. But when he saw the jewel blazing on his shield he appeared so amazed that Charlemagne questioned Roland, and soon learned how it had been obtained. In reward for his bravery in this encounter, Roland was knighted and allowed to take his place among his uncle's paladins, of which he soon became the most renowned.

Charlemagne, according to the old *chanson de geste* entitled "Ogier le Danois," made war against the King of Denmark, defeated him, and received his son Ogier (Olger or Holger Danske) as hostage. The young Danish prince was favored by the fairies from the time of his birth, six of them having appeared to bring him gifts while he was in his cradle. The first five promised him every earthly bliss; while the sixth, Morgana, foretold that he would never die, but would dwell with her in Avalon.

Ogier the Dane, owing to a violation of the treaty on his father's part, was soon confined in the prison of St. Omer. There he beguiled the weariness of captivity by falling in love with, and secretly marrying, the governor's daughter Bellissande. Charlemagne, being about to depart for war, and wishing for the hero's help, released him from captivity; and when Ogier returned again to France he heard that Bellissande had borne him a son, and that, his father having died, he was now the lawful king of Denmark.

Ogier the Dane then obtained permission to return to his native land, where he spent several years, reigning so wisely that he was adored by all his subjects. Such is the admiration of the Danes for this hero that the common people still declare that he is either in Avalon, or sleeping in the vaults of Elsinore, and that he will awaken, like Frederick Barbarossa, to save his country in the time of its direst need.

> "'Thou know'st it, peasant! I am not dead;
> I come back to thee in my glory.
> I am thy faithful helper in need,
> As in Denmark's ancient story.'"
> INGEMANN, *Holder Danske.*

After some years spent in Denmark, Ogier returned to France, where his son, now grown up, had a dispute with Prince Chariot [Ogier and Charlemagne.] over a game of chess. The dispute became so bitter that the prince used the chessboard as weapon, and killed his antagonist with it. Ogier, indignant at the murder, and unable to find redress at the hands of Charlemagne, insulted him grossly, and fled to Didier (Desiderius), King of Lombardy, with whom the Franks were then at feud.

Several ancient poems represent Didier on his tower, anxiously watching the approach of the enemy, and questioning his guest as to the personal appearance of Charlemagne. These poems have been imitated by Longfellow in one of his "Tales of a Wayside Inn."

> "Olger the Dane, and Desiderio,
> King of the Lombards, on a lofty tower
> Stood gazing northward o'er the rolling plains,
> League after league of harvests, to the foot
> Of the snow-crested Alps, and saw approach
> A mighty army, thronging all the roads
> That led into the city. And the King
> Said unto Olger, who had passed his youth
> As hostage at the court of France, and knew
> The Emperor's form and face, 'Is Charlemagne
> Among that host?' And Olger answered, 'No.'"
>
> LONGFELLOW, *Tales of a Wayside Inn.*

This poet, who has made this part of the legend familiar to all English readers, then describes the vanguard of the army, the paladins, the clergy, all in full panoply, and the gradually increasing terror of the Lombard king, who, long before the emperor's approach, would fain have hidden himself underground. Finally Charlemagne appears in iron mail, brandishing aloft his invincible sword "Joyeuse," and escorted by the main body of his army, grim fighting men, at the mere sight of whom even Ogier the Dane is struck with fear.

> "This at a single glance Olger the Dane
> Saw from the tower; and, turning to the King,
> Exclaimed in haste: 'Behold! this is the man
> You looked for with such eagerness!' and then
> Fell as one dead at Desiderio's feet."
>
> LONGFELLOW, *Tales of a Wayside Inn.*

Charlemagne soon overpowered the Lombard king, and assumed the iron crown, while Ogier escaped from the castle in which he was besieged. Shortly after, however, when asleep near a fountain, the

Danish hero was surprised by Turpin. When led before Charlemagne, he obstinately refused all proffers of reconciliation, and insisted upon Charlot's death, until an angel from heaven forbade his asking the life of Charlemagne's son. Then, foregoing his revenge and fully reinstated in the royal good graces, Ogier, according to a thirteenth-century epic by Adenet, successfully encountered a Saracenic giant, and in reward for his services received the hand of Clarice, Princess of England, and became king of that realm.

Weary of a peaceful existence, Ogier finally left England, and journeyed to the East, where he successfully besieged Acre, Babylon and Jerusalem. On his way back to France, the ship was attracted by the famous lodestone rock which appears in many mediaeval romances, and, all his companions having perished, Ogier wandered alone ashore. There he came to an adamantine castle, invisible by day, but radiant at night, where he was received by the famous horse Papillon, and sumptuously entertained. On the morrow, while wandering across a flowery meadow, Ogier encountered Morgana the fay, who gave him a magic ring. Although Ogier was then a hundred years old, he no sooner put it on than he became young once more. Then, having donned the golden crown of oblivion, he forgot his home, and joined Arthur, Oberon, Tristan, and Lancelot, with whom he spent two hundred years in unchanged youth, enjoying constant jousting and fighting.

At the end of that time, his crown having accidentally dropped off, Ogier remembered the past, and returned to France, riding on Papillon. He reached the court during the reign of one of the Capetian kings. He was, of course, greatly amazed at the changes which had taken place, but bravely helped to defend Paris against an invasion from the Normans.

Shortly after this, his magic ring was playfully drawn from his finger and put upon her own by the Countess of Senlis, who, seeing that it restored her vanished youth, would fain have kept it always. She therefore sent thirty champions to wrest it from Ogier, who, however, defeated them all, and triumphantly retained his ring. The king having died, Ogier next married the widowed queen, and would thus have become King of France had not Morgana the fay, jealous of his affections, spirited him away in the midst of the marriage ceremony and borne him off to the Isle of Avalon, whence he, like Arthur, will return only when his country needs him.

Another *chanson de geste*, a sort of continuation of "Ogier le Danois," is called "Meurvin," and purports to give a faithful account of the adventures of a son of Ogier and Morgana, an ancestor of Godfrey of Bouillon, King of Jerusalem. In "Guerin de Montglave," we find that Charlemagne, having quarreled with the Duke of Genoa, proposed that each should send a champion to fight in his name. Charlemagne selected Roland, while the Duke of Genoa chose Oliver as his defender. The battle, if we are to believe some versions of the legend, took place on an island in the Rhone, and Durandana, Roland's sword, struck many a spark from Altecler (Hautecler), the blade of Oliver. The two champions were so well matched, and the blows were dealt with such equal strength and courage, that "giving a Roland for an Oliver" has become a proverbial expression.

After fighting all day, with intermissions to interchange boasts and taunts, and to indulge in sundry discussions, neither had gained any advantage. They would probably have continued the struggle indefinitely, however, had not an angel of the Lord interfered, and bidden them embrace and become fast friends. It was on this occasion, we are told, that Charlemagne, fearing for Roland when he saw the strength of Oliver, vowed a pilgrimage to Jerusalem should his nephew escape alive.

The fulfillment of this vow is described in "Galyen Rhetoré." Charlemagne and his peers reached Jerusalem safely in disguise, but their anxiety to secure relics soon betrayed their identity. The King of Jerusalem, Hugues, entertained them sumptuously, and, hoping to hear many praises of his hospitality, concealed himself in their apartment at night. The eavesdropper, however, only heard the vain talk of Charlemagne's peers, who, unable to sleep, beguiled the hours in making extraordinary boasts. Roland declared that he could blow his horn Olivant loud enough to bring down the palace; Ogier, that he could crumble the principal pillar to dust in his grasp; and Oliver, that he could marry the princess in spite of her father.

The king, angry at hearing no praises of his wealth and hospitality, insisted upon his guests fulfilling their boasts on the morrow, under penalty of death. He was satisfied, however, by the success of Oliver's undertaking, and the peers returned to France. Galyen, Oliver's son by Hugues's daughter, followed them thither when he reached manhood, and joined his father in the valley of Roncesvalles, just in time to receive his blessing ere he died. Then, having helped Charlemagne to avenge his peers, Galyen returned to Jerusalem, where he found his grandfather dead and his mother a captive. His first act was, of course, to free his mother, after which he became king of Jerusalem, and his adventures came to an end.

The "Chronicle" of Turpin, whence the materials for many of the poems about Roland were taken, declares that Charlemagne, having conquered nearly the whole of Europe, retired to his palace to seek repose. But one evening, while gazing at the stars, he saw a bright cluster move from the "Friesian sea, by way of Germany and France, into Galicia." This prodigy, twice repeated, greatly excited Charlemagne's wonder, and was explained to him by St. James in a vision. The latter declared that the progress of the stars was emblematic of the advance of the Christian army towards Spain, and twice bade the emperor deliver his land from the hands of the Saracens.

Thus admonished, Charlemagne set out for Spain with a large army, and invested the city of Pamplona, which showed no signs of surrender at the end of a two months' siege. Recourse to prayer on the Christians' part, however, produced a great miracle, for the walls tottered and fell like those of Jericho. All the Saracens who embraced Christianity were spared, but the remainder were slain before the emperor journeyed to the shrine of St. James at Santiago de Compostela to pay his devotions.

A triumphant march through the country then ensued, and Charlemagne returned to France, thinking the Saracens subdued. He had scarcely crossed the border, however, when Aigolandus, one of the pagan monarchs, revolted, and soon recovered nearly all the territory his people had lost. When Charlemagne heard these tidings, he sent back an army, commanded by Milon, Roland's father, who perished gloriously in this campaign. The emperor speedily followed his brother-in-law with great forces, and again besieged Aigolandus in Pamplona. During the course of the siege the two rulers had an interview, which is described at length, and indulged in sundry religious discussions, which, however, culminated in a resumption of hostilities. Several combats now took place, in which the various heroes greatly distinguished themselves, the preference being generally given to Roland, who, if we are to believe the Italian poet, was as terrible in battle as he was gentle in time of peace.

> "On stubborn foes he vengeance wreak'd,
>   And laid about him like a Tartar;
> But if for mercy once they squeak'd,
>   He was the first to grant them quarter.
> The battle won, of Roland's soul
>   Each milder virtue took possession;
> To vanquished foes he o'er a bowl
>   His heart surrender'd at discretion."
>   ARIOSTO, *Orlando Furioso* (Dr. Burney's tr.).

Aigolandus being slain, and the feud against him thus successfully ended, Charlemagne carried the war into Navarre, where he was challenged by the giant Ferracute (Ferragus) to meet him in single combat. Although the metrical "Romances" describe Charlemagne as twenty feet in height, and declare that he slept in a hall, his bed surrounded by one hundred lighted tapers and one hundred knights with drawn swords, the emperor felt himself no match for the giant, whose personal appearance was as follows:—

> "So hard he was to-fond [proved],
> That no dint of brond
> No grieved him, I plight.
> He had twenty men's strength;
> And forty feet of length
> Thilke [each] paynim had;
> And four feet in the face
> Y-meten [measured] on the place;
> And fifteen in brede [breadth].
> His nose was a foot and more;
> His brow as bristles wore;
> (He that saw it said)
> He looked lothliche [loathly],
> And was swart [black] as pitch;
> Of him men might adrede!"
>   *Roland and Ferragus.*

After convincing himself of the danger of meeting this adversary, Charlemagne sent Ogier the Dane to fight him, and with dismay saw his champion not only unhorsed, but borne away like a parcel under the giant's arm, fuming and kicking with impotent rage. Renaud de Montauban met Ferracute on the next day, with the same fate, as did several other champions. Finally Roland took the field, and although the giant pulled him down from his horse, he continued the battle all day. Seeing that his sword Durandana had no effect upon Ferracute, Roland armed himself with a club on the morrow.

In the pauses of the battle the combatants talked together, and Ferracute, relying upon his adversary's keen sense of honor, even laid his head upon Roland's knee during their noonday rest. While resting thus, he revealed that he was vulnerable in only one point of his body. When called upon by Roland to believe in Christianity, he declared that the doctrine of the Trinity was more than he could accept. Roland, in answer, demonstrated that an almond is but one fruit, although composed of rind, shell, and kernel; that a harp is but one instrument, although it consists of wood, strings, and harmony. He also urged the threefold nature of the sun,—i.e., heat, light, and splendor; and these arguments having satisfied Ferracute concerning the Trinity, he removed his doubts concerning the incarnation by equally forcible reasoning. The giant, however, utterly refused to believe in the resurrection, although Roland, in support of his creed, quoted the mediaeval belief that a lion's cubs are born into the world dead, but come to life on the third day at the sound of their father's roar, or under the warm breath of their mother. As Ferracute would not accept this doctrine, but sprang to his feet proposing a continuation of the fight, the struggle was renewed.

> "Quath Ferragus: 'Now ich wot
> Your Christian law every grot;
> Now we will fight;
> Whether law better be,
> Soon we shall y-see,
> Long ere it be night.'"
>
> *Roland and Ferragus.*

THE DEATH OF ROLAND.—Keller.

Roland, weary with his previous efforts, almost succumbed beneath the giant's blows, and in his distress had recourse to prayer. He was immediately strengthened and comforted by an angelic vision and a promise of victory. Thus encouraged, he dealt Ferracute a deadly blow in the vulnerable spot. The giant fell, calling upon Mohammed, while Roland laughed and the Christians triumphed.

The poem of Sir Otuel, in the Auchinleck manuscript, describes how Otuel, a nephew of Ferracute, his equal in size and strength, came to avenge his death, and, after a long battle with Roland, yielded to his theological arguments, and was converted at the sight of a snowy dove alighting on Charlemagne's helmet in answer to prayer. He then became a devoted adherent of Charlemagne, and served him much in war.

Charlemagne, having won Navarre, carried the war to the south of Spain, where the Saracens frightened the horses of his host by beating drums and waving banners. Having suffered a partial defeat on account of this device, Charlemagne had the horses' ears stopped with wax, and their eyes blindfolded, before he resumed the battle. Thanks to this precaution, he succeeded in conquering the Saracen army. The whole country had now been again subdued, and Charlemagne was preparing to return to France, when he remembered that Marsiglio (Marsilius), a Saracen king, was still intrenched at Saragossa.

> "Carle, our most noble Emperor and King,
> Hath tarried now full seven years in Spain,
> Conqu'ring the highland regions to the sea;
> No fortress stands before him unsubdued,
> Nor wall, nor city left, to be destroyed,
> Save Sarraguce, high on a mountain set.
> There rules the King Marsile, who loves not God,
> Apollo worships, and Mohammed serves;
> Nor can he from his evil doom escape."
> *Chanson de Roland* (Rabillon's tr.).

The emperor wished to send an embassy to him to arrange the terms of peace, but discarded Roland's offer of service because of his impetuosity. Then, following the advice of Naismes de Bavière, "the Nestor of the Carolingian legends," he selected Ganelon, Roland's stepfather, as ambassador. This man was a traitor, and accepted a bribe from the Saracen king to betray Roland and the rear guard of the French army into his power. Advised by Ganelon, Charlemagne departed from Spain at the head of his army, leaving Roland to bring up the rear. The main part of the army passed through the Pyrenees unmolested, but the rear guard of twenty thousand men, under Roland, was attacked by a superior force of Saracens in ambush, as it was passing through the denies of Roncesvalles. A terrible encounter took place here.

> "The Count Rollànd rides through the battlefield
> And makes, with Durendal's keen blade in hand,
> A mighty carnage of the Saracens.
> Ah! had you then beheld the valiant Knight
> Heap corse on corse; blood drenching all the ground;
> His own arms, hauberk, all besmeared with gore,
> And his good steed from neck to shoulder bleed!"
> *Chanson de Roland* (Rabillon's tr.).

All the Christians were slain except Roland and a few knights, who succeeded in repulsing the first onslaught of the painims. Roland then bound a Saracen captive to a tree, wrung from him a confession of the dastardly plot, and, discovering where Marsiglio was to be found, rushed into the very midst of the Saracen army and slew him. The Saracens, terrified at the apparition of the hero, beat a hasty retreat, little suspecting that their foe had received a mortal wound, and would shortly breathe his last.

During the first part of the battle, Roland, yielding to Oliver's entreaty, sounded a blast on his horn Olivant, which came even to Charlemagne's ear. Fearing lest his nephew was calling for aid, Charlemagne would fain have gone back had he not been deterred by Ganelon, who assured him that Roland was merely pursuing a stag.

> "Rolland raised to his lips the olifant,
> Drew a deep breath, and blew with all his force.
> High are the mountains, and from peak to peak
> The sound reëchoes; thirty leagues away
> 'Twas heard by Carle and all his brave compeers.
> Cried the king: 'Our men make battle!' Ganelon

Retorts in haste: 'If thus another dared
To speak, we should denounce it as a lie.'
Aoi"

Chanson de Roland (Rabillon's tr.).

Wounded and faint, Roland now slowly dragged himself to the entrance of the pass of Cisaire,—where the Basque peasants aver they have often seen his ghost, and heard the sound of his horn,—and took leave of his faithful steed Veillantif, which he slew with his own hand, to prevent its falling into the hands of the enemy.

"'Ah, nevermore, and nevermore, shall we to battle ride!
Ah, nevermore, and nevermore, shall we sweet comrades be!
And Veillintif, had I the heart to die forgetting thee?
To leave thy mighty heart to break, in slavery to the foe?
I had not rested in the grave, if it had ended so.
Ah, never shall we conquering ride, with banners bright unfurl'd,
A shining light 'mong lesser lights, a wonder to the world.'"
BUCHANAN, *Death of Roland*.

Then the hero gazed upon his sword Durandana, which had served him faithfully for so many years, and to prevent its falling into the hands of the pagans, he tried to dispose of it also. According to varying accounts, he either sank it deep into a poisoned stream, where it is still supposed to lie, or, striking it against the mighty rocks, cleft them in two, without even dinting its bright blade.

"And Roland thought: 'I surely die; but, ere I end,
Let me be sure that thou art ended too, my friend!
For should a heathen hand grasp thee when I am clay,
My ghost would grieve full sore until the judgment day!'
Then to the marble steps, under the tall, bare trees,
Trailing the mighty sword, he crawl'd on hands and knees,
And on the slimy stone he struck the blade with might—
The bright hilt, sounding, shook, the blade flash'd sparks of light;
Wildly again he struck, and his sick head went round,
Again there sparkled fire, again rang hollow sound;
Ten times he struck, and threw strange echoes down the glade,
Yet still unbroken, sparkling fire, glitter'd the peerless blade."
BUCHANAN, *Death of Roland*.

Finally, despairing of disposing of it in any other way, the hero, strong in death, broke Durandana in his powerful hands and threw the shards away.

Horse and sword were now disposed of, and the dying hero, summoning his last strength, again put his marvelous horn Olivant to his lips, and blew such a resounding blast that the sound was heard far and near. The effort, however, was such that his temples burst, as he again sank fainting to the ground.

One version of the story (Turpin's) relates that the blast brought, not Charlemagne, but the sole surviving knight, Theodoricus, who, as Roland had been shriven before the battle, merely heard his last prayer and reverently closed his eyes. Then Turpin, while celebrating mass before Charlemagne, was suddenly favored by a vision, in which he beheld a shrieking crew of demons bearing Marsiglio's soul to hell, while an angelic host conveyed Roland's to heaven.

Turpin immediately imparted these revelations to Charlemagne, who, knowing now that his fears were not without foundation, hastened back to Roncesvalles. Here the scriptural miracle was repeated, for the sun stayed its course until the emperor had routed the Saracens and found the body of his nephew. He pronounced a learned funeral discourse or lament over the hero's remains, which were then embalmed and conveyed to Blaive for interment.

Another version relates that Bishop Turpin himself remained with Roland in the rear, and, after hearing a general confession and granting full absolution to all the heroes, fought beside them to the end. It was he who heard the last blast of Roland's horn instead of Theodoricus, and came to close his eyes before he too expired.

The most celebrated of all the poems, however, the French epic "Chanson de Roland," gives a different version and relates that, in stumbling over the battlefield, Roland came across the body of his friend Oliver, over which he uttered a touching lament.

> "'Alas for all thy valor, comrade dear!
> Year after year, day after day, a life
> Of love we led; ne'er didst thou wrong to me,
> Nor I to thee. If death takes thee away,
> My life is but a pain.'"
>
> *Chanson de Roland* (Rabillon's tr.).

Slowly and painfully now—for his death was near—Roland climbed up a slope, laid himself down under a pine tree, and placed his sword and horn beneath him. Then, when he had breathed a last prayer, to commit his soul to God, he held up his glove in token of his surrender.

> "His right hand glove he offered up to God;
> Saint Gabriel took the glove.—With head reclined
> Upon his arm, with hands devoutly joined,
> He breathed his last. God sent his Cherubim,
> Saint Raphael, *Saint Michiel del Peril.*
> The soul of Count Rolland to Paradise.
> Aoi."
> *Chanson de Roland* (Rabillon's tr.).

It was here, under the pine, that Charlemagne found his nephew ere he started out to punish the Saracens, as already related. Not far off lay the bodies of Ogier, Oliver, and Renaud, who, according to this version, were all among the slain.

> "Here endeth Otuel, Roland, and Olyvere,
> And of the twelve dussypere,
> That dieden in the batayle of Runcyvale:
> Jesu lord, heaven king,
> To his bliss hem and us both bring,
> To liven withouten bale!"
> *Sir Otuel.*

On his return to France Charlemagne suspected Ganelon of treachery, and had him tried by twelve peers, who, unable to decide the question, bade him prove his innocence in single combat with Roland's squire, Thiedric. Ganelon, taking advantage of the usual privilege to have his cause defended by a champion, selected Pinabel, the most famous swordsman of the time. In spite of all his valor, however, this champion was defeated, and the "judgment of God"—the term generally applied to those judicial combats—was in favor of Thiedric. Ganelon, thus convicted of treason, was sentenced to be drawn and quartered, and was executed at Aix-la-Chapelle, in punishment for his sins.

"Ere long for this he lost
Both limb and life, judged and condemned at Aix,
There to be hanged with thirty of his race
Who were not spared the punishment of death.
Aoi."
Chanson de Roland (Rabillon's tr.).

Roland, having seen Aude, Oliver's sister, at the siege of Viane, where she even fought against him, if the old epics are to be believed, had been so smitten with her charms that he declared that he would marry none but her. When the siege was over, and lifelong friendship had been sworn between Roland and Oliver after their memorable duel on an island in the Rhone, Roland was publicly betrothed to the charming Aude. Before their nuptials could take place, however, he was forced to leave for Spain, where, as we have seen, he died an heroic death. The sad news of his demise was brought to Paris, where the Lady Aude was awaiting him. When she heard that he would never return, she died of grief, and was buried at his side in the chapel of Blaive.

"In Paris Lady Alda sits, Sir Roland's destined bride.
With her three hundred maidens, to tend her, at her side;
Alike their robes and sandals all, and the braid that binds their hair,
And alike the meal, in their Lady's hall, the whole three hundred share.
Around her, in her chair of state, they all their places hold;
A hundred weave the web of silk, and a hundred spin the gold,
And a hundred touch their gentle lutes to sooth that Lady's pain,
As she thinks on him that's far away with the host of Charlemagne.
Lulled by the sound, she sleeps, but soon she wakens with a scream;
And, as her maidens gather round, she thus recounts her dream:
'I sat upon a desert shore, and from the mountain nigh,
Right toward me, I seemed to see a gentle falcon fly;
But close behind an eagle swooped, and struck that falcon down,
And with talons and beak he rent the bird, as he cowered beneath my gown.'
The chief of her maidens smiled, and said; 'To me it doth not seem
That the Lady Alda reads aright the boding of her dream.
Thou art the falcon, and thy knight is the eagle in his pride,
As he comes in triumph from the war, and pounces on his bride.'
The maiden laughed, but Alda sighed, and gravely shook her head.
'Full rich,' quoth she, 'shall thy guerdon be, if thou the truth hast said.'

'Tis morn; her letters, stained with blood, the truth too plainly tell,
How, in the chase of Ronceval, Sir Roland fought and fell."
Lady Alda's Dreams (Sir Edmund Head's tr.).

A later legend, which has given rise to sundry poems, connects the name of Roland with one of the most beautiful places on the Rhine. Popular tradition avers that he sought shelter one evening in the castle of Drachenfels, where he fell in love with Hildegarde, the beautiful daughter of the Lord of Drachenfels. The sudden outbreak of the war in Spain forced him to bid farewell to his betrothed, but he promised to return as soon as possible to celebrate their wedding. During the campaign, many stories of his courage came to Hildegarde's ears, and finally, after a long silence, she heard that Roland had perished at Roncesvalles.

Broken-hearted, the fair young mourner spent her days in tears, and at last prevailed upon her father to allow her to enter the convent on the island of Nonnenworth, in the middle of the river, and within view of the gigantic crag where the castle ruins can still be seen.

"The castled crag of Drachenfels
Frowns o'er the wide and winding Rhine,
Whose breast of water broadly swells
Between the banks which bear the vine,
And hills all rich with blossomed trees,
And fields which promise corn and wine,
And scattered cities crowning these,
Whose fair white walls along them shine."
BYRON, *Childe Harold.*

With pallid cheeks and tear-dimmed eyes, Hildegarde now spent her life either in her tiny cell or in the convent chapel, praying for the soul of her beloved, and longing that death might soon come to set her free to join him. The legend relates, however, that Roland was not dead, as she supposed, but had merely been sorely wounded at Roncesvalles.

When sufficiently recovered to travel, Roland painfully made his way back to Drachenfels, where he presented himself late one evening, eagerly calling for Hildegarde. A few moments later the joyful light left his eyes forever, for he learned that his beloved had taken irrevocable vows, and was now the bride of Heaven.

That selfsame day Roland left the castle of Drachenfels, and riding to an eminence overlooking the island of Nonnenwörth, he gazed long and tearfully at a little light twinkling in one of the convent windows. As he could not but suppose that it illumined Hildegarde's cell and lonely vigils, he watched it all night, and when morning came he recognized his beloved's form in the long procession of nuns on their way to the chapel.

This view of the lady he loved seemed a slight consolation to the hero, who built a retreat on this rock, which is known as Rolandseck. Here he spent his days in penance and prayer, gazing constantly at the island at his feet, and the swift stream which parted him from Hildegarde.

One wintry day, many years after he had taken up his abode on the rocky height, Roland missed the graceful form he loved, and heard, instead of the usual psalm, a dirge for the dead. Then he noticed that six of the nuns were carrying a coffin, which they lowered into an open tomb.

Roland's nameless fears were confirmed in the evening, when the convent priest visited him, and gently announced that Hildegarde was at rest. Calmly Roland listened to these tidings, begged the priest to hear his confession as usual, and, when he had received absolution, expressed a desire to be buried with his face turned toward the convent where Hildegarde had lived and died.

The priest readily promised to observe this request, and departed. When he came on the morrow, he found Roland dead. They buried him reverently on the very spot which bears his name, with his face turned toward Nonnenwörth, where Hildegarde lay at rest.

CHAPTER IX.

THE SONS OF AYMON.

The different *chansons de gestes* relating to Aymon and the necromancer Malagigi (Malagis), probably arose from popular ballads commemorating the struggles of Charles the Bald and his feudatories. These ballads are of course as old as the events which they were intended to record, but the *chansons de gestes* based upon them, and entitled "Duolin de Mayence," "Aymon, Son of Duolin de Mayence," "Maugis," "Rinaldo de Trebizonde," "The Four Sons of Aymon," and "Mabrian," are of much later date, and were particularly admired during the fourteenth and fifteenth centuries.

One of the most famous of Charlemagne's peers was doubtless the noble Aymon of Dordogne; and when the war against the Avars in Hungary had been successfully closed, owing to his bravery, his adherents besought the king to bestow upon this knight some reward. Charlemagne, whom many of these later *chansons de gestes* describe as mean and avaricious, refused to grant any reward, declaring that were he to add still further to his vassal's already extensive territories, Aymon would soon be come more powerful than his sovereign.

This unjust refusal displeased Lord Hug of Dordogne, who had pleaded for his kinsman, so that he ventured a retort, which so incensed the king that he slew him then and there. Aymon, learning of the death of Lord Hug, and aware of the failure of his last embassy, haughtily withdrew to his own estates, whence he now began to wage war against Charlemagne.

Instead of open battle, however, a sort of guerrilla warfare was carried on, in which, thanks to his marvelous steed Bayard, which his cousin Malagigi, the necromancer, had brought him from hell, Aymon always won the advantage. At the end of several years, however, Charlemagne collected a large host, and came to lay siege to the castle where Aymon had intrenched himself with all his adherents.

During that siege, Aymon awoke one morning to find that his beloved steed had vanished. Malagigi, hearing him bewail his loss, bade him be of good cheer, promising to restore Bayard ere long, although he would be obliged to go to Mount Vulcanus, the mouth of hell, to get him. Thus comforted, Aymon ceased to mourn, while Malagigi set to work to fulfill his promise. As a brisk wind was blowing from the castle towards the camp, he flung upon the breeze some powdered hellebore, which caused a violent sneezing throughout the army. Then, while his foes were wiping their streaming eyes, the necromancer, who had learned his black art in the famous school of Toledo, slipped through their ranks unseen, and journeyed on to Mount Vulcanus, where he encountered his Satanic Majesty.

His first act was to offer his services to Satan, who accepted them gladly, bidding him watch the steed Bayard, which he had stolen because he preferred riding a horse to sitting astride a storm cloud as usual. The necromancer artfully pretended great anxiety to serve his new master, but having discovered just where Bayard was to be found, he made use of a sedative powder to lull Satan to sleep. Then, hastening to the angry steed, Malagigi made him tractable by whispering his master's name in his ear; and, springing on his back, rode swiftly away.

Satan was awakened by the joyful whinny of the flying steed, and immediately mounted upon a storm cloud and started in pursuit, hurling a red-hot thunderbolt at Malagigi to check his advance. But the necromancer muttered a magic spell and held up his crucifix, and the bolt fell short; while the devil, losing his balance, fell to the earth, and thus lamed himself permanently.

Count Aymon, in the mean while, had been obliged to flee from his besieged castle, mounted upon a sorry steed instead of his fleet-footed horse. When the enemy detected his flight, they set out in pursuit, tracking him by means of bloodhounds, and were about to overtake and slay him when Malagigi suddenly appeared with Bayard. To bound on the horse's back, draw his famous sword Flamberge, which had been made by the smith Wieland, and charge into the midst of his foes, was the work of a few seconds. The result was that most of Aymon's foes bit the dust, while he rode away unharmed, and gathering many followers, he proceeded to win back all the castles and fortresses he had lost.

Frightened by Aymon's successes, Charlemagne finally sent Roland, his nephew and favorite, bidding him offer a rich ransom to atone for the murder of Lord Hug, and instructing him to secure peace at any price. Aymon at first refused these overtures, but consented at last to cease the feud upon receipt of six times Lord Hug's weight in gold, and the hand of the king's sister, Aya, whom he had long loved.

These demands were granted, peace was concluded, and Aymon, having married Aya, led her to the castle of Pierlepont, where they dwelt most happily together, and became the parents of four brave sons, Renaud, Alard, Guiscard, and Richard. Inactivity, however, was not enjoyable to an inveterate fighter like Aymon, so he soon left home to journey into Spain, where the bitter enmity between the Christians and the Moors would afford him opportunity to fight to his heart's content.

Years now passed by, during which Aymon covered himself with glory; for, mounted on Bayard, he was the foremost in every battle, and always struck terror into the hearts of his foes by the mere flash of his blade Flamberge. Thus he fought until his sons attained manhood, and Aya had long thought him dead, when a messenger came to Pierlepont, telling them that Aymon lay ill in the Pyrenees, and wished to see his wife and his children once more.

In answer to these summons Aya hastened southward, and found her husband old and worn, yet not so changed that she could not recognize him. Aymon, sick as he was, rejoiced at the sight of his manly sons. He gave the three eldest the spoil he had won during those many years' warfare, and promised Renaud (Reinold) his horse and sword, if he could successfully mount and ride the former.

Renaud, who was a skillful horseman, fancied the task very easy, and was somewhat surprised when his father's steed caught him by the garments with his teeth, and tumbled him into the manger. Undismayed by one failure, however, Renaud sprang boldly upon Bayard; and, in spite of all the horse's efforts, kept his seat so well that his father formally gave him the promised mount and sword.

When restored to health by the tender nursing of his loving wife, Aymon returned home with his family. Then, hearing that Charlemagne had returned from his coronation journey to Rome, and was about to celebrate the majority of his heir, Aymon went to court with his four sons.

During the tournament, held as usual on such festive occasions, Renaud unhorsed every opponent, and even defeated the prince. This roused the anger of Charlot, or Berthelot as he is called by some authorities, and made him vow revenge. He soon discovered that Renaud was particularly attached to his brother Alard, so he resolved first to harm the latter. Advised by the traitor Ganelon, Chariot challenged Alard to a game of chess, and insisted that the stakes should be the players' heads.

This proposal was very distasteful to Alard, for he knew that he would never dare lay any claim to the prince's head even if he won the game, and feared to lose his own if he failed to win. Compelled to accept the challenge, however, Alard began the game, and played so well that he won five times in succession. Then Charlot, angry at being so completely checkmated, suddenly seized the board and struck his antagonist such a cruel blow that the blood began to flow. Alard, curbing his wrath, simply withdrew; and it was only when Renaud questioned him very closely that he told how the quarrel had occurred.

Renaud was indignant at the insult offered his brother, and went to the emperor with his complaint. The umpires reluctantly testified that the prince had forfeited his head, so Renaud cut it off in the emperor's presence, and effected his escape with his father and brothers before any one could lay hands upon them. Closely pursued by the imperial troops, Aymon and his sons were soon brought to bay, and fought so bravely that they slew many of their assailants. At last, seeing that all their horses except the incomparable Bayard had been slain, Renaud bade his brothers mount behind him, and they dashed away. The aged Aymon had already fallen into the hands of the emperor's adviser, Turpin, who solemnly promised that no harm should befall him. But in spite of this oath, and of the remonstrances of all his peers, Charlemagne prepared to have Aymon publicly hanged, and consented to release him only upon condition that Aymon would promise to deliver his sons into the emperor's hands, were it ever in his power to do so.

The four young men, knowing their father safe, and unwilling to expose their mother to the unpleasant experiences of the siege which would have followed had they remained at Pierlepont, now journeyed southward, and entered the service of Saforet, King of the Moors. With him they won many victories; but, seeing at the end of three years that this monarch had no intention of giving them the promised reward, they slew him, and offered their swords to Iwo, Prince of Tarasconia.

Afraid of these warriors, yet wishing to bind them to him by indissoluble ties, Iwo gave Renaud his daughter Clarissa in marriage, and helped him build an impregnable fortress at Montauban. This stronghold was scarcely finished when Charlemagne came up with a great army to besiege it; but at the end of a year of fruitless attempts, the emperor reluctantly withdrew, leaving Montauban still in the hands of his enemies.

Seven years had now elapsed since the four young men had seen their mother; and, anxious to embrace her once more, they went in pilgrims' robes to the castle of Pierlepont. Here the chamberlain recognized them and betrayed their presence to Aymon, who, compelled by his oath, prepared to bind his four sons fast and take them captive to his sovereign. The young men, however, defended themselves bravely, secured their father instead, and sent him in chains to Charlemagne. Unfortunately the monarch was much nearer Pierlepont at the time than the young men supposed. Hastening onward, he entered the castle before they had even become aware of his approach, and secured three of them. The fourth, Renaud, aided by his mother, escaped in pilgrim's garb, and returned to Montauban. Here he found Bayard, and without pausing to rest, he rode straight to Paris to deliver his brothers from the emperor's hands.

Overcome by fatigue after this hasty journey, Renaud dismounted shortly before reaching Paris, and fell asleep. When he awoke he found that his steed had vanished, and he reluctantly continued his journey on foot, begging his way. He was joined on the way by his cousin Malagigi, who also wore a pilgrim's garb, and who promised to aid Renaud, not only in freeing his brothers, but also in recovering Bayard.

Unnoticed, the beggars threaded their way through the city of Paris and came to the palace. There a great tournament was to be held, and the emperor had promised to the victor of the day the famous steed Bayard. To stimulate the knights to greater efforts by a view of the promised prize, the emperor bade a groom lead forth the renowned steed. The horse seemed restive, but suddenly paused beside two beggars, with a whinny of joy. The groom, little suspecting that the horse's real master was hidden under the travel-stained pilgrim's robe, laughingly commented upon Bayard's bad taste. Then Malagigi, the second beggar, suddenly cried aloud that his poor companion had been told that he would recover from his lameness were he only once allowed to bestride the famous steed. Anxious to witness a miracle, the emperor gave orders that the beggar should be placed upon Bayard; and Renaud, after feigning to fall off through awkwardness, suddenly sat firmly upon his saddle, and dashed away before any one could stop him.

As for Malagigi, having wandered among the throng unheeded, he remained in Paris until evening. Then, making his way into the prison by means of the necromantic charm "Abracadabra," which he continually repeated, he delivered the other sons of Aymon from their chains. He next entered the palace of the sleeping emperor, spoke to him in his sleep, and forced him, under hypnotic influence, to give up the scepter and crown, which he triumphantly bore away.

[Treachery of Iwo.] When Charlemagne awoke on the morrow, found his prisoners gone, and realized that what had seemed a dream was only too true, and that the insignia of royalty were gone, he was very angry indeed. More than ever before he now longed to secure the sons of Aymon; so he bribed Iwo, with whom the brothers had taken refuge, to send them to him. Clarissa suspected her father's treachery, and implored Renaud not to believe him; but the brave young hero, relying upon Iwo's promise, set out without arms to seek the emperor's pardon. On the way, however, the four sons of Aymon fell into an ambuscade, whence they would scarcely have escaped alive had not one of the brothers drawn from under his robe the weapons Clarissa had given him.

The emperor's warriors, afraid of the valor of these doughty brethren now that they were armed, soon withdrew to a safe distance, whence they could watch the young men and prevent their escape. Suddenly, however, Malagigi came dashing up on Bayard, for Clarissa had warned him of his kinsmen's danger, and implored him to go to their rescue. Renaud immediately mounted his favorite steed, and brandishing Flamberge, which his uncle had brought him, he charged so gallantly into the very midst of the imperial troops that he soon put them to flight.

The emperor, baffled and angry, suspected that Iwo had warned his son-in-law of the danger and provided him with weapons. In his wrath he had Iwo seized, and sentenced him to be hanged. But Renaud, seeing Clarissa's tears, vowed that he would save his father-in-law from such an ignominious death. With his usual bravery he charged into the very midst of the executioners, and unhorsed the valiant champion, Roland. During this encounter, Iwo effected his escape, and Renaud followed him, while Roland slowly picked himself up and prepared to follow his antagonist and once more try his strength against him.

On the way to Montauban, Roland met Richard, one of the four brothers, whom he carried captive to Charlemagne. The emperor immediately ordered the young knight to be hanged, and bade some of his most noble followers to see the sentence executed. They one and all refused, however, declaring death on the gallows too ignominious a punishment for a knight.

The discussions which ensued delayed the execution and enabled Malagigi to warn Renaud of his brother's imminent peril. Mounted upon Bayard, Renaud rode straight to Montfaucon, accompanied by his two other brothers and a few faithful men. There they camped under the gallows, to be at hand when the guard came to hang the prisoner on the morrow. But Renaud and his companions slept so soundly that they would have been surprised had not the intelligent Bayard awakened his master by a very opportune kick. Springing to his feet, Renaud roused his companions, vaulted upon his steed, and charged the guard. He soon delivered his captive brother and carried him off in triumph, after hanging the knight who had volunteered to act as executioner.

Charlemagne, still anxious to seize and punish these refractory subjects, now collected an army and began again to besiege the stronghold of Montauban. Occasional sallies and a few bloody encounters were the only variations in the monotony of a several-years' siege. But finally the provisions of the besieged became very scanty. Malagigi, who knew that a number of provision wagons were expected, advised Renaud to make a bold sally and carry them off, while he, the necromancer, dulled the senses of the imperial army by scattering one of his magic sleeping powders in the air. He had just begun his spell when Oliver perceived him and, pouncing upon him, carried him off to the emperor's tent. Oliver, on the way thither, never once relinquished his grasp, although the magician tried to make him do so by throwing a pinch of hellebore in his face.

While sneezing loudly the paladin told how he had caught the magician, and the emperor vowed that the rascal should be hanged on the very next day. When he heard this decree, Malagigi implored the emperor to give him a good meal, since this was to be his last night on earth, pledging his word not to leave the camp without the emperor. This promise so reassured Charlemagne that he ordered a sumptuous repast, charging a few knights to watch Malagigi, lest, after all, he should effect his escape. The meal over, the necromancer again had recourse to his magic art to plunge the whole camp into a deep sleep. Then, proceeding unmolested to the imperial tent, he bore off the sleeping emperor to the gates of Montauban, which flew open at his well-known voice.

Charlemagne, on awaking, was as surprised as dismayed to find himself in the hands of his foes, who, however, when they saw his uneasiness, gallantly gave him his freedom without exacting any pledge or ransom in return. But when Malagigi heard of this foolhardy act of generosity, he burned up his papers, boxes, and bags, and, when asked why he acted thus, replied that he was about to leave his mad young kinsmen to their own devices, and take refuge in a hermitage, where he intended to spend the remainder of his life in repenting of his sins. Soon after this he disappeared, and Aymon's sons, escaping secretly from Montauban just before it was forced to surrender, took refuge in a castle they owned in the Ardennes.

Here the emperor pursued them, and kept up the siege until Aya sought him, imploring him to forgive her sons and to cease persecuting them. Charlemagne yielded at last to her entreaties, and promised to grant the sons of Aymon full forgiveness provided the demoniacal steed Bayard were given over to him to be put to death. Aya hastened to Renaud to tell him this joyful news, but when he declared that nothing would ever induce him to give up his faithful steed, she besought him not to sacrifice his brothers, wife, and sons, out of love for his horse.

Thus adjured, Renaud, with breaking heart, finally consented. The treaty was signed, and Bayard, with feet heavily weighted, was led to the middle of a bridge over the Seine, where the emperor had decreed that he should be drowned. At a given signal from Charlemagne the noble horse was pushed into the water; but, in spite of the weights on his feet, he rose to the surface twice, casting an agonized glance upon his master, who had been forced to come and witness his death. Aya, seeing her son's grief, drew his head down upon her motherly bosom, and when Bayard rose once more and missed his beloved master's face among the crowd, he sank beneath the waves with a groan of despair, and never rose again.

Renaud, maddened by the needless cruelty of this act, now tore up the treaty and flung it at the emperor's feet. He then broke his sword Flamberge and cast it into the Seine, declaring that he would never wield such a weapon again, and returned to Montauban alone and on foot. There he bade his wife and children farewell, after committing them to the loyal protection of Roland. He then set out for the Holy Land, where he fought against the infidels, using a club as weapon, so as not to break his vow. This evidently proved no less effective in his hands than the noted Flamberge, for he was offered the crown of Jerusalem in reward for his services. As he had vowed to renounce all the pomps and vanities of the world, Renaud passed the crown on to Godfrey of Bouillon. Then, returning home, he found that Clarissa had died, after having been persecuted for years by the unwelcome attentions of many suitors, who would fain have persuaded her that her husband was dead.

According to one version of the story, Renaud died in a hermitage, in the odor of sanctity; but if we are to believe another, he journeyed on to Cologne, where the cathedral was being built, and labored at it night and day. Exasperated by his constant activity, which put them all to shame, his fellow-laborers slew him and flung his body into the Rhine. Strange to relate, however, his body was not carried away by the strong current, but lingered near the city, until it was brought to land and interred by some pious people.

Many miracles having taken place near the spot where he was buried, the emperor gave orders that his remains should be conveyed either to Aix-la-Chapelle or to Paris. The body was therefore laid upon a cart, which moved of its own accord to Dortmund, in Westphalia, where it stopped, and where a church was erected in honor of Renaud in 811. Here the saintly warrior's remains were duly laid to rest, and the church in Dortmund still bears his name. A chapel in Cologne is also dedicated to him, and is supposed to stand on the very spot where he was so treacherously slain after his long and brilliant career.

CHAPTER X.

HUON OF BORDEAUX.

It is supposed that this *chanson de geste* was first composed in the thirteenth century; but the version which has come down to us must have been written shortly before the discovery of printing. Although this poem was deservedly a favorite composition during the middle ages, no manuscript copy of it now exists. Such was the admiration that it excited that Lord Berners translated it into English under Henry VIII. In modern times it has been the theme of Wieland's finest poem, and of one of Weber's operas, both of which works are known by the title of "Oberon." It is from this work that Shakespeare undoubtedly drew some of the principal characters for his "Midsummer-Night's Dream," where Oberon, king of the fairies, plays no unimportant part.

The hero of this poem, Huon of Bordeaux, and his brother Girard, were on their way from Guienne to Paris to do homage to Charlemagne for their estates. Charlot, the monarch's eldest son, who bears a very unenviable reputation in all the mediaeval poems, treacherously waylaid the brothers, intending to put them both to death. He attacked them separately; but, after slaying Girard, was himself slain by Huon, who, quite unconscious of the illustrious birth of his assailant, calmly proceeded on his way.

The rumor of the prince's death soon followed Huon to court, and Charlemagne, incensed, vowed that he would never pardon him until he had proved his loyalty and repentance by journeying to Bagdad, where he was to cut off the head of the great bashaw, to kiss the Sultan's daughter, and whence he was to bring back a lock of that mighty potentate's gray beard and four of his best teeth.

HUON BEFORE THE POPE—Gabriel Max.

"'Yet hear the terms; hear what no earthly power
Shall ever change!' He spoke, and wav'd below
His scepter, bent in anger o'er my brow.—
'Yes, thou may'st live;—but, instant, from this hour,
Away! in exile rove far nations o'er;
Thy foot accurs'd shall tread this soil no more,
Till thou, in due obedience to my will
Shalt, point by point, the word I speak fulfill;
Thou diest, if this unwrought thou touch thy native shore.

"'Go hence to Bagdad; in high festal day
At his round table, when the caliph, plac'd
In stately pomp, with splendid emirs grac'd,
Enjoys the banquet rang'd in proud array,
Slay him who lies the monarch's left beside,
Dash from his headless trunk the purple tide.
Then to the right draw near; with courtly grace
The beauteous heiress of his throne embrace;
And thrice with public kiss salute her as thy bride.

"'And while the caliph, at the monstrous scene,
Such as before ne'er shock'd a caliph's eyes,
Stares at thy confidence in mute surprise,
Then, as the Easterns wont, with lowly mien
Fall on the earth before his golden throne,
And gain (a trifle, proof of love alone)
That it may please him, gift of friend to friend,
Four of his grinders at my bidding send,
And of his beard a lock with silver hair o'ergrown."
WIELAND. *Oberon* (Sotheby's tr.).

Huon regretfully, left his native land to begin this apparently
hopeless quest; and, after visiting his uncle, the Pope, in Rome,
he tried to secure heavenly assistance by a pilgrimage to the holy
sepulcher. Then he set out for Babylon, or Bagdad, for, with the
visual mediaeval scorn for geography, evinced in all the *chansons
de gestes*, these are considered interchangeable names for the same
town. As the hero was journeying towards his goal by way of the
Red Sea, it will not greatly surprise the modern reader to hear
that he lost his way and came to a pathless forest. Darkness soon
overtook him, and Huon was blindly stumbling forward, leading

his weary steed by the bridle, when he perceived a light, toward
which he directed his way.

> "Not long his step the winding way pursued,
> When on his wistful gaze, to him beseems,
> The light of distant fire delightful gleams.
> His cheek flash'd crimson as the flame he view'd.
> Half wild with hope and fear, he rushed to find
> In these lone woods some glimpse of human kind,
> And, ever and anon, at once the ray
> Flash'd on his sight, then sunk at once away,
> While rose and fell the path as hill and valley wind."
> WIELAND, *Oberon* (Sotheby's tr.).

Huon at last reached a cave, and found a gigantic old man all
covered with hair, which was his sole garment. After a few moments'
fruitless attempt at conversation in the language of the country, Huon
impetuously spoke a few words in his mother tongue. Imagine his
surprise when the uncouth inhabitant of the woods answered him
fluently, and when he discovered, after a few rapid questions, that
the man was Sherasmin (Gerasmes), an old servant of his father's!
This old man had escaped from the hands of his Saracen captors, and
had taken refuge in these woods, where he had already dwelt many
years. After relating his adventures, Huon entreated Sherasmin to
point out the nearest way to Bagdad, and learned with surprise that
there were two roads, one very long and comparatively safe, even
for an inexperienced traveler, and the other far shorter, but leading
through an enchanted forest, where countless dangers awaited the
venturesome traveler.

The young knight of course decided to travel along the most perilous way; and, accompanied by Sherasmin, who offered his services
as guide, he set out early upon the morrow to continue his quest. On
the fourth day of their journey they saw a Saracen struggling single-
handed against a band of Arabs, whom Huon soon put to flight with
a few well directed strokes from his mighty sword.

After resting a few moments, Huon bade Sherasmin lead the way
into the neighboring forest, although his guide and mentor again
strove to dissuade him from crossing it by explaining that the forest

was haunted by a goblin who could change men into beasts. The hero, who was on his way to insult the proudest ruler on earth, was not to be deterred by a goblin; and as Sherasmin still refused to enter first, Huon plunged boldly into the enchanted forest. Sherasmin followed him reluctantly, finding cause for alarm in the very silence of the dense shade, and timorously glancing from side to side in the gloomy recesses, where strange forms seemed to glide noiselessly about.

> "Meanwhile the wand'ring travelers onward go
> Unawares within the circuit of a wood,
> Whose mazy windings at each step renew'd,
> In many a serpent-fold, twin'd to and fro,
> So that our pair to lose themselves were fain."
>
> WIELAND, Oberon (Sotheby's tr.).

The travelers lost their way entirely as they penetrated farther into the forest, and they came at last to a little glade, where, resting under the spreading branches of a mighty oak, they were favored with the vision of a castle. Its golden portals opened wide to permit of the egress of Oberon, king of the fairies, the son of Julius Caesar and Morgana the fay. He came to them in the radiant guise of the god of love, sitting in a chariot of silver, drawn by leopards.

Sherasmin, terrified at the appearance of this radiant creature, and under the influence of wild, unreasoning fear, seized the bridle of his master's steed and dragged him into the midst of the forest, in spite of all his remonstrances. At last he paused, out of breath, and thought himself safe from further pursuit; but he was soon made aware of the goblin's wrath by the sudden outbreak of a frightful storm.

> "A tempest, wing'd with lightning, storm, and rain,
> O'ertakes our pair: around them midnight throws
> Darkness that hides the world: it peels, cracks, blows,
> As if the uprooted globe would split in twain;
> The elements in wild confusion flung,
> Each warr'd with each, as fierce from chaos sprung.
> Yet heard from time to time amid the storm,
> The gentle whisper of th' aërial form
> Breath'd forth a lovely tone that died the gales among."
>
> WIELAND, *Oberon* (Sotheby's tr.).

All Sherasmin's efforts to escape from the spirit of the forest had been in vain. Oberon's magic horn had called forth the raging tempest, and his power suddenly stayed its fury as Huon and his companion overtook a company of monks and nuns. These holy people had been celebrating a festival by a picnic, and were now hastening home, drenched, bedraggled, and in a sorry plight. They had scarcely reached the convent yard, however, where Sherasmin fancied all would be quite safe from further enchantment, when Oberon suddenly appeared in their midst like a brilliant meteor.

> "At once the storm is fled; serenely mild
> Heav'n smiles around, bright rays the sky adorn,
> While beauteous as an angel newly born
> Beams in the roseate dayspring, glow'd the child.
> A lily stalk his graceful limbs sustain'd,
> Round his smooth neck an ivory horn was chain'd;
> Yet lovely as he was, on all around
> Strange horror stole, for stern the fairy frown'd,
> And o'er each sadden'd charm a sullen anger reign'd."
> WIELAND, *Oberon* (Sotheby's tr.).

The displeasure of the king of the fairies had been roused by Huon and Sherasmin's discourteous flight, but he merely vented his anger and showed his power by breathing a soft strain on his magic horn. At the same moment, monks, nuns, and Sherasmin, forgetting their age and calling, began to dance in the wildest abandon. Huon alone remained uninfluenced by the music, for he had had no wish to avoid an encounter with Oberon.

The king of the fairies now revealed to Huon that as his life had been pure and his soul true, he would help him in his quest. Then, at a wave from the lily wand the magic music ceased, and the charm was broken. Sherasmin was graciously forgiven by Oberon, who, seeing the old man well-nigh exhausted, offered him a golden beaker of wine, bidding him drink without fear. But Sherasmin was of a suspicious nature, and it was only when he found that the draught had greatly refreshed him that he completely dismissed his fears.

After informing Huon that he was fully aware of the peculiar nature of his quest, Oberon gave him the golden beaker, assuring him that it would always be full of the richest wine for the virtuous, but would burn the evil doer with a devouring fire. He also bestowed his magic horn upon him, telling him that a gentle blast would cause all the hearers to dance, while a loud one would bring to his aid the king of the fairies himself.

> "Does but its snail-like spiral hollow sing,
> A lovely note soft swell'd with gentle breath,
> Though thousand warriors threaten instant death,
> And with advancing weapons round enring;
> Then, as thou late hast seen, in restless dance
> All, all must spin, and every sword and lance
> Fall with th' exhausted warriors to the ground.
> But if thou peal it with impatient sound,
> I at thy call appear, more swift than lightning glance."
>   WIELAND, *Oberon* (Sotheby's tr.).

Another wave of his lily wand, and Oberon disappeared, leaving a subtle fragrance behind him; and had it not been for the golden beaker and the ivory horn which he still held, Huon might have been tempted to consider the whole occurrence a dream.

The journey to Bagdad was now resumed in a more hopeful spirit; and when the travelers reached Tourmont they found that it was governed by one of Huon's uncles, who, captured in his youth by the Saracens, had turned Mussulman, and had gradually risen to the highest dignity. Seeing Huon refresh some of the Christians of his household with a draught of wine from the magic cup, he asked to be allowed to drink from it too. He had no sooner taken hold of it, however, than he was unmercifully burned, for he was a renegade, and the magic cup refreshed only the true believers.

Incensed at what he fancied a deliberate insult, the governor of Tourmont planned to slay Huon at a great banquet. But the young hero defended himself bravely, and, after slaying sundry assailants, disposed of the remainder by breathing a soft note upon his magic horn, and setting them all to dancing wildly, until they sank breathless and exhausted upon their divans.

As Huon had taken advantage of the spell to depart and continue his journey, he soon reached the castle of the giant Angoulaffre. The latter had stolen from Oberon a magic ring which made the wearer invulnerable, and thus suffered him to commit countless crimes with impunity. When Huon came near the castle he met an unfortunate knight who imformed him that the giant detained his promised bride captive, together with several other helpless damsels.

Like a true knight errant, Huon vowed to deliver these helpless ladies, and, in spite of the armed guards at every doorway, he passed unmolested into Angoulaffre's chamber. There he found the giant plunged in a lethargy, but was rapturously welcomed by the knight's fair betrothed, who had long sighed for a deliverer. In a few hurried sentences she told him that her captor constantly forced his unwelcome attentions upon her; but that, owing to the protection of the Virgin, a trance overtook him and made him helpless whenever he tried to force her inclinations and take her to wife.

> "'As oft the hateful battle he renews,
> As oft the miracle his force subdues;
> The ring no virtue boasts whene'er that sleep assails.'"
> WIELAND, *Oberon* (Sotheby's tr.).

Prompted by this fair princess, whose name was Angela, Huon secured the ring, and donned a magic hauberk hanging near. But, as he scorned to take any further advantage of a sleeping foe, he patiently awaited the giant's awakening to engage in one of those combats which the mediaeval poets loved to describe.

Of course Huon was victorious, and after slaying Angoulaffre, he restored the fair Angela to her lover, Alexis, and gave a great banquet, which was attended by the fifty rescued damsels, and by fifty knights who had come to help Alexis. Although this gay company would fain have had him remain with them, Huon traveled on. When too exhausted to continue his way, he again rested under a tree, where Oberon caused a tent to be raised by invisible hands. Here Huon had a wonderful dream, in which he beheld his future ladylove, and was warned of some of the perils which still awaited him before he could claim her as his own.

The journey was then resumed, and when they reached the banks of the Red Sea, Oberon sent one of his spirits, Malebron, to carry them safely over. They traveled through burning wastes of sand, refreshed and strengthened by occasional draughts from the magic goblet, and came at last to a forest, where they saw a Saracen about to succumb beneath the attack of a monstrous lion. Huon immediately flew to his rescue, slew the lion, and, having drunk deeply from his magic cup, handed it to the Saracen, on whose lips the refreshing wine turned to liquid flame.

> "With evil eye, from Huon's courteous hand,
> Filled to the brim, the heathen takes the bowl—
> Back from his lip th' indignant bubbles roll!
> The spring is dried, and hot as fiery brand,
> Proof of internal guilt, the metal glows.
> Far from his grasp the wretch the goblet throws,
> Raves, roars, and stamps."
> WIELAND, *Oberon* (Sotheby's tr.).

With a blasphemous exclamation the Saracen flung aside the cup, and seeing that his own steed had been slain by the lion, he sprang unceremoniously upon Huon's horse, and rode rapidly away.

As there was but one mount left for them both, Huon and Sherasmin were now obliged to proceed more slowly to Bagdad, where they found every hostelry full, as the people were all coming thither to witness the approaching nuptials of the princess, Rezia (Esclamonde), and Babican, King of Hyrcania. Huon and Sherasmin, after a long search, finally found entertainment in a little hut, where an old woman, the mother of the princess's attendant, entertained them by relating that the princess was very reluctant to marry. She also told them that Rezia had lately been troubled by a dream, in which she had seen herself in the guise of a hind and pursued through a pathless forest by Babican. In this dream she was saved and restored to her former shape by a radiant little creature, who rode in a glistening silver car, drawn by leopards. He was accompanied by a fair-haired knight, whom he presented to her as her future bridegroom.

> "The shadow flies; but from her heart again
> He never fades—the youth with golden hair;
> Eternally his image hovers there,

> Exhaustless source of sweetly pensive pain,
> In nightly visions, and in daydreams shown."
> WIELAND, *Oberon* (Sotheby's tr.).

Huon listened in breathless rapture, for he now felt assured that the princess Rezia was the radiant creature he had seen in his dream, and that Oberon intended them for each other. He therefore assured the old woman that the princess should never marry the detested Babican. Then, although Sherasmin pointed out to him that the way to a lady's favor seldom consists in cutting off the head of her intended bridegroom, depriving her father of four teeth and a lock of his beard, and kissing her without the usual preliminary of "by your leave," the young hero persisted in his resolution to visit the palace on the morrow.

That selfsame night, Huon and Rezia were again visited by sweet dreams, in which Oberon, their guardian spirit, promised them his aid. While the princess was arraying herself for her nuptials on the morrow, the old woman rushed into her apartment and announced that a fair-haired knight, evidently the promised deliverer, had slept in her humble dwelling the night before. Comforted by these tidings, Rezia made a triumphant entrance into the palace hall, where her father, the bridegroom, and all the principal dignitaries of the court, awaited her appearance.

> "Emirs and viziers, all the courtly crowd
> Meantime attendant at the sultan's call,
> With festal splendor grace the nuptial hall.
> The banquet waits, the cymbals clang aloud.
> The gray-beard caliph from his golden door
> Stalks mid the slaves that fall his path before;
> Behind, of stately gesture, proud to view,
> The Druse prince, though somewhat pale of hue,
> Comes as a bridegroom deck'd with jewels blazing o'er."
> WIELAND, *Oberon* (Sotheby's tr.).

In the mean while Huon, awaking at early dawn, found a complete suit of Saracenic apparel at his bedside. He donned it joyfully, entered the palace unchallenged, and passed into the banquet hall, where he perceived the gray-bearded caliph, and recognized in the bridegroom at his left the Saracen whom he had delivered from the lion, and who had so discourteously stolen his horse.

One stride forward, a flash of his curved scimitar, and the first part of Charlemagne's order was fulfilled, for the Saracen's head rolled to the ground. The sudden movement caused Huon's turban to fall off, however, and the princess, seated at the caliph's right, gazed spellbound upon the knight, whose golden locks fell in rich curls about his shoulders.

There are several widely different versions of this part of the story. The most popular, however, states that Huon, taking advantage of the first moments of surprise, kissed Rezia thrice, slipping on her finger, in sign of betrothal, the magic ring which he had taken from Angoulaffre. Then, seeing the caliph's guards about to fall upon him, he gently breathed soft music on his magic horn, and set caliph and court a-dancing.

> "The whole divan, one swimming circle glides
> Swift without stop: the old bashaws click time,
> As if on polish'd ice; in trance sublime
> The iman hoar with some spruce courtier slides.
> Nor rank nor age from capering refrain;
> Nor can the king his royal foot restrain!
> He too must reel amid the frolic row,
> Grasp the grand vizier by his beard of snow,
> And teach the aged man once more to bound amain!"
> WIELAND, *Oberon* (Sotheby's tr.).

While they were thus occupied, Huon conducted the willing Rezia to the door, where Sherasmin was waiting for them with fleet steeds, and with Fatima, the princess's favorite attendant. While Sherasmin helped the ladies to mount, Huon hastened back to the palace hall, and found that the exhausted caliph had sunk upon a divan. With the prescribed ceremonies, our hero politely craved a lock of his beard and four of his teeth as a present for Charlemagne. This impudent request so incensed the caliph that he vociferated orders to his guards to slay the stranger. Huon was now forced to defend himself with a curtain pole and a golden bowl, until, needing aid, he suddenly blew

a resounding peal upon his magic horn. The earth shook, the palace
rocked, Oberon appeared in the midst of rolling thunder and flashing
lightning, and with a wave of his lily wand plunged caliph and people
into a deep sleep. Then he placed his silver car at Huon's disposal, to
bear him and his bride and attendants to Ascalon, where a ship was
waiting to take them back to France.

> "'So haste, thou matchless pair!
> On wings of love, my car, that cuts the air,
> Shall waft you high above terrestrial sight,
> And place, ere morning melt the shades of night,
> On Askalon's far shore, beneath my guardian care.'"
> WIELAND, *Oberon* (Sotheby's tr.).

When Huon and Rezia were about to embark at Ascalon, Oberon
appeared. He claimed his chariot, which had brought them thither,
and gave the knight a golden and jeweled casket, which contained
the teeth of the caliph and a lock of his beard. One last test of Huon's
loyalty was required, however; for Oberon, at parting, warned him to
make no attempt to claim Rezia as his wife until their union had been
blessed at Rome by the Pope.

> "'And deep, O Huon! grave it in your brain!
> Till good Sylvester, pious father, sheds
> Heaven's holy consecration on your heads,
> As brother and as sister chaste remain!
> Oh, may ye not, with inauspicious haste,
> The fruit forbidden prematurely taste!
> Know, if ye rashly venture ere the time,
> That Oberon, in vengeance of your crime,
> Leaves you, without a friend, on life's deserted waste!'"
> WIELAND, *Oberon* (Sotheby's tr.).

The first part of the journey was safely accomplished; but when
they stopped at Lepanto, on the way, Huon insisted upon his mentor,
Sherasmin, taking passage on another vessel, which sailed direct to
France, that he might hasten ahead, lay the golden casket at Charlemagne's feet, and announce Huon's coming with his Oriental bride.

When Sherasmin had reluctantly departed, and they were again on

HUON AND AMANDA LEAP OVERBOARD.—Gabriel Max.

the high seas, Huon expounded the Christian faith to Rezia, who not only was converted, but was also baptized by a priest on board. He gave her the Christian name of Amanda, in exchange for her pagan name of Rezia or Esclarmonde. This same priest also consecrated their marriage; and while Huon intended to await the Pope's blessing ere he claimed Amanda as his wife, his good resolutions were soon forgotten, and the last injunction of Oberon disregarded.

This disobedience was immediately punished, for a frightful tempest suddenly arose, threatening to destroy the vessel and all on board. The sailors, full of superstitious fears, cast lots to discover who should be sacrificed to allay the fury of the storm. When the choice fell upon Huon, Amanda flung herself with him into the tumultuous waves. As the lovers vanished overboard the storm was suddenly appeased, and, instead of drowning together, Huon and Amanda, by the magic of the ring she wore, drifted to a volcanic island, where they almost perished from hunger and thirst.

Much search among the rocks was finally rewarded by the discovery of some dates, which were particularly welcome, as the lovers had been bitterly deluded by the sight of some apples of Sodom. The fruit, however, was soon exhausted, and, after untold exertions, Huon made his way over the mountains to a fertile valley, the retreat of Titania, queen of the fairies, who had quarreled with Oberon, and who was waiting here until recalled to fairyland.

The only visible inhabitant of the valley, however, was a hermit, who welcomed Huon, and showed him a short and convenient way to bring Amanda thither. After listening attentively to the story of Huon's adventures, the hermit bade him endeavor to recover the favor of Oberon by voluntarily living apart from his wife, and leading a life of toil and abstinence.

> "'Blest,' says the hermit, 'blest the man whom fate
> Guides with strict hand, but not unfriendly aim!
> How blest! whose slightest fault is doom'd to shame!
> Him, trained to virtue, purest joys await,—
> Earth's purest joys reward each trying pain!
> Think not the fairy will for aye remain
> Inexorable foe to hearts like thine:
> Still o'er you hangs his viewless hand divine;
> Do but deserve his grace, and ye his grace obtain."
> WIELAND, *Oberon* (Sotheby's tr.).

Huon was ready and willing to undergo any penance which would enable him to deliver his beloved Amanda from the isle, and after building her a little hut, within call of the cell he occupied with the hermit, he spent all his time in tilling the soil for their sustenance, and in listening to the teachings of the holy man.

Time passed on. One day Amanda restlessly wandered a little way up the mountain, and fell asleep in a lovely grotto, which she now for the first time discovered. When she awoke from a blissful dream she found herself clasping her new-born babe, who, during her slumbers, had been cared for by the fairies. This child, Huonet, was, of course, a great comfort to Amanda, who was devoted to him.

When the babe was a little more than a year old the aged monk died. Huon and Amanda, despairing of release from the desert island, were weary of living apart; and Titania, who foresaw that Oberon would send new misfortunes upon them to punish them in case they did not stand the second test, carried little Huonet off to fairyland, lest he should suffer for his parents' sins.

Huon and Amanda, in the mean time, searched frantically for the missing babe, fancying it had wandered off into the woods. During their search they became separated, and Amanda, while walking along the seashore, was seized by pirates. They intended to carry her away and sell her as a slave to the Sultan. Huon heard her cries of distress, and rushed to her rescue; but in spite of his utmost efforts to join her he saw her borne away to the waiting vessel, while he was bound to a tree in the woods, and left there to die.

"Deep in the wood, at distance from the shore,
They drag their victim, that his loudest word
Pour'd on the desert air may pass unheard.
Then bind the wretch, and fasten o'er and o'er
Arm, leg, and neck, and shoulders, to a tree.
To heaven he looks in speechless agony,
O'ercome by woe's unutterable weigfit.
Thus he—the while, with jocund shout elate
The crew bear off their prey, and bound along the sea."
WIELAND, *Oberon* (Sotheby's tr.).

Oberon, however, had pity at last upon the unfortunate knight, and sent one of his invisible servants, who not only unbound him, but transported him, with miraculous rapidity, over land and sea, and deposited him at the door of a gardener's house in Tunis.

After parting from his master at Lepanto, Sherasmin traveled on until he came to the gates of the palace with his precious casket. Then only did he realize that Charlemagne would never credit his tale unless Huon were there with his bride to vouch for its truth. Instead of entering the royal abode he therefore hastened back to Rome, where for two months he awaited the arrival of the young couple. Then, sure that some misfortune had overtaken them, the faithful Sherasmin wandered in pilgrim guise from place to place seeking them, until he finally came to Tunis, where Fatima, Amanda's maid, had been sold into slavery, and where he sorrowfully learned of his master's death.

To be near Fatima, Sherasmin took a gardener's position in the Sultan's palace, and when he opened the door of his humble dwelling one morning he was overjoyed to find Huon, who had been brought there by the messenger of Oberon. An explanation ensued, and Huon, under the assumed name of Hassan, became Sherasmin's assistant in the Sultan's gardens.

The pirates, in the mean while, hoping to sell Amanda to the Sultan himself, had treated her with the utmost deference; but as they neared the shore of Tunis their vessel suffered shipwreck, and all on board perished miserably, except Amanda. She was washed ashore at the Sultan's feet. Charmed by her beauty, the Sultan conveyed her to his palace, where he would immediately have married her had she not told him that she had made a vow of chastity which she was bound to keep for two years.

Huon, unconscious of Amanda's presence, worked in the garden, where the Sultan's daughter saw him and fell in love with him. As she failed to win him, she became very jealous. Soon after this Fatima discovered Amanda's presence in the palace, and informed Huon, who made a desperate effort to reach her. This was discovered by the jealous princess, and since Huon would not love her, she was determined that he should not love another. She therefore artfully laid her plans, and accused him of a heinous crime, for which the

Sultan, finding appearances against him, condemned him to death. Amanda, who was warned by Fatima of Huon's danger, rushed into the Sultan's presence to plead for her husband's life; but when she discovered that she could obtain it only at the price of renouncing him forever and marrying the Sultan, she declared that she preferred to die, and elected to be burned with her beloved. The flames were already rising around them both, when Oberon, touched by their sufferings and their constancy, suddenly appeared, and again hung his horn about Huon's neck.

The knight hailed this sign of recovered favor with rapture, and, putting the magic horn to his lips, showed his magnanimity by blowing only a soft note and making all the pagans dance.

> "No sooner had the grateful knight beheld,
> With joyful ardor seen, the ivory horn,
> Sweet pledge of fairy grace, his neck adorn,
> Than with melodious whisper gently swell'd,
> His lip entices forth the sweetest tone
> That ever breath'd through magic ivory blown:
> He scorns to doom a coward race to death.
> 'Dance! till ye weary gasp, depriv'd of breath—
> Huon permits himself this slight revenge alone'"
> WIELAND, *Oberon* (Sotheby's tr.).

While all were dancing, much against their will, Huon and Amanda, Sherasmin and Fatima, promptly stepped into the silvery car which Oberon placed at their disposal, and were rapidly transported to fairyland. There they found little Huonet in perfect health. Great happiness now reigned, for Titania, having secured the ring which Amanda had lost in her struggle with the pirates on the sandy shore, had given it back to Oberon. He was propitiated by the gift, and as the sight of Huon and Amanda's fidelity had convinced him that wives could be true, he took Titania back into favor, and reinstated her as queen of his realm.

When Huon and Amanda had sojourned as long as they wished in fairyland, they were wafted in Oberon's car to the gates of Paris. There Huon arrived just in time to win, at the point of his lance, his patrimony of Guienne, which Charlemagne had offered as prize at a tournament. Bending low before his monarch, the young hero then revealed his name, presented his wife, gave him the golden casket containing the lock of hair and the four teeth, and said that he had accomplished his quest.

> "Our hero lifts the helmet from his head;
> And boldly ent'ring, like the god of day,
> His golden ringlets down his armor play.
> All, wond'ring, greet the youth long mourn'd as dead,
> Before the king his spirit seems to stand!
> Sir Huon with Amanda, hand in hand,
> Salutes the emperor with respectful bow—
> 'Behold, obedient to his plighted vow,
> Thy vassal, sovereign liege, returning to thy land!
>
> "'For by the help of Heaven this arm has done
> What thou enjoin'dst—and lo! before thine eye
> The beard and teeth of Asia's monarch lie,
> At hazard of my life, to please thee, won;
> And in this fair, by every peril tried,
> The heiress of his throne, my love, my bride!'
> He spoke; and lo! at once her knight to grace,
> Off falls the veil that hid Amanda's face,
> And a new radiance gilds the hall from side to side."
>   WIELAND, *Oberon* (Sotheby's tr.).

The young couple, entirely restored to favor, sojourned a short time at court and then traveled southward to Guienne, where their subjects received them with every demonstration of extravagant joy. Here they spent the remainder of their lives together in happiness and comparative peace.

According to an earlier version of the story, Esclarmonde, whom the pirates intended to convey to the court of her uncle, Yvoirin of Montbrand, was wrecked near the palace of Galafre, King of Tunis, who respected her vow of chastity but obstinately refused to give her up to her uncle when he claimed her. Huon, delivered from his fetters on the island, was borne by Malebron, Oberon's servant, to Yvoirin's court, where he immediately offered himself as champion to defy Galafre and win back his beloved wife at the point of the sword.

No sooner did Huon appear in martial array at Tunis than Galafre selected Sherasmin (who had also been shipwrecked off his coast, and had thus become his slave) as his champion. Huon and Sherasmin met, but, recognizing each other after a few moments' struggle, they suddenly embraced, and, joining forces, slew the pagans and carried off Esclarmonde and Fatima. They embarked upon a swift sailing vessel, and soon arrived at Rome, where Huon related his adventures to the Pope, who gave him his blessing.

As they were on their way to Charlemagne's court, Girard, a knight who had taken possession of Huon's estates, stole the golden casket from Sherasmin, and sent Huon and Esclarmonde in chains to Bordeaux. Then, going to court, he informed Charlemagne that although Huon had failed in his quest, he had dared to return to France. Charlemagne, whose anger had not yet cooled, proceeded to Bordeaux, tried Huon, and condemned him to death. But just as the knight was about to perish, Oberon appeared, bound the emperor and Girard fast, and only consented to restore them to freedom when Charlemagne promised to reinstate Huon.

Oberon then produced the missing casket, revealed Girard's treachery, and, after seeing him punished, bore Huon and Esclarmonde off to fairyland. Huon eventually became ruler of this realm in Oberon's stead; and his daughter, Claretie, whose equally marvelous adventures are told at great length in another, but far less celebrated, *chanson de geste*, is represented as the ancestress of all the Capetian kings of France.

CHAPTER XI.

TITUREL AND THE HOLY GRAIL.

The most mystical and spiritual of all the romances of chivalry is doubtless the legend of the Holy Grail. Rooted in the mythology of all primitive races is the belief in a land of peace and happiness, a sort of earthly paradise, once possessed by man, but now lost, and only to be attained again by the virtuous. The legend of the Holy Grail, which some authorities declare was first known in Europe by the Moors, and christianized by the Spaniards, was soon introduced into France, where Robert de Borron and Chrestien de Troyes wrote lengthy poems about it. Other writers took up the same theme, among them Walter Map, Archdeacon of Oxford, who connected it with the Arthurian legends. It soon became known in Germany, where, in the hands of Gottfried von Strassburg, and especially of Wolfram von Eschenbach, it assumed its most perfect and popular form. The "Parzival" of Eschenbach also forms the basis of a recent work, the much-discussed last opera of the great German composer, Wagner.[6] [

The story of the Grail is somewhat confused, owing to the many changes made by the different authors. The account here given, while mentioning the most striking incidents of other versions, is in general an outline of the "Titurel" and "Parzival" of Von Eschenbach.

When Lucifer was cast out of heaven, one stone of great beauty as detached from the marvelous crown which sixty thousand angels had tendered him. This stone fell upon earth, and from it was carved a vessel of great beauty, which came, after many ages, into the hands of Joseph of Arimathea. He offered it to the Savior, who made use of it in the Last Supper. When the blood flowed from the Redeemer's side, Joseph of Arimathea caught a few drops of it in this wonderful

6   See Guerber's Stories of the Wagner Opera.

vessel; and, owing to this circumstance, it was thought to be endowed with marvelous powers. "Wherever it was there were good things in abundance. Whoever looked upon it, even though he were sick unto death, could not die that week; whoever looked at it continually, his cheeks never grew pale, nor his hair gray."

Once a year, on the anniversary of the Savior's death, a white dove brought a fresh host down from heaven, and placed it on the vessel, which was borne by a host of angels, or by spotless virgins. The care of it was at times intrusted to mortals, who, however, had to prove themselves worthy of this exalted honor by leading immaculate lives. This vessel, called the "Holy Grail," remained, after the crucifixion, in the hands of Joseph of Arimathea. The Jews, angry because Joseph had helped to bury Christ, cast him into a dungeon, and left him there for a whole year without food or drink. Their purpose in doing so was to slay Joseph, as they had already slain Nicodemus, so that should the Romans ever ask them to produce Christ's body, they might declare that it had been stolen by Joseph of Arimathea.

The Jews little suspected, however, that Joseph, having the Holy Grail with him, could suffer no lack. When Vespasian, the Roman emperor, heard the story of Christ's passion, as related by a knight who had just returned from the Holy Land, he sent a commission to Jerusalem to investigate the matter and bring back some holy relic to cure his son Titus of leprosy.

In due time the ambassadors returned, giving Pilate's version of the story, and bringing with them an old woman (known after her death as St. Veronica). She produced the cloth with which she had wiped the Lord's face, and upon which his likeness had been stamped by miracle. The mere sight of this holy relic sufficed to restore Titus, who now proceeded with Vespasian to Jerusalem. There they vainly tried to compel the Jews to produce the body of Christ, until one of them revealed, under pressure of torture, the place where Joseph was imprisoned. Vespasian proceeded in person to the dungeon, and was hailed by name by the perfectly healthy prisoner. Joseph was set free, but, fearing further persecution from the Jews, soon departed with his sister, Enigée, and her husband, Brons, for a distant land. The pilgrims found a place of refuge near Marseilles, where the

Holy Grail supplied all their needs, until one of them committed a sin. Then divine displeasure became manifest by a terrible famine.

As none knew who had sinned, Joseph was instructed in a vision to discover the culprit by the same means with which the Lord had revealed the guilt of Judas. Still following divine commands, Joseph made a table, and directed Brons to catch a fish. The Grail was placed before Joseph's seat at table, where all who implicitly believed were invited to take a seat. Eleven seats were soon occupied, and only Judas's place remained empty. Moses, a hypocrite and sinner, attempted to sit there, but the earth opened wide beneath him and ingulfed him.

In another vision Joseph was now informed that the vacancy would only be filled on the day of doom. He was also told that a similar table would be constructed by Merlin. Here the grandson of Brons would honorably occupy the vacant place, which is designated in the legend as the "Siege Perilous," because it proved fatal to all for whom it was not intended.

In the "Great St. Grail," one of the longest poems on this theme, there are countless adventures and journeys, "transformations of fair females into foul fiends, conversions wholesale and individual, allegorical visions, miracles, and portents. Eastern splendor and northern weirdness, angelry and deviltry, together with abundant fighting and quite a phenomenal amount of swooning, which seem to reflect a strange medley of Celtic, pagan, and mythological traditions, and Christian legends and mysticism, alternate in a kaleidoscopic maze that defies the symmetry which modern aesthetic canons associate with every artistic production."

The Holy Grail was, we are further told, transported by Joseph of Arimathea to Glastonbury, where it long remained visible, and whence it vanished only when men became too sinful to be permitted to retain it in their midst.

Another legend relates that a rich man from Cappadocia, Berillus, followed Vespasian to Rome, where he won great estates. He was a very virtuous man, and his good qualities were inherited by all his descendants. One of them, called Titurisone, greatly regretted having no son to continue his race. When advised by a soothsayer to make a pilgrimage to the holy sepulcher, and there to lay a crucifix of pure gold upon the altar, the pious Titurisone hastened to do so. On his return he was rewarded for his pilgrimage by the birth of a son, called Titurel.

This child, when he had attained manhood, spent all his time in warring against the Saracens, as all pagans are called in these metrical romances. The booty he won he gave either to the church or to the poor, and his courage and virtue were only equaled by his piety and extreme humility.

One day, when Titurel was walking alone in the woods, he was favored by the vision of an angel. The celestial messenger sailed down to earth out of the blue, and announced in musical tones that the Lord had chosen him to be the guardian of the Holy Grail on Montsalvatch (which some authors believe to have been in Spain), and that it behooved him to set his house in order and obey the voice of God.

When the angel had floated upward and out of sight, Titurel returned home. After disposing of all his property, reserving nothing but his armor and trusty sword, he again returned to the spot where he had been favored with the divine message. There he saw a mysterious white cloud, which seemed to beckon him onward. Titurel followed it, passed through vast solitudes and almost impenetrable woods, and eventually began to climb a steep mountain, whose ascent at first seemed impossible. Clinging to the rocks, and gazing ever ahead at the guiding cloud, Titurel came at last to the top of the mountain, where, in a beam of refulgent light, he beheld the Holy Grail, borne in the air by invisible hands. He raised his heart in passionate prayer that he might be found worthy to guard the emerald-colored wonder which was thus intrusted to his care, and in his rapture hardly heeded the welcoming cries of a number of knights in shining armor, who hailed him as their king.

The vision of the Holy Grail was as evanescent as beautiful, and soon disappeared; but Titurel, knowing that the spot was holy, guarded it with all his might against the infidels, who would fain have climbed the mountain.

After several years had passed without the Holy Grail's coming down to earth, Titurel conceived the plan of building a temple suitable for its reception. The knights who helped to build and afterward guarded this temple were called "Templars." Their first effort was to clear the mountain top, which they found was one single onyx of enormous size. This they leveled and polished until it shone like a mirror, and upon this foundation they prepared to build their temple.

As Titurel was hesitating what plan to adopt for the building, he prayed for guidance, and when he arose on the morrow he found the ground plan all traced out and the building materials ready for use. The knights labored piously from morning till night, and when they ceased, invisible hands continued to work all night. Thus pushed onward, the work was soon completed, and the temple rose on the mountain top in all its splendor. "The temple itself was one hundred fathoms in diameter. Around it were seventy-two chapels of an octagonal shape. To every pair of chapels there was a tower six stories high, approachable by a winding stair on the outside. In the center stood a tower twice as big as the others, which rested on arches. The vaulting was of blue sapphire, and in the center was a plate of emerald, with the lamb and the banner of the cross in enamel. All the altar stones were of sapphire, as symbols of the propitiation of sins. Upon the inside of the cupola surmounting the temple, the sun and moon were represented in diamonds and topazes, and shed a light as of day even in the darkness of the night. The windows were of crystal, beryl, and other transparent stones. The floor was of translucent crystal, under which all the fishes of the sea were carved out of onyx, just like life. The towers were of precious stones inlaid with gold; their roofs of gold and blue enamel. Upon every tower there was a crystal cross, and upon it a golden eagle with expanded wings, which, at a distance, appeared to be flying. At the summit of the main tower was an immense carbuncle, which served, like a star, to guide the Templars thither at night. In the center of the building, under the dome, was a miniature representation, of the whole, and in this the holy vessel was kept."

When all the work was finished, the temple was solemnly consecrated, and as the priests chanted the psalms a sweet perfume filled the air, and the holy vessel was seen to glide down on a beam of light. While it hovered just above the altar the wondering assembly heard the choir of the angels singing the praises of the Most High. The Holy Grail, which had thus come down upon earth, was faithfully guarded by Titurel and his knights, who were fed and sustained by its marvelous power, and whose wounds were healed as soon as they gazed upon it. From time to time it also delivered a divine message, which

PARZIVAL UNCOVERING THE HOLY GRAIL.—Pixis.

appeared in letters of fire inscribed about its rim, and which none of the Templars ever ventured to disregard.

By virtue of the miraculous preservative influence of the Holy Grail, Titurel seemed but forty when he was in reality more than four hundred years old. His every thought had been so engrossed by the care of the precious vessel that he was somewhat surprised when he read upon its rim a luminous command to marry, so that his race might not become extinct. When the knights of the temple had been summoned, and had all perused the divine command, they began to consider where a suitable helpmate could be found for their beloved king. They soon advised him to woe Richoude, the daughter of a Spaniard. An imposing embassy was sent to the maiden, who, being piously inclined, immediately consented to the marriage.

Richoude was a faithful wife for twenty years, and when she died she left two children,—a son, Frimoutel, and a daughter, Richoude,—to comfort the sorrowing Titurel for her loss. These children both married in their turn, and Frimoutel had two sons, Amfortas and Trevrezent, and three daughters, Herzeloide, Josiane, and Repanse de Joie. As these children grew up, Titurel became too old to bear the weight of his armor, and spent all his days in the temple, where he finally read on the Holy Grail a command to anoint Frimoutel king. Joyfully the old man obeyed, for he had long felt that the defense of the Holy Grail should be intrusted to a younger man than he.

Although he renounced the throne in favor of his son, Titurel lived on, witnessed the marriage of Josiane, and mourned for her when she died in giving birth to a little daughter, called Sigune. This child, being thus deprived of a mother's care, was intrusted to Herzeloide, who brought her up with Tchionatulander, the orphaned son of a friend. Herzeloide married a prince named Gamuret, and became the happy mother of Parzival, who, however, soon lost his father in a terrible battle.

Fearful lest her son, when grown up, should want to follow his father's example, and make war against even the most formidable foes, Herzeloide carried him off into the forest of Soltane (which some authors locate in Brittany), and there brought him up in complete solitude and ignorance.

"The child her falling tears bedew;
No wife was ever found more true.
She teemed with joy and uttered sighs;
And tears midst laughter filled her eyes
Her heart delighted in his birth;
In sorrow deep was drowned her mirth."
      WOLFRAM VON ESCHENBACH, *Parzival* (Dippold's tr.).

While she was living there, Frimoutel, weary of the dull life on Montsalvatch, went out into the world, and died of a lance wound when far away from home. Amfortas, his son, who was now crowned in obedience to the command of the Holy Grail, proved equally restless, and went out also in search of adventures. Like his father, he too was wounded by a poisoned lance; but, instead of dying, he lived to return to the Holy Grail. But since his wound had not been received in defense of the holy vessel, it never healed, and caused him untold suffering.

Titurel, seeing this suffering, prayed ardently for his grandson's release from the pain which imbittered every moment of his life, and was finally informed by the glowing letters on the rim of the Holy Grail that a chosen hero would climb the mountain and inquire the cause of Amfortas's pain. At this question the evil spell would be broken, Amfortas healed, and the newcomer appointed king and guardian of the Holy Grail.

This promise of ultimate cure saved Amfortas from utter despair, and all the Templars lived in constant anticipation of the coming hero, and of the question which would put an end to the torment which they daily witnessed.

Parzival, in the mean while, was growing up in the forest, where he amused himself with a bow and arrow of his own manufacture. But when for the first time he killed a tiny bird, and saw it lying limp and helpless in his hand, he brought it tearfully to his mother and inquired what it meant. In answering him she, for the first time also, mentioned the name of God; and when he eagerly questioned her about the Creator, she said to him: "Brighter is God than e'en the brightest day; yet once he took the form and face of man."

Thus brought up in complete ignorance, it is no wonder that when young Parzival encountered some knights in brilliant armor in the forest, he fell down and offered to worship them. Amused at the lad's simplicity, the knights told him all about the gay world of chivalry beyond the forest, and advised him to ride to Arthur's court, where, if worthy, he would receive the order of knighthood, and perchance be admitted to the Round Table. Beside himself with joy at hearing all these marvelous things, and eager to set out immediately, Parzival returned to his mother to relate what he had seen, and to implore her to give him a horse, that he might ride after the knights.

> "'I saw four men, dear mother mine;
> Not brighter is the Lord divine.
> They spoke to me of chivalry;
> Through Arthur's power of royalty,
> In knightly honor well arrayed,
> I shall receive the accolade.'"
> WOLFRAM VON ESCHENBACH, *Parzival* (Dippold's tr.).

The mother, finding herself unable to detain him any longer, reluctantly consented to his departure, and, hoping that ridicule and lack of success would soon drive him back to her, prepared for him the motley garb of a fool and gave him a very sorry nag to ride.

> "The boy, silly yet brave indeed,
> Oft from his mother begged a steed.
> That in her heart she did lament;
> She thought: 'Him must I make content,
> Yet must the thing an evil be.'
> Thereafter further pondered she:
> 'The folk are prone to ridicule.
> My child the garments of a fool
> Shall on his shining body wear.
> If he be scoffed and beaten there,
> Perchance he'll come to me again.'"
> WOLFRAM VON ESCHENBACH, *Parzival* (Bayard Taylor's tr.).

Thus equipped, his mind well stored with all manner of unpractical advice given by his mother in further hopes of making a worldly career impossible for him, the young hero set out. As he rode away from home, his heart was filled with regret at leaving and with an ardent desire to seek adventures abroad,—conflicting emotions which he experienced for the first time in his life. Herzeloide accompanied her son part way, kissed him good-by, and, as his beloved form disappeared from view in the forest paths, her heart broke and she breathed her last!

Parzival rode onward and soon came to a meadow, in which some tents were pitched. He saw a beautiful lady asleep in one of these tents, and, dismounting, he wakened her with a kiss, thus obeying one of his mother's injunctions—to kiss every fair lady he met. To his surprise, however, the lady seemed indignant; so he tried to pacify her by telling her that he had often thus saluted his mother. Then, slipping the bracelet from off her arm, and carrying it away as a proof that she was not angry, he rode on. Lord Orilus, the lady's husband, hearing from her that a youth had kissed her, flew into a towering rage, and rode speedily away, hoping to overtake the impudent varlet and punish him.

Parzival, in the mean while, had journeyed on, and, passing through the forest, had seen a maiden weeping over the body of her slain lover. In answer to his inquiries she told him that she was his cousin, Sigune, and that the dead man, Tchionatulander, had been killed in trying to fulfill a trifling request—to recover her pet dog, which had been stolen. Parzival promised to avenge Tchionatulander as soon as possible, and to remember that the name of the murderer was Orilus.

Next he came to a river, where he was ferried across, and repaid the boatman by giving him the bracelet he had taken from Orilus's wife. Then, hearing that Arthur was holding his court at Nantes, he proceeded thither without further delay.

On entering the city, Parzival encountered the Red Knight, who mockingly asked him where he was going. The unabashed youth immediately retorted, "To Arthur's court to ask him for your arms and steed!"

A little farther on the youth's motley garb attracted much attention, and the town boys made fun of him until Iwanet, one of the king's squires, came to inquire the cause of the tumult. He took Parzival under his protection, and conducted him to the great hall, where, if we are to believe some accounts, Parzival boldly presented himself on horseback. The sight of the gay company so dazzled the inexperienced youth that he wonderingly inquired why there were so many Arthurs. When Iwanet told him that the wearer of the crown was the sole king, Parzival boldly stepped up to him and asked for the arms and steed of the Red Knight.

Arthur wonderingly gazed at the youth, and then replied that he could have them provided he could win them. This was enough. Parzival sped after the knight, overtook him, and loudly bade him surrender weapons and steed. The Red Knight, thus challenged, began to fight; but Parzival, notwithstanding his inexperience, wielded his spear so successfully that he soon slew his opponent. To secure the steed was an easy matter, but how to remove the armor the youth did not know. By good fortune, however, Iwanet soon came up and helped Parzival to don the armor. He put it on over his motley garb, which he would not set aside because his mother had made it for him.

Some time after, Parzival came to the castle of Gurnemanz, a noble knight, with whom he remained for some time. Here he received valuable instructions in all a knight need know. When Parzival left this place, about a year later, he was an accomplished knight, clad as beseemed his calling, and ready to fulfill all the duties which chivalry imposed upon its votaries.

He soon heard that Queen Conduiramour was hard pressed, in her capital of Belripar, by an unwelcome suitor. As he had pledged his word to defend all ladies in distress, Parzival immediately set out to rescue this queen. A series of brilliant single fights disposed of the besiegers, and the citizens of Belripar, to show their gratitude to their deliverer, offered him the hand of their queen, Conduiramour, which he gladly accepted. But Parzival, even in this new home, could not forget his sorrowing mother, and he soon left his wife to go in search of Herzeloide, hoping to comfort her. He promised his wife that he would return soon, however, and would bring his mother to Belripar to share their joy. In the course of this journey homeward Parzival came to a lake, where a richly dressed fisherman, in answer to his inquiry, directed him to a neighboring castle where he might find shelter.

Although Parzival did not know it, he had come to the temple and castle on Montsalvatch. The drawbridge was immediately lowered at his call, and richly clad servants bade him welcome with joyful mien. They told him that he had long been expected, and after arraying him in a jeweled garment, sent by Queen Repanse de Joie, they conducted him into a large, brilliantly illumined hall. There four hundred knights were seated on soft cushions, before small tables each laid for four guests; and as they saw him enter a flash of joy passed over their grave and melancholy faces. The high seat was occupied by a man wrapped in furs, who was evidently suffering from some painful disease. He made a sign to Parzival to draw near, gave him a seat beside him, and presented him with a sword of exquisite workmanship. To Parzival's surprise this man bade him welcome also, and repeated that he had long been expected. The young knight, amazed by all he heard and saw, remained silent, for he did not wish to seem inquisitive,—a failing unworthy of a knight. Suddenly the great doors opened, and a servant appeared bearing the bloody head of a lance, with which he silently walked around the hall, while all gazed upon it and groaned aloud.

The servant had scarcely vanished when the doors again opened, and beautiful virgins came marching in, two by two. They bore an embroidered cushion, an ebony stand, and sundry other articles, which they laid before the fur-clad king. Last of all came the beautiful maiden, Repanse de Joie, bearing a glowing vessel; and as she entered and laid it before the king, Parzival heard the assembled knights whisper that this was the Holy Grail.

> "Now after them advanced the Queen,
> With countenance of so bright a sheen,
> They all imagined day would dawn.
> One saw the maiden was clothed on
> With muslin stuffs of Araby.
> On a green silk cushion she
> The pearl of Paradise did bear.
>
> *   *   *   *   *
>
> The blameless Queen, proud, pure, and calm,
> Before the host put down the Grail;
> And Percival, so runs the tale,
> To gaze upon her did not fail,
> Who thither bore the Holy Grail."
> WOLFRAM VON ESCHENBACH, *Parzival* (Bayard Taylor's tr.).

The maidens then slowly retired, the knights and squires drew near, and now from the shining vessel streamed forth a supply of the daintiest dishes and richest wines, each guest being served with the viands which he liked best. All ate sadly and in silence, while Parzival wondered what it might all mean, yet remained mute. The meal ended, the sufferer rose from his seat, gazed reproachfully at the visitor, who, by asking a question, could have saved him such pain, and slowly left the room, uttering a deep sigh.

With angry glances the knights also left the hall, and sad-faced servants conducted Parzival past a sleeping room, where they showed him an old white-haired man who lay in a troubled sleep. Parzival wondered still more, but did not venture to ask who it might be. Next the servants took him to an apartment where he could spend the night. The tapestry hangings of this room were all embroidered with gorgeous pictures. Among them the young hero noticed one in particular, because it represented his host borne down to the ground by a spear thrust into his bleeding side. Parzival's curiosity was even greater than before; but, scorning to ask a servant what he had not ventured to demand of the master, he went quietly to bed, thinking that he would try to secure an explanation on the morrow.

When he awoke he found himself alone. No servant answered his call. All the doors were fastened except those which led outside, where he found his steed awaiting him. When he had passed the drawbridge it rose up slowly behind him, and a voice called out from the tower, "Thou art accursed; for thou hadst been chosen to do a great work, which thou hast left undone!" Then looking upward, Parzival saw a horrible face gazing after him with a fiendish grin, and making a gesture as of malediction.

At the end of that day's journey, Parzival came to a lonely cell in the desert, where he found Sigune weeping over a shrine in which lay Tchionatulander's embalmed remains. She too received him with curses, and revealed to him that by one sympathetic question only he might have ended Amfortas's prolonged pain, broken an evil spell, and won for himself a glorious crown.

Horrified, now that he knew what harm he had done, Parzival rode away, feeling as if he were indeed accursed. His greatest wish was to return to the mysterious castle and atone for his remissness by asking the question which would release the king from further pain. But alas! the castle had vanished; and our hero was forced to journey from place to place, seeking diligently, and meeting with many adventures on the way.

At times the longing to give up the quest and return home to his young wife was almost unendurable. His thoughts were ever with her, and the poem relates that even a drop of blood fallen on the snow reminded, him most vividly of the dazzling complexion of Conduiramour, and of her sorrow when he departed.

> "'Conduiramour, thine image is
> Here in the snow now dyed with red
> And in the blood on snowy bed.
> Conduiramour, to them compare
> Thy forms of grace and beauty rare.'"
> WOLFRAM VON ESCHENBACH, *Parzival* (Dippold's tr.).

Although exposed to countless temptations, Parzival remained true to his wife as he rode from place to place, constantly seeking the Holy Grail. His oft-reiterated questions concerning it caused him to be considered a madman or a fool by all he met.

In the course of his journeys, he encountered a lady in chains, led by a knight who seemed to take pleasure in torturing her. Taught by Gurnemanz to rescue all ladies in distress, Parzival challenged and defeated this knight. Then only did he discover that it was Sir Orilus, who had led his wife about in chains to punish her for accepting a kiss from a strange youth. Of course Parzival now hastened to give an explanation of the whole affair, and the defeated knight, at his request, promised to treat his wife with all kindness in future.

As Parzival had ordered all the knights whom he had defeated to journey immediately to Arthur's court and tender him their services, the king had won many brave warriors. He was so pleased by these constant arrivals, and so delighted at the repeated accounts of Parzival's valor, that he became very anxious to see him once more.

To gratify this wish several knights were sent in search of the wanderer, and when they finally found him they bade him come to court. Parzival obeyed, was knighted by Arthur's own hand, and, according to some accounts, occupied the "Siege Perilous" at the Round Table. Other versions state, however, that just as he was about to take this seat the witch Kundrie, a messenger of the Holy Grail, appeared in the hall. She vehemently denounced him, related how sorely he had failed in his duty, and cursed him, as the gate keeper had done, for his lack of sympathy. Thus reminded of his dereliction, Parzival immediately left the hall, to renew the quest which had already lasted for many months. He was closely followed by Gawain, one of Arthur's knights, who thought that Parzival had been too harshly dealt with.

Four years now elapsed,—four years of penance and suffering for Parzival, and of brilliant fighting and thrilling adventures for Gawain. Seeking Parzival, meeting many whom he had helped or defeated, Gawain journeyed from land to land, until at last he decided that his quest would end sooner if he too sought the Holy Grail, the goal of all his friend's hopes.

On the way to Montsalvatch Gawain met a beautiful woman, to whom he made a declaration of love; but she merely answered that those who loved her must serve her, and bade him fetch her palfrey from a neighboring garden. The gardener told him that this lady was the Duchess Orgueilleuse; that her beauty had fired many a knight; that many had died for her sake; and that Amfortas, King of the Holy Grail, had braved the poisoned spear which wounded him, only to win her favor. Gawain, undeterred by this warning, brought out the lady's palfrey, helped her to mount, and followed her submissively through many lands. Everywhere they went the proud lady stirred up some quarrel, and always called upon Gawain to fight the enemies whom she had thus wantonly made. After much wandering, Gawain and his ladylove reached the top of a hill, whence they could look across a valley to a gigantic castle, perched on a rock, near which was a pine tree. Orgueilleuse now informed Gawain that the castle belonged to her mortal enemy, Gramoflaus. She bade him bring her a twig of the tree, and conquer the owner of the castle, who would challenge him as soon as he touched it, and promised that if he obeyed her exactly she would be his faithful wife.

Gawain, emboldened by this promise, dashed down into the valley, swam across the moat, plucked a branch from the tree, and accepted the challenge which Gramoflaus promptly offered. The meeting was appointed for eight days later, in front of Klingsor's castle, whither Gawain immediately proceeded with the Lady Orgueilleuse. On the way she told him that this castle, which faced her father's, was occupied by a magician who kept many noble ladies in close confinement, and had even cruelly laden them with heavy chains.

Gawain, on hearing this, vowed that he would punish the magician; and, having seen Orgueilleuse safely enter her ancestral home, he crossed the river and rode toward Klingsor's castle. As night drew on the windows were brilliantly illumined, and at each one he beheld the pallid, tear-stained faces of some of the captives, whose years ranged from early childhood to withered old age.

Calling for admittance at this castle, Gawain was allowed to enter, but, to his surprise, found hall and court deserted. He wandered from room to room, meeting no one; and, weary of his vain search, prepared at last to occupy a comfortable couch in one of the chambers. To his utter amazement, however, the bed retreated as he advanced, until, impatient at this trickery, he sprang boldly upon it. A moment later a rain of sharp spears and daggers fell upon his couch, but did him no harm, for he had not removed his heavy armor. When the rain of weapons was over, a gigantic peasant, armed with a huge club, stalked into the room, closely followed by a fierce lion. When the peasant perceived that the knight was not dead, as he expected, he beat a hasty retreat, leaving the lion to attack him alone.

In spite of the size and fury of the lion, Gawain defended himself so bravely that he finally slew the beast, which was Klingsor in disguise. As the monster expired the spell was broken, the captives were released, and the exhausted Gawain was tenderly cared for by his mother and sister Itonie, who were among those whom his courage had set free. The news of this victory was immediately sent to Arthur, who now came to witness the battle between Gawain and a champion who was to appear for Gramoflaus.

Gawain's strength and courage were about to give way before the stranger's terrible onslaught, when Itonie implored the latter to spare Gawain, whose name and valor were so well known. At the sound of this name the knight sheathed his sword, and, raising his visor, revealed the sad but beautiful countenance of Parzival.

The joy of reunion over, Parzival remained there long enough to witness the marriage of Gawain and Orgueilleuse, and of Itonie and Gramoflaus, and to be solemnly admitted to the Round Table. Still, the general rejoicing could not dispel his sadness or the recollection of Amfortas and his grievous wound; and as soon as possible Parzival again departed, humbly praying that he might at last find the Holy Grail, and right the wrong he had unconsciously done.

Some months later, exhausted by constant journeys, Parzival painfully dragged himself to a hermit's hut. There he learned that the lonely penitent was Trevrezent, the brother of Amfortas, who, having also preferred worldly pleasures to the service of the Holy Grail, had accompanied him on his fatal excursion. When Trevrezent saw his brother sorely wounded, he repented of his sins, and, retiring into the woods, spent his days and nights in penance and prayer. He told Parzival of the expected stranger, whose question would break the evil spell, and related how grievously he and all the Templars had been disappointed when such a man had actually come and gone, but without fulfilling their hopes. Parzival then penitently confessed that it was he who had thus disappointed them, related his sorrow and ceaseless quest, and told the story of his early youth and adventures. Trevrezent, on hearing his guest's name, exclaimed that they must be uncle and nephew, as his sister's name was Herzeloide. He then informed Parzival of his mother's death, and, after blessing him and giving him some hope that sincere repentance would sometime bring its own reward, allowed him to continue his search for the Holy Grail.

Soon after this meeting Parzival encountered a knight, who, laying lance in rest, challenged him to fight. In one of the pauses of the battle he learned that his brave opponent was his stepbrother, Fierefiss, whom he joyfully embraced, and who now followed him on his almost endless quest. At last they came to a mountain, painfully climbed its steep side, and, after much exertion, found themselves in front of a castle, which seemed strangely familiar to Parzival.

The doors opened, willing squires waited upon both brothers, and led them into the great hall, where the pageant already described was repeated. When Queen Repanse de Joie entered bearing the Holy Grail, Parzival, mindful of his former failure to do the right thing, humbly prayed aloud for divine guidance to bring about the promised redemption. An angel voice now seemed to answer, "Ask!" Then Parzival bent kindly over the wounded king, and gently inquired what ailed him. At those words the spell was broken, and a long cry of joy arose as Amfortas, strong and well, sprang to his feet.

A very aged man, Parzival's great-grandfather, Titurel, now drew near, bearing the crown, which he placed on the young hero's head, as he hailed him as guardian and defender of the Holy Grail. This cry was taken up by all present, and even echoed by the angelic choir.

> "'Hail to thee, Percival, king of the Grail!
> Seemingly lost forever,
> Now thou art blessed forever.
> Hail to thee, Percival, king of the Grail!'"
> WOLFRAM VON ESCHENBACH (McDowall's tr.).

The doors now opened wide once more to admit Conduiramour and her twin sons, summoned thither by the power of the Holy Grail, that Parzival's happiness might be complete. All the witnesses of this happy reunion were flooded with the light of the Holy Grail, except Fierefiss, who, being a Moor and a pagan, still remained in outer darkness. These miracles, however, converted him to the Christian faith, and made him beg for immediate baptism. The christening was no sooner performed than he too beheld and was illumined by the holy vase. Fierefiss, now a true believer, married Repanse de Joie, and they were the parents of a son named John, who became a noted warrior, and was the founder of the historic order of the Knights Templars.

Titurel, having lived to see the recovery of his son, blessed all his descendants, told them that Sigune had joined her lover's spirit in the heavenly abode, and, passing out of the great hall, was never seen again; and the witch Kundrie died of joy.

Another version of the legend of the Holy Grail relates that Parzival, having cured his uncle, went to Arthur's court. There he remained until Amfortas died, when he was called back to Montsalvatch to inherit his possessions, among which was the Holy Grail. Arthur and all the knights of the Round Table were present at his coronation, and paid him a yearly visit. When he died, "the Sangreal, the sacred lance, and the silver trencher or paten which covered the Grail, were carried up to the holy heavens in presence of the attendants, and since that time have never anywhere been seen on earth."

Other versions relate that Arthur and his knights sought the Holy Grail in vain, for their hearts were not pure enough to behold it. Still others declare that the sacred vessel was conveyed to the far East, and committed to the care of Prester John.

ARRIVAL OF LOHENGRIN.—Pixis.

The legend of Lohengrin, which is connected with the Holy Grail, is in outline as follows:

Parzival and Conduiramour dwelt in the castle of the Holy Grail. When their sons had grown to man's estate, Kardeiss, the elder, became ruler of his mother's kingdom of Belripar, while Lohengrin, the younger, remained in the service of the Holy Grail, which was now borne into the hall by his young sister, Aribadale, Repanse de Joie having married.

Whenever a danger threatened, or when the services of one of the knights were required, a silver bell rang loudly, and the letters of flame around the rim of the holy vessel revealed the nature of the deed to be performed. One day the sound of the silvery bell was heard pealing ever louder and louder, and when the knights entered the hall, they read on the vase that Lohengrin had been chosen to defend the rights of an innocent person, and would be conveyed to his destination by a swan. As the knights of the Grail never disputed its commands, the young man immediately donned the armor of silver which Amfortas had worn, and, bidding farewell to his mother and sister, left the temple. Parzival, his father, accompanied him to the foot of the mountain, where, swimming gracefully over the smooth waters of the lake, they saw a snowy swan drawing a little boat after her.

Lohengrin received a horn from his father, who bade him sound it thrice on arriving at his destination, and an equal number of times when he wished to return to Montsalvatch. Then he also reminded him that a servant of the Grail must reveal neither his name nor his origin unless asked to do so, and that, having once made himself known, he was bound to return without delay to the holy mountain.

Thus reminded of the custom of all the Templars, Lohengrin sprang into the boat, and was rapidly borne away, to the sound of mysterious music.

While Lohengrin was swiftly wafted over the waters, Else, Duchess of Brabant, spent her days in tears. She was an orphan, and, as she possessed great wealth and extensive lands, many were anxious to secure her hand. Among these suitors her guardian, Frederick of Telramund, was the most importunate; and when he saw that she would never consent to marry him, he resolved to obtain her inheritance in a different way.

One day, while Else was wandering alone in the forest, she rested for a moment under a tree, where she dreamed that a radiant knight came to greet her, and offered her a little bell, saying that she need but ring it whenever she required a champion. The maiden awoke, and as she opened her eyes a falcon came gently sailing down from the sky and perched upon her shoulder. Seeing that he wore a tiny bell like the one she had noticed in her dream, Else unfastened it; and as the falcon flew away, she hung it on her rosary.

A few days later Else was in prison, for Frederick of Telramund had accused her of a great crime. He said that she had received the attentions of a man beneath her, or, according to another version, that she had been guilty of the murder of her brother. Henry the Fowler, Emperor of Germany, hearing of this accusation, came to Cleves, where, as the witnesses could not agree, he ordered that the matter should be settled by a judicial duel.

Frederick of Telramund, proud of his strength, challenged any man to prove him mistaken at the point of the sword. But no champion appeared to fight for Else, who, kneeling in her cell, beat her breast with her rosary, until the little silver bell attached to it rang loudly as she fervently prayed, "O Lord, send me a champion." The faint tinkling of the bell floated out of the window, and was wafted away to Montsalvatch. It grew louder and louder the farther it traveled, and its sound called the knights into the temple, where Lohengrin received his orders from the Holy Grail.

The day appointed for the duel dawned, and just as the heralds sounded the last call for Else's champion to appear, the swan boat glided up the Rhine, and Lohengrin sprang into the lists, after thrice blowing his magic horn.

With a God-sent champion opposed to a liar, the issue of the combat could not long remain doubtful. Soon Frederick of Telramund lay in the dust and confessed his guilt, while the people hailed the Swan Knight as victor. Else, touched by his prompt response to her appeal, and won by his passionate wooing, then consented to become his wife, without even knowing his name. Their nuptials were celebrated at Antwerp, whither the emperor went with them and witnessed their marriage.

Lohengrin had cautioned Else that she must never ask his name; but she wished to show that he was above the people who, envying his lot, sought to injure him by circulating malicious rumors, so she finally asked the fatal question. Regretfully Lohengrin led her into the great hall, where, in the presence of the assembled knights, he told her that he was Lohengrin, son of Parzival, the guardian of the Holy Grail. Then, embracing her tenderly, he told her that "love cannot live without faith," and that he must now leave her and return to the holy mountain. When he had thrice blown his magic horn, the sound of faint music again heralded the approach of the swan; Lohengrin sprang into the boat, and soon vanished, leaving Else alone.

Some versions of the story relate that she did not long survive his departure, but that her released spirit followed him to Montsalvatch, where they dwelt happy forever. Other accounts, however, aver that when Lohengrin vanished Else's brother returned to champion her cause and prevent her ever being molested again.

CHAPTER XII.

MERLIN.

As Saintsbury so ably expressed it, "The origin of the legends of King Arthur, of the Round Table, of the Holy Grail, and of all the adventures and traditions connected with these centers, is one of the most intricate questions in the history of mediaeval literature." Owing to the loss of many ancient manuscripts, the real origin of all these tales may never be discovered; and whether the legends owe their birth to Celtic, Breton, or Welsh poetry we may never know, as the authorities fail to agree. These tales, apparently almost unknown before the twelfth century, soon became so popular that in the course of the next two centuries they had given birth to more than a dozen poems and prose romances, whence Malory drew the materials for his version of the story of King Arthur. Nennius, Geoffrey of Monmouth, Walter Map, Chrestien de Troyes, Robert de Borron, Gottfried von Strassburg, Wolfram von Eschenbach, Hartmann von Aue, Tennyson, Matthew Arnold, Swinburne, and Wagner have all written of these legends in turn, and to these writers we owe the most noted versions of the tales forming the Arthurian cycle. They include, besides the story of Arthur himself, an account of Merlin, of Lancelot, of Parzival, of the love of Tristan and Iseult, and of the quest of the Holy Grail.

The majority of these works were written in French, which was the court language of England in the mediaeval ages; but the story was "Englished" by Malory in the fourteenth century. In every European language there are versions of these stories, which interested all hearers alike, and which exerted a softening influence upon the rude customs of the age, "communicated a romantic spirit to literature," and taught all men courtesy.

[The Real Merlin] The first of these romances is that of Merlin the enchanter, in very old French, ascribed to Robert de Borron. The following outline of the story is modified and supplemented from other sources. The real Merlin is said to have been a bard of the fifth century, and is supposed to have served the British chief Ambrosius Aurelianus, and then King Arthur. This Merlin lost his reason after the battle of Solway Firth, broke his sword, and retired into the forest, where he was soon after found dead by a river bank.

The mythical Merlin had a more exciting and interesting career, however. King Constans, who drove Hengist from England, was the father of three sons,—Constantine, Aurelius Ambrosius, and Uther Pendragon. When dying he left the throne to his eldest son, Constantine, who chose Vortigern as his prime minister. Shortly after Constantine's accession, Hengist again invaded England, and Constantine, deserted by his minister, was treacherously slain. In reward for his defection at this critical moment, Vortigern was offered the crown, which he accepted, and which he hoped to retain, although Constans's two other sons, who, according to another version of the story, were called Uther and Pendragon, were still in existence.

To defend himself against any army which might try to deprive him of the throne, Vortigern resolved to build a great fortress on the Salisbury plains. But, although the masons worked diligently by day, and built walls wide and thick, they always found them overturned in the morning. The astrologers, when consulted in reference to this strange occurrence, declared that the walls would not stand until the ground had been watered with the blood of a child who could claim no human father.

Five years previous to this prediction, the demons, seeing that so many souls escaped them owing to the redemption procured by a child of divine origin, thought that they could regain lost ground by engendering a demon child upon a human virgin. A beautiful, pious maiden was chosen for this purpose; and as she daily went to confess her every deed and thought to a holy man, Blaise, he soon discovered the plot of the demons, and resolved to frustrate it.

By his advice the girl, instead of being immediately put to death, as the law required, was locked up in a tower, where she gave birth to her son. Blaise, the priest, more watchful than the demons, no sooner heard of the child's birth than he hastened to baptize him, giving him the name of Merlin. The holy rite annulled the evil purpose of the demons, but, owing to his uncanny origin, the child was gifted with all manner of strange powers, of which he made use on sundry occasions.

> "To him
> Great light from God gave sight of all things dim,
> And wisdom of all wondrous things, to say
> What root should bear what fruit of night or day;
> And sovereign speech and counsel above man:
> Wherefore his youth like age was wise and wan,
> And his age sorrowful and fain to sleep."
> SWINBURNE, *Tristram of Lyonesse*.

The child thus baptized soon gave the first proof of his marvelous power; for, when his mother embraced him and declared that she must soon die, he comforted her by speaking aloud and promising to prove her innocent of all crime. The trial took place soon after this occurrence, and although Merlin was but a few days old, he sat up boldly in his mother's lap and spoke so forcibly to the judges that he soon secured her acquittal. Once when he was five years old, while playing in the street, he saw the messengers of Vortigern. Warned by his prophetic instinct that they were seeking him, he ran to meet them, and offered to accompany them to the king. On the way thither he saw a youth buying shoes, and laughed aloud. When questioned concerning the cause of his mirth, he predicted that the youth would die within a few hours.

> "Then said Merlin, 'See ye nought
> That young man, that hath shoon bought,
> And strong leather to do hem clout [patch],
> And grease to smear hem all about?
> He weeneth to live hem to wear:
> But, by my soul, I dare well swear,
> His wretched life he shall for-let [lose],
> Ere he come to his own gate.'"
> ELLIS, *Merlin*.

A few more predictions of an equally uncanny and unpleasant nature firmly established his reputation as a prophet even before he reached court. There he boldly told the king that the astrologers, wishing to destroy the demon's offspring, who was wiser than they, had demanded his blood under pretext that the walls of Salisbury would stand were it only shed. When asked why the walls continually fell during the night, Merlin attributed it to the nightly conflict of a red and a white dragon concealed underground. In obedience to his instructions, search was made for these monsters, and the assembled court soon saw a frightful struggle between them. This battle finally resulted in the death of the red dragon and the triumph of the white.

> "With long tailis, fele [many] fold,
> And found right as Merlin told.
> That one dragon was red as fire,
> With eyen bright, as basin clear;
> His tail was great and nothing small;
> His body was a rood withal.
> His shaft may no man tell;
> He looked as a fiend from hell.
> The white dragon lay him by,
> Stern of look, and griesly.
> His mouth and throat yawned wide;
> The fire brast [burst] out on ilka [each] side.
> His tail was ragged as a fiend,
> And, upon his tail's end,
> There was y-shaped a griesly head,
> To fight with the dragon red."
> ELLIS, *Merlin*.

The white dragon soon disappeared also, and the work of the castle now proceeded without further hindrance. Vortigern, however, was very uneasy, because Merlin had not only said that the struggle of the red and the white dragon represented his coming conflict with Constans's sons, but further added that he would suffer defeat. This prediction was soon fulfilled. Uther and his brother Pendragon landed in Britain with the army they had assembled, and Vortigern was burned in the castle he had just completed.

Shortly after this victory a war arose between the Britons under Uther and Pendragon, and the Saxons under Hengist. Merlin, who had by this time become the prime minister and chief adviser of the

British kings, predicted that they would win the victory, but that one would be slain. This prediction was soon verified, and Uther, adding his brother's name to his own, remained sole king. His first care was to bury his brother, and he implored Merlin to erect a suitable monument to his memory; so the enchanter conveyed great stones from Ireland to England in the course of a single night, and set them up at Stonehenge, where they can still be seen.

> "How Merlin by his skill, and magic's wondrous might,
> From Ireland hither brought the Stonendge in a night."
> DRAYTON, *Polyolbion*.

Proceeding now to Carduel (Carlisle), Merlin, who is represented as a great architect and wonder-worker, built Uther Pendragon a beautiful castle, and established the Round Table, in imitation of the one which Joseph of Arimathea had once instituted. There were places for a large number of knights around this board (the number varying greatly with different writers), and a special place was reserved for the Holy Grail, which, having vanished from Britain because of the sinfulness of the people, the knights still hoped to have restored when they became sufficiently pure.

> "This table gan [began] Uther the wight;
> Ac [but] it to ende had he no might.
> For, theygh [though] alle the kinges under our lord
> Hadde y-sitten [sat] at that bord,
> Knight by knight, ich you telle,
> The table might nought fulfille,
> Till they were born that should do all
> Fulfill the mervaile of the Greal."
> ELLIS, *Merlin*.

A great festival was announced for the institution of the Round Table, and all the knights came to Carduel, accompanied by their wives. Among the latter the fairest was Yguerne, wife of Gorlois, Lord of Tintagel in Cornwall, and with her Uther fell desperately in love.

"This fest was noble ynow, and nobliche y-do [done];
For mony was the faire ledy, that y-come was thereto.
Yguerne, Gorloys wyf, was fairest of echon [each one],
That was contasse of Cornewail, for so fair was there non."
ROBERT OF GLOUCESTER.

Yguerne had already three or four daughters, famous in the Arthurian legends as mothers of the knights Gawain, Gravain, Ywain, and others. One of the king's councilors, Ulfin, revealed the king's passion to Yguerne, and she told her husband. Indignant at the insult offered him, Gorlois promptly left court, locked his wife up in the impregnable fortress of Tintagel, and, gathering together an army, began to fight against Uther Pendragon.

The day before the battle, Merlin changed Uther into the form of Gorlois, and himself and Ulfin into those of the squires of the Duke of Cornwall. Thus disguised, the three went to Tintagel, where Yguerne threw the gates open at their call and received Uther as her husband, without suspecting the deception practiced upon her.

On the morrow the battle took place. Gorlois was slain. Shortly after, Uther married Yguerne, who never suspected that the child which was soon born, and which Uther immediately confided to Merlin, was not a son of Gorlois. Arthur, the child who had thus come into the world, was intrusted to the care of Sir Hector, who brought him up with his own son, Sir Kay, little suspecting his royal descent. This child grew up rapidly, and when but fifteen years of age was handsome, accomplished, and dearly loved by all around him.

"He was fair, and well agré [agreeable],
And was a thild [child] of gret noblay.
He was curteys, faire and gent,
And wight [brave], and hardi, veramen [truly].
Curteyslich [courteously] and fair he spac [spake].
With him was none evil lack [fault]."
ELLIS, *Merlin*.

When Uther died without leaving any heir, there was an interregnum, for Merlin had promised that the true king should be revealed by a miracle. This prophecy was duly fulfilled, as will be shown hereafter. Merlin became the royal adviser as soon as Arthur ascended the throne,

THE BEGUILING OF MERLIN.—Burne-Jones.

helped him win signal victories over twelve kings, and in the course of a single night conveyed armies over from France to help him.

As Merlin could assume any shape he pleased, Arthur often used him as messenger; and one of the romances relates that the magician, in the guise of a stag, once went to Rome to bear the king's challenge to Julius Caesar (not the conqueror of Gaul but the mythical father of Oberon) to single combat. Merlin was also renowned for the good advice which he gave, not only to Vortigern and Uther Pendragon, but also to Arthur, and for his numerous predictions concerning the glorious future of England, all of which, if we are to believe tradition, have been fulfilled.

> "O goodly River! near unto thy sacred spring
> Prophetic Merlin sate, when to the British King
> The changes long to come, auspiciously he told."
> DRAYTON, *Polyolbion*.

Merlin also won great renown as a builder and architect. Besides the construction of Stonehenge, and of the castle for Uther Pendragon, he is said to have built Arthur's beautiful palace at Camelot. He also devised sundry magic fountains, which are mentioned in other mediaeval romances. One of these is referred to by Spenser in the "Faerie Queene," and another by Ariosto in his "Orlando Furioso."

> "This Spring was one of those four fountains rare,
> Of those in France produced by Merlin's sleight,
> Encompassed round about with marble fair,
> Shining and polished, and than milk more white.
> There in the stones choice figures chiseled were,
> By that magician's god-like labour dight;
> Some voice was wanting, these you might have thought
> Were living, and with nerve and spirit fraught."
> ARIOSTO, *Orlando Furioso* (Rose's tr.).

Merlin was also supposed to have made all kinds of magic objects, among which the poets often mention a cup. This would, reveal whether the drinker had led a pure life, for it always overflowed when touched by polluted lips. He was also the artificer of Arthur's armor, which no weapon could pierce, and of a magic mirror in which one could see whatever one wished.

> "It Merlin was, which whylome did excel
> All living wightes in might of magicke spell:
> Both shield, and sword, and armour all he wrought
> For this young Prince, when first to armes he fell."
> SPENSER, *Faerie Queene.*

Merlin, in spite of all his knowledge and skill, yielded often to the entreaties of his fair mistress, Vivian, the Lady of the Lake. She followed him wherever he went, and made countless efforts to learn all his arts and to discover all his magic spells. In order to beguile the aged Merlin into telling her all she wished to know, Vivian pretended great devotion, which is admirably related in Tennyson's "Idylls of the King," one of which treats exclusively of Merlin and Vivian.

This enchantress even went with him to the fairy-haunted forest of Broceliande, in Brittany, where she finally beguiled him into revealing a magic spell whereby a human being could be inclosed in a hawthorn tree, where he must dwell forever.

> "And then she follow'd Merlin all the way,
> E'en to the wild woods of Broceliande.
> For Merlin once had told her of a charm,
> The which if any wrought on any one
> With woven paces and with waving arms,
> The man so wrought on ever seem'd to lie
> Closed in the four walls of a hollow tower,
> From which was no escape for evermore;
> And none could find that man for evermore,
> Nor could he see but him who wrought the charm
> Coming and going; and he lay as dead
> And lost to life and use and name and fame."
> TENNYSON, *Merlin and Vivien.*

This charm having been duly revealed, the Lady of the Lake, weary of her aged lover, and wishing to rid herself of him forever now that she had learned all he could teach her, lured him into the depths of the forest. There, by aid of the spell, she imprisoned him in a thorn bush, whence, if the tales of the Breton peasants can be believed, his voice can be heard to issue from time to time.

"They sate them down together, and a sleep
Fell upon Merlin, more like death, so deep.
Her finger on her lips, then Vivian rose,
And from her brown-lock'd head the wimple throws,
And takes it in her hand, and waves it over
The blossom'd thorn tree and her sleeping lover.
Nine times she waved the fluttering wimple round,
And made a little plot of magic ground.
And in that daised circle, as men say,
Is Merlin prisoner till the judgment day;
But she herself whither she will can rove—
For she was passing weary of his love."
MATTHEW ARNOLD, Tristram and Iseult.

According to another version of the tale, Merlin, having grown very old indeed, once sat down on the "Siege Perilous," forgetting that none but a sinless man could occupy it with impunity. He was immediately swallowed up by the earth, which yawned wide beneath his feet, and he never visited the earth again.

A third version says that Vivian through love imprisoned Merlin in an underground palace, where she alone could visit him. There he dwells, unchanged by the flight of time, and daily increasing the store of knowledge for which he was noted.

CHAPTER XIII.

THE ROUND TABLE.

Fortunately "the question of the actual existence and acts of Arthur has very little to do with the question of the origin of the Arthurian cycle." But although some authorities entirely deny his existence, it is probable that he was a Briton, for many places in Wales, Scotland, and England are connected with his name.

On the very slightest basis, many of the mediaeval writers constructed long and fabulous tales about this hero. Such was the popularity of the Arthurian legends all over Europe that prose romances concerning him were among the first works printed, and were thus brought into general circulation. An outline of the principal adventures of Arthur and of his knights is given here. It has been taken from many works, whose authors will often be mentioned as we proceed.

King Uther Pendragon, as we have already seen, intrusted his new-born son, Arthur, to the care of the enchanter Merlin, who carried him to the castle of Sir Hector (Anton), where the young prince was brought up as a child of the house.

> "Wherefore Merlin took the child,
> And gave him to Sir Anton, an old knight
> And ancient friend of Uther; and his wife
> Nursed the young prince, and rear'd him with her own;
> And no man knew."
> TENNYSON, *The Coming of Arthur.*

Two years later King Uther Pendragon died, and the noblemen, not knowing whom to choose as his successor, consulted Merlin, promising to abide by his decision. By his advice they all assembled in St. Stephen's Church, in London, on Christmas Day. When mass was over they beheld a large stone which had mysteriously appeared in the churchyard. This stone was surmounted by a ponderous anvil, in which the blade of a sword was deeply sunk. Drawing near to examine the wonder, they read an inscription upon the jeweled hilt, to the effect that none but the man who could draw out the sword should dare to take possession of the throne. Of course all present immediately tried to accomplish this feat, but all failed.

Several years passed by ere Sir Hector came to London with his son, Sir Kay, and his foster son, young Arthur. Sir Kay, who, for the first time in his life, was to take part in a tournament, was greatly chagrined, on arriving there, to discover that he had forgotten his sword; so Arthur volunteered to ride back and get it. He found the house closed; yet, being determined to secure a sword for his foster brother, he strode hastily into the churchyard, and easily drew from the anvil the weapon which all had vainly tried to secure.

This mysterious sword was handed to Sir Kay, and Sir Hector, perceiving it, and knowing whence it came, immediately inquired how Arthur had secured it. He even refused at first to believe the evidence of his own eyes; but when he and all the principal nobles of the realm had seen Arthur replace and draw out the sword, after all had again vainly tried their strength, they gladly hailed the young man king.

As Merlin was an enchanter, it was popularly rumored that Arthur was not, as he now declared, the son of Uther Pendragon and Yguerne, but a babe mysteriously brought up from the depths of the sea, on the crest of the ninth wave, and cast ashore at the wizard's feet. Hence many people distrusted the young king, and at first refused to obey him.

> "Watch'd the great sea fall,
> Wave after wave, each mightier than the last,
> Till last, a ninth one, gathering half the deep,
> And full of voices, slowly rose and plunged
> Roaring, and all the wave was in a flame:
> And down the wave and in the flame was borne
> A naked babe, and rode to Merlin's feet,
> Who stoopt and caught the babe, and cried 'The King!
> Here is an heir for Uther!'"
>
> TENNYSON, *The Coming of Arthur.*

Among the unbelievers were some of the king's own kindred, and notably his four nephews, Gawain, Gaheris, Agravaine, and Gareth. Arthur was therefore obliged to make war against them; but although Gawain's strength increased in a truly marvelous fashion from nine to twelve in the morning, and from three to six in the afternoon, the king succeeded in defeating him by following Merlin's advice and taking advantage of his comparatively weak moments.

Arthur, aided by Merlin, ruled over the land wisely and well, redressed many wrongs, reëstablished order and security, which a long interregnum had destroyed, and brandished his sword in many a fight, in which he invariably proved victor. But one day, having drawn his blade upon Sir Pellinore, who did not deserve to be thus attacked, it suddenly failed him and broke. Left thus without any means of defense, the king would surely have perished had not Merlin used his magic arts to put Sir Pellinore to sleep and to bear his charge to a place of safety.

Arthur, thus deprived of his magic sword, bewailed its loss; but while he stood by a lake, wondering how he should procure another, he beheld a white-draped hand and arm rise out of the water, holding aloft a jeweled sword which the Lady of the Lake, who appeared beside him, told him was intended for his use.

> "'Thou rememberest how
> In those old days, one summer noon, an arm
> Rose up from out the bosom of the lake,
> Clothed in white samite, mystic, wonderful,
> Holding the sword—and how I row'd across
> And took it, and have worn it, like a king;
> And, wheresoever I am sung or told
> In aftertime, this also shall be known.'"
> TENNYSON, *The Passing of Arthur.*

Arthur rowed out into the middle of the lake and secured the sword which is known by the name Excalibur. He was then told by the Lady of the Lake that it was gifted with magic powers, and that as long as the scabbard remained in his possession he would suffer neither wound nor defeat.

Thus armed, Arthur went back to his palace, where, hearing that the Saxons had again invaded the country, he went to wage war against them, and won many victories. Shortly after this Arthur heard that Leodegraunce, King of Scotland, was threatened by his brother Ryance, King of Ireland, who was determined to complete a mantle furred with the beards of kings, and wanted to secure one more at any price. Arthur hastened to this monarch's assistance, and delivered him from the clutches of Ryance. He not only killed this savage monarch, but appropriated his mantle and carried it away in triumph as a trophy of the war.

> "And for a trophy brought the Giant's coat away
> Made of the beards of Kings."
> DRAYTON, *Polyolbion.*

After these martial exploits Arthur returned to the court of Leodegraunce, where he fell in love with the latter's fair daughter, Guinevere. The king sued successfully for her hand, but Merlin would not allow him to marry this princess until he had distinguished himself by a campaign in Brittany. The wedding was then celebrated with true mediaeval pomp; and Arthur, having received, besides the princess, the Round Table once made for his father, conveyed his bride and wedding gift to Camelot (Winchester), where he bade all his court be present for a great feast at Pentecost.

> "The nearest neighboring flood to Arthur's ancient seat,
> Which made the Britons' name through all the world so great.
> Like Camelot, what place was ever yet renown'd?
> Where, as at Carlion, oft, he kept the Table-Round,
> Most famous for the sports at Pentecost so long,
> From whence all knightly deeds, and brave achievements sprong."
> DRAYTON,—*Polyolbion.*

Arthur had already warred successfully against twelve revolted kings, whose remains were interred at Camelot by his order. There Merlin erected a marvelous castle, containing a special hall for the reception of the Round Table. This hall was adorned with the lifelike statues of all the conquered kings, each holding a burning taper which the magician declared would burn brightly until the Holy Grail should appear. Hoping to bring that desirable event to pass, Arthur bade Merlin frame laws for the knights of the Round Table. As distinctive mark, each of the noblemen admitted to a seat at this marvelous table adopted some heraldic device. The number of these knights varies from twelve to several hundred, according to the different poets or romancers.

> "The fellowshipp of the Table Round,
> Soe famous in those dayes;
> Whereatt a hundred noble knights
> And thirty sat alwayes;
> Who for their deeds and martiall feates,
> As bookes done yett record,
> Amongst all other nations
> Wer feared through the world."
>
> *Legend of King Arthur* (Old Ballad).

Merlin, by virtue of his magic powers, easily selected the knights worthy to belong to this noble institution, and the Archbishop of Canterbury duly blessed them and the board around which they sat. All the places were soon filled except two; and as the knights arose from their seats after the first meal they noticed that their names were inscribed in letters of gold in the places they had occupied. But one of the empty seats was marked "Siege Perilous," and could only be occupied by a peerless knight.

Among all the knights of the Round Table, Sir Lancelot du Lac, who is the hero of several lengthy poems and romances bearing his name, was the most popular. Chrestien de Troyes, Geoffrey de Ligny, Robert de Borron, and Map have all written about him, and he was so well known that his name was given to one of the knaves on the playing cards invented at about this time. Malory, in his prose version of the "Morte d'Arthur," has drawn principally from the poems treating of Lancelot, whose early life was somewhat extraordinary, too.

Some accounts relate that Lancelot was the son of King Ban and Helen. When he was but a babe, his parents were obliged to flee from their besieged castle in Brittany. Before they had gone far, the aged Ban, seeing his home in flames, sank dying to the ground. Helen, eager to minister to her husband, laid her baby boy down on

SIR LANCELOT DU LAC.—Sir John Gilbert.

the grass near a lake, and when she again turned around, she saw him in the arms of Vivian, the Lady of the Lake, who plunged with him into the waters.

> "In the wife's woe, the mother was forgot.
> At last (for I was all earth held of him
> Who had been all to her, and now was not)
> She rose, and looked with tearless eyes, but dim,
> In the babe's face the father still to see;
> And lo! the babe was on another's knee!
>
> "Another's lips had kissed it into sleep,
> And o'er the sleep another watchful smiled;
> The Fairy sate beside the lake's still deep,
> And hush'd with chaunted charms the orphan child!
> Scared at the mother's cry, as fleets a dream,
> Both Child and Fairy melt into the stream."
> BULWER LYTTON, *King Arthur.*

The bereaved wife and mother now sorrowfully withdrew into a convent, while Lancelot was brought up in the palace of the Lady of the Lake, with his two cousins, Lyonel and Bohort. Here he remained until he was eighteen, when the fairy herself brought him to court and presented him to the king. Arthur then and there made him his friend and confidant, and gave him an honored place at the Round Table. He was warmly welcomed by all the other knights also, whom he far excelled in beauty and courage.

> "But one Sir Lancelot du Lake,
> Who was approved well,
> He for his deeds and feats of armes
> All others did excell."
> *Sir Lancelot du Lake* (Old Ballad).

Lancelot, however, was doomed to much sorrow, for he had no sooner beheld Queen Guinevere than he fell deeply in love with her. The queen fully returned his affection, granted him many marks of her favor, and encouraged him to betray his friend and king on sundry occasions, which form the themes of various episodes in the romances of the time. Lancelot, urged in one direction by passion, in another by loyalty, led a very unhappy life, which made him relapse into occasional fits of insanity, during which he roamed aimlessly about for many years. When restored to his senses, he always returned to court, where he accomplished unheard-of deeds of valor, delivered many maidens in distress, righted the wrong wherever he found it, won all the honors at the tournaments, and ever remained faithful in his devotion to the queen, although many fair ladies tried to make him forget her.

Some of the poems, anxious to vindicate the queen, declare that there were two Guineveres, one pure, lovely, and worthy of all admiration, who suffered for the sins of the other, an unprincipled woman. When Arthur discovered his wife's intrigue with Lancelot, he sent her away, and Guinevere took refuge with her lover in Joyeuse Garde (Berwick), a castle he had won at the point of his lance to please her. But the king, having ascertained some time after that the real Guinevere had been wrongfully accused, reinstated her in his favor, and Lancelot again returned to court, where he continued to love and serve the queen.

On one occasion, hearing that she had been made captive by Meleagans, Lancelot rushed after Guinevere to rescue her, tracing her by a comb and ringlet she had dropped on the way. His horse was taken from him by enchantment, so Lancelot, in order sooner to overtake the queen, rode on in a cart. This was considered a disgraceful mode of progress for a knight, as a nobleman in those days was condemned to ride in a cart in punishment for crimes for which common people were sentenced to the pillory.

Lancelot succeeded in reaching the castle of Guinevere's kidnaper, whom he challenged and defeated. The queen, instead of showing herself grateful for this devotion, soon became needlessly jealous, and in a fit of anger taunted her lover about his journey in the cart. This remark sufficed to unsettle the hero's evidently very tottering reason, and he roamed wildly about until the queen recognized her error, and sent twenty-three knights in search of him. They journeyed far and wide for two whole years without finding him.

> "Then Sir Bors had ridden on
> Softly, and sorrowing for our Lancelot,
> Because his former madness, once the talk

> And scandal of our table, had return'd;
> For Lancelot's kith and kin so worship him
> That ill to him is ill to them.'"
>
> TENNYSON, *The Holy Grail.*

Finally a fair and pious damsel took pity upon the frenzied knight, and seeing that he had atoned by suffering for all his sins, she had him borne into the chamber where the Holy Grail was kept; "and then there came a holy man, who uncovered the vessel, and so by miracle, and by virtue of that holy vessel, Sir Lancelot was all healed and recovered."

Sane once more, Lancelot now returned to Camelot, where the king, queen, and all the knights of the Round Table rejoiced to see him. Here Lancelot knighted Sir Gareth, who, to please his mother, had concealed his true name, and had acted as kitchen vassal for a whole year. The new-made knight immediately started out with a fair maiden called Lynette, to deliver her captive sister. Thinking him nothing but the kitchen vassal he seemed, the damsel insulted Gareth in every possible way. He bravely endured her taunts, courageously defeated all her adversaries, and finally won her admiration and respect to such a degree that she bade him ride beside her, and humbly asked his pardon for having so grievously misjudged him.

> "'Sir,—and, good faith, I fain had added Knight,
> But that I heard thee call thyself a knave,—
> Shamed am I that I so rebuked, reviled,
> Missaid thee; noble I am; and thought the King
> Scorn'd me and mine; and now thy pardon, friend,
> For thou hast ever answer'd courteously,
> And wholly bold thou art, and meek withal
> As any of Arthur's best, but, being knave,
> Hast mazed my wit: I marvel what thou art.'"
>
> TENNYSON, *Gareth and Lynette.*

Granting her full forgiveness, Gareth now rode beside her, fought more bravely still, and, after defeating many knights, delivered her sister from captivity, and secured Lynette's promise to become his wife as soon as he had been admitted to the Round Table. When he returned to Arthur's court this honor was immediately awarded him, for his prowess had won the admiration of all, and he was duly married on St. Michaelmas Day.

> "And he that told the tale in older times
> Says that Sir Gareth wedded Lyoners,
> But he that told it later, says Lynette."
>> TENNYSON, *Gareth and Lynette.*

Gareth's brother, Geraint, was also an honored member of the Round Table. After distinguishing himself by many deeds of valor he married Enid the Fair, the only daughter of an old and impoverished knight whom he delivered from the tyranny of his oppressor and restored to all his former state. Taking his fair wife away with him to his lonely manor, Geraint surrounded her with every comfort, and, forgetting his former high aspirations, spent all his time at home, hoping thereby to please her.

> "He compass'd her with sweet observances
> And worship, never leaving her, and grew
> Forgetful of his promise to the King.
> Forgetful of the falcon and the hunt,
> Forgetful of the tilt and tournament,
> Forgetful of his glory and his name,
> Forgetful of his princedom and its cares.
> And this forgetfulness was hateful to her."
>> TENNYSON, *Geraint and Enid.*

Enid, however, soon perceived that her husband was forgetting both honor and duty to linger by her side. One day, while he lay asleep before her, she, in an outburst of wifely love, poured out her heart, and ended her confession by declaring that since Geraint neglected everything for her sake only, she must be an unworthy wife.

Geraint awoke too late to overhear the first part of her speech; but, seeing her tears, and catching the words "unworthy wife," he immediately imagined that she had ceased to love him, and that she received the attentions of another. In his anger Geraint (whom the French and German poems call Erec) rose from his couch, and sternly bade his wife don her meanest apparel and silently follow him through the world.

"The page he bade with speed
Prepare his own strong steed,
Dame Enid's palfrey there beside;
He said that he would ride
For pastime far away:
So forward hastened they."
　　　　HARTMANN VON AVE, *Erek and Enid* (Bayard Taylor's tr.)

Patiently Enid did her husband's bidding, watched him fight the knights by the way, and bound up his wounds. She suffered intensely from his incomprehensible coldness and displeasure; but she stood all his tests so nobly that he finally recognized how greatly he had misjudged her. He then restored her to her rightful place, and loved her more dearly than ever before.

"Nor did he doubt her more,
But rested in her fealty, till he crown'd
A happy life with a fair death, and fell
Against the heathen of the Northern Sea
In battle, fighting for the blameless King."
　　　　TENNYSON,—*Geraint and Enid.*

One Pentecost Day, when all the knights were assembled, as usual, around the table at Camelot, a distressed damsel suddenly entered the hall and implored Lancelot to accompany her to the neighboring forest, where a young warrior was hoping to receive knighthood at his hands. This youth was Sir Galahad, the peerless knight, whom some authorities call Lancelot's son, while others declare that he was not of mortal birth.

On reëntering the hall after performing this ceremony, Lancelot heard that a miracle had occurred, and rushed with the king and his companions down to the riverside. There the rumor was verified, for they all saw a heavy stone floating down the stream, and perceived that a costly weapon was sunk deep in the stone. On this weapon was an inscription, declaring that none but a peerless knight should attempt to draw it out, upon penalty of a grievous punishment. As all the knights of the Round Table felt guilty of some sin, they modestly refused to touch it.

When they returned into the hall an aged man came in, accompanied by Galahad, and the latter, fearless by right of innocence, sat down in the "Siege Perilous." As his name then appeared upon it, all knew that he was the rightful occupant, and hailed his advent with joy. Then, noticing that he wore an empty scabbard, and hearing him state that he had been promised a marvelous sword, they one and all escorted him down to the river, where he easily drew the sword out of the stone. This fitted exactly in his empty sheath, and all vowed that it was evidently meant for him.

That selfsame night, after evensong, when all the knights were seated about the Round Table at Camelot, they heard a long roll of thunder, and felt the palace shake. The brilliant lights held by the statues of the twelve conquered kings grew strangely dim, and then, gliding down upon a beam of refulgent celestial light, they all beheld a dazzling vision of the Holy Grail. Covered by white samite, and borne by invisible hands, the sacred vessel was slowly carried all around the great hall, while a delicious perfume was wafted throughout the huge edifice. All the knights of the Round Table gazed in silent awe at this resplendent vision, and when it vanished as suddenly and as mysteriously as it had come, each saw before him the food which he liked best.

Speechless at first, and motionless until the wonted light again illumined the hall, the knights gave fervent thanks for the mercy which had been vouchsafed them, and then Lancelot, springing impetuously to his feet, vowed that he would ride forth in search of the Holy Grail and would know no rest until he had beheld it unveiled. This vow was echoed by all the knights of the Round Table; and when Arthur now questioned them closely, he discovered that none had seen the vessel unveiled. Still he could not prevent his knights from setting out in quest of it, because they had solemnly vowed to do so.

> "'Nay, lord, I heard the sound, I saw the light,
> But since I did not see the Holy Thing,
> I sware a vow to follow it till I saw.'
> "Then when he ask'd us, knight by knight, if any
> Had seen it, all their answers were as one:
> 'Nay, lord, and therefore have we sworn our vows.'"
> TENNYSON, *The Holy Grail.*

During this quest the knights traveled separately or in pairs all through the world, encountered many dangers, and in true mediaeval fashion defended damsels in distress, challenged knights, and covered themselves with scars and glory. Some of the legends declare that

Parzival alone saw the Holy Grail, while others aver that Lancelot saw it through a veil faintly. The pure Galahad, having never sinned at all, and having spent years in prayer and fasting, finally beheld it just as his immaculate soul was borne to heaven by the angels.

The rest of the knights, realizing after many years' fruitless search that they were unworthy of the boon, finally returned to Camelot, where they were duly entertained by the queen. While they were feasting at her table, one of their number, having partaken of a poisonous draught, fell lifeless to the ground. As the incident had happened at the queen's side, some of her detractors accused her of the crime, and bade her confess, or prove her innocence by a judicial duel. Being her husband, Arthur was debarred by law of the privilege of fighting for her in the lists of Camelot, and the poor queen would have been condemned to be burned alive for lack of a champion had not Lancelot appeared incognito, and forced her accuser to retract his words.

Throughout his reign Arthur had been wont to encourage his knights by yearly tournaments, the victor's prize being each time a precious jewel. It seems that these jewels had come into his possession in a peculiar way. While wandering as a lad in Lyonesse, Arthur found the moldering bones of two kings. Tradition related that these monarchs had slain each other, and, as they were brothers, the murder seemed so heinous that none dared touch their remains. There among the rusty armor lay a kingly crown studded with diamonds, which Arthur picked up and carelessly set upon his own head. At that very moment a prophetic voice was heard declaring to him that he should rule. Arthur kept the crown, and made each jewel set in it the object of a brilliant pageant when the prophecy had been fulfilled.

> "And Arthur came, and laboring up the pass,
> All in a misty moonshine, unawares
> Had trodden that crown'd skeleton, and the skull
> Brake from the nape, and from the skull the crown
> Roll'd into light, and turning on its rims
> Fled like a glittering rivulet to the tarn.
> And down the shingly scaur he plunged, and caught,
> And set it on his head, and in his heart
> Heard murmurs,—'Lo! thou likewise shalt be King.'"
> TENNYSON, *Lancelot and Elaine.*

ELAINE—Rosenthal.

Lancelot had been present at every one of these knightly games, and had easily borne away the prize, for his very name was almost enough to secure him the victory. When the time for the last tournament came, he pretended to take no interest in it; but, riding off to Astolat (Guildford), he asked Elaine, the fair maiden who dwelt there, to guard his blazoned shield and give him another in exchange.

This fair lady, who had fallen in love with Lancelot at first sight, immediately complied with his request, and even timidly suggested that he should wear her colors in the coming fray. Lancelot had never worn any favors except Guinevere's, but thinking that it would help to conceal his identity, he accepted the crimson, pearl-embroidered sleeve she offered, and fastened it to his helmet in the usual way.

> "'Lady, thy sleeve thou shalt off-shear,
> I wol it take for the love of thee;
> So did I never no lady's ere [before]
> But one, that most hath loved me.'"
> ELLIS, *Lancelot du Lac.*

Thus effectually disguised, and accompanied by Sir Lawaine, Elaine's brother, Lancelot rode on to the tournament, where, still unknown, he unhorsed every knight and won the prize. His last encounter, however, nearly proved fatal, for in it he received a grievous wound. As he felt faint, and was afraid to be recognized, Lancelot did not wait to claim the prize, but rode immediately out of the town. He soon fainted, but was conveyed to the cell of a neighboring hermit. Here his wound was dressed, and he was carefully nursed by Elaine, who had heard that he was wounded, and had immediately set out in search of him.

When Lancelot, entirely recovered, was about to leave Elaine after claiming his own shield, she timidly confessed her love, hoping that it was returned. Gently and sorrowfully Lancelot repulsed her, and, by her father's advice, was even so discourteous as to leave her without a special farewell. Unrequited love soon proved too much for the "lily maid of Astolat," who pined away very rapidly. Feeling that her end was near, she dictated a farewell letter to Lancelot, which she made her father promise to put in her dead hand. She also directed that her body should be laid in state on a barge, and sent in charge of a mute boatman to Camelot, where she was sure she would receive a suitable burial from the hands of Lancelot.

In the meanwhile the hero of the tournament had been sought everywhere by Gawain, who was the bearer of the diamond won at such a cost. Coming to Astolat before Lancelot was cured, Gawain had learned the name of the victor, which he immediately proclaimed to Guinevere. The queen, however, hearing a vague rumor that Lancelot had worn the colors of the maiden of Astolat, and was about to marry her, grew so jealous that when Lancelot reappeared at court she received him very coldly, and carelessly flung his present (a necklace studded with the diamonds he had won at various tournaments) into the river flowing beneath the castle walls.

> "She seized,
> And, thro' the casement standing wide for heat,
> Flung them, and down they flash'd, and smote the stream.
> Then from the smitten surface flash'd, as it were,
> Diamonds to meet them, and they passed away."
> TENNYSON, *Lancelot and Elaine.*

As he leaned out of the window to trace them in their fall, Lancelot saw a barge slowly drifting down the stream. Its peculiar appearance attracted his attention, and as it passed close by him he saw that it bore a corpse. A moment later he had recognized the features of the dead Elaine. The mute boatman paused at the castle steps, and Arthur had the corpse borne into his presence. The letter was found and read aloud in the midst of the awestruck court. Arthur, touched by the girl's love, bade Lancelot fulfill her last request and lay her to rest. Lancelot then related the brief story of the maiden, whose love he could not return, but whose death he sincerely mourned.

> "'My lord liege Arthur, and all ye that hear,
> Know that for this most gentle maiden's death
> Right heavy am I; for good she was and true,
> But loved me with a love beyond all love
> In women, whomsoever I have known.
> Yet to be loved makes not to love again;
> Not at my years, however it hold in youth.

I swear by truth and knighthood that I gave
No cause, not willingly, for such a love:
To this I call my friends in testimony,
Her brethren, and her father, who himself
Besought me to be plain and blunt, and use,
To break her passion, some discourtesy
Against my nature: what I could, I did.
I left her and I bade her no farewell;
Tho', had I dreamt the damsel would have died,
I might have put my wits to some rough use,
And help'd her from herself.'"
TENNYSON, Lancelot and Elaine.

Haunted by remorse for this involuntary crime, Lancelot again wandered away from Camelot, but returned in time to save Guinevere, who had again been falsely accused. In his indignation at the treatment to which she had been exposed, Lancelot bore her off to Joyeuse Garde, where he swore he would defend her even against the king. Arthur, whose mind, in the mean while, had been poisoned by officious courtiers, besieged his recreant wife and knight; but although repeatedly challenged, the loyal Lancelot ever refused to bear arms directly against his king.

When the Pope heard of the dissension in England he finally interfered; and Lancelot, assured that Guinevere would henceforth be treated with all due respect, surrendered her to the king and retreated to his paternal estate in Brittany. As Arthur's resentment against Lancelot had not yet cooled, he left Guinevere under the care and protection of Mordred, his nephew,—some versions say his son,—and then, at the head of a large force, departed for Brittany.

Mordred the traitor immediately took advantage of his uncle's absence to lay claim to the throne; and loudly declaring that Arthur had been slain, he tried to force Guinevere to marry him. As she demurred, he kept her a close prisoner, and set her free only when she pretended to agree with his wishes, and asked permission to go to London to buy wedding finery.

When Guinevere arrived in that city she intrenched herself

in the Tower, and sent word to her husband of her perilous position. Without any delay Arthur abandoned the siege of Lancelot's stronghold, and, crossing the channel, encountered Mordred's army near Dover.

Negotiations now took place, and it was finally agreed that Arthur and a certain number of knights should meet Mordred with an equal number, and discuss the terms of peace. It had been strictly enjoined on both parties that no weapon should be drawn, and all would have gone well had not an adder been lurking in the grass. One of the knights drew his sword to kill it, and this unexpected movement proved the signal for one of the bloodiest battles described in mediaeval poetry.

> "An addere crept forth of a bushe,
> Stunge one o' th' king's knightes on the knee.
> Alacke! it was a woefulle chance,
> As ever was in Christientie;
> When the knighte founde him wounded sore,
> And sawe the wild worme hanginge there,
> His sworde he from the scabbarde drewe;
> A piteous case, as ye shall heare;
> For when the two hostes saw the sworde,
> They joyned in battayle instantlye;
> Till of so manye noble knightes,
> On one side there was left but three."
> *King Arthur's Death.*

On both sides the knights fought with the utmost courage, and when nearly all were slain, Arthur encountered the traitor Mordred. Summoning all his strength, the exhausted king finally slew the usurper, who, in dying, dealt Arthur a mortal blow. This would never have occurred, however, had not Morgana the fay, Arthur's sister, purloined his magic scabbard and substituted another. All the enemy's host had perished, and of Arthur's noble army only one man remained alive, Sir Bedivere, a knight of the Round Table. He hastened to the side of his fallen master, who in faltering accents now bade him take the brand Excalibur, cast it far from him into the waters of the lake, and return to report what he should see. The knight, thinking it a pity to throw away so valuable a sword, concealed it twice; but the dying monarch detected the fraud, and finally prevailed upon Bedivere to fulfill his wishes. As the magic blade touched the waters Sir Bedivere saw a hand and arm rise up from the depths to seize it, brandish it thrice, and disappear.

> "'Sir King, I closed mine eyelids, lest the gems
> Should blind my purpose; for I never saw,
> Nor shall see, here or elsewhere, till I die,
> Not tho' I live three lives of mortal men,
> So great a miracle as yonder hilt.
> Then with both hands I flung him, wheeling him;
> But when I look'd again, behold an arm,
> Clothed in white samite, mystic, wonderful,
> That caught him by the hilt, and brandish'd him
> Three times, and drew him under in the mere.'"
>   TENNYSON, *The Passing of Arthur.*

Arthur gave a sigh of relief when he heard this report; and after telling his faithful squire that Merlin had declared that he should not die, he bade the knight lay him in a barge, all hung with black, wherein he would find Morgana the fay, the Queen of Northgallis, and the Queen of the Westerlands.

Sir Bedivere obeyed all these orders exactly; and then, seeing his beloved king about to leave him, he implored permission to accompany him. This, however, Arthur could not grant, for it had been decreed that he should go alone to the island of Avalon, where he hoped to be cured of his grievous wound, and some day to return to his sorrowing people.

> "'But now farewell. I am going a long way
> With these thou seest—if indeed I go
> (For all my mind is clouded with a doubt)—
> To the island-valley of Avilion;
> Where falls not hail, or rain, or any snow,
> Nor ever wind blows loudly; but it lies
> Deep-meadow'd, happy, fair with orchard lawns
> And bowery hollows crown'd with summer sea,
> Where I will heal me of my grievous wound.'"
>   TENNYSON, *The Passing of Arthur.*

It was because Arthur thus disappeared and was never seen again, according to one version of the myth, and because none knew whether he were living or dead, that he was popularly supposed to be enjoying perpetual youth and bliss in the fabled island of Avalon, whence they averred he would return when his people needed him. This belief was so deeply rooted in England that Philip of Spain, upon marrying Mary, was compelled to take a solemn oath whereby he bound himself to relinquish the crown in favor of Arthur should he appear to claim it.

> "Still look the Britons for the day
> Of Arthur's coming o'er the sea."
> LAYAMON, *Brut*.

Other romances and poems relate that Arthur was borne in the sable-hung barge to Glastonbury, where his remains were laid in the tomb, while Guinevere retired into the nunnery at Almesbury. There she was once more visited by the sorrowing Lancelot, who, in spite of all his haste, had come upon the scene too late to save or be reconciled to the king, to whom he was still devotedly attached. In his sorrow and remorse the knight withdrew into a hermitage, where he spent six years in constant penance and prayer. At last he was warned in a vision that Guinevere was no more. He hastened to Almesbury, and found her really dead. After burying her by Arthur's side, in the chapel of Glastonbury, Lancelot again withdrew to his cell. Six weeks later, worn to a shadow by abstinence and night watches, he peacefully passed away, and a priest watching near him said that he had seen the angels receive and bear his ransomed spirit straight up to heaven.

Lancelot was buried either at Arthur's feet or at Joyeuse Garde. He was deeply mourned by all his friends, and especially by his heir, Sir Ector de Maris, who eulogized him in the following touching terms: "'Ah, Sir Lancelot,' he said, 'thou were head of all Christian knights; and now I dare say,' said Sir Ector, 'that, Sir Lancelot, there thou liest, thou were never matched of none earthly knight's hands; and thou were the courtliest knight that ever bare shield; and thou were the truest friend to thy lover that ever bestrode horse; and thou

were the truest lover of a sinful man that ever loved woman; and
thou were the kindest man that ever struck with sword; and thou
were the goodliest person that ever came among press of knights;
and thou were the meekest man, and the gentlest, that ever ate in
hall among ladies; and thou were the sternest knight to thy mortal
foe that ever put spear in rest.'"

CHAPTER XIV

TRISTAN AND ISEULT.

The story of Tristan, which seems to have been current from earliest times, refers, perhaps, to the adventures of a knight, the contemporary of Arthur or of Cassivellaunus. The tale seems to have already been known in the sixth century, and was soon seized upon by the bards, who found it a rich theme for their metrical romances. It is quite unknown whether it was first turned into Latin, French, or Welsh verse; but an established fact is that it has been translated into every European language, and was listened to with as much interest by the inhabitants of Iceland as by those of the sunny plains of Greece.

We know that there are metrical versions, or remains of metrical versions, attributed to Thomas of Ercildoune (the Rhymer), to Raoul de Beauvais, Chrestien de Troyes, Rusticien de Pise, Luces de Cast, Robert and Hélie de Borron, and Gottfried von Strassburg, and that in our day it has been retold by Matthew Arnold and Swinburne, and made the subject of an opera by Wagner. These old metrical versions, recited with manifold variations by the minstrels, were finally collected into a prose romance, like most of the mediaeval poems of this kind.

The outline of the story, collected from many different sources, is as follows:

Meliadus (Rivalin, or Roland Rise) was Lord of Lyonesse (Ermonie, or Parmenia), and after warring for some time against Morgan, he entered into a seven-years' truce. This time of respite was employed by Meliadus in visiting Mark, King of Cornwall, who dwelt at Tintagel, where he was holding a great tournament. Many knights of tried valor hurried thither to win laurels, but none were able to unhorse Meliadus, who obtained every prize.

His courage was such that he even won the heart of Blanchefleur, the sister of the king. As the monarch refused to consent to their union, the young people were secretly married, or eloped, if we are to believe another version of the story.

According to the first account, Blanchefleur remained at court, where, hearing that her husband had died, she breathed her last in giving birth to a son, whom she called Tristan (Tristrem), because he had come into the world under such sad circumstances. The second version relates that Blanchefleur died as Morgan entered the castle over her husband's dead body, and that her faithful retainer, Kurvenal (Rohand, Rual), in order to save her son, claimed him as his own.

The child Tristan grew up without knowing his real parentage, learned all that a knight was expected to know, and became especially expert as a hunter and as a harp player. One day he strolled on board of a Norwegian vessel which had anchored in the harbor near his ancestral home, and accepted the challenge of the Norsemen to play a game of chess for a certain wager.

As Tristan played at chess as well as upon the harp, he soon won the game; but the Northmen, rather than pay their forfeited wager, suddenly raised the anchor and sailed away, intending to sell the kidnaped youth as a slave.

> "Ther com a ship of Norway,
>   To Sir Rohandes hold,
> With haukes white and grey,
>   And panes fair y-fold:
> Tristrem herd it say,
>   On his playing he wold
> Tventi schilling to lay,
>   Sir Rohand him told,
> And taught;
>   For hauke silver he gold;
> The fairest men him raught."
>   SCOTT, *Sir Tristrem.*

They had not gone far, however, before a terrible tempest arose, which threatened to sink the vessel and drown all on board. The mariners, supposing in their terror that this peril had come upon them because they had acted dishonorably, made a solemn vow to liberate the youth if they escaped.

The vow having been made, the wind ceased to blow; and anchoring in the nearest bay, the Norsemen bade Tristan land, and paid him the sum he had won at chess.

Thus forsaken on an unknown shore, with nothing but his harp and bow, Tristan wandered through an extensive forest, where, coming across a party of huntsmen who had just slain a deer, he gave them valuable and lengthy instructions in matters pertaining to the chase, and taught them how to flay and divide their quarry according to the most approved mediaeval style. Then, accompanying them to the court of their master, King Mark, he charmed every one with his minstrelsy, and was invited to tarry there as long as he pleased. His foster father, Kurvenal, in the mean while, had set out to seek him; and in the course of his wanderings he too came to Mark's court, where he was overjoyed to find Tristan, whose parentage he revealed to the king.

Tristan now for the first time heard the story of his father's death, and refused to rest until he had avenged him. He immediately set out, slew Morgan, and recovered his father's estate of Lyonesse, which he intrusted to Kurvenal's care, while he himself went back to Cornwall. On arriving at Tintagel he was surprised to find all the court plunged in sorrow. Upon inquiring the cause he was informed that Morold, brother of the King of Ireland, had come to claim the usual tribute of three hundred pounds of silver and tin and three hundred promising youths to be sold into slavery.

Indignant at this claim, which had been enforced ever since Mark had been defeated in battle by the Irish king, Tristan boldly strode up to the emissary, tore the treaty in two, flung the pieces in his face, and challenged him to single combat. Morold, confident in his strength,— for he was a giant,—and relying particularly upon his poisoned sword, immediately accepted the challenge. When the usual preliminaries had been settled, the battle began.

> "Sir Morold rode upon his steed,
> And flew against Tristan with speed
> Still greater than is falcons' flight;
> But warlike too was Tristan's might."
>
> GOTTFRIED VON STRASSBURG (Dippold's tr.).

Terrible blows were given and received, and at last Tristan sank to the ground on one knee, for his opponent's poisoned weapon had pierced his side.

Morold then called upon him to acknowledge himself beaten, promising to obtain a balsam from his sister Iseult (Isolde, Ysolde), who knew a remedy for such a dangerous wound. But Tristan, remembering that, if he surrendered, three hundred innocent children would be sold as slaves, made a last despairing effort, and slew Morold. Such was the force of the blow he dealt that he cut through the helmet and pierced Morold's skull, which was so hard that a fragment of his sword remained imbedded within the wound.

The people of Cornwall were, of course, delighted; and while the Irish heralds returned empty-handed to Dublin with Morold's remains, the King of Cornwall loudly proclaimed that as he had no son, Tristan should be his heir.

Tristan, however, was far from happy, for the wound in his side refused to heal, and gradually became so offensive that no one could bear his presence. As none of the court doctors could relieve him, he remembered Morold's words, and resolved to go to Ireland, in hopes that Iseult would cure him. Conscious, however, that she would never consent to help him if she suspected his identity, he embarked alone, or with Kurvenal, in a small vessel, taking only his harp, and drifted toward Ireland, where he arrived at the end of fifteen days. When he appeared at court, Tristan declared that he was a wandering minstrel called Tantris, and bespoke the kind offices of the queen, Iseult. Charmed by his music, she hastened to cure him of the grievous wound from which he had suffered so much.

Tristan, still unknown, remained at the Irish court for some time, spending many hours with Iseult, the daughter and namesake of the queen, whom he instructed daily in the art of music. After some months passed thus in pleasant intercourse, Tristan returned to Cornwall, where he related to Mark the story of his cure, and so extolled the beauty of young Iseult that the king finally expressed a desire to marry her. By the advice of the courtiers, who were jealous of Tristan, and who hoped that this mission would cost him his life, the young hero was sent to Ireland with an imposing retinue, to sue for the maiden's hand and to escort her safely to Cornwall.

On landing in Dublin, Tristan immediately became aware that the people were laboring under an unusual excitement. Upon questioning them he learned that a terrible dragon had taken up its station near the city, that it was devastating the country, and that the king had promised the hand of Iseult to the man who would slay the monster. Tristan immediately concluded that by killing the dragon he would have the best chance of successfully carrying out his uncle's wishes, so he sallied forth alone to attack it.

> "This dragon had two furious wings,
>   Each one upon each shoulder;
> With a sting in his tayl as long as a flayl,
>   Which made him bolder and bolder.
> "He had long claws, and in his jaws
>   Four and forty teeth of iron;
> With a hide as tough as any buff
>   Which did him round environ."
> *Dragon of Wantly* (Old Ballad).

In spite of the fearful appearance of this dragon, and of the volumes of fire and venom which it belched forth, Tristan encountered it bravely, and finally slew it. Then, cutting out the monster's tongue, he thrust it into his pocket, intending to produce it at the right moment. He had gone only a few steps, however, when, exhausted by his prolonged conflict, stunned by the poisonous fumes which he had inhaled, and overcome by the close contact with the dragon's tongue, he sank fainting to the ground. A few moments later the butler of the Irish king rode up. He saw the dragon dead, with his conqueror lifeless beside him, and quickly resolved to take advantage of this fortunate chance to secure the hand of the fair princess. He therefore cut off the dragon's head, and, going to court, boasted of having slain the monster just as it had killed a strange knight. Iseult and her mother, well aware that the man was a coward, refused to believe his story, and hastened off to the scene of the conflict, where they found the fainting Tristan with the dragon's tongue in his pocket.

To remove the poisonous substance, (which they, however, preserved,) convey the knight to the palace, and restore him by tender care, was the next impulse of these brave women. Then, while Iseult the younger sat beside her patient, watching his slumbers, she idly drew his sword from the scabbard. Suddenly her eye was caught by a dint in the blade, which she soon discovered was of exactly the same shape and size as the fragment of steel which she had found in her uncle's skull.

> "Then all at once her heart grew cold
> In thinking of that deed of old.
> Her color changed through grief and ire
> From deadly pale to glowing fire.
> With sorrow she exclaimed: 'Alas!
> Oh, woe! what has now come to pass?
> Who carried here this weapon dread,
> By which mine uncle was struck dead?
> And he who slew him, Tristan hight.
> Who gave it to this minstrel knight?'"
>   GOTTFRIED VON STRASSBURG (Dippold's tr.).

Morold's murderer lay helpless before her, and Iseult, animated by the spirit of vengeance, which was considered a sacred duty among the people of the time, was about to slay Tristan, when he opened his eyes and disarmed her by a glance. Her mother further hindered her carrying out her hostile intentions by telling her that Tristan had atoned for his crime by delivering the people from the power of the dragon.

As soon as Tristan had quite recovered, he appeared at court, where he offered to prove at the point of his sword that the butler had no claim to the princess's hand. A duel was arranged, and the butler, disarmed by Tristan, confessed his lie. Tristan then produced the dragon's tongue and told his adventures; but, to the general surprise, instead of suing for Iseult's hand for himself, he now asked it in the name of his uncle, King Mark of Cornwall.

The young princess was none too well pleased at this unexpected turn of affairs; but, as princesses never had much to say about the choice of a husband, she obediently prepared to accompany the embassy to Tintagel. Her mother, wishing to preserve her from a loveless marriage, now sought out all manner of herbs wherewith to brew one of those magic love potions which were popularly supposed to have unlimited powers.

> "Bethought her with her secret soul alone
> To work some charm for marriage unison,
> And strike the heart of Iseult to her lord
> With power compulsive more than stroke of sword."
> SWINBURNE, *Tristram of Lyonesse.*

This magic potion was put in a golden cup and intrusted to Brangwaine, the attendant of Iseult, with strict injunctions to guard the secret well, and to give the draught to her mistress and Mark to quaff together on their wedding day.

> "Therefore with marvelous herbs and spells she wrought
> To win the very wonder of her thought,
> And brewed it with her secret hands, and blest
> And drew and gave out of her secret breast
> To one her chosen and Iseult's handmaiden,
> Brangwain, and bade her hide from sight of men
> This marvel covered in a golden cup,
> So covering in her heart the counsel up
> As in the gold the wondrous wine lay close."
> SWINBURNE, *Tristram of Lyonesse.*

Brangwaine carefully carried this potion on board the ship, and placed it in a cupboard, whence she intended to produce it when the suitable moment came. Iseult embarked with the escort sent from Cornwall, and Tristan, in order to beguile the long, weary hours of the journey, entertained her with all the songs and stories that he knew. One day, after singing for some time, he asked his fair young mistress for a drink; and she, going to the cupboard, drew out the magic potion, little guessing its power.

As was customary in those days in offering wine to an honored guest, she first put it to her own lips and then handed it to the thirsty minstrel, who drained it greedily. They had no sooner drunk, however, than the draught, working with subtle power, suddenly kindled in their hearts a passionate love, destined to last as long as they both lived.

"Now that the maiden and the man,
Fair Iseult and Tristan,
Both drank the drink, upon them pressed
What gives the world such sore unrest,—
Love, skilled in sly and prowling arts,—
And swiftly crept in both their hearts;
So, ere of him they were aware,
Stood his victorious banners there.
He drew them both into his power;
One and single were they that hour
That two and twofold were before."
      GOTTFRIED VON STRASSBURG (Bayard Taylor's tr.).

After the first few hours of rapture had passed, the young people, who honorably intended to keep their word and conquer the fatal passion which had overwhelmed them, remained apart, and when Iseult landed in Cornwall her marriage was celebrated with Mark. Brangwaine, who knew all that had passed, tried to shield her mistress in every way, and blind the king, who is depicted as a very unheroic monarch, but little fitted to secure the affections of the proud young Iseult.

This story of a love potion whose magic power none could resist, and of the undying love which it kindled in the unsuspecting hearts of Tristan and Iseult, has been treated in many ways by the different poets and prose writers who have handled it. In many of the older versions we have lengthy descriptions of stolen interviews, hairbreadth escapes, and tests of love, truth, and fidelity without number.

In many respects the story is a parallel of that of Lancelot and Guinevere, although it contains some incidents which are duplicated in the "Nibelungenlied" only. But throughout, the writers all aver that, owing to the magic draught, the lovers, however good their intentions, could not long exist without seeing each other.

By means of this boundless love Tristan is said to have had an intuitive knowledge of Iseult's peril, for he hastened to rescue her from danger whenever events took a turn which might prove fatal to her. There are in some of these old romances pretty descriptions of scenery and of the signals used by the lovers to communicate with each other when forced by adverse circumstances to remain apart. One of the poems, for instance, says that Tristan's love messages were written on chips of wood, which he floated down the little stream which flowed past his sylvan lodge and crossed the garden of the queen.

The inevitable villain of the tale is one of Mark's squires, the spy Meliadus, also a very unheroic character, who told the king of Tristan's love for Iseult. Mark, who all through the story seems strangely indifferent to his beautiful wife, was not aware of the magic draught and its powerful effect, but Meliadus roused him temporarily from his apathy.

As the queen had been publicly accused, he compelled her to prove her innocence by undergoing the ordeal of fire, or by taking a public oath that she had shown favor to none but him. On her way to the place where this ceremony was to take place, Iseult was carried across a stream by Tristan disguised as a beggar, and, at his request, kissed him in reward for this service.

When called upon to take her oath before the judges and assembled court, Iseult could truthfully swear that, with the exception of the beggar whom she had just publicly kissed, no other man than the king could ever boast of having received any special mark of her favor.

Thus made aware of their danger, the lovers again decided to part, and Tristan, deprived for a time of the sight of Iseult, went mad, and performed many extraordinary feats; for mediaeval poets generally drove their heroes into a frenzy when they did not know what else to do with them. Having recovered, and hoping to forget the fatal passion which had already caused him so much sorrow, Tristan now wandered off to Arthur's court, where he performed many deeds of valor. Thence he went on to various strange lands, distinguishing himself greatly everywhere, until he received from a poisoned arrow a wound which no doctor could heal.

Afraid to expose himself again to the fascinations of Iseult of Cornwall, Tristan went to Brittany, where another Iseult,—with the White Hands,—equally well skilled in medicine, tenderly nursed him back to health. This maiden, as good and gentle as she was beautiful, soon fell in love with the handsome knight, and hearing him sing a passionate lay in honor of Iseult, she fancied that her affections were returned, and that it was intended for her ear.

ISEULT SIGNALS TRISTAN.—Pixis.

> "I know her by her mildness rare,
> Her snow-white hands, her golden hair;
> I know her by her rich silk dress,
> And her fragile loveliness,—
> The sweetest Christian soul alive,
> Iseult of Brittany."
> MATTHEW ARNOLD, *Tristram and Iseult*.

The brother of this fair Iseult saw her love for Tristan, and offered him her hand, which he accepted more out of gratitude than love, and in the hope that he might at last overcome the effects of the fatal draught. But, in spite of all his good resolutions, he could not forget Iseult of Cornwall, and treated his wife with such polite coolness that her brother's suspicions were finally roused.

Tristan, having conquered a neighboring giant and magician by the name of Beliagog, had granted him his life only upon condition that he would build a marvelous palace in the forest, and adorn it with paintings and sculptures, true to life, and representing all the different stages of his passion for Iseult of Cornwall. When his brother-in-law, therefore, asked why he seemed to find no pleasure in the society of his young wife, Tristan led him to the palace, showed him the works of art, and told him all. Ganhardin, the brother-in-law, must evidently have considered the excuse a good one, for he not only forgave Tristan, but implored him to take him to Cornwall, for he had fallen in love with the picture of Brangwaine, and hoped to win her for wife. On the way thither the young knights met with sundry adventures, delivered Arthur from the power of the Lady of the Lake, and carried off Iseult, whom the cowardly Mark was ill treating, to Lancelot's castle of Joyeuse Garde. There she became acquainted with Guinevere, and remained with her until Arthur brought about a general reconciliation.

Then Tristan once more returned to Brittany, resumed his wonted knightly existence, and fought until he was wounded so sorely that Iseult of Brittany could not cure him. His faithful steward Kurvenal, hoping yet to save him, sailed for Cornwall to bring the other Iseult to the rescue; and as he left he promised his master to change the black sails of the vessel for white in case his quest were successful.

Tristan now watched impatiently for the returning sail, but just as it came into view he breathed his last. Some ill-advised writers have ventured to state that Iseult of Brittany, whose jealousy had been aroused, was guilty of Tristan's death by falsely averring, in answer to his feverish inquiry, that the long-expected vessel was wafted along by black sails; but, according to other authorities, she remained gentle and lovable to the end.

Iseult of Cornwall, speeding to the rescue of her lover, whom nothing could make her forget, and finding him dead, breathed her last upon his corpse. Both bodies were then carried to Cornwall, where they were interred in separate graves by order of King Mark. But from the tomb of the dead minstrel there soon sprang a creeper, which, finding its way along the walls, descended into Iseult's grave. Thrice cut down by Mark's orders, the plant persisted in growing, thus emphasizing by a miracle the passionate love which made this couple proverbial in the middle ages. There are in subsequent literature many parallels of the miracle of the plant which sprang from Tristan's tomb, as is seen by the Ballad of Lord Thomas and Fair Annet, and of Lord Lovel, where, as in later versions of the Tristan legend, a rose and a vine grew out of the respective graves and twined tenderly around each other.

> "And out of her breast there grew a red rose,
> And out of his breast a brier."
>
> *Ballad of Lord Lovel.*

CHAPTER XV.

THE STORY OF FRITHIOF.

Norse, Danish, and Swedish writers have frequently called public attention to the vast literary treasures which are contained in the old sagas or tales of their forefathers. The work of northern scalds whose names in most cases are unknown to us, these stories relate the lives and adventures of the gods and heroes of the North. Many of these old sagas have been translated into various other European languages; but Tegnér, a Swedish writer of this century, has done most to revive a taste for them by making one of them the basis of a poem which is generally considered a masterpiece.

Tegnér's "Frithiof Saga" has been translated once at least into every European tongue, and more than eighteen times into English and German. Goethe spoke of the work with the greatest enthusiasm, and the tale, which gives a matchless picture of the life of our heathen ancestors in the North, has been the source of inspiration for important works of art.

Although Tegnér has chosen for his theme the Frithiof saga only, we find that that tale is the sequel to the older but less interesting Thorsten saga, of which we give here a very brief outline, merely to enable the reader to understand clearly every allusion in the more modern poem.

As is so frequently the case with these ancient tales, the story begins with Haloge (Loki), who came north with Odin, and began to reign over north Norway, which from him was called Halogaland. According to northern mythology, this god had two lovely daughters. They were carried off by bold suitors, who, banished from the mainland by Haloge's curses and magic spells, took refuge with their newly won wives upon neighboring islands.

Thus it happened that Haloge's grandson, Viking, was born upon the island of Bornholm, in the Balitic Sea, where he dwelt until he was fifteen, and where he became the largest and strongest man of his time. Rumors of his valor finally reached Hunvor, a Swedish princess; and, as she was oppressed by the attentions of a gigantic suitor whom none dared drive away, she quickly sent for Viking to deliver her.

Thus summoned, the youth departed, after having received from his father a magic sword named Angurvadel, whose blows would prove fatal even to the giant suitor of Hunvor. A "holmgang," the northern name for a duel, ensued, and Viking, having slain his antagonist, could have married the princess had it not been considered disgraceful for a Northman to marry before he was twenty.

To beguile the time of waiting, Viking set out in a well-manned dragon ship; and, cruising about the northern and southern seas, he met with countless adventures. During this time he was particularly persecuted by the slain giant's kin, who were adepts in magic, and caused him to encounter innumerable perils by land and by sea.

Aided and abetted by his bosom friend, Halfdan, Viking escaped every danger, slew many of his foes, and, after recovering his promised bride, Hunvor, whom the enemy had carried off to India, he settled down in Sweden. His friend, faithful in peace as well as in war, settled near him, and married also, choosing for his wife Ingeborg, Hunvor's attendant.

The saga now describes the long, peaceful winters, when the warriors feasted and listened to the tales of the scalds, rousing themselves to energetic efforts only when returning spring again permitted them to launch their dragon ships and set out once more upon their favorite piratical expeditions. In the olden story the bards relate with great gusto every phase of attack and defense during cruise and raid, describe every blow given and received, and spare us none of carnage, or lurid flames which envelop both enemies and ships in common ruin. A fierce fight is often an earnest of future friendship, however, for we are told that Halfdan and Viking, having failed to conquer Njorfe, even after a most obstinate struggle, sheathed their swords and accepted him as a third in their close bond of friendship.

On returning home after one of these customary raids, Viking lost his beloved wife; and, after intrusting her child, Ring, to the care of a foster father, and undergoing a short period of mourning, the brave warrior married again. This time his marital bliss was more lasting, for the saga reports that his second wife bore him nine stalwart sons.

Njorfe, King of Uplands, in Norway, had, in the mean while, followed Viking's example, and he too rejoiced in a large family, numbering also nine brave sons. Now, although their fathers were united in bonds of the closest friendship, having sworn blood brotherhood according to the true northern rites, the young men were jealous of one another, and greatly inclined to quarrel.

Notwithstanding this smoldering animosity, these youths often met; and the saga relates that they used to play ball together, and gives a description of the earliest ball game on record in the northern annals. Viking's sons, as tall and strong as he, were inclined to be rather reckless of their opponents' welfare, and, judging from the following account, translated from the old saga, the players were often left in as sorry a condition as after a modern game.

"The next morning the brothers went to the games, and generally had the ball during the day; they pushed men and let them fall roughly, and beat others. At night three men had their arms broken, and many were bruised or maimed."

The game between Njorfe's and Viking's sons culminated in a disagreement, and one of the former nine struck one of the latter a dangerous and treacherous blow. Prevented from taking his revenge then and there by the interference of the spectators, the injured man made a trivial excuse to return to the ball ground alone; and, meeting his assailant there, he killed him.

When Viking heard that one of his sons had slain one of his friend's children, he was very indignant, and, mindful of his oath to avenge all Njorfe's wrongs, he banished the young murderer. The other brothers, on hearing this sentence, all vowed that they would accompany the exile, and so Viking sorrowfully bade them farewell, giving his sword Angurvadel to Thorsten, the eldest, and cautioning him to remain quietly on an island in Lake Wener until all danger of retaliation on the part of Njorfe's remaining sons was over.

The young men obeyed; but Njorfe's sons, who had no boats to take them across the lake, soon made use of a conjuror's art to bring about a great frost, and, accompanied by many armed men, stole noiselessly over the ice to attack Thorsten and his brothers. A terrible carnage ensued, and only two of the attacking party managed to escape, leaving, as they fancied, all their foes among the dead.

But when Viking came to bury his sons, he found that two of them, Thorsten and Thorer, were still alive, and he secretly conveyed them to a cellar beneath his dwelling, where they recovered from their wounds.

By magic arts Njorfe's two sons discovered that their opponents were not dead, and soon made a second desperate but vain attempt to kill them. Viking saw that the quarrel would be incessantly renewed if his sons remained at home; so he now sent them to Halfdan, whose court they reached after a series of adventures which in many points resemble those of Theseus on his way to Athens.

When spring came Thorsten embarked on a piratical excursion, and encountered Jokul, Njorfe's eldest son, who, in the mean while, had taken forcible possession of the kingdom of Sogn, after killing the king, banishing his heir, Belé, and changing his beautiful daughter, Ingeborg, into the form of an old witch.

Throughout the story Jokul is represented as somewhat of a coward, for he resorted by preference to magic when he wished to injure Viking's sons. Thus he stirred up great tempests, and Thorsten, after twice suffering shipwreck, was saved from the waves by the witch Ingeborg, whom he promised to marry in gratitude for her good services.

Thorsten, advised by her, went in search of Belé, replaced him on his hereditary throne, swore eternal friendship with him, and, the baleful spell being removed, married the beautiful Ingeborg, who dwelt with him at Framnäs.

Every spring Thorsten and Belé now set out together in their ships; and, joining forces with Angantyr, a foe whose mettle they had duly tested, they proceeded to recover possession of a priceless treasure, a magic dragon ship named Ellida, which Aegir, god of the sea, had once given to Viking in reward for hospitable treatment, and which had been stolen from him.

> "A royal gift to behold, for the swelling planks of its framework
> Were not fastened with nails, as is wont, but *grown* in together.
> Its shape was that of a dragon when swimming, but forward
> Its head rose proudly on high, the throat with yellow gold flaming;
> Its belly was spotted with red and yellow, but back by the rudder
> Coiled out its mighty tail in circles, all scaly with silver;
> Black wings with edges of red; when all were expanded
> Ellida raced with the whistling storm, but outstript the eagle.
> When filled to the edge with warriors, it sailed o'er the waters,
> You'd deem it a floating fortress, or warlike abode of a monarch.
> The ship was famed far and wide, and of ships was first in the North."
> TEGNÉR, *Frithiof Saga* (Spalding's tr.).

The next season, Thorsten, Belé, and Angantyr conquered the Orkney Islands, which were given as kingdom to the latter, he voluntarily pledging himself to pay a yearly tribute to Belé. Next Thorsten and Belé went in quest of a magic ring, or armlet, once forged by Völund, the smith, and stolen by Soté, a famous pirate.

This bold robber was so afraid lest some one should gain possession of the magic ring, that he had buried himself alive with it in a mound in Bretland. Here his ghost was said to keep constant watch over it, and when Thorsten entered his tomb, Belé heard the frightful blows given and received, and saw lurid gleams of supernatural fire.

When Thorsten finally staggered out of the mound, pale and bloody, but triumphant, he refused to speak of the horrors he had encountered to win the coveted treasure, nor would he ever vouchsafe further information than this:

> "'Dearly bought is the prize,' said he often,
> 'For I trembled but once in my life, and 'twas when I seized it!'"
> TEGNÉR, *Frithiof Saga* (Spalding's tr.).

Thus owner of the three greatest treasures in the North, Thorsten returned home to Framnäs, where Ingeborg bore him a fine boy, Frithiof, the playmate of Halfdan and Helgé, Belé's sons. The three youths were already well grown when Ingeborg, Belé's little daughter, was born, and as she was intrusted to the care of Hilding, Frithiof's foster father, the children grew up in perfect amity.

> "Jocund they grew, in guileless glee;
> Young Frithiof was the sapling tree;
> In budding beauty by his side,
> Sweet Ingeborg, the garden's pride."
> TEGNÉR, *Frithiof Saga* (Longfellow's tr.).

Frithiof soon became hardy and fearless under his foster father's training, and Ingeborg rapidly developed all the sweetest traits of female loveliness. Both, however, were happiest when together; and as they grew older their childish affection daily became deeper and more intense, until Hilding, perceiving this state of affairs, bade the youth remember that he was only a subject, and therefore no mate for the king's only daughter.

> "But Hilding said, 'O foster son,
> Set not thy heart her love upon,
> For Destiny thy wish gainsaid;
> King Belé's daughter is the maid!
> "From Odin's self, in starry sky,
> Descends her ancestry so high;
> But thou art Thorsten's son, so yield,
> And leave to mightier names the field.'"
>   TEGNÉR, *Frithiof Saga* (Spalding's tr.)

These wise admonitions came too late, however, and Frithiof vehemently declared that he would win the fair Ingeborg for his bride in spite of all obstacles and his comparatively humble origin.

Shortly after this Belé and Thorsten met for the last time, near the magnificent shrine of Balder, where the king, feeling that his end was near, had convened a solemn assembly, or Thing, of all his principal subjects, in order to present his sons Helgé and Halfdan to the people as his chosen successors. The young heirs were very coldly received on this occasion, for Helgé was of a somber and taciturn disposition, and inclined to the life of a priest, and Halfdan was of a weak, effeminate nature, and noted for his cowardice. Frithiof, who was present, and stood beside them, cast them both in the shade, and won many admiring glances from the throng.

> "But after them came Frithiof, in mantle blue—
> He by a head was taller than th' other two.
> He stood between the brethren, as day should light
> Between the rosy morning and darksome night."
>   TEGNÉR, *Frithiof Saga* (Spalding's tr.)

After giving his last instructions to his sons, and speaking kindly to Frithiof, who was his favorite, the old king turned to his lifelong companion, Thorsten, to take leave of him, but the old warrior declared that they would not long be parted. Belé then spoke again to his sons, and bade them erect his howe, or funeral mound, within sight of that of Thorsten, that their spirits might commune, and not be sundered even in death.

> "'But lay us gently, children, where the blue wave,
> Beating harmonious cadence, the shore doth lave;
> Its murmuring song is pleasant unto the soul,
> And like a lamentation its ceaseless roll.
> "'And when the moon's pale luster around us streams,
> And midnight dim grows radiant with silver beams,
> There will we sit, O Thorsten, upon our graves,
> And talk of bygone battles by the dark waves.
> "'And now, farewell, my children! Come here no more;
> Our road lies to Allfather's far-distant shore,
> E'en as the troubled river sweeps to the sea:
> By Frey and Thor and Odin blessed may ye be.'"
> TEGNÉR, *Frithiof Saga* (Spalding's tr.).

These instructions were all piously obeyed when the aged companions had breathed their last. Then the brothers, Helgé and Halfdan, began to rule their kingdom, while Frithiof, their former playmate, withdrew to his own place at Framnäs, a very fertile homestead, lying in a snug valley closed in by the towering mountains and the ever-changing ocean.

> "Three miles extended around the fields of the homestead; on three sides
> Valleys and mountains and hills, but on the fourth side was the ocean.
> Birch-woods crowned the summits, but over the down-sloping hillsides
> Flourished the golden corn, and man-high was waving the ryefield."
> TEGNÉR, *Frithiof Saga* (Longfellow's tr.).

But although surrounded by faithful retainers, and blessed with much wealth and the possession of the famous sword Angurvadel, the Völund ring, and the matchless dragon ship Ellida, Frithiof was unhappy, because he could no longer see the fair Ingeborg daily. With the returning spring, however, all his former spirits returned, for both kings came to visit him, accompanied by their fair sister, with whom he lived over the happy childish years, and spent long hours in cheerful companionship. As they were thus constantly thrown together, Frithiof soon made known to Ingeborg his deep affection, and received in return an avowal of her love.

> "He sat by her side, and he pressed her soft hand,
> And he felt a soft pressure responsive and bland;
> Whilst his love-beaming gaze
> Was returned as the sun's in the moon's placid rays."
> TEGNÉR, *Frithiof Saga* (Longfellow's tr.).

When the visit was over and the guests had departed, Frithiof informed his confidant and chief companion, Björn, of his determination to follow them and openly ask for Ingeborg's hand. His ship was prepared, and after a swift sail touched the shore near Balder's shrine. Discerning the royal brothers seated in state on Belé's tomb to listen to the petitions of their subjects, Frithiof immediately presented himself before them, and manfully made his request, adding that the old king had always loved him and would surely have granted his prayer.

> "They were seated on Belè's tomb, and o'er
> The common folk administered law.
> But Frithiof speaks,
> And his voice re-echoes round valleys and peaks.
> "'Ye kings, my love is Ingborg fair;
> To ask her in marriage I here repair;
> And what I require
> I here maintain was King Belè's desire.
> "'He let us grow in Hilding's care,
> Like two young saplings, year by year;
> And therefore, kings,
> Unite the full-grown trees with golden rings.'"
> TEGNÉR, *Frithiof Saga* (Spalding's tr.).

But although he promised lifelong fealty and the service of his strong right arm in exchange for the boon he craved, Helgé contemptuously dismissed him. Enraged at the insult thus publicly received, Frithiof raised his invincible sword; but, remembering that he stood on a consecrated spot, he spared the king, only cutting the royal shield in two to show the strength of his blade, and striding back to his ship, he embarked and sailed away in sullen silence.

> "And lo! cloven in twain at a stroke
> Fell King Helgé's gold shield from its pillar of oak:
> At the clang of the blow,
> The live started above, the dead started below."
> TEGNÉR, *Frithiof Saga* (Longfellow's tr.).

Just after his departure came messengers from Sigurd Ring, the aged King of Ringric, in Norway, who, having lost his wife, sent to Helgé and Halfdan to ask Ingeborg's hand in marriage. Before answering this royal suitor, Helgé consulted the Vala, or prophetess, and the priests, and as they all declared that the omens were not in favor of this marriage, he gave an insolent refusal to the messengers. This impolitic conduct so offended the would-be suitor that he immediately collected an army and prepared to march against the Kings of Sogn to avenge the insult with his sword. When the rumor of his approach reached the cowardly brothers they were terrified, and fearing to encounter the foe alone, they sent Hilding to Frithiof to implore his aid.

Hilding gladly undertook the mission, although he had not much hope of its success. He found Frithiof playing chess with a friend, Björn, and immediately made known his errand.

> "'From Belé's high heirs
> I come with courteous words and prayers:
> Disastrous tidings rouse the brave;
> On thee a nation's hope relies.
>
> *   *   *   *   *
>
> In Balder's fane, grief's loveliest prey,
> Sweet Ing'borg weeps the livelong day:
> Say, can her tears unheeded fall,
> Nor call her champion to her side?'"
> TEGNÉR, *Frithiof Saga* (Longfellow's tr.).

THE LOVERS AT BALDER'S SHRINE. —Kepler.

But Frithiof was so deeply offended that even this appeal in the name of his beloved could not move him. Quietly he continued his game of chess, and, when it was ended, told Hilding that he had no answer to give. Rightly concluding that Frithiof would lend the kings no aid, Hilding returned to Helgé and Halfdan, who, forced to fight without their bravest leader, preferred to make a treaty with Sigurd Ring, promising to give him not only their sister Ingeborg, but also a yearly tribute.

While they were thus engaged at Sogn Sound, Frithiof hastened to Balder's temple, where, as Hilding had declared, he found Ingeborg a prey to grief. Now although it was considered a sacrilege for man and woman to exchange a word in the sacred building, Frithiof could not see his beloved in tears without attempting to console her; and, forgetting all else, he spoke to her and comforted her. He repeated how dearly he loved her, quieted all her apprehensions of the gods' anger by assuring her that Balder, the good, must view their innocent passion with approving eyes, said that love as pure as theirs could defile no sanctuary, and plighted his troth to her before the shrine.

> "'What whisper you of Balder's ire?
> The pious god—he is not wrath.
> He loves himself, and doth inspire
> Our love—the purest he calls forth.
> The god with true and steadfast heart,
> The sun upon his glittering form,
> Is not his love for Nanna part
> Of his own nature, pure and warm?
> "'There is his image; he is near.
> How mild he looks on me—how kind!
> A sacrifice to him I'll bear,
> The offer of a loving mind.
> Kneel down with me; no better gift,
> No fairer sure for Balder is,
> Than two young hearts, whose love doth lift
> Above the world almost like his.'"
>
> TEGNÉR, *Frithiof Saga* (Spalding's tr.).

Reassured by this reasoning, Ingeborg no longer refused to see and converse with Frithiof; and during the kings' absence the young lovers met every day, and plighted their troth with Volund's ring, which Ingeborg solemnly promised to send back to her lover should she break her promise to live for him alone. Frithiof lingered there until the kings' return, when, for love of Ingeborg the fair, he again appeared before them, and pledged himself to free them from their thraldom to Sigurd Ring if they would only reconsider their decision and promise him their sister's hand.

> "War is abroad,
> And strikes his echoing shield within our borders;
> Thy crown and land, King Helgé, are in danger;
> Give me thy sister's hand, and I will use
> Henceforth my warlike force in thy defense.
> Let then the wrath between us be forgotten,
> Unwillingly I strive 'gainst Ingborg's brother.
> Secure, O king, by one fraternal act
> Thy golden crown and save thy sister's heart.
> Here is my hand. By Thor, I ne'er again
> Present it here for reconciliation.'"
>
> TEGNÉR, *Frithiof Saga* (Spalding's tr.).

But although this offer was hailed with rapture by the assembled warriors, it was again scornfully rejected by Helgé, who declared that he would have granted it had not Frithiof proved himself unworthy of all confidence by defiling the temple of the gods. Frithiof tried to defend himself; but as he had to plead guilty to the accusation of having conversed with Ingeborg at Balder's shrine, he was convicted of having broken the law, and, in punishment therefor, condemned to sail off to the Orkney Islands to claim tribute from the king, Angantyr.

Before he sailed, however, he once more sought Ingeborg, and vainly tried to induce her to elope with him by promising her a home in the sunny south, where her happiness should be his law, and where she should rule over his subjects as his honored wife. Ingeborg sorrowfully refused to accompany him, saying that, since her father was no more, she was in duty bound to obey her brothers implicitly, and could not marry without their consent.

"'But Helgé is my father,
Stands in my father's place; on his consent
Depends my hand, and Belé's daughter steals not
Her earthly happiness, how near it be.'"
TEGNÉR, *Frithiof Saga* (Spalding's tr.).

After a heartrending parting scene, Frithiof embarked upon Ellida, and sorrowfully sailed out of the harbor, while Ingeborg wept at his departure. When the vessel was barely out of sight, Helgé sent for two witches named Heid and Ham, bidding them begin their incantations, and stir up such a tempest at sea that it would be impossible for even the god-given vessel Ellida to withstand its fury, and all on board would perish. The witches immediately complied; and with Helgé's aid they soon stirred up a storm unparalleled in history.

"Helgé on the strand
Chants his wizard-spell,
Potent to command
Fiends of earth or hell.
Gathering darkness shrouds the sky;
Hark, the thunder's distant roll!
Lurid lightnings, as they fly,
Streak with blood the sable pole.
Ocean, boiling to its base,
Scatters wide its wave of foam;
Screaming, as in fleetest chase,
Sea-birds seek their island home."
TEGNÉR, *Frithiof Saga* (Longfellow's tr.).

In spite of tossing waves and whistling blasts, Frithiof sang a cheery song to reassure his frightened crew; but when the peril grew so great that his exhausted men gave themselves up for lost, he bade Björn hold the rudder, and himself climbed up to the mast top to view the horizon. While perched up there he descried a whale, upon which the two witches were riding at ease. Speaking to his good ship, which was gifted with the power of understanding and obeying his words, he now ran down both witches and whale, and the sea was reddened with their blood. No sooner had they sunk than the wind fell, the waves ceased to heave and toss as before, and soon fair weather again smiled over the seas.

"Now the storm has flown,
The sea is calm awhile;
A gentle swell is blown
Against the neighboring isle.

"Then at once the sun arose,
Like a king who mounts his throne,
Vivifies the world and throws
His light on billow, field, and stone.
His new-born beams adorn awhile
A dark green grove on rocky top,
All recognize a sea-girt isle,
Amongst the distant Orkney's group."
　　　　　TEGNÉR, *Frithiof Saga* (Spalding's tr.).

Exhausted by their previous superhuman efforts and by the bailing of their water-logged vessel, the men were too weak to land when they at last reached the Orkney Islands, and had to be carried ashore by Björn and Frithiof, who gently laid them down on the sand, bidding them rest and refresh themselves after all the hardships they had endured.

"Tired indeed are all on board,
All the crew of Frithiofs men,
Scarce supported by a sword,
Can they raise themselves again.
Björn takes four of them ashore,
On his mighty shoulders wide,
Frithiof singly takes twice four,
Places them the fire beside.
'Blush not, ye pale ones,
The sea's a valiant viking;
'Tis hard indeed to fight
Against the rough sea waves.
Lo! there comes the mead horn
On golden feet descending,
To warm our frozen limbs.
Hail to Ingeborg!'"
　　　　　TEGNÉR, *Frithiof Saga* (Spalding's tr.).

The arrival of Frithiof and his men had been seen by the watchman of Angantyr's castle, who immediately informed his master of all he had seen. The jarl exclaimed that the ship which had weathered such a gale could be none but Ellida, and that its captain was doubtless Frithiof, Thorsten's gallant son. At these words one of his Berserkers, Atlé, caught up his weapons and strode out of the hall, vowing that he would challenge Frithiof, and thus satisfy himself concerning the veracity of the tales he had heard of the young hero's courage.

Although still greatly exhausted, Frithiof immediately accepted Atlé's challenge, and, after a sharp encounter, threw his antagonist, whom he would have slain then and there had his sword been within reach. Atlé saw his intention, and bade him go in search of a weapon, promising to remain motionless during his absence. Frithiof, knowing that such a warrior's promise was inviolable, immediately obeyed; but when he returned with his sword, and found his antagonist calmly awaiting death, he relented, and bade Atlé rise and live.

> "With patience long not gifted,
> Frithiof the foe would kill,
> And Angurvadel lifted,
> But Atlé yet lay still.
> This touched the hero's soul;
> He stayed the sweeping brand
> Before it reached its goal,
> And took the fall'n one's hand."
>
> TEGNÉR, *Frithiof Saga* (Spalding's tr.).

Together these doughty warriors then wended their way to Angantyr's halls, where they found a festal board awaiting them, and there they ate and drank, sang songs, and recounted stories of thrilling adventure by land and by sea.

At last, however, Frithiof made known his errand. Angantyr said that he owed no tribute to Helgé, and would pay him none; but that he would give the required sum as a free gift to his old friend Thorsten's son, leaving him at liberty to dispose of it as he pleased. Then, since the season was unpropitious, and storms continually swept over the sea, the king invited Frithiof to tarry with him; and it was only when the gentle spring breezes were blowing once more that he at last allowed him to depart.

After sailing over summer seas, wafted along by favorable winds for six days, Frithiof came in sight of his home, Framnäs, which had been reduced to a shapeless heap of ashes by Helgé's orders. Sadly steering past the ruins, he arrived at Baldershage, where Hilding met him and informed him that Ingeborg was now the wife of Sigurd Ring. When Frithiof heard these tidings he flew into a Berserker rage, and bade his men destroy all the vessels in the harbor, while he strode up to the temple alone in search of Helgé. He found him there before the god's image, roughly flung Angantyr's heavy purse of gold in his face, and when, as he was about to leave the temple, he saw the ring he had given Ingeborg on the arm of Helgé's wife, he snatched it away from her. In trying to recover it she dropped the god's image, which she had just been anointing, into the fire, where it was rapidly consumed, and the rising flames soon set the temple roof in a blaze.

Frithiof, horror-stricken at the sacrilege which he had involuntarily occasioned, after vainly trying to extinguish the flames and save the costly sanctuary, escaped to his ship and waiting companions, to begin the weary life of an outcast and exile.

> "The temple soon in ashes lay,
> Ashes the temple's bower;
> Wofully Frithiof goes his way,
> Weeps in the morning hour."
>
> TEGNÉR, *Frithiof Saga* (Spalding's tr.).

Helgé's men started in pursuit, hoping to overtake and punish him; but when they reached the harbor they could not find a single seaworthy craft, and were forced to stand on the shore in helpless inactivity while Ellida's great sails slowly sank beneath the horizon. It was thus that Frithiof sadly saw his native land vanish from sight; and as it disappeared he breathed a tender farewell to the beloved country which he never expected to see again.

"'World-circle's brow,
Thou mighty North!
I may not go
Upon thine earth;
But in no other
I love to dwell;
Now, hero-mother,
Farewell, farewell!

"'Farewell, thou high
And heavenly one,
Night's sleeping eye,
Midsummer sun.
Thou clear blue sky,
Like hero's soul,
Ye stars on high,
Farewell, farewell!

"'Farewell, ye mounts
Where Honour thrives,
And Thor recounts
Good warriors' lives.
Ye azure lakes,
I know so well,
Ye woods and brakes,
Farewell, farewell!

"'Farewell, ye tombs,
By billows blue,
The lime tree blooms
Its snow on you.
The Saga sets
In judgment-veil
What earth forgets;
Farewell, farewell!

"'Farewell the heath,
The forest hoar
I played beneath,
By streamlet's roar.
To childhood's friends

Who loved me well,
Remembrance sends
A fond farewell!

"'My love is foiled,
My rooftree rent,
Mine honour soiled,
In exile sent!
We turn from earth,
On ocean dwell,
But, joy and mirth,
Farewell, farewell!'"

TEGNÉR, *Frithiof Saga* (Spalding's tr.).

After thus parting from his native land, Frithiof took up the life of a pirate, rover, or viking, whose code was never to settle anywhere, to sleep on his shield, to fight and neither give nor take quarter, to protect the ships which paid him tribute and sack the others, and to distribute all the booty to his men, reserving for himself nothing but the glory of the enterprise. Sailing and fighting thus, Frithiof visited many lands, and came to the sunny isles of Greece, whither he would fain have carried Ingeborg as his bride; but wherever he went and whatever he did, he was always haunted by the recollection of his beloved and of his native land.

Overcome at last by homesickness, Frithiof returned north-ward, determined to visit Sigurd Ring's court and ascertain whether Ingeborg was really well and happy. Steering his vessel up the Vik (the main part of the Christiania-Fiord), he intrusted it to Björn's care, and alone, on foot, and enveloped in a tat-tered mantle, which he used as disguise, he went to the court of Sigurd Ring, arriving there just as the Yuletide festivities were being held. As if in reality nothing more than the aged beggar he appeared, Frithiof sat down upon the bench near the door, where he became the butt of the courtiers' rough jokes; but when one of his tormentors approached too closely he caught him in his powerful grasp and swung him high above his head.

Terrified by this proof of great strength, the courtiers silently withdrew, while Sigurd Ring invited the old man to remove his mantle, take a seat beside him, and share his good cheer. Frithiof accepted the invitation thus cordially given, and when he had laid aside his squalid outward apparel all started with surprise to see a handsome warrior, richly clad, and adorned with a beautiful ring.

"Now from the old man's stooping head is loosed the sable hood,
When lo! a young man smiling stands, where erst the old one stood.
See! From his lofty forehead, round shoulders broad and strong, The
golden locks flow glistening, like sunlight waves along.

"He stood before them glorious in velvet mantle blue, His baldrics broad, with silver worked, the artist's skill did shew; For round about the hero's breast and round about his waist, The beasts and birds of forest wild, embossed, each other chased.

"The armlet's yellow luster shone rich upon his arm; His war sword by his side—in strife a thunderbolt alarm. Serene the hero cast his glance around the men of war; Bright stood he there as Balder, as tall as Asa Thor."

TEGNÉR, *Frithiof Saga* (Spalding's tr.).

But although his appearance was so unusual, none of the people present recognized him save Ingeborg only; and when the king asked him who he was he evasively replied that he was Thiolf (a thief), that he came from Ulf's (the wolf's), and had been brought up in Anger (sorrow or grief). Notwithstanding this unenticing account of himself, Sigurd Ring invited him to remain; and Frithiof, accepting the proffered hospitality, became the constant companion of the king and queen, whom he accompanied wherever they went.

One day, when the royal couple were seated in a sleigh and skimming along a frozen stream, Frithiof sped on his skates before them, performing graceful evolutions, and cutting Ingeborg's name deep in the ice. All at once the ice broke and the sleigh disappeared; but Frithiof, springing forward, caught the horse by the bridle, and by main force dragged them all out of their perilous position.

When spring came, Sigurd Ring invited Frithiof to accompany

FRITHIOF AT THE COURT OF KING RING.—Kepler.

him on a hunting expedition. The king became separated from all the rest of his suite, and saying that he was too weary to continue the chase, he lay down to rest upon the cloak which Frithiof spread out for him, resting his head upon his young guest's knee.

> "Then threw Frithiof down his mantle, and upon the greensward spread,
> And the ancient king so trustful laid on Frithiof's knee his head;
> Slept, as calmly as the hero sleepeth after war's alarms
> On his shield, calm as an infant sleepeth in its mother's arms."
> TEGNÉR, *Frithiof Saga* (Longfellow's tr.).

While the aged king was thus reposing, the birds and beasts of the forest softly drew near, bidding Frithiof take advantage of his host's unconsciousness to slay him and recover the bride of whom he had been unfairly deprived. But although Frithiof understood the language of birds and beasts, and his hot young heart clamored for his beloved, he utterly refused to listen to them; and, fearing lest he should involuntarily harm his trusting host, he impulsively flung his sword far from him into a neighboring thicket.

A few moments later Sigurd Ring awoke from his feigned sleep, and after telling Frithiof that he had recognized him from the first, had tested him in many ways, and had always found his honor fully equal to his vaunted courage, he bade him be patient a little longer, for his end was very near, and said that he would die happy if he could leave Ingeborg, his infant heir, and his kingdom in such good hands. Then, taking the astonished Frithiof's arm, Sigurd Ring returned home, where, feeling death draw near, he dedicated himself anew to Odin by carving the Geirs-odd, or sacrificial runes, deeply in his aged chest.

> "Bravely he slashes
> Odin's red letters,
> Blood-runes of heroes, on arm and on breast.
> Brightly the splashes
> Of life's flowing fetters
> Drip from the silver of hair-covered chest."
> TEGNÉR, *Frithiof Saga* (Spalding's tr.).

When this ceremony was finished, Sigurd Ring laid Ingeborg's hand in Frithiof's, and, once more commending her to the young hero's loving care, closed his eyes and breathed his last.

All the nation assembled to raise a mound for Sigurd Ring; and by his own request the funeral feast was closed by a banquet to celebrate the betrothal of Ingeborg and Frithiof. The latter had won the people's enthusiastic admiration; but when they would fain have elected him king, Frithiof raised Sigurd Ring's little son up on his shield and presented him to the assembled nobles as their future king, publicly swearing to uphold him until he was of age to defend himself. The child, weary of his cramped position on the shield, boldly sprang to the ground as soon as Frithiof's speech was ended, and alighted upon his feet. This act of daring in so small a child was enough to win the affection and admiration of all his rude subjects.

According to some accounts, Frithiof now made war against Ingeborg's brothers, and after conquering them, allowed them to retain their kingdom only upon condition of their paying him a yearly tribute. Then he and Ingeborg remained in Ringric until the young king was able to assume the government, when they repaired to Hordaland, a kingdom Frithiof had obtained by conquest, and which he left to his sons Gungthiof and Hunthiof.

But according to Tegnér's poem, Frithiof, soon after his second betrothal to Ingeborg, made a pious pilgrimage to his father's resting place, and while seated on the latter's funeral mound, plunged in melancholy and remorse at the sight of the desolation about him, he was favored by a vision of a new temple, more beautiful than the first, within whose portals he beheld the three Norns.

> "And lo! reclining on their runic shields
> The mighty Nornas now the portal fill;
> Three rosebuds fair which the same garden yields,
> With aspect serious, but charming still.
> Whilst Urda points upon the blackened fields,
> The fairy temple Skulda doth reveal.
> When Frithiof first his dazzled senses cleared,
> Rejoiced, admired, the vision disappeared."
>
> TEGNÉR, *Frithiof Saga* (Spalding's tr.).

The hero immediately understood that the gods had thus pointed out to him a means of atonement, and spared neither wealth nor pains to restore Balder's temple and grove, which soon rose out of the ashes in more than their former splendor.

When the temple was all finished, and duly consecrated to Balder's service, Frithiof received Ingeborg at the altar from her brothers' hands, and ever after lived on amicable terms with them.

> "Now stepped Halfdan in
> Over the brazen threshold, and with wistful look
> Stood silent, at a distance from the dreaded one.
> Then Frithiof loosed the Harness-hater from his thigh,
> Against the altar placed the golden buckler round,
> And forward came unarmed to meet his enemy:
> 'In such a strife,' thus he commenced, with friendly voice,
> 'The noblest he who first extends the hand of peace.'
> Then blushed King Halfdan deep, and drew his gauntlet off,
> And long-divided hands now firmly clasped each other,
> A mighty pressure, steadfast as the mountain's base.
> The old man then absolved him from the curse which lay
> Upon the Varg i Veum,[7] on the outlawed man.
> And as he spake the words, fair Ingeborg came in,
> Arrayed in bridal dress, and followed by fair maids,
> E'en as the stars escort the moon in heaven's vault.
> Whilst tears suffused her soft and lovely eyes, she fell
> Into her brother's arms, but deeply moved he led
> His cherished sister unto Frithiof's faithful breast,
> And o'er the altar of the god she gave her hand
> Unto her childhood's friend, the darling of her heart."
> TEGNÉR, *Frithiof Saga* (Spalding's tr.).

7   Wolf in the sanctuaries.

CHAPTER XVI

RAGNAR LODBROK.

"Last from among the Heroes one came near,
No God, but of the hero troop the chief—
Regner, who swept the northern sea with fleets,
And ruled o'er Denmark and the heathy isles,
Living; but Ella captured him and slew;—
A king whose fame then fill'd the vast of Heaven,
Now time obscures it, and men's later deeds."
MATTHEW ARNOLD, *Balder Dead.*

Ragnar Lodbrok, who figures in history as the contemporary of Charlemagne, is one of the great northern heroes, to whom many mythical deeds of valor are ascribed. His story has given rise not only to the celebrated Ragnar Lodbrok saga, so popular in the thirteenth century, but also to many poems and songs by ancient scalds and modern poets. The material of the Ragnar Lodbrok saga was probably largely borrowed from the Volsunga saga and from the saga of Dietrich von Bern, the chief aim of the ancient composers being to connect the Danish dynasty of kings with the great hero Sigurd, the slayer of Fafnir, and thereby to prove that their ancestor was no less a person than Odin.

The hero of this saga was Ragnar, the son of Sigurd Ring and his first wife, Alfild. According to one version of the story, as we have seen, Sigurd Ring married Ingeborg, and died, leaving Frithiof to protect his young son. According to another, Sigurd Ring appointed Ragnar as his successor, and had him recognized as future ruler by the Thing before he set out upon his last military expedition.

This was a quest for a new wife named Alfsol, a princess of Jutland, with whom, in spite of his advanced years, he had fallen passionately in love. Her family, however, rudely refused Sigurd Ring's request.

When he came to win his bride by the force of arms, and they saw themselves defeated, they poisoned Alfsol rather than have her fall alive into the viking's hands.

Sigurd Ring, finding a corpse where he had hoped to clasp a living and loving woman, was so overcome with grief that he now resolved to die too. By his orders Alfsol's body was laid in state on a funeral pyre on his best ship. Then, when the fire had been kindled, and the ship cut adrift from its moorings, Sigurd Ring sprang on board, and, stabbing himself, was burned with the fair maiden he loved.

Ragnar was but fifteen years old when he found himself called upon to reign; but just as he outshone all his companions in beauty and intelligence, so he could match the bravest heroes in courage and daring, and generally escaped uninjured from every battle, owing to a magic shirt which his mother had woven for him.

> "'I give thee the long shirt,
> Nowhere sewn,
> Woven with a loving mind,
> Of hair——[obscure word].
> Wounds will not bleed
> Nor will edges bite thee
> In the holy garment;
> It was consecrated to the gods.'"
> *Ragnar Lodbrok Saga.*

Of course the young hero led out his men every summer upon some exciting viking expedition, to test their courage and supply them with plunder; for all the northern heroes proudly boasted that the sword was their god and gold was their goddess.

On one occasion Ragnar landed in a remote part of Norway, and having climbed one of the neighboring mountains, he looked down upon a fruitful valley inhabited by Lodgerda, a warrior maiden who delighted in the chase and all athletic exercises, and ruled over all that part of the country. Ragnar immediately resolved to visit this fair maiden; and, seeing her manifold attractions, he soon fell in love with her and married her. She joined him in all his active pursuits; but in spite of all his entreaties, she would not consent to leave her native land and accompany him home.

After spending three years in Norway with Lodgerda, the young viking became restless and unhappy; and learning that his kingdom had been raided during his prolonged absence, he parted from his wife in hot haste. He pursued his enemies to Whitaby and to Lym-Fiord, winning a signal victory over them in both places, and then reentered his capital of Hledra in triumph, amid the acclamations of his joyful people.

He had not been resting long upon his newly won laurels when a northern seer came to his court, and showed him in a magic mirror the image of Thora, the beautiful daughter of Jarl Herrand in East Gothland. Ragnar, who evidently considered himself freed from all matrimonial bonds by his wife's refusal to accompany him home, eagerly questioned the seer concerning the radiant vision.

This man then revealed to him that Thora, having at her father's request carefully brought up a dragon from an egg hatched by a swan, had at last seen it assume such colossal proportions that it coiled itself all around the house where she dwelt. Here it watched over her with jealous care, allowing none to approach except the servant who brought the princess her meals and who provided an ox daily for the monster's sustenance. Jarl Herrand had offered Thora's hand in marriage, and immense sums of gold, to any hero brave enough to slay this dragon; but none dared venture within reach of its powerful jaws, whence came fire, venom, and noxious vapors.

Ragnar, who as usual thirsted for adventure, immediately made up his mind to go and fight this dragon; and, after donning a peculiar leather and woolen garment, all smeared over with pitch, he attacked and successfully slew the monster.

> "'Nor long before
> In arms I reached the Gothic shore,
> To work the loathly serpent's death.
> I slew the reptile of the heath.'"
>
> *Death Song of Regner Lodbrock* (Herbert's tr.).

In commemoration of this victory, Ragnar ever after bore also the name of Lodbrok (Leather Hose), although he laid aside this garment as soon as possible, and appeared in royal garb, to receive his prize, the beautiful maiden Thora, whom he had delivered, and whom he now took to be his wife.

> "'My prize was Thora; from that fight,
> 'Mongst warriors am I Lodbrock hight.
> I pierced the monster's scaly side
> With steel, the soldier's wealth and pride.'"
>
> *Death Song of Regner Lodbrock* (Herbert's tr.).

Thora gladly accompanied Ragnar back to Hledra, lived happily with him for several years, and bore him two sturdy sons, Agnar and Erik, who soon gave proof of uncommon courage. Such was Ragnar's devotion to his new wife that he even forbore to take part in the usual viking expeditions, to linger by her side. All his love could not long avail to keep her with him, however, for she soon sickened and died, leaving him an inconsolable widower.

To divert him from his great sorrow, his subjects finally proposed that he should resume his former adventurous career, and prevailed upon him to launch his dragon ship once more and to set sail for foreign shores. Some time during the cruise their bread supply failed, and Ragnar steered his vessel into the port of Spangarhede, where he bade his men carry their flour ashore and ask the people in a hut which he descried there to help them knead and bake their bread. The sailors obeyed; but when they entered the lowly hut and saw the filthy old woman who appeared to be its sole occupant, they hesitated to bespeak her aid.

While they were deliberating what they should do, a beautiful girl, poorly clad, but immaculately clean, entered the hut; and the old woman, addressing her as Krake (Crow), bade her see what the strangers wanted. They told her, and admiringly watched her as she deftly fashioned the dough into loaves and slipped them into the hot oven. She bade the sailors watch them closely, lest they should burn; but these men forgot all about their loaves to gaze upon her as she flitted about the house, and the result was that their bread was badly burned.

When they returned to the vessel, Ragnar Lodbrok reproved them severely for their carelessness, until the men, to justify themselves, began describing the maiden Krake in such glowing terms that the chief finally expressed a desire to see her. With the view of testing her wit and intelligence, as well as her beauty, Ragnar sent a message bidding her appear before him neither naked nor clad, neither alone nor unaccompanied, neither fasting nor yet having partaken of any food.

This singular message was punctually delivered, and Krake, who was as clever as beautiful, soon presented herself, with a fish net wound several times around her graceful form, her sheep dog beside her, and the odor of the leek she had bitten into still hovering over her ruby lips.

Ragnar, charmed by her ingenuity no less than by her extreme beauty, then and there proposed to marry her. But Krake, who was not to be so lightly won, declared that he must first prove the depth of his affection by remaining constant to her for one whole year, at the end of which time she would marry him if he still cared to claim her hand.

The year passed by; Ragnar returned to renew his suit, and Krake, satisfied that she had inspired no momentary passion, forsook the aged couple and accompanied the great viking to Hledra, where she became queen of Denmark. She bore Ragnar four sons—Ivar, Björn, Hvitserk, and Rogenwald,—who from earliest infancy longed to emulate the prowess of their father, Ragnar, and of their step-brothers, Erik and Agnar, who even in their youth were already great vikings.

The Danes, however, had never fully approved of Ragnar's last marriage, and murmured frequently because they were obliged to obey a lowborn queen, and one who bore the vulgar name of Krake. Little by little these murmurs grew louder, and finally they came to Ragnar's ears while he was visiting Eystein, King of Svithiod (Sweden). Craftily his courtiers went to work, and finally prevailed upon him to sue for the princess's hand. He did so, and left Sweden promising to divorce Krake when he reached home, and to return as soon as possible to claim his bride.

As Ragnar entered the palace at Hledra, Krake came, as usual, to meet him. His conscience smote him, and he answered all her tender inquiries so roughly that she suddenly turned and asked him why he had made arrangements to divorce her and take a new wife. Surprised at her knowledge, for he fancied the matter still a secret, Ragnar Lodbrok asked who had told her. Thereupon Krake explained that, feeling anxious about him, she had sent her pet magpies after him, and that the birds had come home and revealed all.

This answer, which perhaps gave rise to the common expression, "A little bird told me," greatly astonished Ragnar. He was about to try to excuse himself when Krake, drawing herself up proudly, declared that while she was perfectly ready to depart, it was but just that he should now learn that her extraction was far less humble than he thought. She then proceeded to tell him that her real name was Aslaug, and that she was the daughter of Sigurd Fafnisbane (the slayer of Fafnir) and the beautiful Valkyr Brunhild. Her grandfather, or her foster father, Heimir, to protect her from the foes who would fain have taken her life, had hidden her in his hollow harp when she was but a babe. He had tenderly cared for her until he was treacherously murdered by peasants, who had found her in the hollow harp instead of the treasure they sought there.

> "Let be—as ancient stories tell—
> Full knowledge upon Ragnar fell
> In lapse of time, that this was she
> Begot in the felicity
> Swift-fleeting of the wondrous twain,
> Who afterwards through change and pain
> Must live apart to meet in death."
> WILLIAM MORRIS, *The Fostering of Aslaug.*

In proof of her assertion, Aslaug then produced a ring and a letter which had belonged to her illustrious mother, and foretold that her next child, a son, would bear the image of a dragon in his right eye, as a sign that he was a grandson of the Dragon Slayer, whose memory was honored by all.

Convinced of the truth of these statements, Ragnar no longer showed any desire to repudiate his wife; but, on the contrary, he besought her to remain with him, and bade his subjects call her Aslaug.

Shortly after this reconciliation the queen gave birth to a fifth son, who, as she had predicted, came into the world with a peculiar birthmark, to which he owed his name—Sigurd the Snake-eyed. As it was customary for kings to intrust their sons to some noted warrior to foster, this child was given to the celebrated Norman pirate, Hastings, who, as soon as his charge had attained a suitable age, taught him the art of viking warfare, and took him, with his four elder brothers, to raid the coasts of all the southern countries.

Ivar, the eldest of Ragnar and Aslaug's sons, although crippled from birth, and unable to walk a step, was always ready to join in the fray, into the midst of which he was borne on a shield. From this point of vantage he shot arrow after arrow, with fatal accuracy of aim. As he had employed much of his leisure time in learning runes [8]and all kinds of magic arts, he was often of great assistance to his brothers, who generally chose him leader of their expeditions.

While Ragnar's five sons were engaged in fighting the English at Whitaby to punish them for plundering and setting fire to some Danish ships, Rogenwald fell to rise no more.

Eystein, the Swedish king, now assembled a large army and declared war against the Danes, because their monarch had failed to return at the appointed time and claim the bride for whom he had sued. Ragnar would fain have gone forth to meet the enemy in person, but Agnar and Erik, his two eldest sons, craved permission to go in his stead. They met the Swedish king, but in spite of their valor they soon succumbed to an attack made by an enchanted cow.

> "'We smote with swords; at dawn of day
> Hundred spearmen gasping lay,
> Bent beneath the arrowy strife.
> Egill reft my son of life;
> Too soon my Agnar's youth was spent,
> The scabbard thorn his bosom rent.'"
> *Death Song of Regner Lodbrock* (Herbert's tr.).

Ragnar was about to sally forth to avenge them, when Hastings and the other sons returned. Then Aslaug prevailed upon her husband to linger by her side and delegate the duty of revenge to his sons. In this battle Ivar made use of his magic to slay Eystein's cow, which could make more havoc than an army of warriors. His brothers, having slain Eystein and raided the country, then sailed off to renew their depredations elsewhere.

This band of vikings visited the coasts of England, Ireland, France,

8   See Guerber's Myths of Northern Lands, p. 39.

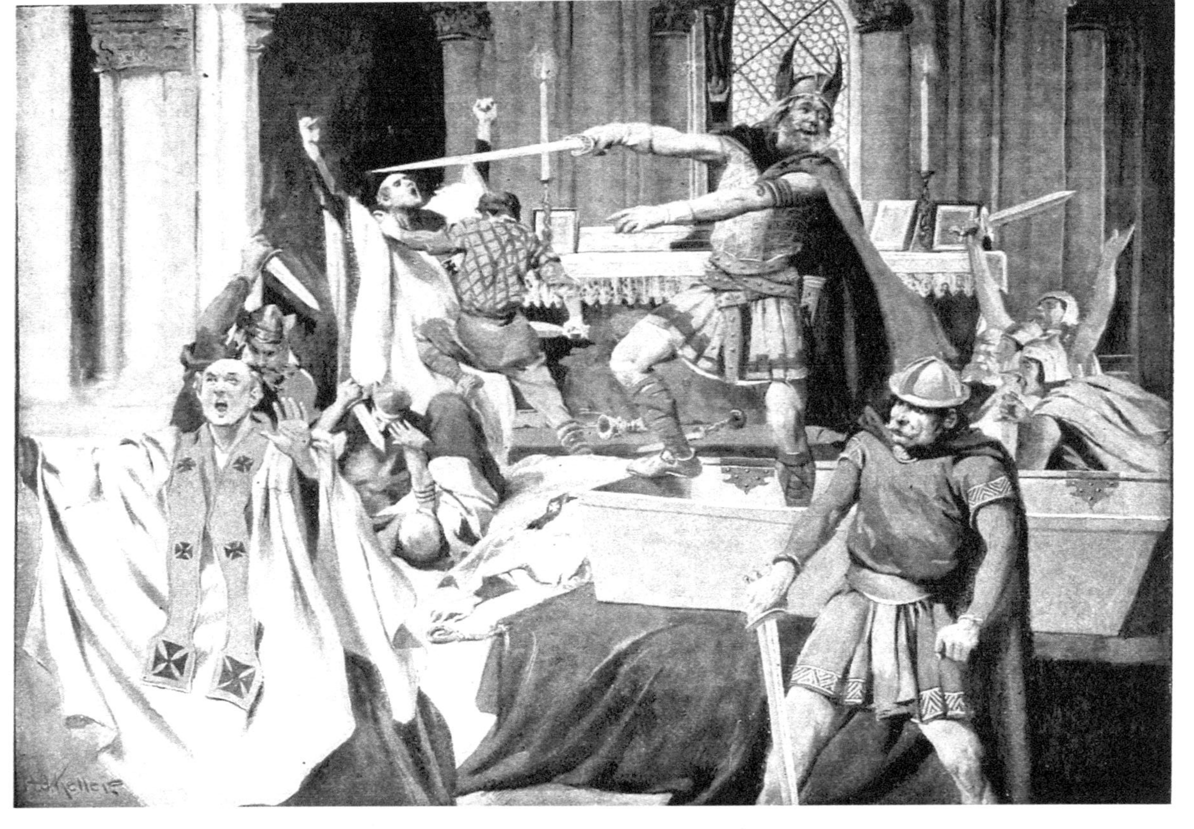

STRATEGY OF HASTINGS—Keller.

Italy, Greece, and the Greek isles, plundering, murdering, and burning wherever they went. Assisted by Hastings, the brothers took Wiflisburg (probably the Roman Aventicum), and even besieged Luna in Etruria.

As this city was too strongly fortified and too well garrisoned to yield to an assault, the Normans (as all the northern pirates were indiscriminately called in the South) resolved to secure it by stratagem. They therefore pretended that Hastings, their leader, was desperately ill, and induced a bishop to come out of the town to baptize him, so that he might die in the Christian faith. Three days later they again sent a herald to say that Hastings had died, and that his last wish had been to be buried in a Christian church. They therefore asked permission to enter the city unarmed, and bear their leader to his last resting place, promising not only to receive baptism, but also to endow with great wealth the church where Hastings was buried.

The inhabitants of Luna, won by these specious promises, immediately opened their gates, and the funeral procession filed solemnly into the city. But, in the midst of the mass, the coffin lid flew open, and Hastings sprang out, sword in hand, and killed the officiating bishop and priests. This example was followed by his soldiers, who produced the weapons they had concealed upon their persons, and slew all the inhabitants of the town.

These lawless invaders were about to proceed to Romaburg (Rome), and sack that city also, but were deterred by a pilgrim whom they met. He told them that the city was so far away that he had worn out two pairs of iron-soled shoes in coming from thence. The Normans, believing this tale, which was only a stratagem devised by the quick-witted pilgrim, spared the Eternal City, and, reembarking in their vessels, sailed home.

Ragnar Lodbrok, in the mean while, had not been inactive, but had continued his adventurous career, winning numerous battles, and bringing home much plunder to enrich his kingdom and subjects.

> "I have fought battles
> Fifty and one
> Which were famous;
> I have wounded many men."
> *Ragnar's Sons' Saga.*

The hero's last expedition was against Ella, King of Northumberland. From the very outset the gods seemed to have decided that Ragnar should not prove as successful as usual. The poets tell us that they even sent the Valkyrs (battle maidens of northern mythology) to warn him of his coming defeat, and to tell him of the bliss awaiting him in Valhalla.

> "'Regner! tell thy fair-hair'd bride
> She must slumber at thy side!
> Tell the brother of thy breast
> Even for him thy grave hath rest!
> Tell the raven steed which bore thee
> When the wild wolf fled before thee,
> He too with his lord must fall,—
> There is room in Odin's Hall!'"
>   MRS. HEMANS, *Valkyriur Song.*

In spite of this warning, Ragnar went on. Owing to the magic shirt he wore, he stood unharmed in the midst of the slain long after all his brave followers had perished; and it was only after a whole day's fighting that the enemy finally succeeded in making him a prisoner. Then the followers of Ella vainly besought Ragnar to speak and tell his name. As he remained obstinately silent they finally flung him into a den of snakes, where the reptiles crawled all over him, vainly trying to pierce the magic shirt with their venomous fangs. Ella perceived at last that it was this garment which preserved his captive from death, and had it forcibly removed. Ragnar was then thrust back amid the writhing, hissing snakes, which bit him many times. Now that death was near, the hero's tongue was loosened, not to give vent to weak complaints, but to chant a triumphant death song, in which he recounted his manifold battles, and foretold that his brave sons would avenge his cruel death.

> "'Grim stings the adder's forked dart;
> The vipers nestle in my heart.
> But soon, I wot, shall Vider's wand,
> Fixed in Ella's bosom stand.
> My youthful sons with rage will swell,

> Listening how their father fell;
> Those gallant boys in peace unbroken
> Will never rest, till I be wroken [avenged].'"
>
> *Death Song of Regner Lodbrock* (Herbert's tr.).

This heroic strain has been immortalized by ancient scalds and modern poets. They have all felt the same admiration for the dauntless old viking, who, even amid the pangs of death, gloried in his past achievements, and looked ardently forward to his sojourn in Valhalla. There, he fancied, he would still be able to indulge in warfare, his favorite pastime, and would lead the einheriar (spirits of dead warriors) to their daily battles.

> '"Cease, my strain! I hear a voice
> From realms where martial souls rejoice;
> I hear the maids of slaughter call,
> Who bid me hence to Odin's hall:
> High seated in their blest abodes
> I soon shall quaff the drink of gods.
> The hours of life have glided by;
> I fall, but smiling shall I die.'"
>
> *Death Song of Regner Lodbrock* (Herbert's tr.).

Ragnar Lodbrok's sons had reached home, and were peacefully occupied in playing chess, when a messenger came to announce their father's sad end. In their impatience to avenge him they started out without waiting to collect a large force, and in spite of many inauspicious omens. Ella, who expected them, met them with a great host, composed not only of all his own subjects but also of many allies, among whom was King Alfred. In spite of their valor the Normans were completely defeated by the superior forces of the enemy, and only a few of them survived. Ivar and his remaining followers consented to surrender at last, provided that Ella would atone for their losses by giving them as much land as an oxhide would inclose. This seemingly trifling request was granted without demur, nor could the king retract his promise when he saw that the oxhide, cut into tiny strips, inclosed a vast space of land, upon which the Normans now proceeded to construct an almost impregnable fortress, called Lunduna Burg (London).

Here Ivar took up his permanent abode, while his brothers returned to Hledra. Little by little he alienated the affections of Ella's subjects, and won them over to him by rich gifts and artful flattery. When sure of their allegiance, he incited them to revolt against the king; and as he had solemnly sworn never to bear arms against Ella, he kept the letter of his promise by sending for his brothers to act as their leaders.

As a result of this revolution Ella was made prisoner. Then the fierce vikings stretched him out upon one of those rude stone altars which can still be seen in England, and ruthlessly avenged their father's cruel death by cutting the bloody eagle upon him.[9] After Ella's death, Ivar became even more powerful than before, while his younger brothers continued their viking expeditions, took an active part in all the piratical incursions of the time, and even, we are told, besieged Paris in the reign of Louis the Fat.

Other Danish and Scandinavian vikings were equally venturesome and successful, and many eventually settled in the lands which they had conquered. Among these was the famous Rollo (Rolf Ganger), who, too gigantic in stature to ride horseback, always went on foot. He settled with his followers in a fertile province in northern France, which owes to them its name of Normandy.

The rude independence of the Northmen is well illustrated by their behavior when called to court to do homage for this new fief. Rollo was directed to place both his hands between those of the king, and take his vow of allegiance; so he submitted with indifferent grace. But when he was told that he must conclude the ceremony by kissing the monarch's foot, he obstinately refused to do so. A proxy was finally suggested, and Rollo, calling one of his Berserkers, bade him take his place. The stalwart giant strode forward, but instead of kneeling, he grasped the king's foot and raised it to his lips. As the king did not expect such a jerk, he lost his balance and fell heavily backward. All the Frenchmen present were, of course, scandalized; but the barbarian refused to make any apology, and strode haughtily out of the place, vowing he would never come to court again.

All the northern pirates were, as we have seen, called Normans. They did not all settle in the North, however, for many of them found their way

9   See Guerber's Myths of Northern Lands, p. 85.

into Italy, and even to Constantinople. There they formed the celebrated Varangian Guard, and faithfully watched over the safety of the emperor. It was probably one of these soldiers who traced the runes upon the stone lion which was subsequently transferred to Venice, where it now adorns the Piazza of St. Mark's.

> "Rose the Norseman chief Hardrada, like a lion from his lair;
> His the fearless soul to conquer, his the willing soul to dare.
> Gathered Skald and wild Varingar, where the raven banner shone,
> And the dread steeds of the ocean, left the Northland's frozen zone."
> VAIL, Marri's Vision.

CHAPTER XVII

THE CID.

The ballads of the Cid, which number about two hundred, and some of which are of undoubted antiquity, were not committed to writing until the twelfth century, when a poem of about three thousand lines was composed. This poem, descriptive of a national hero's exploits, was probably written about half a century after his death. The earliest manuscript of it now extant bears the date either 1245 or 1345. The Cid was a real personage, named Rodrigo Diaz, or Ruy Diaz. He was born in Burgos, in the eleventh century, and won the name of "Cid" (Conqueror) by defeating five Moorish kings, when Spain had been in the hands of the Arabs for more than three centuries.

> "Mighty victor, never vanquish'd,
>   Bulwark of our native land,
> Shield of Spain, her boast and glory,
>   Knight of the far-dreaded brand,
> Venging scourge of Moors and traitors,
>   Mighty thunderbolt of war,
> Mirror bright of chivalry,
>   Ruy, my Cid Campeador!"
>   *Ancient Spanish Ballads* (Lockhart's tr.).

Rodrigo was still a young and untried warrior when his aged father, Diego Laynez, was grossly and publicly insulted by Don Gomez, who gave him a blow in the face. Diego was far too feeble to seek the usual redress, arms in hand; but the insult rankled deep in his heart, preventing him from either sleeping or eating, and imbittering every moment of his life.

> "Sleep was banish'd from his eyelids;
>   Not a mouthful could he taste;
> There he sat with downcast visage,—
>   Direly had he been disgrac'd.
>
> "Never stirr'd he from his chamber;
>   With no friends would he converse,
> Lest the breath of his dishonor
>   Should pollute them with its curse."
>   *Ancient Spanish Ballads* (Lockhart's tr.).

At last, however, Diego confessed his shame to his son Rodrigo, who impetuously vowed to avenge him. Armed with his father's cross-hilted sword, and encouraged by his solemn blessing, Rodrigo marched into the hall of Don Gomez, and challenged him to fight. In spite of his youth, Rodrigo conducted himself so bravely in this his first encounter that he slew his opponent, and by shedding his blood washed out the stain upon his father's honor, according to the chivalric creed of the time. Then, to convince Diego that he had been duly avenged, the young hero cut off the head of Don Gomez, and triumphantly laid it before him.

> "'Ne'er again thy foe can harm thee;
>   All his pride is now laid low;
> Vain his hand is now to smite thee,
>   And this tongue is silent now.'"
>   *Ancient Spanish Ballads* (Lockhart's tr.).

Happy once more, old Diego again left home, and went to King Ferdinand's court, where he bade Rodrigo do homage to the king. The proud youth obeyed this command with indifferent grace, and his bearing was so defiant that the frightened monarch banished him from his presence. Rodrigo therefore departed with three hundred kindred spirits. He soon encountered the Moors, who were invading Castile, defeated them in battle, took five of their kings prisoners, and released them only after they had promised to pay tribute and to refrain from further warfare. They were so grateful for their liberty that they pledged themselves to do his will, and departed, calling him "Cid," the name by which he was thenceforth known.

As Rodrigo had delivered the land from a great danger, King Ferdinand now restored him to favor and gave him an honorable place among his courtiers, who, however, were all somewhat inclined to be jealous of the fame the young man had won. Shortly after his triumphant return, Doña Ximena, daughter of Don Gomez, also appeared in Burgos, and, falling at the king's feet, demanded justice. Then, seeing the Cid among the courtiers, she vehemently denounced him for having slain her father, and bade him take her life also, as she had no wish to survive a parent whom she adored.

> "'Thou hast slain the best and bravest
>   That e'er set a lance in rest;
> Of our holy faith the bulwark,—
>   Terror of each Paynim breast.
>
> "'Traitorous murderer, slay me also!
>   Though a woman, slaughter me!
> Spare not—I'm Ximena Gomez,
>   Thine eternal enemy!
>
> "'Here's my throat—smite, I beseech thee!
>   Smite, and fatal be thy blow!
> Death is all I ask, thou caitiff,—
>   Grant this boon unto thy foe.'"
>   *Ancient Spanish Ballads* (Lockhart's tr.).

As this denunciation and appeal remained without effect (for the king had been too well served by the Cid to listen to any accusation against him), the distressed damsel departed, only to return to court three times upon the same fruitless errand. During this time the valor and services of the Cid had been so frequently discussed in her presence that on her fifth visit to Ferdinand she consented to forego all further thoughts of vengeance, if the king would but order the young hero to marry her instead.

> "'I am daughter of Don Gomez,
>   Count of Gormaz was he hight,
> Him Rodrigo by his valor
>   Did o'erthrow in mortal fight.

> "'King, I come to crave a favor—
> This the boon for which I pray,
> That thou give me this Rodrigo
> For my wedded lord this day.'"
> *Ancient Spanish Ballads* (Lockhart's tr.).

The king, who had suspected for some time past that the Cid had fallen in love with his fair foe, immediately sent for him. Rodrigo entered the city with his suite of three hundred men, proposed marriage to Ximena, and was accepted on the spot. His men then proceeded to array him richly for his wedding, and bound on him his famous sword Tizona, which he had won from the Moors. The marriage was celebrated with much pomp and rejoicing, the king giving Rodrigo the cities of Valduerna, Soldañia, Belforado, and San Pedro de Cardeña as a marriage portion. When the marriage ceremony was finished, Rodrigo, wishing to show his wife all honor, declared that he would not rest until he had won five battles, and would only then really consider himself entitled, to claim her love.

> "'A man I slew—a man I give thee—
> Here I stand thy will to bide!
> Thou, in place of a dead father,
> Hast a husband at thy side.'"
> *Ancient Spanish Ballads* (Lockhart's tr.).

Before beginning this war, however, the Cid remembered a vow he had made; and, accompanied by twenty brave young hidalgos, he set out for a pious pilgrimage to Santiago de Compostela, the shrine of the patron saint of Spain. On his way thither he frequently distributed alms, paused to recite a prayer at every church and wayside shrine, and, meeting a leper, ate, drank, and even slept with him in a village inn. When Rodrigo awoke in the middle of the night, he found his bedfellow gone, but was favored by a vision of St. Lazarus, who praised his charity, and promised him great temporal prosperity and eternal life.

> "'Life shall bring thee no dishonor—
> Thou shalt ever conqueror be;

Death shall find thee still victorious,
    For God's blessing rests on thee.'"
        Ancient Spanish Ballads (Lockhart's tr.).

When his pilgrimage was ended, Rodrigo further showed his piety by setting aside a large sum of money for the establishment of a leper house, which, in honor of the saint who visited him, was called "St. Lazarus." He then hastened off to Calahorra, a frontier town of Castile and Aragon, which was a bone of contention between two monarchs.

Just before the Cid's arrival, Don Ramiro of Aragon had arranged with Ferdinand of Castile that their quarrel should be decided by a duel between two knights. Don Ramiro therefore selected as his champion Martin Gonzalez, while Ferdinand intrusted his cause to the Cid. The duel took place; and when the two champions found themselves face to face, Martin Gonzalez began to taunt Rodrigo, telling him that he would never again be able to mount his favorite steed Babieça, or see his wife, as he was doomed to die.

    "'Sore, Rodrigo, must thou tremble
        Now to meet me in the fight,
    Since thy head will soon be sever'd
        For a trophy of my might.

    "'Never more to thine own castle
        Wilt thou turn Babieça's rein;
    Never will thy lov'd Ximena
        See thee at her side again.'"
        Ancient Spanish Ballads (Lockhart's tr.).

This boasting did not in the least dismay the Cid, who fought so bravely that he defeated Martin Gonzalez, and won such plaudits that the jealousy of the Castilian knights was further excited. In their envy they even plotted with the Moors to slay Rodrigo by treachery. This plan did not succeed, however, because the Moorish kings whom he had captured and released gave him a timely warning of the threatening danger.

The king, angry at this treachery, banished the jealous courtiers, and, aided by Rodrigo, defeated the hostile Moors in Estremadura.

There the Christian army besieged Coimbra in vain for seven whole months, and were about to give up in despair of securing the city, when St. James appeared to a pilgrim, promising his help on the morrow.

When the battle began, the Christian knights were fired by the example of a radiant warrior, mounted on a snow-white steed, who led them into the thickest of the fray and helped them win a signal victory. This knight, whom no one recognized as one of their own warriors, was immediately hailed as St. James, and it was his name which the Spaniards then and there adopted as their favorite battle cry.

The city of Coimbra having been taken, Don Rodrigo was duly knighted by the king; while the queen and princesses vied with one another in helping him don the different pieces of his armor, for they too were anxious to show how highly they valued his services.

After a few more victories over his country's enemies, the triumphant Cid returned to Zamora, where Ximena, his wife, was waiting for him, and where the five Moorish kings sent not only the promised tribute, but rich gifts to their generous conqueror. Although the Cid rejoiced in these tokens, he gave all the tribute and the main part of the spoil to Ferdinand, his liege lord, for he considered the glory of success a sufficient reward for himself.

While the Cid was thus resting upon his laurels, a great council had been held at Florence, where the Emperor (Henry III.) of Germany complained to the Pope that King Ferdinand had not done him homage for his crown, and that he refused to acknowledge his superiority. The Pope immediately sent a message to King Ferdinand asking for homage and tribute, and threatening a crusade in case of disobedience. This unwelcome message greatly displeased the Spanish ruler, and roused the indignation of the Cid, who declared that his king was the vassal of no monarch, and offered to fight any one who dared maintain a contrary opinion.

> "'Never yet have we done homage—
> Shall we to a stranger bow?
> Great the honor God hath given us—
> Shall we lose that honor now?
>
> "'Send then to the Holy Father,

> Proudly thus to him reply—
> Thou, the king, and I, Rodrigo,
> Him and all his power defy.'"
>> *Ancient Spanish Ballads* (Lockhart's tr.).

This challenge was sent to the Pope, who, not averse to having the question settled by the judgment of God, bade the emperor send a champion to meet Rodrigo. This imperial champion was of course defeated, and all King Ferdinand's enemies were so grievously routed by the ever-victorious Cid that no further demands of homage or tribute were ever made.

Old age had now come on, and King Ferdinand, after receiving divine warning of his speedy demise, died. He left Castile to his eldest son, Don Sancho, Leon to Don Alfonso, Galicia to Don Garcia, and gave his daughters, Doña Urraca and Doña Elvira, the wealthy cities of Zamora and Toro. Of course this disposal of property did not prove satisfactory to all his heirs, and Don Sancho was especially displeased, because he coveted the whole realm. He, however, had the Cid to serve him, and selected this doughty champion to accompany him on a visit to Rome, knowing that he would brook no insult to his lord. These previsions were fully justified, for the Cid, on noticing that a less exalted seat had been prepared for Don Sancho than for the King of France, became so violent that the Pope excommunicated him. But when the seats had been made of even height, the Cid, who was a good Catholic, humbled himself before the Pope, and the latter, knowing the hero's value as a bulwark against the heathen Moors, immediately granted him full absolution.

> "'I absolve thee, Don Ruy Diaz,
> I absolve thee cheerfully,
> If, while at my court, thou showest
> Due respect and courtesy.'"
>> *Ancient Spanish Ballads* (Lockhart's tr.).

On his return to Castile, Don Sancho found himself threatened by his namesake, the King of Navarre, and by Don Ramiro of Aragon. They both invaded Castile, but were ignominiously repulsed by the Cid. As some of the Moors had helped the invaders, the Cid next proceeded to punish them, and gave up the siege of Saragossa only when the inhabitants made terms with him. This campaign won for the Cid the title of "Campeador" (Champion), which he well deserved, as he was always ready to do battle for his king.

While Don Sancho and his invaluable ally were thus engaged, Don Garcia, King of Galicia, who was also anxious to increase his kingdom, deprived his sister Doña Urraca of her city of Zamora. In her distress the infanta came to Don Sancho and made her lament, thereby affording him the long-sought pretext to wage war against his brother, and rob him of his kingdom.

This war, in which the Cid reluctantly joined, threatened at one time to have serious consequences for Sancho. He even once found himself a prisoner of Garcia's army, shortly after Garcia had been captured by his. The Cid, occupied in another part of the field, no sooner heard of this occurrence than he hastened to the Galician nobles to offer an exchange of prisoners; but, as they rejected his offer with contempt, he soon left them in anger.

> "'Hie thee hence, Rodrigo Diaz,
>   An thou love thy liberty;
> Lest, with this thy king, we take thee
>   Into dire captivity.'"
>   *Ancient Spanish Ballads* (Lockhart's tr.).

The wrath which the Cid Campeador experienced at this discourteous treatment so increased his usual strength that he soon put the enemy to flight, recovered possession of his king, and not only made Don Garcia a prisoner, but also secured Don Alfonso who had joined in the revolt. Don Garcia was sent in chains to the castle of Luna, where he eventually died, entreating that he might be buried, with his fetters, in the city of Leon.

As for Don Alfonso, Doña Urraca pleaded his cause so successfully that he was allowed to retire into a monastery, whence he soon effected his escape and joined the Moors at Toledo. There he became the companion and ally of Alimaymon, learned all his secrets, and once, during a pretended nap, overheard the Moor state that even Toledo could be taken by the Christians, provided they had the patience to begin a seven-years' siege, and to destroy all the harvests so as to reduce the people to starvation. The information thus accidentally obtained proved invaluable to Alfonso, as will be seen, and enabled him subsequently to drive the Moors out of the city Toledo.

In the mean while Sancho, not satisfied with his triple kingdom, robbed Doña Elvira of Toro, and began to besiege Doña Urraca in Zamora, which he hoped to take also in spite of it almost impregnable position.

> "'See! where on yon cliff Zamora
>   Lifteth up her haughty brow;
> Walls of strength on high begird her,
>   Duero swift and deep below.'"
>   *Ancient Spanish Ballads* (Lockhart's tr.).

The king, utterly regardless of the Cid's openly expressed opinion that it was unworthy of a knight to attempt to deprive a woman of her inheritance, now bade him carry a message to Doña Urraca, summoning her to surrender at once. The hero went reluctantly, but only to be bitterly reproached by Urraca. She dismissed him after consulting her assembled people, who vowed to die ere they would surrender.

> "Then did swear all her brave vassals
>   In Zamora's walls to die,
> Ere unto the king they'd yield it,
>   And disgrace their chivalry."
>   *Ancient Spanish Ballads* (Lockhart's tr.).

This message so enraged Don Sancho that he banished the Cid. The latter departed for Toledo, whence he was soon recalled, however, for his monarch could do nothing without him. Thus restored to favor, the Cid began the siege of Zamora, which lasted so long that the inhabitants began to suffer all the pangs of famine.

At last a Zamoran by the name of Vellido (Bellido) Dolfos came out of the town in secret, and, under pretense of betraying the city into Don Sancho's hands, obtained a private interview with him. Dolfos availed himself of this opportunity to murder the king, and rushed back to the city before the crime was discovered. He entered the gates just in time to escape from the Cid, who had mounted hastily, without spurs, and thus could not urge Babieça on to his utmost speed and overtake the murderer.

> "'Cursed be the wretch! and cursed
> He who mounteth without spur!
> Had I arm'd my heels with rowels,
> I had slain the treacherous cur.'"
> *Ancient Spanish Ballads* (Lockhart's tr.).

The grief in the camp at the violent death of the king was very great. Don Diego Ordoñez immediately sent a challenge to Don Arìas Gonzalo, who, while accepting the combat for his son, swore that none of the Zamorans knew of the dastardly deed, which Dolfos alone had planned.

> "'Fire consume us, Count Gonzalo,
> If in this we guilty be!
> None of us within Zamora
> Of this deed had privity.
>
> "'Dolfos only is the traitor;
> None but he the king did slay.
> Thou canst safely go to battle,
> God will be thy shield and stay.'"
> *Ancient Spanish Ballads* (Lockhart's tr.).

This oath was confirmed by the outcome of the duel, and none of the besiegers ever again ventured to doubt the honor of the Zamorans.

As Don Sancho had left no children to inherit his kingdom, it came by right of inheritance to Don Alfonso, who was still at Toledo, a nominal guest, but in reality a prisoner. Doña Urraca, who was deeply attached to her brother, now managed to convey to him secret information of Don Sancho's death, and Don Alfonso cleverly effected his escape, turning his pursuers off his track by reversing his horse's shoes. When he arrived at Zamora, all were ready to do him homage except the Cid, who proudly held aloof until Don Alfonso had publicly sworn that he had not bribed Dolfos to commit the dastardly crime which had called him to the throne.

> "'Wherefore, if thou be but guiltless,
>   Straight I pray of thee to swear,—
> Thou and twelve of these thy liegemen,
>   Who with thee in exile were,—
> That in thy late brother's death
>   Thou hadst neither part nor share
> That none of ye to his murder
>   Privy or consenting were.'"
>   *Ancient Spanish Ballads* (Lockhart's tr.).

The king, angry at being thus called upon to answer for his conduct to a mere subject, viewed the Cid with great dislike, and only awaited a suitable occasion to take his revenge. During a war with the Moors he made use of a trifling pretext to banish him, allowing him only nine days to prepare for departure. The Cid accepted this cruel decree with dignity, hoping that the time would never come when the king would regret his absence, and his country need his right arm.

> "'I obey, O King Alfonso,
>   Guilty though in naught I be,
> For it doth behoove a vassal
>   To obey his lord's decree;
> Prompter far am I to serve thee
>   Than thou art to guerdon me.
>
> "'I do pray our Holy Lady
>   Her protection to afford,
> That thou never mayst in battle
>   Need the Cid's right arm and sword.'"
>   *Ancient Spanish Ballads* (Lockhart's tr.).

Amid the weeping people of Burgos, who dared not offer him help and shelter lest they should incur the king's wrath, lose all their property, and even forfeit their eyesight, the Cid slowly rode away, and camped without the city to make his final arrangements. Here a devoted follower supplied him with the necessary food, remarking that he cared "not a fig" for Alfonso's prohibitions, which is probably the first written record of the use of this now popular expression.

To obtain the necessary money the Cid pledged two locked coffers full of sand to the Jews. They, thinking that the boxes contained vast treasures, or relying upon the Cid's promise to release them for a stipulated sum, advanced him six hundred marks of gold. The Cid then took leave of his beloved wife Ximena, and of his two infant daughters, whom he intrusted to the care of a worthy ecclesiastic, and, followed by three hundred men, he rode slowly away from his native land, vowing that he would yet return, covered with glory, and bringing great spoil.

> "'Comrades, should it please high Heaven
>   That we see Castile once more,—
> Though we now go forth as outcasts,
>   Sad, dishonor'd, homeless, poor,—
> We'll return with glory laden
>   And the spellings of the Moor.'"
>   *Ancient Spanish Ballads* (Lockhart's tr.).

Such success attended the little band of exiles that within the next three weeks they won two strongholds from the Moors, and much spoil, among which was the sword Colada, which was second only to Tizona. From the spoil the Cid selected a truly regal present, which he sent to Alfonso, who in return granted a general pardon to the Cid's followers, and published an edict allowing all who wished to fight against the Moors to join him. A few more victories and another present so entirely dispelled Alfonso's displeasure that he restored the Cid to favor, and, moreover, promised that thereafter thirty days should be allowed to every exile to prepare for his departure.

When Alimaymon, King of Toledo, died, leaving Toledo in the hands of his grandson Yahia, who was generally disliked, Alfonso thought the time propitious for carrying out his long-cherished scheme of taking the city. Thanks to the valor of the Cid and the destruction of all the crops, the siege of the city progressed favorably, and it finally fell into the hands of the Christian king.

A second misunderstanding, occasioned principally by the jealous courtiers, caused Alfonso to insult the Cid, who in anger left the army and made a sudden raid in Castile. During his absence, the Moors resumed courage, and became masters of Valencia. Hearing of this disaster, the Cid promptly returned, recaptured the city, and, establishing his headquarters there, asked Alfonso to send him his wife and daughters. At the same time he sent more than the promised sum of money to the Jews to redeem the chests which, as they now first learned, were filled with nothing but sand.

> "'Say, albeit within the coffers
>   Naught but sand they can espy,
> That the pure gold of my truth
>   Deep beneath that sand doth lie."'
>   *Ancient Spanish Ballads* (Lockhart's tr.).

As the Cid was now master of Valencia and of untold wealth, his daughters were soon sought in marriage by many suitors. Among them were the Counts of Carrion, whose proposals were warmly encouraged by Alfonso. To please his royal master, the Cid consented to an alliance with them, and the marriage of both his daughters was celebrated with much pomp. In the "Chronicle of the Cid," compiled from all the ancient ballads, these festivities are recorded thus: "Who can tell the great nobleness which the Cid displayed at that wedding! the feasts and the bullfights, and the throwing at the target, and the throwing canes, and how many joculars were there, and all the sports which are proper at such weddings!"

Pleased with their sumptuous entertainment, the Infantes of Carrion lingered at Valencia two years, during which time the Cid had ample opportunity to convince himself that they were not the brave and upright husbands he would fain have secured for his daughters. In fact, all soon became aware of the young men's cowardice, for when a lion broke loose from the Cid's private menagerie and entered the hall where he was sleeping, while his guests were playing chess, the princes fled, one falling into an empty vat in his haste, and the other taking refuge behind the Cid's couch. Awakened by the noise, the Cid seized his sword, twisted his cloak around his arm, and, grasping the lion by its mane, thrust it back into its cage, and calmly returned to his place.

> "Till the good Cid awoke; he rose without alarm;
> He went to meet the lion, with his mantle on his arm.
> The lion was abash'd the noble Cid to meet,
> He bow'd his mane to earth, his muzzle at his feet.
> The Cid by the neck and mane drew him to his den,
> He thrust him in at the hatch, and came to the hall again;
> He found his knights, his vassals, and all his valiant men.
> He ask'd for his sons-in-law, they were neither of them there."
> *Chronicles of the Cid* (Southey's tr.).

This cowardly conduct of the Infantes of Carrion could not fail to call forth some gibes from the Cid's followers. The young men, however, concealed their anger, biding their time to take their revenge. During the siege of Valencia, which took place shortly after this adventure, the Infantes did not manage to show much courage either; and it was only through the kindness of Felez Muñoz, a nephew of the Cid, that one of them could exhibit a war horse which he falsely claimed to have taken from the enemy.

Thanks to the valor of the Cid, the Moors were driven away from Valencia with great loss, and peace was restored. The Infantes of Carrion then asked permission to return home with their brides, and the spoil and presents the Cid had given them, among which were the swords Colada and Tizona. The Cid escorted them part way on their journey, bade farewell to his daughters with much sorrow, and returned alone to Valencia, which appeared deserted without the presence of the children he loved.

> "The Cid he parted from his daughters,
>   Naught could he his grief disguise;
> As he clasped them to his bosom,
>   Tears did stream from out his eyes."
> *Ancient Spanish Ballads* (Lockhart's tr.).

After journeying on for some time with their brides and Felez Muñoz, who was acting as escort, the Infantes of Carrion camped near the Douro. Early the next day they sent all their suite ahead, and, being left alone with their wives, stripped them of their garments, lashed them with thorns, kicked them with their spurs, and finally left them for dead on the blood-stained ground, and rode on to join their escort.

Suspecting foul play, and fearing the worst, Felez Muñoz cleverly managed to separate himself from the party, and, riding swiftly back to the banks of the Douro, found his unhappy cousins in a sorry plight. He tenderly cared for their wounds, placed them upon his horse, and took them to the house of a poor man, whose wife and daughters undertook to nurse them, while Felez Muñoz hastened back to Valencia to tell the Cid what had occurred. The Cid Campeador then swore that he would be avenged; and as Alfonso was responsible for the marriage, he applied to him for redress.

> "'Lo! my daughters have been outrag'd!
> For thine own, thy kingdom's sake,
> Look, Alfonso, to mine honor!
> Vengeance thou or I must take.'"
> *Ancient Spanish Ballads* (Lockhart's tr.).

The king, who had by this time learned to value the Cid's services, was very angry when he heard how the Infantes of Carrion had insulted their wives, and immediately summoned them to appear before the Cortes, the Spanish assembly, at Toledo, and justify themselves, if it were possible. The Cid was also summoned to the same assembly, where he began by claiming the two precious blades Tizona and Colada, and the large dowry he had given with his daughters. Then he challenged the young cowards to fight. When questioned, they tried to excuse themselves by declaring that the Cid's daughters, being of inferior birth, were not fit to mate with them.

The falseness of this excuse was shown, however, by an embassy from Navarre, asking the hands of the Cid's daughters for the Infantes of that kingdom, who were far superior in rank to the Infantes of Carrion. The Cid consented to this new alliance, and after a combat had been appointed between three champions of his selection and the Infantes of Carrion and their uncle, he prepared to return home.

As proof of his loyalty, however, he offered to give to Alfonso his favorite steed Babieça, an offer which the king wisely refused, telling him that the best of warriors alone deserved that peerless war horse.

"'Tis the noble Babieça that is fam'd for speed and force,
Among the Christians nor the Moors there is not such another one,
My Sovereign, Lord, and Sire, he is fit for you alone;
Give orders to your people, and take him for your own.'
The King replied, 'It cannot be; Cid, you shall keep your horse;
He must not leave his master, nor change him for a worse;
Our kingdom has been honor'd by you and by your steed—
The man that would take him from you, evil may he speed.
A courser such as he is fit for such a knight,
To beat down Moors in battle, and follow them in flight.'"
Chronicles of the Cid (Southey's tr.).

Shortly after, in the presence of the king, the Cid, and the assembled Cortes, the appointed battle took place. The Infantes of Carrion and their uncle were defeated and banished, and the Cid returned in triumph to Valencia. Here his daughters' second marriage took place, and here he received an embassy bringing him rich gifts from the Sultan of Persia, who had heard of his fame.

Five years later the Moors returned, under the leadership of Bucar, King of Morocco, to besiege Valencia. The Cid was about to prepare to do battle against this overwhelming force when he was favored by a vision of St. Peter. The saint predicted his death within thirty days, but assured him that, even though he were dead, he would still triumph over the enemy whom he had fought against for so many years.

"'Dear art thou to God, Rodrigo,
        And this grace he granteth thee:
When thy soul hath fled, thy body
        Still shall cause the Moors to flee;
And, by aid of Santiago,
        Gain a glorious victory.'"
Ancient Spanish Ballads (Lockhart's tr.).

The pious and simple-hearted warrior immediately began to prepare for the other world. He appointed a successor, gave instructions that none should bewail his death lest the news should encourage the Moors, and directed that his embalmed body should be set upon Babieça, and that, with Tizona in his hand, he should be led against the enemy on a certain day, when he promised a signal victory.

THE CID'S LAST VICTORY.—Rochegrosse.

> "'Saddle next my Babieça,
>   Arm him well as for the fight;
> On his back then tie my body,
>   In my well-known armor dight.
>
> "'In my right hand place Tizona;
>   Lead me forth unto the war;
> Bear my standard fast behind me,
>   As it was my wont of yore.'"
>   *Ancient Spanish Ballads* (Lockhart's tr.).

When these instructions had all been given, the hero died at the appointed time, and his successor and the brave Ximena strove to carry out his every wish. A sortie was planned, and the Cid, fastened upon his war horse, rode in the van. Such was the terror which his mere presence inspired that the Moors fled before him. Most of them were slain, and Bucar beat a hasty retreat, thinking that seventy thousand Christians were about to fall upon him, led by the patron saint of Spain.

> "Seventy thousand Christian warriors,
>   All in snowy garments dight,
> Led by one of giant stature,
>   Mounted on a charger white;
>
> "On his breast a cross of crimson,
>   In his hand a sword of fire,
> With it hew'd he down the Paynims,
>   As they fled, with slaughter dire."
>   *Ancient Spanish Ballads* (Lockhart's tr.).

The Christians, having routed the enemy, yet knowing, as the Cid had told them, that they would never be able to hold Valencia when he was gone, now marched on into Castile, the dead hero still riding Babieça in their midst. Then Ximena sent word to her daughters of their father's demise, and they came to meet him, but could scarcely believe that he was dead when they saw him so unchanged.

By Alfonso's order the Cid's body was placed in the Church of San Pedro de Cardeña, where for ten years it remained seated in a chair of state, and in plain view of all. Such was the respect which the dead hero inspired that none dared lay a finger upon him, except a sacrilegious Jew, who, remembering the Cid's proud boast that no man had ever dared lay a hand upon his beard, once attempted to do so. Before he could touch it, however, the hero's lifeless hand clasped the sword hilt and drew Tizona a few inches out of its scabbard.

> "Ere the beard his fingers touched,
>   Lo! the silent man of death
> Grasp'd the hilt, and drew Tizona
>   Full a span from out the sheath!"
>   *Ancient Spanish Ballads* (Lockhart's tr.).

Of course, in the face of such a miracle, the Jew desisted, and the Cid Campeador was reverently laid in the grave only when his body began to show signs of decay. His steed Babieça continued to be held in great honor, but no one was ever again allowed to bestride him.

As for the Moors, they rallied around Valencia. After hovering near for several days, wondering at the strange silence, they entered the open gates of the city, which they had not dared to cross for fear of an ambuscade, and penetrated into the court of the palace. Here they found a notice, left by the order of the Cid, announcing his death and the complete evacuation of the city by the Christian army. The Cid's sword Tizona became an heirloom in the family of the Marquis of Falies, and is said to bear the following inscriptions, one on either side of the blade: "I am Tizona, made in era 1040," and "Hail Maria, full of grace."

CHAPTER XVIII.

GENERAL SURVEY OF ROMANCE LITERATURE.

In the preceding chapters we have given an outline of the principal epics which formed the staple of romance literature in the middle ages. As has been seen, this style of composition was used to extol the merits and describe the great deeds of certain famous heroes, and by being gradually extended it was made to include the prowess of the friends and contemporaries of these more or less fabulous personages. All these writings, clustering thus about some great character, eventually formed the so-called "cycles of romance."

There were current in those days not only classical romances, but stories of love, adventure, and chivalry, all bearing a marked resemblance to one another, and prevailing in all the European states during the four centuries when knighthood flourished everywhere. Some of these tales, such as those of the Holy Grail, were intended, besides, to glorify the most celebrated orders of knighthood,—the Templars and Knights of St. John.

Other styles of imaginative writing were known at the same time also, yet the main feature of the literature of the age is first the metrical, and later the prose, romance, the direct outcome of the great national epics.

We have outlined very briefly, as a work of this character requires, the principal features of the Arthurian, Carolingian, and Teutonic cycles. We have also touched somewhat upon the Anglo-Danish and Scandinavian contributions to our literature.

Of the extensive Spanish cycle we have given only a short sketch of the romance, or rather the chronicle, of the Cid, leaving out entirely the vast and deservedly popular cycles of Amadis of Gaul and of the Palmerins. This omission has been intentional, however, because these romances have left but few traces in our literature. As they are seldom even alluded to, they are not of so great importance to the English student of letters as the Franco-German, Celto-Briton, and Scandinavian tales.

The stories of Amadis of Gaul and of the Palmerins are, moreover, very evident imitations of the principal romances of chivalry which we have already considered. They are formed of an intricate series of adventures and enchantments, are, if anything, more extravagant than the other mediaeval romances, and are further distinguished by a tinge of Oriental mysticism and imagery, the result of the Crusades.

The Italian cycle, which we have not treated separately because it relates principally to Charlemagne and Roland, is particularly noted for its felicity of expression and richness of description. Like the Spanish writers, the Italians love to revel in magic, as is best seen in the greatest gems of that age, the poems of "Orlando Innamorato" and "Orlando Furioso," by Boiardo and Ariosto.

Mediaeval literature includes also a very large and so-called "unaffiliated cycle" of romances. This is composed of many stories, the precursors of the novel and "short story" of the present age. We are indebted to this cycle for several well-known works of fiction, such as the tale of patient Griseldis, the gentle and meek-spirited heroine who has become the personification of long-suffering and charity. After the mediaeval writers had made much use of this tale, it was taken up in turn by Boccaccio and Chaucer, who have made it immortal.

The Norman tale of King Robert of Sicily, so beautifully rendered in verse by Longfellow in his "Tales of a Wayside Inn," also belongs to this cycle, and some authorities claim that it includes the famous animal epic "Reynard the Fox," of which we have given an outline. The story of Reynard the Fox is one of the most important mediaeval contributions to the literature of the world, and is the source from which many subsequent writers have drawn the themes for their fables.

A very large class of romances, common to all European nations during the middle ages, has also been purposely omitted from the foregoing pages. This is the so-called "classical cycle," or the romances based on the Greek and Latin epics, which were very popular during the age of chivalry. They occupy so prominent a place in mediaeval literature, however, that we must bespeak a few moments' attention to their subjects.

In these classical romances the heroes of antiquity have lost many of their native characteristics, and are generally represented as knight-errants, and made to talk and act as such knights would. Christianity and mythology are jumbled up together in a most peculiar way, and history, chronology, and geography are set at defiance and treated with the same scorn of probabilities.

The classical romances forming this great general cycle are subdivided into several classes or cycles. The interest of the first is mainly centered upon the heroes of Homer and Hesiod. The best-known and most popular of these mediaeval works was the "Roman de Troie," relating the siege and downfall of Troy.

Based upon post-classical Greek and Latin writings rather than upon the great Homeric epic itself, the story, which had already undergone many changes to suit the ever-varying public taste, was further transformed by the Anglo-Norman trouvère, Benoît de Sainte-More, about 1184. He composed a poem of thirty thousand lines, in which he related not only the siege and downfall of Troy, but also the Argonautic expedition, the wanderings of Ulysses, the story of Aeneas, and many other mythological tales.

This poet, following the custom of the age, naïvely reproduced the manners, customs, and, in general, the beliefs of the twelfth century. There is plenty of local color in his work, only the color belongs to his own locality, and not to that of the heroes whose adventures he purports to relate. In his work the old classical heroes are transformed into typical mediaeval knights, and heroines such as Helen and Medea, for instance, are portrayed as damsels in distress.

This prevalent custom of viewing the ancients solely from the mediaeval point of view gave rise not only to grotesque pen pictures, but also to a number of paintings, such as Gozzoli's kidnapping of Helen. In this composition, Paris, in trunk hose, is carrying off the fair Helen pickaback, notwithstanding the evident clamor raised by the assembled court ladies, who are attired in very full skirts and mediaeval headdresses.

On account of these peculiarities, and because the customs, dress, festivities, weapons, manners, landscapes, etc., of the middle ages are so minutely described, these romances have, with much justice, been considered as really original works.

The "Roman de Troie" was quite as popular in mediaeval Europe as the "Iliad" had been in Hellenic countries during the palmy days of Greece, and was translated into every dialect. There are still extant many versions of the romance in every European tongue, for it penetrated even into the frozen regions of Scandinavia and Iceland. It was therefore recited in every castle and town by the wandering minstrels, trouvères, troubadours, minnesingers, and scalds, who thus individually and collectively continued the work begun so many years before by the Greek rhapsodists. Thus for more than two thousand years the story which still delights us has been familiar among high and low, and has served to beguile the hours for old and young.

This cycle further includes a revised and much-transformed edition of the adventures of Aeneas and of the early history of Rome. But although all these tales were first embodied in metrical romances, these soon gave way to prose versions of equally interminable length, which each relator varied and embellished according to his taste and skill.

The extreme popularity of Benoît de Sainte-More's work induced many imitations, and the numerous *chansons de gestes*, constructed on the same general plan, soon became current everywhere. Sundry episodes of these tales, having been particularly liked, were worked over, added to, and elaborated, until they assumed the proportions of romances in themselves. Such was, for example, the case with the story of Troilus and Cressida, which was treated by countless mediaeval poets, and finally given the form in which we know it best, first by Chaucer in his "Canterbury Tales," and lastly by Shakespeare in his well-known play.

Another great romance of the classical cycle is the one known as "Alexandre le Grant." First written in verse by Lambert le Cort, in a meter which is now exclusively known as Alexandrine, because it was first used to set forth the charms and describe the deeds of this hero, it was recast by many poets, and finally turned into a prose romance also.

The first poetical version was probably composed in the eleventh century, and is said to have been twenty-two thousand six hundred lines long. Drawn from many sources,—for the Greek and Latin writers had been all more or less occupied with describing the career of the youthful conqueror and the marvels he discovered in the far East,—the mediaeval writers still further added to this heterogeneous material.

The romance of "Alexandre le Grant," therefore, purports to relate the life and adventures of the King of Macedon; but as Lambert le Cort and his numerous predecessors and successors were rather inclined to draw on imagination, the result is a very extravagant tale.

In the romance, as we know it, Alexander is described as a mediaeval rather than an ancient hero. After giving the early history of Macedon, the poet tells of the birth of Alexander,—which is ascribed to divine intervention,—and dwells eloquently upon the hero's youthful prowess. Philip's death and the consequent reign of Alexander next claim our attention. The conquest of the world is, in this romance, introduced by the siege and submission of Rome, after which the young monarch starts upon his expedition into Asia Minor, and the conquest of Persia. The war with Porus and the fighting in India are dwelt upon at great length, as are the riches and magnificence of the East. Alexander visits Amazons and cannibals, views all the possible and impossible wonders, and in his fabulous history we find the first mention, in European literature, of the marvelous "Fountain of Youth," the object of Ponce de Leon's search in Florida many years later.

When, in the course of this lengthy romance, Alexander has triumphantly reached the ends of the earth, he sighs for new worlds to conquer, and even aspires to the dominion of the realm of the air. To wish is to obtain. A magic glass cage, rapidly borne aloft by eight griffins, conveys the conqueror through the aërial kingdom, where all the birds in turn do homage to him, and where he is enabled to understand their language, thanks to the kind intervention of a magician.

But Alexander's ambition is still insatiable; and, earth and air having both submitted to his sway, and all the living creatures therein having recognized him as master and promised their allegiance, he next proposes to annex the empire of the sea. Magic is again employed to gratify this wish, and Alexander sinks to the bottom of the sea in a peculiarly fashioned diving bell. Here all the finny tribe press around to do him homage; and after receiving their oaths of fealty, and viewing all the marvels of the deep, as conceived by the mediaeval writer's fancy, Alexander returns to Babylon.

Earth, air, and sea having all been subdued, the writer, unable to follow the course of Alexander's conquests any further, now minutely describes a grand coronation scene at Babylon, where, with the usual disregard for chronology which characterizes all the productions of this age, he makes the hero participate in a solemn mass!

The story ends with a highly sensational description of the death of Alexander by poisoning, and an elaborate enumeration of the pomps of his obsequies.

A third order of romances, also belonging to this cycle, includes a lengthy poem known as "Rome la Grant." Here Virgil appears as a common enchanter. With the exception of a few well-known names, all trace of antiquity is lost. The heroes are now exposed to hairbreadth escapes; wonderful adventures succeed one another without any pause; and there is a constant series of enchantments, such as the Italian poets loved to revel in, as is shown in the works by Boiardo and Ariosto already mentioned.

These tales, and those on the same theme which had preceded them, gave rise to a generally accepted theory of European colonization subsequent to the Trojan war; and every man of note and royal family claimed to descend from the line of Priam.

As the Romans insisted that their city owed its existence to the descendants of Aeneas, so the French kings Dagobert and Charles the Bald claimed to belong to the illustrious Trojan race. The same tradition appeared in England about the third century, and from Gildas and Nennius was adopted by Geoffrey of Monmouth. It is from this historian that Wace drew the materials for the metrical tale of Brutus (Brute), the supposed founder of the British race and kingdom. This poem is twenty thousand lines long, and relates the adventures and life of Brutus, the great-grandson of Aeneas.

At the time of Brutus' birth his parents were frightened by an oracle predicting that he would be the cause of the death of both parents, and only after long wanderings would attain the highest pitch of glory. This prophecy was duly fulfilled. Brutus' mother, a niece of Lavinia, died at his birth. Fifteen years later, while hunting, he accidentally slew his father; and, expelled from Italy on account of this involuntary crime, he began his wanderings.

In the course of time Brutus went to Greece, where he found the descendants of Helenus, one of Priam's sons, languishing in captivity.

Brutus headed the revolted Trojans, and after helping them to defeat Pandrasus, King of Greece, obtained their freedom, and invited them to accompany him to some distant land, where they could found a new kingdom.

Led by Brutus, who in the mean while had married the daughter of Pandrasus, the Trojans sailed away, and, landing on the deserted island of Leogecia, visited the temple of Diana, and questioned her statue, which gave the following oracle:

> "'Brutus! there lies beyond the Gallic bounds
> An island which the western sea surrounds,
> By giants once possessed; now few remain
> To bar thy entrance, or obstruct thy reign.
> To reach that happy shore thy sails employ;
> There fate decrees to raise a second Troy,
> And found an empire in thy royal line,
> Which time shall ne'er destroy, nor bounds confine.'"
> GEOFFREY OF MONMOUTH (Giles's tr.).

Thus directed by miracle, Brutus sailed on, meeting with many adventures, and landed twice on the coast of Africa. The Pillars of Hercules once passed, the travelers beheld the sirens, and, landing once more, were joined by Corineus, who proposed to accompany them.

Brutus then coasted along the shores of the kingdom of Aquitaine and up the Loire, where his men quarreled with the inhabitants. He found himself involved in a fierce conflict, in which, owing to his personal valor and to the marvelous strength of Corineus, he came off victor in spite of the odds against him.

In this battle Brutus' nephew, Turonus, fell, and was buried on the spot where the city of Tours was subsequently built and named after the dead hero. After having subdued his foes, Brutus embarked again and landed on an island called Albion. Here he forced the giants to make way for him, and in the encounters with them Corineus again covered himself with glory.

We are told that the first germ of the nursery tale of Jack the Giant Killer is found in this poem, for Corineus, having chosen Corinea (Cornwall) as his own province, defeated there the giant Goëmagot, who was twelve cubits high and pulled up an oak as if it were but a weed. Corineus, after a famous wrestling bout, flung this Goëmagot into the sea, at a place long known as Lam Goëmagot, but now called Plymouth.

Brutus pursued his way, and finally came to the Thames, on whose banks he founded New Troy, a city whose name was changed in honor of Lud, one of his descendants, to London. Brutus called the newly won kingdom Britain, and his eldest sons, Locrine and Camber, gave their names to the provinces of Locria and Cambria when they became joint rulers of their father's kingdom, while Albanact, his third son, took possession of the northern part, which he called Albania (Scotland).

Albanact was not allowed to reign in peace, however, but was soon called upon to war against Humber, King of the Huns. The latter was defeated, and drowned in the stream which still bears his name. Locrine's daughter, Sabrina, also met with a watery death, and gave her name to the Severn.

The posterity of Brutus now underwent many other vicissitudes. There was fighting at home and abroad; and after attributing the founding of all the principal cities to some ruler of this line, the historian relates the story of King Leir, the founder of Leicester. As this monarch's life has been used by Shakespeare for one of his dramas,—the tragedy of "King Lear,"—and is familiar to all students of English literature, there is no need to outline Geoffrey of Monmouth's version of the tale.

The chronicler then resumes the account of Brutus' illustrious descendants, enumerating them all, and relating their adventures, till we come to the reign of Cassivellaunus and the invasion of Britain by the Romans. Shortly after, under the reign of Cymbelinus, he mentions the birth of Christ, and then resumes the thread of his fabulous history, and brings it down to the reign of Uther Pendragon, where it has been taken up in the Arthurian cycle.

This chronicle, which gave rise to many romances, was still considered reliable even in Shakespeare's time, and many poets have drawn freely from it. The mediaeval poets long used it as a mental quarry, and it has been further utilized by some more recent poets, among whom we must count Drayton, who makes frequent mention of these ancient names in his poem "Polyolbion," and Spenser, who immortalizes many of the old legends in his "Faerie Queene."

There are, of course, many other mediaeval tales and romances;

but our aim has been to enable the reader to gain some general idea of the principal examples, leaving him to pursue the study in its many branches if he wishes a more complete idea of the literature of the past and of the influence it has exerted and still exerts upon the writers of our own day.